GWEN

ALWAYS IN MY HEART

First edition

ISBN: 978-1-0683688-0-6

This book was professionally typeset on Reedsy.
Find out more at reedsy.com

Foreword

The poem incorporated within this manuscript was not written by me and I therefore cannot claim copyright for it. This poem was told to me by a friend, who had lived through the war and remembered it. However she was unable to remember the whole poem except the excerpt in this book. Apparently it was quite a long-involved poem, I have no idea who wrote it or where it came from, but I have decided to include it in this book as I thought it was very apt of how a lot of people felt at the time.

Acknowledgments

I would like to thank Gillian, a colleague who does charity work with me, for the idea for this book which is inspired by a remark she made to me one day. I would also like to thank Bobby who have both read this and enjoyed it and therefore gave me encouragement to have it published. Also my brother Graham, who has read all my books and enjoyed them and encourages me. Last, but by no means least, my wonderful Partner Tony, who has given me constant encouragement and always drives away any self-doubt I have.

Chapter 1

The moon hung low and sharp above the rooftops, bathing the narrow street in silver. Jenny strolled through the sleeping village, her scarf tugged gently by the breeze, her smile a private thing.

A bomber's moon, the airmen called it. She remembered the first time she'd heard the phrase—how the Americans had laughed at her confusion.

"Means we can see the target," a lieutenant had told her, his grin both easy and edged. "But so can they, honey. That's why it's dangerous."

She'd blushed at her own naivety. Of course it made sense. Tonight's moonlight was merciless—every chimney, every shadow drawn with a blade's precision.

A voice sliced through the quiet.

"Ah yes, you—girl! You're the Jackson girl, aren't you?"

Jenny stopped. Of all people, it had to be Mrs. Frances *Flaming* Davies—village tyrant in silk gloves.

"Yes," Jenny said, smoothing her tone. "Good evening, Mrs. Davies."

The woman's greeting was a brisk flick of the wrist, as though even words were too dear to spend.

"Has the new collection come in yet?"

"No, I'm afraid not. It's the war—materials are—"

Mrs. Davies rolled her eyes heavenward. "Oh, this is too bad. I need a dress for the Lord Mayor's dinner next Thursday. Outrageous, the whole business. Why must I suffer because some stupid little German insists on waging war on us? And for the second time in twenty years!"

Jenny murmured agreement, as one does when trapped with a snake.

"You'll inform me the *moment* it arrives. Understood?"

"Yes, Mrs. Davies."

"Good. Run along now."

Dismissed like a servant, Jenny walked on, biting back the retort that burned her tongue. In a village this small, crossing Frances Davies was like lighting a fire in your own kitchen—you'd only end up choking on the smoke.

Her husband, the council head, was no better—thundering through the lanes in his Bentley as if the road were his personal runway. His wife was equally lethal behind the wheel, though with more flair.

No children, of course. Jenny's mother said it was no mystery—what child could survive in that household of sharp words and sharper silences?

Jenny shook them from her thoughts. The night was too beautiful to waste on such people. Somewhere overhead, the bomber's moon glared down, bright as a searchlight, and she wondered—not for the first time—what it might reveal before morning.

The village was hardly more than a clutch of houses and shops clinging to a single road, its life anchored by the church, the school, the pub, and the police house—which doubled as the station. At its heart, the village green sagged under the weight of time: a faded bench, a weathered bus stop, grass worn thin where generations of boots had passed. Here, the days seemed to drift slower, as though the war beyond its hedgerows were happening in another country altogether.

Everyone knew everyone. The butcher's son had married the baker's daughter; the ironmonger still whistled the same tune his father had. Jenny's own father kept the greengrocer's, just as his father had before him, the crates of apples and potatoes stacked exactly where they'd always been. The shop sat halfway down the main street, the pub squatting comfortably beside the church—a pairing Jenny still found faintly scandalous.

Across the road stood the butcher's, the baker's, a narrow café with steamed-up windows, and the ironmonger's that smelled of oil and dust. At one end of the street was the school; at the other, the police station. Beyond, a narrow lane led to the American airbase. Only a few years ago it had been open fields—now it was all concrete, fences, and the endless snarl of engines. At night, the roar of departing bombers rattled the crockery in the cupboards.

A mile further on sat the railway station—three trains a day, and nothing on Sundays.

Jenny sighed. She loved her family, the safe familiarity of the village, but sometimes the sameness pressed in around her. She wanted the thrum of cities, the salt wind of foreign shores—something that would make her heart race.

Across the street, Margaret Thompson strode towards the

station in her crisp ATS uniform, her cap angled just so. She'd been home on leave, visiting her parents. Jenny watched her go, a knot of envy tightening in her chest. *How I wish I could go too.*

At seventeen, she was three years shy of call-up—if the war even lasted that long. Women between twenty and thirty were being enlisted, while boys marched off at eighteen. Perhaps they'd lower the age for girls. She hoped so. The thought of the war ending before she could be part of it felt, absurdly, like a personal loss.

She'd even considered lying about her age, but her father would sniff out the truth in a heartbeat. He and her mother were kind, but their rules were carved in stone. Out in the evenings until ten—no later. At the stroke of the hour, the door would be locked, and if she knocked to be let in, she'd get the full weight of one of his lectures.

He'd never raised a hand to her or her sister, but his words could grind away at a person. "Nagging," she called it; he called it guidance. Either way, the punishments—no trips to the pictures, no dancing at the Air Force base—stung.

And dancing was the thing she loved most. The swirl of skirts, the hot brass of American swing, the ripple of laughter—it was a taste of the world she dreamed about, pressed into a few precious hours.

Her days were spent in the dress department of the department store in the nearby town. It wasn't thrilling work, but the staff discount softened the edges, and she liked seeing the latest fashions before anyone else. She'd been there two years now, long enough to know the stockroom like her own bedroom, and to collect a small circle of good friends—girls who also watched the station, wondering what it would be like to be on the next train out.

Most of her friends from the store were gone now—off to the forces or the Land Army. Before the war, they'd been like a little family: chattering over tea breaks, swapping secrets in the stockroom, laughing until Miss Penheart's shadow darkened the doorway. Now the air felt thinner without them. Some mornings, Jenny half-expected to find herself the only one left—apart from Miss Penheart, of course.

Miss Amelia Penheart was far too old for the forces—possibly too old for anything human, Jenny often thought. Her iron-grey hair was scraped into a bun so tight it might have been holding her head together, and she peered at people over her spectacles like a scientist examining a particularly disappointing beetle.

She'd begun at the store as a junior assistant at fourteen—back in 1900, when the elder Mr. Tobias Findley was still in charge—and she never let anyone forget it. Tea breaks were peppered with her reminiscences, each one polished like a medal she wore in her own honour.

Jenny remembered the staff Christmas party one year, held in the grand upstairs room usually forbidden to mere mortals. High on the wall had hung a portrait of Mr. Findley himself—side-whiskers bristling, pince-nez perched on his nose. She and the other girls had been unable to stifle their giggles, until Miss Penheart silenced them with a glance that could have stopped a clock.

She smiled at the memory as she strolled through the fading light, the last streaks of gold stretching the shadows across the street she both loved and longed to leave.

"Hey, wait up!"

She turned, her smile breaking wide when she saw him—the young American lieutenant who'd once explained what a bomber's moon was. Tall, trim in his uniform, with a smile that seemed to belong in the pictures—Cary Grant with a dash of mischief.

"You're out late, aren't you?" he teased.

"It's only nine," she said, matching his easy stride. "I've just come from my friend's house."

"Then I'll walk you home. Keep you safe."

She laughed. "Safe? In this village? The worst crime we've had is someone letting the butcher's boy's tyres down. And I'm fairly sure it was schoolkids."

"Oh, dangerous stuff," he deadpanned. "Sounds like hardened criminals on the loose."

Their laughter mingled in the cool evening air.

"You must think it's dreadfully dull here after America," she said.

He shook his head. "Not really. I'm from Vermont—a little town called Norwich. Not so different."

She grinned. "It's not Nor-wich, it's Norritch. We've got one here too. I'll have to take you."

"I'd like that," he said.

They reached her father's grocery shop all too soon.

"Well, this is me. Thanks for the escort."

"You're welcome." He hesitated, then: "What are you doing

Friday night?"

"Nothing special. Why?"

"There's another dance at the base. I've seen you there with your friends… I thought maybe this time, you and I could go together."

Her heart gave a small, startled jump. "Oh—I'd have to ask my dad. Going with the girls is one thing, but with a boy—especially one who's not local—"

"Then let's ask him. Now."

She stared. "Now? It's after nine."

He grinned, eyes glinting green in the lamplight. "No time like the present."

She should have said no. Instead, she found herself unlocking the shop door, leading him inside.

"Oh," she said, pausing in the hallway, "I don't even know your name. I've seen you around, but—"

He gave a small, mock-formal bow, his smile warm and certain, as though he'd known her far longer than she'd guessed.

"Marcus Philbert Potter the Third, at your service, ma'am."

Jenny stared at him for half a beat—then dissolved into giggles.

"Really? *Marcus Philbert Potter the Third*? That's quite a mouthful!"

He gave a sheepish smile. "Old family name."

"Goodness. Well, my name is—"

"I know who you are," he said softly. "Jenny Jackson."

Her brows rose. "How do you know that?"

"I asked," he admitted. "I noticed you some time ago… and I wanted to meet you."

"Goodness… why?"

Before he could answer, a voice came from the hallway.

"Oh, Jenny—I thought I heard you come in."

Her mother stepped into view, then stopped short when she saw Marcus. One eyebrow arched high.

"And who do we have here?"

Marcus straightened to full height, tucking his cap under his arm with military precision. "First Lieutenant Marcus Philbert Potter, ma'am."

Jenny was almost certain her mother swallowed a laugh. For a moment, she simply regarded him as if he'd just stepped out of a recruiting poster.

"I see. And how do you know my daughter, Marcus?"

"We've only met briefly, ma'am—at the base dances. Once, we shared a dance. Tonight, I saw her walking home and offered to see her back safely."

Jenny blinked—he remembered? That night had stayed with her too, but she'd never imagined he would hold onto it.

Her mother's expression softened. "Well, that was thoughtful of you. I'm grateful."

"I have two sisters," he said, his voice steady. "I like to think someone would do the same for them. And… I was hoping to speak with your husband. I'd like permission to take Miss Jackson to the dance at the base this Friday—if it's no trouble."

Jenny bit back another giggle. *Miss Jackson*—so formal! But she could tell her mother was impressed.

"Well then," Veronica Jackson said, "we'd better see him. Would you like some tea?"

"Oh, I wouldn't want to trouble you—"

"It's no trouble at all. We always have a cup before bed. Come along."

In the living room, Ronald Jackson looked up from his paper. His wife gave him a look that said *you'll want to hear this.*

"Ron, this is Marcus," she said. "He'd like a word with you. I'll put the kettle on."

Ronald stood, folding his paper neatly before offering a firm handshake. Marcus matched it without hesitation—respect meeting respect.

The room smelled faintly of polish. Every surface gleamed. The furniture was well-worn but cared for, the carpets faded but spotless. To Marcus, it felt worlds away from the manicured luxury of his family's Vermont estate. But he found he liked this better—because she was here.

From the first week at the base, he'd noticed her. That one dance—Glenn Miller's *Always in My Heart*—had been enough to lodge her firmly in his thoughts. She'd fitted in his arms as though she'd always belonged there. Since then, he'd watched for her in the crowd, trying to get close, but she was always swept up with friends.

He'd never been the sort to fall hard. But now, at twenty-one, he was certain of one thing: he wanted Jenny Jackson in his life. Always.

Ronald's voice brought him back.

"I understand you want to ask me something, young man?"

"Yes, sir." Marcus leaned forward slightly. "I'd like your permission to escort Jenny to the dance this Friday night."

Ronald looked from Marcus to his daughter, noting her wide eyes and unguarded smile. He remembered when Veronica had looked at him that way—sixteen years old, brimming with hope. And he remembered her father's wary expression.

This boy was polite, steady, and there was something in his manner—an honesty Ronald found himself respecting. He gave a slow nod.

At that moment, Veronica returned with the tea tray. Marcus rose at once, taking it from her with careful hands and setting it on the table.

Ronald watched, quietly impressed.

"Well," Ronald said at last, "I see no reason why not. She usually goes with her friends anyway. But you'll have her home by ten—or there won't be a second time. Understand?"

"Yes, sir. Understood," Marcus said without hesitation.

"Good. And if anything happens to her—" Ronald's gaze sharpened—"you'll wish you'd never been born."

"I'll take good care of her, sir. You have my word."

Veronica smiled into her teacup. Marcus was everything she'd hoped a young man might be if he ever came calling for Jenny—courteous, respectful, and so obviously smitten. And Jenny? She was practically glowing.

Inside, Jenny was bursting. She wanted to fling her arms around her father, hug her mother, and—most of all—wrap herself around Marcus. Of all the girls in the village—and plenty had noticed him—it was *her* he wanted. Jenny Jackson. She'd be the envy of every friend she had. And here he was, in her living room, drinking tea with her parents.

It felt like stepping into a dream.

She thought of that first dance—Glenn Miller's *Always in My Heart*. She'd claimed it as their song in her own mind, but until tonight she'd wondered if she'd imagined the connection. Now, here he was, asking her father's permission. It was more than she'd dared hope.

"So, what does your father do, Marcus?" Ronald asked, his voice casual but his eyes measuring.

Marcus paused for the briefest beat. The truth—that his father owned a bank and several businesses—felt like bragging. So he kept it simple.

"He works in a bank, sir."

"A good position?"

"Yes, sir."

"And your mother?" Veronica asked warmly.

"She looks after the home, ma'am," Marcus replied with a fond smile. He left out the part about her committees, luncheons, and elegant dinner parties.

"And siblings?"

"Yes, ma'am—two sisters, Sally and Susan, and a younger brother, Richard. He's in college now. The girls are still in school."

"My, your mother must have her hands full."

Marcus nodded. "She'll miss them when they go. They miss me too, but—someone has to do their part. Hitler has to be stopped. I felt it should be me."

Ronald gave an approving grunt. "A good profession, banking. And good for you—fighting. I was in the last lot myself. Too old for this one, or I'd go again."

Marcus stood. "I'd better be off before I'm late for roll call." He turned to Veronica. "Thank you for the tea, Mrs. Jackson." Then to Ronald: "And thank you, sir, for allowing me to take Jenny to the dance."

"You're welcome. And tell your parents they've raised a fine young man." Ronald's tone held genuine respect. "Jenny, see him out—and mind the blackout."

Jenny felt weightless as she walked him to the door. Marcus paused, eyes searching hers. He wanted to kiss her properly, but not here, not with her parents just feet away. Instead, he brushed a gentle kiss against her cheek.

Jenny's breath caught. She'd been kissed only by relatives before—never by a handsome man in uniform.

Marcus took her hand, holding it just a moment longer than necessary. "Only a few more days," he said quietly, "and you'll be mine for two and a half hours."

Her cheeks warmed. "I'll look forward to it."

"I'll pick you up at seven-thirty."

She nodded. "Goodnight, Marcus."

"Goodnight, Jenny."

She stood in the doorway, watching him walk away, whistling under his breath. Only when he vanished around the corner did she close the door, still in a haze of joy.

The next morning at work, Jenny's best friend Ruth nearly dropped the blouse she was folding.

"And your dad said yes?" she gasped.

Jenny nodded, her grin unstoppable. "I know—I couldn't believe it either."

"Honestly, Jen, you only left my house for a two-minute walk home—and in that time, you meet the best-looking boy on the entire base *and* land a date? How do you do it?"

Jenny giggled. "I didn't do anything! Well… apart from being ambushed by Mrs. Flaming Davies, demanding to know if her frock had come in. You'd think I had a sewing machine in the back room, stitching it myself."

Ruth groaned. "Oh, I bet she gave you the full treatment."

"She did! As if it's my fault the dress hasn't arrived. 'Let me know the moment it comes in,' she said—as if I've got a direct line to the War Office. Doesn't she realise there's a war on?"

"She just likes having something to moan about. But what's so urgent about this frock?"

"Lord Mayor's dinner next Thursday."

"Well, with the number of dresses she owns, surely she's got something decent to wear?"

"You'd think so, wouldn't you? But no—she probably doesn't want to be seen in the same outfit twice."

Ruth scoffed. "Crikey, I've worn mine hundreds of times. Where's she even getting all the coupons to buy that many?"

Jenny shrugged. "No idea. But I wish she'd spend a few on patience."

At the base, Marcus sat with a mug of coffee cooling beside him, his pen hovering over the letter he'd been reading and rereading for the past ten minutes. The words on the page felt too small for what he was feeling.

I actually have a date with Jenny.

Even thinking it made his mouth curve into a smile. It hardly seemed real.

He wondered if her parents thought him too forward—he'd only been stationed here a short while—but wartime didn't allow for slow steps. Life could change—or end—in an instant. If you wanted something, you reached for it. And Marcus wanted Jenny. He wanted to know her laugh, her thoughts, her dreams—everything.

He wanted to tell his parents. He wanted them to know he'd met their future daughter-in-law.

The certainty of the thought struck him like a clear bell.

Absurd? Perhaps. They'd only shared one real dance, a handful of conversations. But his parents had fallen in love almost instantly—his mother swore it had been love at first sight. Now he knew what she meant.

On Friday night, he'd ask the base photographer for a picture of them together. He'd keep one copy and send the other home. He could already see his mother's reaction—her delight, her approval. His sisters would adore Jenny too.

Richard... well, Richard was another matter.

Marcus's pen tapped lightly against the table. He loved his younger brother, but Richard had inherited too much of their grandfather's arrogance—quick to sneer, slow to respect. Marcus could already hear it: *Good lord, Marcus—a greengrocer's daughter?*

Too bad. Jenny was the one, and Marcus would not tolerate anything less than complete respect toward her. If Richard couldn't manage that, Marcus would make sure he kept his opinions to himself.

His parents would back him. So would his sisters. And if not—there was always Great Aunt Clementine.

The smile returned at that thought. Clementine Potter had no patience for snobbery, not even within her own family. Her tongue was sharper than her knitting needles, and Richard had learned the hard way not to cross her. If she took a liking to Jenny—and Marcus was sure she would—that would settle the matter.

He dipped his pen again and wrote the line that had been pressing against his mind all morning.

There's someone I want you to meet...

Chapter 2

Marcus sipped his coffee, rereading the letter he'd been drafting to his parents. A smile tugged at the corner of his mouth—particularly at the section where he'd written about Richard and how he might react to Jenny.

I know Richard thinks I ought to marry one of the girls back home. Truth is, I have no feelings for any of them. They bore me. Jenny doesn't. She has real depth, and she's down to earth in a way that's rare. I know you'll love her—and the girls will too. I think you'll especially love her accent. It has this soft burr to it, and her laugh... well, it's the kind of laugh that makes you want to laugh too. She loves life, even in these hard times.

He paused, imagining his family reading those words, seeing Jenny through his eyes.

The rationing here is dreadful—no chocolate, no candy at all really. Butter, sugar, meat... everything is in short supply. But still, they manage. They carry on with quiet resilience. Honestly, I think it would do Richard the world of good to live through times like this. Maybe then he'd stop expecting the world to hand him everything on a silver platter.

Just as he signed off the sentence, the air raid siren pierced the morning solitude. Marcus dropped his pen, stuffed the half-finished letter into the drawer of his bureau, and grabbed his flight jacket. In seconds, he was out the door, sprinting towards the aircraft.

All around him, crews were racing toward their planes. He spotted his co-pilot, Alvin Peterson, already hauling himself into the cockpit. Dickie Phillips, the navigator, was aboard and doing pre-flight checks. Marcus climbed in and slid into his seat as the rest of the crew scrambled into position.

As usual, Danny Butchers was the last. He sauntered across the tarmac as if out for a leisurely stroll through Central Park.

"Get your sorry ass in this plane, Butchers! We don't have all day—move it!" Alvin yelled.

At last, Danny pulled himself aboard, slamming the hatch shut behind him. Final checks were completed in record time, and soon they were airborne.

As the engines roared and the countryside fell away beneath them, Marcus's thoughts returned to Jenny. He hoped she was safe. Surely the store had a proper air raid shelter?

At that precise moment, Jenny was crouched in the cellar beneath Findley's Department Store, wedged between Ruby from Perfume and Sheila from Shoes. The room smelled of damp earth, perfume samples, and floor polish.

She hugged her knees and closed her eyes, thinking of Marcus.

Please God, keep him safe. And please look after Mum, Dad, and my baby sister too.

The all-clear sounded not long after, echoing eerily through the narrow space. Slowly, the women began to stir, brushing themselves off as they prepared to return to their departments.

"Is this bloody war ever going to end?" Sheila muttered as she stood.

"Miss Bracken, moderate your language!" Miss Penheart's clipped voice cut through the room like a whip. "That is not the sort of vocabulary we expect from our young ladies."

Sheila blushed. "Sorry, Miss Penheart. But honestly... I'm so fed up. Every day it's this. Then at night I can't sleep."

"We are *all* suffering, Miss Bracken," Amelia Penheart replied firmly. "But that is no excuse for lowering standards or using vulgar language."

"Yes, Miss Penheart. Sorry, Miss Penheart," Sheila mumbled.

"I know exactly how she feels," Ruth whispered to Jenny as they filed up the stairs. "It's enough to make a saint swear. I hope Hitler gets bombed to hell and back."

Jenny smiled. She couldn't help it—she agreed entirely.

Later that evening, Marcus and Alvin were nursing pints in the base bar when Danny Butchers swaggered across the floor toward them. Marcus stiffened slightly. Neither he nor Alvin had much time for Danny. He was a cocky kid from the Bronx—barely nineteen—and he seemed to think he knew everything. Worse, he took reckless chances no one else dared. Marcus often thanked God the boy didn't have control of the aircraft.

"What d'ya say, Skip?" Danny asked, flashing his usual wide grin as he reached them.

"Say about what?" Marcus replied, guarded.

"You crack me up, Skip. You really do," Danny said, still

grinning. "Looking forward to the dance Friday?"

"Are you?" Alvin asked coolly.

"Hell yeah. All those chicks—it's gonna be a good night."

Something snapped in Marcus. He had sisters. The idea of one of them being treated like a casual fling by someone like Butchers made his blood boil.

"You listen to me," he said sharply. "You treat those girls with respect. They're not here for your gratification. Leave them alone, you hear?"

Danny blinked. "Blimey, Skip, I was just saying. Life's for living, right? It's short. Look what happened to Pete's crew last week—*gone*, just like that." He snapped his fingers to drive the point home. "I'm just trying to get my living in while I can."

Alvin stepped in before things could escalate.

"What the Skip means is that these girls are *decent.* Good girls. And like you just said—we could be gone tomorrow. But that's no reason to ruin a girl's name, or worse—get her pregnant. She'd be an outcast in her community. Is that really what you want?"

Alvin leaned in slightly.

"And let's be honest, Butchers—would you *marry* a girl you got into trouble? I doubt it. And if you did... what kind of life would she have, married to you?"

Danny bristled. "No need for that. I just want to have some fun, that's all. And if a girl's willing, well... she knows the score." He winked and sauntered off, drink in hand.

"Slimeball," Alvin muttered.

"One of these days, I swear I'll have him," Marcus said

darkly.

"Take a number," Alvin replied. "I think there are half a dozen men on this base already biding their time with Danny Butchers."

Jenny looked at the dress her mother was holding up.

"Well, what do you think?" Veronica asked, a hint of anticipation in her voice.

Jenny's eyes lit up. "Oh, Mum, it's *lovely*. It'll be perfect for Friday."

"That's what I thought." Veronica smiled and studied her daughter carefully. She looked so young still—but she was already a year older than Veronica had been when she first met Ronald.

She had noticed the change in Jenny lately. That sparkle in her eyes when she mentioned Marcus, the way her expression softened at the sound of his name—even if she barely used it. Clearly, this boy had made quite the impression. And from what Veronica had seen of Marcus, the feeling was mutual. He had looked at Jenny with such warmth, such quiet admiration.

"It's strange," Veronica said now, "but I don't recall you ever mentioning Marcus before. How long have you known him?"

Jenny hesitated. "Well… I don't really. I've seen him around the base at the dances. We've even had a couple of dances—but I didn't really know him. To be honest, I didn't even know his *name* until the other night."

Veronica raised an eyebrow in surprise. "Good heavens, I thought you two had been friends for some time."

Jenny shook her head, brushing a loose strand of hair behind her ear. "No… I just bumped into him on my way home from Ruth's the other night. He walked me home and asked me to the dance. I was honestly surprised he even *noticed* me. But apparently, he'd asked around about me—my friends told him my name."

Veronica laughed softly. "Well, I'll give him full marks for determination." Then her tone turned tender as she lifted a strand of Jenny's hair and brushed it gently away from her face. "He must really be smitten. And he seems like a nice lad. Your father and I were both impressed with him."

She paused, looking at her daughter—not just seeing her, but *really* seeing her. It seemed like only yesterday that Jenny had clung to her skirts, wide-eyed and chattering about dolls and storybooks. And now, here she was, a young woman in love.

Veronica sighed softly. *Where had the years gone?*

When Jenny opened the door to Marcus on Friday evening, he was momentarily speechless.

He would never forget the way she looked in that moment. One side of her hair was swept back with a sparkling diamanté clip, cascading in soft waves over her shoulder in the perfect imitation of Veronica Lake. Her dress was a pale pastel mauve, with elegant three-quarter-length sleeves, a fitted button-down bodice, and a pleated skirt that moved delicately with every breath of air.

She was breathtaking.

"I brought you a corsage," Marcus said finally, holding it out with a slightly bashful smile. "I thought it might go with your dress."

Jenny beamed as she took it. "Oh, Marcus, it's beautiful. Thank you." She carefully slipped it onto her wrist.

Just then, a small voice piped up behind her.

"Who's that man?"

Jenny turned and smiled. A little girl stood in the hallway in her pink nightdress, thumb in her mouth and a teddy bear tucked firmly under one arm.

Squatting down to her level, Jenny said gently, "Betty, this is Marcus. Say hello."

"Hello," the little girl mumbled, peering at him with curious brown eyes.

Marcus smiled down at the tiny figure in pink. She had dark hair like her father and the same serious, soulful expression. Her feet were clad in fluffy pink slippers, and her nightdress was covered in teddy bears.

He looked at Jenny, eyebrows raised. "I didn't know you had a sister."

Jenny laughed. "Yes—meet my baby sister, Betty. She was a bit of a late arrival... but a very welcome one."

"I can see that," Marcus said warmly.

He bent to Betty's level, mirroring Jenny's position. "How do you do, Miss Betty? I'm Marcus."

Betty looked at him solemnly for a moment, then lifted her teddy and held it out. "This is Mr. Cuddles. He's my teddy."

Marcus extended his hand and gently shook the teddy's paw. "Well, how do you do, Mr. Cuddles?"

Betty giggled. "You talk funny."

"Betty!" Jenny chided, eyes wide. "That's rude."

Betty's smile faded, and she looked crestfallen. But Marcus only laughed softly.

"No, she's right. I *do* talk funny—it's because I'm from America."

Betty's eyes widened. "What's America?"

"It's a place a long, long way away."

"Like the town? Mummy took me to town to buy my shoes."

Marcus grinned. "Even farther than the town. Much farther."

Veronica came into the hallway, her voice gently scolding. "Oh, you little scamp," she said, scooping up her youngest daughter. "I thought you were playing in the front room."

She turned to Marcus with an apologetic smile. "Hello, Marcus. I hope she hasn't been bothering you—she's at that inquisitive stage and wants to know *everything*."

Marcus stood politely. "No, ma'am, not at all. She's been delightful. We were just getting acquainted. I've even had the pleasure of meeting Mr. Cuddles."

"Mummy," Betty chimed in, "he talks funny 'cause he comes from *Merica*! Can we go to Merica, Mummy?"

Veronica chuckled. "No, darling, I don't think so. The only place *you're* going right now is to bed—it's well past your bedtime." She lifted Betty into her arms. "Come along, say goodnight to Daddy, and I'll read you a story and tuck you in."

Jenny and Marcus followed her into the sitting room, where Ronald was seated, listening to the wireless. He greeted Marcus with a firm handshake, then took Betty onto his lap.

"Well, young lady," he said, kissing her forehead, "it's bedtime for you."

As Veronica carried Betty off, Jenny went to fetch her coat. When she returned, Marcus and Ronald were deep in conversation.

"Bataan is dreadful," Ronald was saying. "And so soon after Pearl Harbor."

Marcus nodded. "I know. My parents are worried they'll lower the draft age again. My brother's just eighteen... they're afraid he'll be next."

"Yes, having one son in the fight is hard enough. Two—well, let's hope it doesn't come to that."

He turned to his daughter with a warm smile, then clapped Marcus lightly on the back.

"Anyway, it's time you youngsters forgot about the war for a bit. Go out, have some fun, and enjoy yourselves while you can."

The evening was crisp and clear—the kind of cold that only came at the turn of the year. Jenny was grateful for her fur-lined boots and warm winter coat. The fur wasn't real, of course—her shop assistant's wage wouldn't stretch that far—but it was warm and well-loved, even if it had seen better days.

Marcus noticed the wear in her coat and made a silent promise to himself. Somehow, without offending her pride, he'd find a way to replace it.

They walked hand in hand toward the base, the music already floating on the still night air. It carried further on nights like this—soft and haunting.

They walked mostly in silence. It wasn't awkward. It was companionable, comfortable. They were in step, in sync, like they'd known each other far longer than a few days.

Jenny let out a soft sigh.

Marcus glanced over, concerned. "You alright?"

She looked up at him and smiled. "Yes, very much so."

"You sighed—I thought maybe you were bored."

She laughed, shaking her head. "Bored? With *you*? No, not at all. That was a *happy* sigh."

Relieved, Marcus smiled and gave her hand a gentle squeeze. "That's good. That's exactly how I feel too.

So… tell me more about your little sister. There's quite an age gap there."

"Yes, thirteen years and six months to be exact."

"That's quite something. Have you ever asked your mum why?"

Jenny shrugged. "No. I suppose I just accepted it. If Mum ever wanted me to know, I'm sure she'd tell me."

"Maybe… or maybe it's too painful to talk about. Even after all these years."

Jenny stopped in her tracks and looked up at him, frowning slightly. "What do you mean?"

Marcus hesitated. "Well… if she lost babies between you and Betty, or had any difficult times, it might not be something she's ready to talk about."

Jenny's expression softened. "Oh… I hadn't thought of that. Maybe one day she'll tell me. Or maybe… maybe I'll ask."

The warmth of the mess hall was a welcome contrast to the chill outside. Jenny changed from her boots into her dancing shoes and tucked them neatly under her coat on the peg. Marcus hung up his greatcoat, then offered her his arm as they entered the crowded room.

He guided her to a table near the bandstand where his crew was already seated. As he pulled out a chair for her, the men all stood out of courtesy.

"Well, well," one of them said with a grin. "Aren't you the dark horse, Skip? You kept this little doll well under wraps."

Marcus stiffened.

Jenny flushed to the roots of her blonde hair, unsure how to respond. But before the awkward silence could stretch any longer, Dickie Phillips stood and grabbed the offending man—Danny Butchers—firmly by the arm.

"Let's take some air, Danny," he said through clenched teeth.

Danny tried to resist, but Dickie's grip was unrelenting—and Alvin had risen to flank his other side. With no way to save face, Danny allowed himself to be led out.

Marcus turned to Jenny, placing a hand gently on her shoulder. "I'm so sorry, Jenny. You shouldn't have been subjected to that. Believe me, I'll be having words with Butchers."

She smiled, embarrassed but touched by his protectiveness. "It's alright."

"No, it isn't. No lady should be spoken to—or *about*—like that. Ever."

Chuck Brierly, the radioman, leaned in. "I think Butchers is about to get what's coming to him, Skip."

Then, turning to Jenny, he added, "I'm sorry for the way he spoke to you, ma'am. But don't judge the rest of us by *him*. He's just never learned any manners. To prove it, may I buy you a drink?"

He looked to Marcus. "If that's alright with the Skip, of course."

Marcus laughed. "Seeing as *you're* buying, Chuck—sure. We'll take two sodas, please."

Chuck raised his eyebrows. "No beer?"

Marcus shook his head. "British law—Jenny's too young to drink. And I wouldn't insult her by drinking when she can't. Soda's fine."

Jenny touched his arm. "Marcus, really, if you want a beer, I don't mind. My dad has one every Sunday afternoon."

Marcus looked down at her with affection. "No. Honestly, a soda is just right."

A moment later, Alvin and Dickie returned, both looking satisfied.

"We've educated Butchers on how to treat a lady," Dickie said mildly. "And I think he got the message."

As if on cue, Danny appeared at the edge of the table. He looked unharmed, but his arm was cradled slightly and he was holding his side. His face was flushed, and he avoided everyone's eyes.

He cleared his throat awkwardly. "Um… I just wanted to say, ma'am," he said to Jenny, "I'm sorry if I insulted you. I wasn't thinking. I apologise."

Before Jenny could respond, Marcus cut in, voice cold.

"No, Butchers—you *weren't* thinking. And if you *ever* speak to a lady like that again in my hearing, you'll be sorry. Understood?"

Danny nodded, murmured something indistinct, and turned on his heel, walking stiffly out of the hall.

That evening was the best Jenny had ever known.

Ruth and the other girls had come over to join them, and Marjory had seemed to hit it off with Chuck Brierly. The two of them shared several dances, laughing and chatting like old friends. Dickie and Alvin also danced with the girls, though as married men, they kept a respectful distance, ever polite and proper.

Then, the band began to play *Always in My Heart*—Glenn Miller's familiar melody drifting like a soft breeze through the air.

Marcus turned to Jenny, took her hand gently, and whispered, “They’re playing *our* song. Shall we dance?”

He led her onto the floor, slipping an arm around her waist as the first few notes filled the room. She melted into his embrace. She felt safe there, cherished—as though she belonged nowhere else but in his arms.

Marcus inhaled the soft floral scent of her hair and closed his eyes briefly. *She feels so right,* he thought. *Please let this moment last forever.*

Jenny tilted her head up to look at him. “It’s funny,” she said shyly, “but I always think of this as our song when I hear it. I didn’t know you did too.”

He smiled, his voice low and husky. “Oh yes. This was playing the first time we danced. In fact, the *only* time—until now. I’ve always thought of it as our song.”

Jenny sighed softly, the music swirling around them. She felt like she was dreaming.

Eventually, the evening drew to a close. Chuck offered to walk Marjory and Ruth home, and the group left the base together, chatting and laughing as they strolled through the quiet streets. Despite the war, despite the hardships, it felt good to be young, alive, and happy—if only for a night.

They reached Jenny’s house first.

“See you in the morning,” she called as her friends walked on.

“Yes, see you in the morning!” Ruth and Marjory echoed.

“See you next week, Chuck,” Jenny added with a smile.

“It was a pleasure to meet you, Jenny,” he said kindly, tipping his cap before disappearing into the night.

Marcus turned to her, taking both of her hands in his. "Well, I'll see you in then I'd better head back. Thank you for a wonderful evening, Jenny. I honestly can't remember the last time I enjoyed myself so much."

He hesitated, then added, "Would you like to go to the pictures with me tomorrow? There's a new film playing—it's a comedy. I thought you might like it."

"I'd love that," she said, beaming. "What's it called?"

"To Be or Not to Be."

Jenny frowned. "That sounds like Shakespeare. Is it Shakespeare?"

Marcus laughed. "No—it's not Shakespeare. Like I said, it's a comedy. You'll enjoy it, I promise."

Jenny glanced at the clock through the front window. "I'd better go in—it's five to ten, and if I'm late, Dad won't let me out for a while. He's quite strict about that."

"He has every right to be," Marcus said gently. "He's just trying to protect you, and that's what fathers are meant to do."

He leaned in and kissed her lightly on the forehead, then opened the door for her.

"Goodnight, Jenny. Sweet dreams."

"Goodnight, Marcus... and thank *you*—for a lovely evening."

Inside the sitting room, her parents looked up as she entered. Both were smiling.

"Did you have a nice evening, dear?" Veronica asked.

"Oh, I did, Mum," Jenny said, glowing. "Marcus's friends are all so nice. Marjory and Chuck really hit it off—he even walked her and Ruth home. We all walked together—it was lovely."

"That's nice," Veronica replied. "Marjory's a lovely girl. Didn't Ruth get on with any of the boys?"

"Oh yes—she did. But the others are married, so it was friendly, but nothing more. And to be honest, I think Ruth's still holding a candle for Raymond—you know, from school."

Veronica frowned in thought. "Raymond… do I know his mother?"

"Yes—Mrs. Merrett. She runs the haberdashery counter at Findley's."

"Oh yes! Dark hair, glasses. I know who you mean. Nice woman."

"That's her."

"So young Ruth likes her boy, does she?"

Jenny nodded. "Always did. Had a terrible crush on him in school—still does, as far as I know. She blushes every time she sees him. Was heartbroken when he joined up."

"Oh dear," Veronica sighed. "Well, let's hope he comes home safely. Maybe they'll have a happy life together yet."

Ronald chuckled. "Your mother—ever the romantic," he said fondly, smiling at her.

"There's nothing wrong with a bit of romance," Veronica replied, giving his arm a playful tap.

Ronald looked at Jenny. "So, are you seeing Marcus again?"

"Yes," she said, barely able to hide her excitement. "He's asked me to go to the pictures tomorrow. There's a new comedy out, and he thought I might like it."

"What's it called?" he asked.

"To Be or Not to Be."

Ronald raised an eyebrow. "Sounds like Shakespeare."

"That's what I said! But Marcus says it's not—it's a comedy.

I'll let you know what it's like. Maybe you and Dad could go and see it too. Ruth and I could babysit Betty."

"That's very thoughtful of you, love," Veronica said. "We'll see."

"Now," she added, "off to bed with you. You've got work in the morning."

Jenny kissed them both goodnight and headed upstairs, her heart still dancing to the rhythm of *Always in My Heart*.

She went to bed floating on a cloud of happiness.

Chapter 3

All day Saturday, Jenny found herself glancing at the clock. Again and again. *Would this day ever end?*

Marjory was floating on air. "Oh, Jenny, Chuck is just *lovely*! We really hit it off — and he's asked to see me again. We're going to the pictures tonight. There's a new comedy on."

Jenny's eyes lit up. "Oh, Marcus and I are going to the pictures too. What's the film?"

"*To Be or Not to Be*. I thought it was Shakespeare, but apparently not."

Jenny laughed. "That's the one we're seeing! I thought it was Shakespeare too. We'll probably run into each other."

"We should meet for a drink afterwards — before heading home."

"Good idea!"

"Ladies," came a sharp voice behind them. "Are you *working*, or just enjoying a chat?"

Neither of them had seen Miss Penheart approach. The girls jumped guiltily and quickly returned to their tasks, scattering in opposite directions.

At last, five o'clock arrived. Jenny and Marjory sighed with relief and practically flew out the door. If they were quick, they'd catch the quarter-past bus — the direct route home, instead of the half-past that looped 'round the houses and added another thirty minutes to the journey.

They ran for it, shoes clacking on the pavement.

The driver, one of the regulars, spotted them and waited with a grin.

"Just made it in time, girls," he called as they clambered aboard, breathless and laughing. "Need to be quicker off the mark next time."

"Thank you!" they panted in unison.

"Got a hot date, have you?" he chuckled, putting the bus in gear.

"Yes — something like that," Jenny said, cheeks flushed. "We're off to the pictures."

"Well, enjoy it. You're only young once, love."

When Jenny arrived home, she was greeted by the delicious smell of her mother's shepherd's pie — cheesy, crispy topping and all. It wasn't quite what it had been before the war — rationing made sure of that — but her mother still managed to work culinary miracles with what little they had.

After dinner, her father went for his usual Saturday evening stroll down to the pub for a couple of pints with his mates. Jenny took her turn at the sink for a strip wash — proper baths were a luxury saved for once a week now, but the big kitchen sink made things easier and less messy than the bathroom basin.

She hurried upstairs to get ready. She was applying the final touches to her makeup when a knock sounded at the front door. Her heart skipped.

Marcus.

She ran lightly down the stairs, only to pause as her mother put a finger to her lips and motioned for her to stay quiet. Together, they crept towards the sitting room door.

There, on the rug, was Marcus — sitting cross-legged beside Betty, who was surrounded by her toys.

"Are you a soldier?" Betty asked, gazing up at him with wide eyes.

He shook his head gently. "No, honey, I'm an airman."

She frowned. "What's an airman?"

"Well, I fly in an airplane."

Her eyes widened. "Ooh — an airplane? Up in the sky?"

Marcus chuckled. "Yes, way up in the sky."

Betty's voice turned pleading. "Can I come in your airplane and fly in the sky too?"

He smiled. "I'm afraid not, sweetheart — my airplane's already full. But one day, I *promise* you'll fly."

"With Mummy and Daddy and Jenny?"

"Yes, with all of them."

"Will it be soon?"

Marcus's smile softened. "I sure hope so, Betty."

Veronica stepped into the room. "Come on, rascal. It's well past your bedtime," she said, scooping the little girl into her arms.

Jenny stepped forward and kissed Betty goodnight. To everyone's surprise, Betty leaned over and flung her chubby arms around Marcus's neck, planting a kiss on his cheek.

He hugged her gently, kissing her back. "Goodnight, sweetheart. Sweet dreams."

Veronica smiled and carried Betty upstairs.

Marcus turned to Jenny. "We'd better get going, or we'll miss the bus."

He helped her on with her coat, and they stepped out into the cool evening.

"What you did just now — with Betty — that was sweet," Jenny said as they walked.

Marcus looked puzzled. "Sweet? In what way?"

"Telling her she'd fly one day. That was kind."

"Well, I meant it," he said simply. "There's no reason she can't. In fact, after this war's over, I think everyone will be flying. You, your parents, Betty — all of you."

The bus arrived, ending the conversation for the moment. They found seats near the back, and Marcus reached over to take Jenny's hand. She smiled, fingers interlacing with his.

They rode in comfortable silence, the quiet hum of the engine and the rhythmic bounce of the journey lulling them into calm.

As the bus pulled up near the cinema, they spotted Marjory and Chuck waiting out front.

"How did *you* get here before us?" Jenny asked in surprise. "You weren't on the bus."

Marjory grinned. "We caught the earlier one."

"Heavens! You must've eaten your tea in record time."

"I had a proper lunch in the canteen, so I only needed a sandwich tonight. Gave me more time to get ready. Good thing too—Chuck was at the door before I'd even finished dressing!"

Chuck looked sheepish. "I was just eager to see you again. Honestly, I forgot you had to work and wouldn't be home until after five."

They entered the cinema, and after collecting their tickets, the usherette led them down the dim aisle to their seats. The place was already filling fast, the low murmur of conversation and the rustling of coats and sweet wrappers creating a gentle hum.

"Looks like it's going to be a full house," Jenny whispered, glancing around. "Let's just hope Hitler doesn't decide to launch an raid during the film."

Everyone murmured agreement, half-joking, but half-serious too. It was never far from anyone's mind.

Just under two hours later, they stepped out into the cool night air, wiping away tears of laughter.

"Oh, I *ache* from laughing!" Marjory gasped. "That's one of the funniest films I've ever seen! Jack Benny is *hilarious*... but it's such a shame about Carole Lombard. It's so sad she never lived to see it released."

"Yes, a real shame," Chuck added. "She was so young—and such a good actress."

Marcus turned to the group. "What do you say—shall we catch the bus back to Codly and maybe pop into the pub for a quick drink?"

"Oh... I've never been in a pub," Jenny said, suddenly hesitant.

"Neither have I," Marjory admitted.

The two men exchanged a glance, having momentarily forgotten that the girls were only seventeen.

"Alright," Chuck said quickly, adapting. "How about we see if the little coffee shop's still open? We can grab a coffee instead."

Both girls nodded gratefully. They weren't entirely sure

how their fathers would react if they heard they'd been in the pub—even if it was just for a lemonade. And with it being the *local*, word would definitely get back.

As they stepped off the bus, they spotted the café still lit up. Since the arrival of the Americans, the café had been staying open later to take advantage of the extra business. Not all the servicemen wanted to drink; some just wanted somewhere quieter to escape the noise of the base.

They found a table in the corner and ordered coffee all around.

"So," Chuck asked, "where do you girls work?"

"Findley's Department Store in town," Marjory replied. "Ruth works with us too—you remember Ruth from last night?"

"Oh yeah, sure. Nice girl."

"She is. We all went to school together—Ruth, Marjory, and me," Jenny added.

"So was it planned that you'd all end up at the same place, or just luck?" Marcus asked, sipping his coffee.

Jenny and Marjory both laughed.

"There isn't anywhere else to go!" Marjory said. "Everyone ends up at Findley's sooner or later. Our mums worked there too before they married."

"So what happens if there aren't any vacancies when the school leavers come out?" Marcus asked.

"Well," Jenny replied, "there are a few other smaller shops in the village, and some girls go into office work or domestic service. And of course, there's the hospital if someone wants to train as a nurse. But Findley's is by far the biggest employer in the area."

Marjory glanced at her watch. "We'd better get going. Looks like they're closing up."

Marcus paid the bill, and they all stepped back into the cool night. After saying goodnight to Chuck and Marjory, Marcus and Jenny strolled slowly along the road, hand in hand.

When they reached her front door, Marcus hesitated. He wanted to pull her into his arms and kiss her properly, but it still felt a little soon. He didn't want to come across as pushy. So instead, he leaned in and kissed her softly on the cheek.

"Good night, Jenny. And thank you for a wonderful evening. May I take you to the dance on Friday?"

She nodded, smiling. "Of course you can. I'll look forward to it. Thank you for tonight—I really enjoyed it."

Then, gathering her courage, she stood on tiptoe and kissed his cheek. She'd wanted to kiss him on the lips but held back. She didn't want him to get the wrong idea about her.

Inside, her parents looked up from their chairs as she came in. Veronica set down her knitting with a smile.

"Oh good, you're home. I'll pop the kettle on, and you can tell us all about the film."

"Did you have a nice time, love?" her father asked.

"Oh, it was great, Dad. We bumped into Marjory and Chuck outside the cinema, so we sat together. Afterwards, we went for a coffee."

Veronica returned with the tea tray and poured them each a cup.

"So, was the film good?" she asked.

"Oh, Mum, it was *hilarious*! You'd both love it. Jack Benny is so funny. But it's sad too—Carole Lombard was brilliant in it, but she died before the film was released. She never got to see it."

"Well, that's an idea," Ronald said. "We should go—maybe one evening this week."

"Yes," Veronica agreed. "I'd love to see it. Would you babysit Betty for us, Jenny?"

"Of course! I'll ask Ruth to come round too. She's working on a dress, so she can bring it with her. We could even use your sewing machine, Mum—if you don't mind."

"Not at all. Just don't break it," Veronica said with a chuckle.

"How about Wednesday?" Jenny suggested. "It's my half-day, so I'll be home just after two. I can give Betty her tea, and then you can meet Dad from work, get fish and chips, and have a proper evening out."

Veronica looked touched. "Oh, love, that's such a lovely thought."

Ronald nodded. "Yes, let's do that. It's been ages since we had a night out. Thank you, Jenny—that's very thoughtful."

Jenny stretched and yawned. "Well, I'm off to bed. See you in the morning."

She kissed them both goodnight and headed upstairs, her steps light, her heart full.

That night she dreamt of Marcus, and when she woke up on Sunday morning, the world seemed full of light and promise. For the first time in a long while, the future felt like something to look forward to.

Ruth was more than happy to help with the babysitting on Wednesday.

"My dress is nearly finished," she said, as they walked home from work together. "I think we'll get it done Wednesday night and then I can try it on. You'll have to tell me what you think."

"Is it for a special occasion?" Jenny asked.

Ruth shook her head. "Not really. I just saw the pattern and loved it. Mum had the material tucked away in the cupboard for ages. She said I could have it. She'd meant to make something with it but never got around to it."

Jenny smiled, then hesitated. "I spoke to Mrs. Merrett this morning. She said Raymond's coming home on leave—he's got a forty-eight-hour pass before being shipped out again. It feels like ages since he was last home."

She glanced at her friend and felt a pang of sympathy. Back at school, Jenny had always thought Ruth's crush on Raymond was just that—a schoolgirl crush. But now, she realised it was something deeper. The way Ruth had gone quiet at the mention of his name said more than words ever could.

"Why don't you ask him if he'd like to go to the pictures with you?" Jenny suggested gently.

Ruth froze. "Ask a boy out?" she whispered, wide-eyed. "I couldn't do that! He'd think I was being awfully forward. Ooo no, Jenny—I couldn't possibly."

"Ruth," Jenny said patiently, "there's a war on. Who knows when you'll see him again—or even *if* you will. I bet he'd be thrilled to go with you. It'd be a nice evening for him to remember before he ships out again. And it's not like he doesn't know you. You grew up together."

But Ruth was already shaking her head. "No. I couldn't. And anyway, what if he *has* a girlfriend now? What if he says no? That'd be humiliating."

Jenny looked at her fondly. Their mothers had been friends since before either of them was born, and she loved Ruth like a sister. She sighed.

If Ruth wouldn't ask him, then she—Jenny—would.

Later that evening, Jenny looked down at her baby sister with a smile. "Right, Betty. How about beans on toast for tea?"

Betty nodded enthusiastically, her big dark eyes shining. "I *like* beans on toast."

Jenny laughed. "So do I, Betty. Beans on toast it is."

Once they'd eaten and the dishes were done, Jenny bathed Betty—just a quick strip wash in the big kitchen sink. At just over three years old, she still fitted comfortably, and it was much easier than splashing about upstairs. After helping her brush her teeth, Jenny tucked her into bed and read *Peter Rabbit,* her favourite story.

Betty was fast asleep before Jenny had finished the final page.

She tiptoed out, pulling the door mostly shut behind her—just enough so she could hear if the little one cried out.

When Ruth arrived, she was carrying a neatly folded piece of pale blue fabric in her arms.

"The material I told you about," she said, holding it out for Jenny to admire.

The print was charming—a soft blue background with tiny yellow flowers scattered across it. The dress pattern was a button-through design with a flared skirt, cap sleeves, and a smart stand-up collar.

"Oh, Ruth, it's *lovely,*" Jenny said.

"I fell in love with it the moment I saw it. I've just got to finish the collar, sew in the sleeves, and add the buttons, then it's done."

As Ruth worked at the sewing machine, Jenny picked up her knitting, and the two girls settled into a comfortable rhythm, chatting as they went.

"Do you think it'll get serious with Marcus?" Ruth asked after a while.

Jenny let out a slow sigh. "I hope so. He's so kind, and I've never felt this way about anyone before. But… it frightens me a bit. Him being a flyer—and what'll happen after the war."

"What do you mean?"

Jenny shrugged. "He'll go back to America, won't he? And then what? Will he find someone back home? Or will he want to take me with him? And if he *did*… how could I leave everyone? My family, my friends. *You.*"

Ruth fell quiet.

Jenny continued, voice soft. "I'd never see you all again. And my parents could never afford to come and visit. I'd miss Betty growing up. She'd forget me."

Ruth nodded slowly. "It's true. It's the other side of the world. And for girls like us, who've never been further than the next town, it's… well, it's a long way. Could you even afford to come home for visits?"

"No," Jenny said sadly. "And my parents certainly couldn't visit me."

She sighed again. "But I shouldn't get ahead of myself. We've only had two dates."

"Still," Ruth said with a smile, "I'd say the way he looks at you, he's completely *smitten*."

With a little flourish, she pulled the dress from the machine and held it up.

"Well? What do you think?"

"Oh, Ruth—it's *gorgeous*. Try it on!"

Ruth stripped down to her underwear and slipped into the dress. It fitted perfectly, hugging her slender frame in all the right places. With her auburn hair and green eyes, the pale blue fabric made her glow.

She quickly changed back into her clothes and laid the dress carefully on the table to mark out the buttonholes and sew on the buttons.

"All I need now is a nice belt," she said. "I'll check the haberdashery tomorrow—there's bound to be something."

Jenny smiled. "And while you're there, you can ask Mrs. Merrett when Raymond's coming home."

Ruth blushed. "I'll do no such thing, Jenny Jackson. I'll find out when I see him in the village."

Jenny laughed. "Oh Ruth, you'll end up an old maid if you're not careful. *Seize the moment!*"

Ruth snorted. "Yes—seize the moment and make a complete fool of myself, more like. What if he *doesn't* like me? If he did, he'd have asked me out last time he was home. We could've gone to the Christmas dances at the village hall."

Jenny didn't argue. But she made a silent decision right there: if the opportunity presented itself, she'd give Raymond a little nudge in Ruth's direction.

Ruth had just sewn the final button in place when Jenny's parents came in. She held up the finished dress with pride, and Veronica beamed.

"Oh, Ruth, it's lovely, dear—and such a beautiful colour for you too."

"It really suits her, Mum," Jenny agreed. "Ruth tried it on

earlier before finishing the buttons, and it's a perfect fit."

"Well, it's a credit to you," Veronica said warmly. "And was Betty all right going to bed?"

"No trouble at all," Jenny replied. "I read *Peter Rabbit*, and she was asleep before I'd even got halfway through."

"Oh, I'm not surprised. I think she knows that story by heart—heaven knows I do." Veronica smiled as she began taking off her coat.

Ronald joined them, rubbing his hands together from the cold. "Anyway, what did you think of the film?" Jenny asked.

"Oh, it was great—and as you said, Jenny, so funny," her mother said, chuckling. "We really enjoyed it. And fish and chips before we went in—it was a lovely evening. Thank you, girls. We do appreciate it."

"No need to thank us, Mrs Jackson," Ruth said. "I don't know about Jenny, but I've had a lovely evening."

"Me too," Jenny agreed.

"Would you like a cup of tea before you go, Ruth?" Veronica asked.

"Oh no, thank you. I'd best be getting off—I don't like to keep Mum and Dad up too late on a weeknight."

"Of course, dear," Veronica said kindly.

"I'll walk you home, Ruth. It's pitch-black out there," Ronald offered, already reaching for his coat again.

"Oh, Mr Jackson, there's no need. I don't want to trouble you—"

"Nonsense. No trouble at all. As I said—it's pitch black. I'll see you get home safe."

"Thank you. I appreciate it."

"I'll come too, Dad," Jenny said, grabbing her own coat. "I'll give you company on the way back."

"I'll put the kettle on," Veronica called after them. "Tea will be ready when you get back."

Outside, the night air was bitterly cold, and a thick layer of snow crunched under their feet. They hugged their coats tightly around them as they stepped into the still, dark evening.

"I swear it's getting colder," Jenny muttered. "I do hope we have a good summer to make up for this."

"So do we all, love," Ronald replied.

As they turned a corner, a couple of airmen on leave spotted the girls and whistled.

"Hey, fancy a drink, sweetheart?" one of them called.

Then they saw Ronald striding beside them and froze in place.

Ronald gave them a firm look. "No, son, they don't. They're both underage. And this young lady's my daughter. So, off you go—home with you."

"Oh—yes, sir. Right," one of them mumbled before both airmen broke into an awkward trot and vanished down the street.

The girls giggled.

Ronald chuckled too. "Just high spirits," he said, "but that's why I didn't want young Ruth walking home alone."

"No, you're quite right, Dad," Jenny said. "It could've got out of hand if she'd been by herself."

"I'm glad you came," Ruth agreed sincerely. "Thank you, Mr Jackson."

Meanwhile, at the local pub, Marcus sat nursing a pint with Dickie and Alvin, deep in conversation.

"So," he said, a teasing glint in his eyes, "what *exactly* did you two do to him?"

Dickie leaned back innocently. "Us, Skip? Nothing. Did we, Alvin?"

Alvin gave a mock-serious nod. "Nope. Not much, anyway. I just… enlightened him."

"Well, didn't *look* like nothing," Marcus said, raising an eyebrow. "He was clutching his side and clearly in pain."

Dickie chuckled. "Ah, the art of karate. Subtle but effective. No bruises, just a lesson learned."

Marcus turned to him curiously. "So how'd you get into it?"

"My dad was in the Diplomatic Corps. We spent time in China when I was a kid. I got friendly with some of the local lads and started going to lessons with them. Been practising ever since. Must say, it's come in handy."

"I can see that," Marcus said, impressed. "I might take it up after the war."

"Good idea, Skip," Dickie said.

"But first," Alvin added dryly, "we need to defeat that strutting little maniac."

Marcus raised his glass. "I'll drink to that."

Just then, the bell rang for last orders. Marcus looked toward the bar.

"One more for the road?" he asked, already sliding out of his seat.

He didn't wait for an answer—he knew exactly what it would be. A few minutes later, he returned with three fresh pints, and the men settled back, their laughter subdued but steady.

Fifteen minutes until time was called. Just long enough to

sit, talk, and forget the war for a little while.

As the three men made their way back to base, their breath clouding in the frosty night air, conversation turned inevitably to the war.

"What do you reckon will happen in Bataan?" Dickie asked, kicking at a patch of snow. "Think we're making any real headway?"

Alvin exhaled slowly, his brow furrowed. "Hard to say. It could go either way, but… to be honest, it doesn't look good."

He didn't say more than that, but Marcus and Dickie knew why his tone had turned grim. Alvin's older brother was stationed there, and his parents were beside themselves with worry. Having both their sons serving in different theatres of war was a burden no family should have to bear.

Marcus nodded solemnly. "Let's just hope they can pull a rabbit out of the hat and push through. The alternative…" He didn't finish the sentence. He didn't have to. None of them wanted to voice what that might mean.

Sensing the heavy silence settling between them, Dickie quickly steered the conversation in another direction. "Heard about the SS *Normandie*?" he asked. "Such a shame. Could've been a huge asset to the war effort."

"Yeah," Marcus said. "Hell of a loss. At least there weren't many casualties—just the one, I heard."

"One too many," Alvin muttered. "And all down to someone being careless. Damn shame."

The others murmured their agreement as the lights of the base came into view. Snow crunched beneath their boots as they passed through the checkpoint, the guards nodding them through with a tired salute.

"Well," Marcus said, rubbing his hands together to keep the cold at bay, "tomorrow's another day. Let's hope it's a quiet one."

"Quiet sounds good," Dickie said. "I've had my fill of excitement this week."

"Same here," Alvin added. "Let's hope we all get a decent night's sleep."

They parted ways at the barracks, each heading off into the dark to their own quarters. The base had settled into its nighttime hush—just the distant hum of generators and the occasional clatter of boots on concrete.

As Marcus climbed into his bunk and pulled the coarse military blanket over him, his thoughts drifted to Jenny. He smiled to himself in the dark, remembering the feel of her hand in his, the light in her eyes when she laughed.

Outside, the wind howled faintly, and somewhere in the distance a dog barked. But inside the dormitory, silence reigned—for now.

Tomorrow, the war would still be there. But for tonight, they slept.

Chapter 4

Veronica and Ronald sat quietly in the sitting room, the soft crackle of the wireless filling the air as the announcer read out the latest headlines.

"Do you think the Germans really did sink the *Normandie*?" Veronica asked, glancing at her husband with furrowed brows.

Ron shook his head slowly. "No, love. I doubt it. The official word is it was a spark from a welder's torch that started the fire. I know the papers are full of rumours—whispers of sabotage by the Germans, or even the Japs—but I don't buy it. Best to stick with what the news on the wireless says, not get caught up in all the gossip and scare stories."

"Yes... I suppose you're right," Veronica said quietly.

She leaned back in her chair, her eyes distant. "Still, I worry about the girls. They're so young, and they've had their youth stolen by this war—just like we did. It's so terribly unfair."

Ron reached over and gently patted her hand. "I know, love. We've seen it before, haven't we? But we got through it last time—and we'll get through this one too. At least little Betty's too young to really understand what's going on."

Veronica gave a small, sad smile. "Thank goodness for that." Her smile faltered as another thought struck her. "But now with Singapore fallen… all those boys out there. Just children, some of them."

Tears welled in her eyes, and Ron gave her hand a gentle squeeze.

"I know. I used to think it would've been lovely to have a son, but now… I'm not so sure. He'd be out there, like the rest of them. We'd never sleep, never stop worrying."

She nodded silently. "They called the last one the war to end all wars," she whispered. "Let's hope this time they're right."

There was a pause, and then Ron brightened and gave her a smile. "How about I make us a nice cup of tea?"

She leaned in and kissed his cheek. "I'll put the kettle on."

The following morning at Findley's department store, Jenny stepped into the staff room for her tea break and spotted Mrs Merrett sitting alone at one of the corner tables, a cup of tea in front of her and a half-finished crossword beside it. Gathering her courage, Jenny approached.

"Mrs Merrett, could I have a word, please?"

Victoria Merrett looked up, her expression softening. "Of course, dear. Sit down."

Jenny pulled out a chair and perched nervously on the edge of it. "You're Raymond's mother, aren't you?" she asked. "I'm Jenny Jackson. My parents run the grocer's in the village."

"Yes, of course, I know who you are," Victoria said with a warm smile. "What can I do for you?"

Jenny hesitated, fiddling with the corner of the tablecloth. "Well… it's about Raymond."

Victoria's eyebrows lifted in interest. "Raymond? Goodness, what about him?"

Jenny flushed and rushed out the words. "It's a bit awkward, really, but it's about my friend Ruth. She's—well, she's always liked him. Ever since school. And I know he's coming home on leave soon, and I thought… I mean, maybe he might ask her to go to the pictures while he's home?"

Victoria blinked, surprised by the flurry of words and the earnestness on Jenny's face. She smiled to herself, but kept her tone gentle. "Well now, that's very sweet of you to say. But why hasn't Ruth asked me herself—or even spoken to Raymond when he gets home?"

"Oh, she'd never do that," Jenny said quickly. "She'd be far too shy. She'd be mortified if she knew I was talking to you. But she really does care for him. I used to think it was just a schoolgirl thing, but it's more than that. And with the war, well… nothing's guaranteed, is it?"

Victoria's smile faded slightly. "No," she murmured. "You're right about that." Her voice turned thoughtful. "Funny you should mention Ruth. He used to talk about her all the time when he was at school. And even now, he still mentions her in his letters."

Jenny's eyes lit up. "Really? Oh, that's wonderful! But why didn't he ever ask her to the Christmas dance at the village hall? She was so disappointed."

Victoria chuckled. "He thought she didn't like him. He was afraid to ask, in case she said no. Didn't want to look foolish, bless him."

"Oh, poor Ruth," Jenny sighed. "She's been pining for him all this time. Please tell him she likes him—really likes him—and if he asked her out, she'd say yes in a heartbeat."

"I'll be sure to let him know," Victoria said, reaching across the table to pat Jenny's hand. "Thank you, dear. That will mean a lot to him—it'll give him something to hold on to when he's out there."

Jenny stood. "I'd best be getting back to work. Please don't say anything to Ruth. She'd be furious with me if she knew I said anything."

"Don't worry, I won't breathe a word," Victoria promised with a wink.

"Thank you, Mrs Merrett."

Jenny left the room with a smile on her face, hoping she'd helped set something special in motion.

When Raymond arrived home on his forty-eight-hour embarkation leave, his mother greeted him with a tight hug and a warm smile.

"I think you should ask young Ruth out while you're home," Victoria said casually as she hung up his coat.

Raymond raised an eyebrow. "Ruth? No, Mum… she's not interested. I'd rather not make a fool of myself."

Victoria crossed her arms and gave him a knowing look. "That's where you're wrong, my lad. I happen to have it on very good authority that she's *very* interested—and has been since school."

He stared at her in disbelief. "You're serious? She *likes* me?"

"I wouldn't say it if I didn't mean it," she said gently. "You won't embarrass yourself or her, I promise. Just go round and ask the girl."

He hesitated. "Whose authority are we talking about?"

"Jenny Jackson," she said with a small smile. "And if *anyone* would know, it's her—they've been inseparable since they were babies."

"Jenny," Raymond murmured. "Yes… she would know."

"One thing though," Victoria added. "You *mustn't* tell Ruth that Jenny said anything. Just say you thought you'd like to take her out."

"Alright. I won't say a word. And... well, no time like the present." He kissed her cheek and practically bounded out the door, leaving his mother smiling wistfully after him.

As the door closed behind him, Victoria sighed. Her heart ached for all the young people caught up in this war—so much hope and promise, shadowed by uncertainty. It wasn't fair.

When Ruth opened her front door and saw Raymond standing there in his uniform, she very nearly lost her footing. He looked taller, older, more confident—and so handsome her breath caught in her throat.

He offered a small smile. "Hello, Ruth. I was wondering... would you like to go out with me while I'm home? I've only got a couple of days, but I thought maybe we could go to the pictures tomorrow night?"

For a moment, Ruth was too stunned to speak. Her heart raced. She'd imagined this moment so many times—and now that it was really happening, she could hardly believe it. Then, slowly, her face lit up with the brightest smile he'd ever seen.

"Yes, Raymond," she said breathlessly. "I'd really like that."

His relief was palpable. "Great! I'll meet you after work, we'll grab some fish and chips, then catch the film. That alright?"

"Oh yes," she said, her voice a whisper. "More than alright."

At that moment, her mother appeared in the hallway, wiping her hands on a tea towel. "Well, good heavens! Is that young Raymond? Come in, lad, come in, how are you?"

Raymond gave her a warm smile. "Hello, Mrs Mitchell. I'm

well, thank you. How are you?"

"Oh, fair to middling, son. Ruth, don't keep the lad standing on the doorstep—bring him into the parlour. Your dad will be glad to see him."

"Oh, I don't want to be any bother..." Raymond started.

"Nonsense. You're not bothering anyone. The kettle's just about to boil."

Inside, Stephen Mitchell looked up from his newspaper and stood when he saw Raymond.

"Well, if it isn't Raymond Merrett. Good to see you, lad." He extended a hand, and Raymond shook it firmly.

"It's good to see you too, sir."

"Artillery, right?"

"Yes, sir."

"Same as me," Stephen nodded. "So I know what you're dealing with." The two men sat and talked for a while—about tactics, the state of things, and what might lie ahead.

"So do you know where you're headed next?" Stephen asked.

Raymond shook his head. "No, sir. They don't tell us until the last moment. Loose lips, and all that. They're worried someone might get drunk and say too much, so they keep us in the dark."

"Probably just as well," Stephen said with a grim smile. "Less to worry about that way."

Gillian returned with the tea tray, and conversation turned to lighter matters. When the cups were empty and the clock ticked on, Raymond stood.

"Well, thank you very much for the tea, Mrs Mitchell." He shook hands with Stephen again. "It was good to see you both."

"You take care of yourself, lad," Gillian said, kissing his cheek gently. "Come home safe."

"I will," Raymond promised.

Ruth walked with him to the front door. He looked down at her and smiled.

"We didn't get much chance to talk tonight—but we'll make up for that tomorrow. I'll be outside the shop after work."

She nodded, her cheeks flushed. "I'll look forward to it."

He bent and kissed her cheek. "Goodnight, Ruth. Sweet dreams."

"Goodnight, Raymond," she whispered. "You too."

He left with a light heart; certain those dreams would now come easily.

Back in the parlour, Ruth stood glowing as she took off her coat. Her mother looked up from her knitting.

"Well, that was a lovely surprise. Did you know he was coming?"

Ruth shook her head. "No, I had no idea. I was completely stunned when I opened the door." Her smile widened. "He's asked me to the pictures tomorrow night. We're getting fish and chips first. Is that alright?"

Her mother beamed. "Of course, it is. We're very happy for you."

"I've had an idea," Gillian said. "Why don't you take your new dress and change after work? It's just the occasion for it."

"But what'll I do with my work dress?"

"Leave it in your locker—or ask Jenny to bring it home for you. I'm sure she won't mind."

Ruth smiled brightly. "No, she won't. That's a brilliant idea,

Mum."

The next day, when Ruth told Jenny, Jenny lit up with happiness for her friend.

"Oh Ruth, that's lovely! Did he just turn up?"

Ruth was glowing, her smile lighting up her whole face. "Yes, I couldn't believe it. And he came in and chatted to Dad for ages—had a cup of tea and everything." She sounded like a schoolgirl in love, and she was floating on air.

"I don't know how I'm going to get through the day," she confessed, lowering her voice. "Oh, and I've brought my new dress to wear. Would you take this one home for me, Jen, please?"

"Of course I will. Oh Ruth, it's going to look beautiful on you. I can't wait to hear all about it tomorrow."

The day dragged for both girls. Jenny kept glancing at the clock, not just for Ruth, but because she knew Marcus would likely come by again that evening. He'd started popping around most evenings if he was free—sometimes to play Ludo, sometimes cards—and their friendship was slowly blooming into something deeper. A quiet, comfortable closeness was forming.

Finally, the workday ended, and Ruth dashed off to change. When she emerged from the ladies, Jenny's eyes widened with admiration.

She'd styled her hair with a ribbon that matched the pale blue of her dress, and her new belt from haberdashery tied the whole outfit together perfectly.

"Oh Ruth," Jenny breathed, "you look *lovely*."

"Well, look at you," came a voice. It was Sheila, one of their co-workers, who grinned playfully. "Got a hot date then?"

Ruth grinned back. "Going to the pictures."

"I didn't know you had a boyfriend," Sheila said curiously.

"He's just home on leave—we were all at school together," Jenny explained smoothly.

"Oh, nice! Well, have a great evening."

Raymond was waiting outside, and his face lit up when he saw them. He greeted Jenny politely, but his eyes never strayed from Ruth.

"Hello Jenny, how are you?"

"I'm fine, thank you, Raymond. And you?"

"Oh, well, thanks." But he barely looked at her—he only had eyes for Ruth.

Jenny smiled at them. "Have a lovely evening, you two." She watched as they crossed the road together, Raymond placing a protective hand under Ruth's elbow as they weaved through the traffic. Jenny smiled, her heart full. Seeing them together made it all worthwhile. She was so glad she had spoken to Mrs Merrett.

That evening, after dropping Ruth's dress off at the Mitchells', Jenny returned home and told her parents about the unexpected romance.

"Well, I never," Veronica said, touched by the story. "So he just turned up out of the blue on her doorstep?"

"He's a good lad," Ronald nodded. "He'll have a lot in common with Steve, both artillerymen."

Jenny and her mother rolled their eyes in unison.

"He's come to court the girl, not talk artillery tactics," Veronica scolded gently. "Honestly—men! No sense of romance."

Later, Marcus arrived and joined them for a quiet evening of cards. It was these small, peaceful moments that Jenny had begun to cherish more and more.

Meanwhile, Ruth was in seventh heaven.

They'd gone to a cosy café just around the corner from the cinema. It was warm inside, and the scent of frying fish and vinegar hung in the air. Raymond had ordered them fish and chips, and they sat at a small table by the window, chatting easily as they ate.

"Can I ask you something?" Ruth ventured, her voice soft.

"You can ask me anything," he said sincerely. "What is it?"

"Why did you never ask me to the dances at the village hall?"

He looked sheepish. "Honestly? I didn't think you liked me. You hardly ever spoke to me. You always seemed a bit… distant. I guessed you didn't want to know."

"Oh dear," Ruth said, laughing gently. "I thought the same about *you*! What a pair of clods we are."

He smiled at her, his eyes twinkling. "Well, we're here now. And with any luck, we'll have a few more evenings like this."

"Let's hope so."

During the film, he reached for her hand, and she didn't hesitate. She held it tightly, and all the noise and chaos of the world faded away. She had never felt happier in her life.

Raymond, for his part, committed every detail of the evening to memory. He knew he'd hold onto it during the long nights ahead—something warm and real to keep him anchored.

On the walk home, the streets were quiet. The sound of their footsteps echoed off the buildings, their breath visible in the crisp night air.

"Ruth," he said softly, "would you like to come to tea tomorrow night? I have to go back on Wednesday afternoon, and I want to spend the day with Mum—but I'd really like to spend the evening with you both."

"Oh, I'd love to," she said without hesitation. "But are you sure your mum won't mind?"

"She'll be thrilled. Say you'll come—it's my last night home."

"Of course I'll come," she said, smiling.

At her doorstep, he hesitated for a moment, then gently tilted her chin and kissed her on the lips. It was soft and brief, but it left her breathless. She sighed with contentment.

"I'll see you tomorrow," he said quietly.

She nodded. "Yes. See you tomorrow."

She watched him walk away, her heart full and heavy at the same time. She hoped, with everything in her, that this wasn't all they'd ever have.

As Raymond passed Jenny's front door, it opened, and Jenny and Marcus stepped out into the crisp evening air.

"Evening, Raymond," Jenny greeted him brightly. "Did you have a good time?"

He grinned, still riding the wave of happiness. "Oh, evening, Jenny—yes, smashing, thanks."

She turned to Marcus. "Oh, Marcus, this is Raymond—Ruth's boyfriend. Raymond, this is Marcus."

The two young men shook hands, a quiet understanding passing between them.

"Nice to meet you," Marcus said politely.

"You too," Raymond replied, before tipping his cap and continuing on down the road.

When he was out of earshot, Marcus turned to Jenny with a raised eyebrow. "I didn't know Ruth had a boyfriend."

Jenny smiled to herself. "Oh yes. It's a long story. I'll tell you all about it on Friday."

"Sounds intriguing," he said, his eyes twinkling. Then, after a brief pause, he stepped closer. "I'll see you Friday… sweet dreams, Jenny."

And with that, he leaned in and kissed her—softly, gently—on the lips.

Jenny's heart skipped a beat. It was tender and sweet, and her cheeks glowed with warmth.

"Night, Marcus," she whispered. "See you Friday."

As she watched him walk away, her hand touched her lips, and a smile crept across her face. She stood there for a moment, under the quiet stars, before finally stepping inside, her heart light and full.

Chapter 5

Victoria watched her son slowly pushing food around his plate. Finally, she put down her fork and asked gently, "Is everything all right, son?"

Raymond looked up, his expression serious. "Mum, I've been thinking. I know Ruth and I have only had one proper date, but we've known each other all our lives. Normally, I'd court her for a few years, take things slow… but we might not have a few years. These couple of days could be all we ever get. So I was wondering—do you think it's too soon to ask her to marry me?"

Victoria was taken aback. She knew Raymond had always liked Ruth—ever since they were schoolchildren—but she hadn't realised just how deep his feelings ran. It took her a moment to respond.

"Well," she said carefully, "she's underage, so you'd have to ask her father's permission. But are you sure, love? I mean really sure. Marriage is a big step. You're about to be shipped out, and it's easy to confuse strong feelings with the fear of what's to come. Are you certain it's not just the war talking?"

When he looked up at her, she saw it in his eyes—solid, unwavering, sincere.

"I've never been more sure of anything," he said quietly. "I fell in love with her in the first year at secondary school, and I've never stopped loving her. I've tried going out with other girls, but none of them were Ruth. Nothing felt right. It never will."

She sighed, deeply moved. "Well then," she said, "if that's how you feel, go and speak to her father. He usually comes home for lunch, I've noticed, and he works just down the road. Catch him before you meet Ruth tonight."

"Thanks, Mum," he said, standing up and pacing a little. Then he paused. "But... how am I going to get a ring in time? I've only got today and tomorrow morning."

She gave a little chuckle. "Oh, I thought you meant to *get married* now! An engagement—that's different."

Raymond ran a hand through his hair. "Yeah, no, not married yet—just engaged. A promise. Something real to hold on to."

Victoria nodded thoughtfully. "Well, in that case... I've got an idea. Your grandmother's rings are in my jewel box. When she died, your father gave them to me, and when he died, I just kept them safe."

Raymond's face lit up. "You'd let me give Gran's ring?"

"Of course," Victoria said, her voice soft with emotion. "She'd have liked that. Ruth's a good girl—kind, steady. She'd be proud for her ring to go to someone like her."

The morning dragged for Raymond. He paced, checked the time every few minutes, and was at the window the moment he spotted Stephen Mitchell heading down the street for lunch. Without hesitation, he dashed outside.

"Mr Mitchell!" he called. "Could I have a quick word, please?"

Stephen turned and gave a nod. "Ah, Raymond—yes, lad, what is it? I'm on my break, so make it quick."

Raymond took a deep breath. "I know it's sudden, sir, but I'd like your permission to ask Ruth to marry me. To get engaged before I leave tomorrow."

Stephen stopped walking and turned fully to face him. For a long moment, he said nothing. He simply studied the young man before him, seeing something familiar—the same hopeful urgency he'd once had in his own youth. A memory stirred of standing nervously before Gillian's father all those years ago.

Finally, he cleared his throat. "It's a big step, Raymond. She's only just seventeen, and you're going off to war. This isn't something to rush into lightly."

"I know, sir," Raymond said quickly. "I do. And I promise you—I'll be faithful to her, always. I have nothing but respect for Ruth, and I would never—well, I think you know what I mean."

Stephen gave a small nod. "Aye, I do. And I appreciate you saying it out loud. All right then—you have my permission. But mind you, take care of her heart. It's not an easy thing, this war. She'll be left waiting."

"I will," Raymond said earnestly. "Thank you, sir. I'll do right by her, I promise."

The two men shook hands. "Now off you go," Stephen said. "You've got a girl to propose to—and I've got a lunch to eat."

Raymond laughed, practically floating back down the lane. When he stepped inside the house again, he couldn't contain his joy—he grabbed his mother by the waist, twirled her around the kitchen, and kissed both her cheeks.

"Well," she said, laughing, "I take it that's a yes?"

"It certainly is. He gave me his blessing."

"And now," she said, gently touching his arm, "let's go and choose a ring for Ruth. Something old, something full of love, something that ties the past to the future."

Raymond nodded, eyes shining. "Oh mum that sounds wonderful."

The engagement ring was a tiny ruby surrounded by delicate diamonds, set in white gold. Raymond turned it over in his fingers, hardly able to believe how perfect it was.

"Oh, she'll love it," he breathed. "And the wedding ring... it's white gold too. Mum, they're perfect."

Victoria nodded, her eyes shining. "Yes. I think your father would want you to give it to the girl you're going to marry."

Raymond looked down at the ring again. His father had died just months after his birth; his body weakened beyond repair from being gassed in the Great War. His lungs had never recovered, and by 1922, they had simply given out. Victoria had been left a young widow with a newborn son and had never remarried. She'd never forgiven the Germans—and now, with another war, she feared she might lose her only child to the same enemy.

Her voice trembled only slightly as she added, "Yes, I think she'll love it very much."

She gave his arm a small pat and turned away, busying herself at the sink. She would save her tears for after he'd gone—tomorrow, when the house would fall silent again.

When Raymond met Ruth outside the shop that evening, he felt as if his feet barely touched the ground. Her face lit up when she saw him.

Before taking her home, he asked if they could walk to the green.

"But it's freezing—and it's snowing!" Ruth laughed, pulling her coat tighter.

"I know," he said, grinning. "But this won't take long. I just... I want to ask you something."

She looked at him curiously, eyebrows raised. "Oh? What kind of something?"

"Come on—let's sit for a second," he said, brushing snow off one of the benches under the bare trees. She sat down beside him, her breath showing in little clouds.

Then Raymond took a small velvet box from his coat pocket, and in one smooth movement, dropped to one knee.

Ruth froze. Her gloved hand flew to her mouth.

His voice was steady, but his heart thudded in his chest. "Ruth Mitchell, will you give me the honour of becoming my wife?"

She stared down at him, eyes wide. The ring sparkled even in the dim evening light. She blinked several times, stunned.

"It's beautiful," she whispered. "But... but I'm only seventeen. My dad..."

"I know," Raymond said softly. "I spoke to him at lunchtime. He said yes."

Her eyes welled with tears. "You... already asked him?"

He nodded.

For a moment, all Ruth could do was stare at him. Then the tears spilled over and she laughed through them. "Oh yes. Yes, Raymond—I'll marry you."

His relief was like a wave crashing over him. He slipped the ring onto her finger—it fitted perfectly—then stood, pulled her gently into his arms, and kissed her.

The snow fell around them in soft silence.

Jenny was over the moon when Ruth showed her the ring the next day. She cried and hugged her friend, marvelling at the delicate ruby.

Ruth, glowing and happier than Jenny had ever seen her, made a rare request. "Jen... I need a favour. I'd never ask this normally—but could you tell Miss Penheart I'm sick today? Say I've got a tummy bug or something. Just so I can stay home, spend the day with Raymond. He leaves this afternoon, and I want to go with him and his mum to the station."

Jenny didn't hesitate. "Of course I will. Don't worry—I'll cover for you. And Ruth..." she paused, touching the ring again, "you deserve every minute."

Ruth squeezed her hand. "Thank you, Jenny. I don't know what I'd do without you."

Jenny smiled. "I'd do the same. Just promise you'll tell me everything after."

The war and the year rolled on, the battle for Bataan raged on, the Japanese opened fire on Australian military nurses on the Banka Islands, killing twenty-one, and the world was in shock over such a brutal act; this was one of the most horrendous acts of the war to date. The Japanese attacked Darwine, and so it went on. People became weary, but the Dunkerque spirit prevailed, and they pulled together and got on with it.

In March, the government raised the age of conscription to forty-five for both men and women, Hitler's war machine rumbled on, and the Japanese made many advances in the far east; closer to home the RAF launched a raid on Essen.

At the end of March, Marcus told Jenny he had a couple of weeks' furlough.

"What's furlough?" she asked, puzzled.

"Leave," he smiled. "I'm going home for a couple of weeks to see my folks."

The look of disappointment that flickered across her face made his heart twist. He reached for her hand.

"It's just a couple of weeks, honey—and I'll write. I don't know if the letters will reach you before I'm back, but I'll write all the same."

Jenny tried to smile, determined not to seem clingy. She didn't want him thinking she was the sort of girl who couldn't manage without her chap.

"You need to see your family," she said with a small nod. "It's been so long since you last saw them. Do they know about me?"

"Oh, they know all about you," he said with a grin. "That's why I think we should have our picture taken—something proper. Then we can each have a copy, and I can show them how pretty you are. I've been trying to get the crew photographer to do it, but he's not allowed to use military film for private pictures."

"That's a great idea!" Jenny said. "I'll ask Dad if he still has film in his camera. I'm sure he's got a roll somewhere."

"When are you going?" she asked quietly.

"Next week."

Her face fell again, and Marcus gave her hand a gentle squeeze. "Will you be back in time for my birthday?" she asked, trying to sound casual.

"Your birthday? Heavens, when is it?"

"April sixteenth."

"I get back on the fifteenth," he said, smiling. "Just in time. What would you like me to bring you back for your birthday?"

She looked at him with a soft smile and said, "You."

His eyes lit up, his heart full. "Just me? Nothing else?"

Jenny shook her head. "No, nothing else. Just you."

He leaned in and kissed the tip of her nose, hugging her tightly. But in his mind, he made a note: he'd ask his mother to help him choose something special—a keepsake Jenny could hold onto while he was away.

Danny Butchers lay in his bunk staring at the ceiling, unable to sleep. It was just gone half past six, and he knew there wasn't much point trying to drift off again. The day would be starting soon.

His thoughts turned—as they so often did—to New York. He grinned to himself. It was either leave or end up in a pine box by now. He could almost picture Jake's face, twisted with rage, yelling at the boys to find him—and more importantly, to find the money. Three thousand dollars. A fortune for a lad like him. He hadn't kept all of it, though.

He thought of Sister Angelica and the look on her face when he handed over the five hundred dollars.

"Where did this money come from, Danny?" she'd asked, clutching the crumpled notes.

Danny had simply tapped the side of his nose and said, "Best you don't know, Sister. But trust me—the guy I took it from won't miss it. Just keep stumm about where you got it. You don't want him knowing you have it. Your habit won't protect you from someone like him."

She'd looked torn. "Well… I can't pretend we don't need it. Five hundred dollars… But I can't take illegal money, Danny."

He'd shrugged. "It's not exactly illegal. But if you don't want it, I'll find someone else."

He'd tilted his head, knowing she'd take it in the end. And she had.

"Well… thank you, Danny. It will come in very useful."

He'd wanted to give more—but knew she wouldn't take it. Would start asking questions he couldn't answer.

He'd kissed her cheek on the way out, making her blush. It had been many years since a handsome young man had kissed her, even on the cheek.

As he'd opened the door, he'd turned. "Just one thing, Sister. If anyone comes looking for me—you haven't seen me in months. You don't know where I am. Safer that way. For you and the kids."

She'd sighed deeply. "Oh, Danny… what kind of trouble are you in? Maybe we could go to the police."

Danny had laughed. "The police? I don't think so, Sister? You don't want the cops involved. Just plead ignorance. Besides, it won't be a lie—I'm not telling you where I'm going, because to be honest, I don't know. Not yet."

He'd disappeared into the night, and Sister Angelica had stood there in the hallway, the notes trembling in her hand.

She knew it was the proceeds of crime. But they were desperate. The roof leaked, the pantry was bare, and the children needed shoes.

She looked heavenward and whispered, "Forgive me, Father, for I am about to sin."

Danny grabbed young Tony on his way out and bent to have

a quiet word in his ear. The boy was nine years old, full of attitude and too much street smarts for someone his age. Danny could see himself in Tony—raw, sharp, and already teetering on the edge. If someone didn't step in, he'd end up the same way. And Danny wouldn't be around to pull him back.

"Hey, Tony—c'mere a sec."

"Hi Danny, whatcha doin'?"

Danny rested a hand on the boy's shoulder. "Listen to me, Tony. I've gotta go away for a while, and I want you to promise me something."

Tony looked up, curious. "What?"

"Promise me you'll work hard at school. Listen to the sisters, do what they say, and keep yourself on the straight and narrow. You hear me?"

"Sure, but where you goin'?"

Danny shook his head. "I don't know yet, kid—and it's best you don't know either. But I'll keep in touch with the sisters, and if I hear you've been messin' around or getting into trouble, I'll come back and tan your hide. Got it?"

"I got it," Tony said, eyes wide.

"Yeah, you *hear* me—but are you *listening*, Tony?"

"What d'ya mean? If I hear you, then I'm listening."

Danny chuckled. The kid was sharp. Too sharp. "I mean, are you takin' in what I'm sayin'? Like, really takin' it in."

Tony nodded slowly. "I think so. But Danny—you did okay, and you never worked hard at school."

Danny crouched to meet him eye to eye. "No, Tony. I didn't do okay. It just *looks* like I did. That's why I gotta leave. I got mixed up with some bad people. Real bad. And now I gotta disappear. I don't want that for you."

Tony looked pale.

"I want you to be somebody. Be a doctor, a teacher—heck, even a fireman. Just don't go near the mob, Tony. You do, you'll end up in the gutter with your throat cut, or a bullet in your head. Is that what you want?"

Tony shook his head fast. "No!"

"Then listen to the sisters. They care about you. You're a good kid, Tony—but you need a firm hand. Don't make the mistakes I did."

Danny ruffled his hair and gave him a quick, awkward hug. In another life, Tony could've been the little brother Danny never had. And if he could keep *just one* kid on the right path, maybe that meant his life hadn't been all for nothing.

Now, thousands of miles away, Danny lay in his bunk in a cold English barracks, thinking of that little boy. He wondered how Tony was getting on. Maybe he'd call Sister Angelica, just to check in. Truth be told, Danny wasn't as hard as he acted. He rubbed people the wrong way, sure—but he had a conscience, and Tony had made a mark on him.

His thoughts drifted to the money he'd stolen from Jake and what the money he'd made from the jewellery, plus he still had some jewellery to sell. He had enough put aside to start fresh when the war ended. Maybe Montana—he'd always fancied being a cowboy. Or maybe he'd stay in England. Life here was slower, quieter. It had a certain charm.

A sudden wave of homesickness washed over him. He wanted to hear a familiar voice—someone who didn't judge him. He slipped quietly out of bed, dressed in the dark, and padded through the corridor to the telephone.

He asked the operator to connect him to the Sisters of Mercy Orphanage. After what felt like forever, a sleepy voice answered.

"Sisters of Mercy Orphanage..."

"Sister Angelica? It's Danny. Danny Butchers."

"Good heavens, Danny Butchers! Do you *have* any idea what time it is?"

He glanced at his watch. "Jeez, Sister, I'm sorry. I didn't think."

"Danny," she chided gently, "don't take the Lord's name in vain."

"Sorry, Sister. But I just wanted to hear your voice... and ask how young Tony's doing."

Her tone softened. She missed him, too. Danny wasn't all bad—she'd always seen it.

"He's doing well, Danny. Working hard at his lessons. He's changed—especially since those men came. I think they frightened him."

Danny stiffened. "Men? What men?"

"Two rough-looking fellows. They came asking where you were. If I'd seen you."

His voice went cold. "What did you tell them?"

"I told them the truth. Or at least your truth—I said I hadn't seen you in months and didn't know where you'd gone. Tony was there. He saw them. They got nasty, but I told them I'd call the police. They left, but loitered outside for a while. It scared the children."

Danny's heart pounded. "Are they still coming around?"

"No, not anymore. I spoke to Sergeant Peters—he sent a patrol by every few hours. They stopped turning up after that."

Danny let out a long breath. "That's good. Everyone's okay, though?"

"Yes, Danny. Everyone's fine. But I had to lie to the bishop." Her voice dropped to a whisper. "I told him the money came from an anonymous benefactor. Do you know how many Hail Marys I had to say? I lied—to the *bishop,* Danny. The *bishop!* And I can't even go to confession because I can't tell Father Patrick the truth. Can you imagine?"

Danny chuckled softly. "I'm sorry, Sister. But I just wanted you to have the money. For the kids."

She sighed. "I know, Danny. Your heart was in the right place. But please—what about you? Where are you?"

"You won't believe this," he said, "but I'm in England. Joined the Air Force. Fighting Hitler now."

"Oh, Danny," she breathed, "I'm so pleased. You've finally sorted yourself out. But please—be careful. Don't throw your life away."

He grinned. Good old Sister Angelica.

"I won't, Sister. I promise."

He could hear the other lads stirring in the dorm, voices rising.

"I've got to go. But tell Tony I'm proud of him. And to keep it up."

"I will. You take care, Danny."

"Sorry for waking you."

"Don't worry. I'm used to it."

He hung up and stood there for a moment, hand resting on the phone. He still missed home—but it had done his heart good to hear her voice.

Behind him, a voice barked, "Hey, Butchers! Who the hell are you calling at this hour?"

He turned and grinned. "My tailor. Why, you want his number?"

"Just move it, or you'll be late again."

Chapter 6

Ruth and Victoria had stood on the cold, draughty station platform, waving as Raymond's train pulled away. He had hugged tightly and kissed them both, then he was gone. The two women had cried all the way home.

Now, a week later, neither of them could believe how quickly the time had passed. It had been seven whole days since they'd last seen him. Ruth kept the photo her father had taken of her and Raymond on her bedside table. As soon as he sent her an address, she planned to send him a copy. Veronica had been given one as well, and it now sat proudly on the sideboard—Raymond in his uniform, standing tall and proud, and Ruth beside him in her new blue dress, beaming with happiness.

At work, Ruth had shown her engagement ring to the other girls. They all gathered round to admire it, offering their congratulations.

"We should go out and celebrate," Sheila said, clapping her hands together.

Ruby nodded. "That's a great idea—we don't get much to celebrate these days."

"Well," Jenny chimed in, "why don't we go to that little tea shop round the corner on Wednesday after we close? We can have tea and cakes—my treat."

Sheila raised an eyebrow. "Tea and cakes for an engagement? Come on, Jenny, this is supposed to be a celebration. We should go to the pub and have a *proper* drink."

"I second that," Ruby added with a grin.

Ruth shook her head firmly. "I can't go to a pub—I'm underage. And if I came home smelling of drink, my dad would hit the roof."

Sheila huffed. "But he let you get engaged!"

"Yes, but that's different. That's Raymond. A pub's another matter entirely."

They turned to Jenny.

"I can't either," Jenny said quickly. "Like Ruth said, we're underage, and my dad would go absolutely mad. No, tea and cakes will do us just fine."

Sheila gave a dramatic sigh and glanced at Ruby, who rolled her eyes.

"Alright, tea and cakes it is. I keep forgetting you two are quite a bit younger than us."

Then Ruby brightened suddenly. "Actually—I might have something to celebrate too. I've applied to join the WAAF!"

The others stared at her in surprise.

"You're not serious?" Sheila said, eyes wide.

"I am," Ruby said proudly. "I'm just waiting to hear back. But with the war on, I doubt they'll turn me down. And I turned twenty-two weeks ago, so I'm eligible."

Sheila looked at her in shock. "But if you go, there'll be no one left here—and what'll I do without you? You're my best friend."

Ruby leaned closer. "Well, you could join up too. We're the same age—why not? Come on, it'll be fun."

Sheila frowned, thinking it over for a moment. "Well... why not? Go out, see the world, do something different."

Ruby grinned. "That's the spirit!"

"I'll go during my lunch break," Sheila decided. "Mum and Dad will probably go mad, but they'll get over it. I'll likely be called up soon anyway—had my birthday last week."

"Don't tell them yet," Ruby advised. "Let them think it's your call-up. That's what I'm doing."

Sheila laughed. "Oh, that's a good idea."

Jenny smiled at the two of them, quietly proud. They were stepping into something brave, and though part of her felt a flicker of fear at the thought of them going off to who knew where, she also felt a deep swell of admiration. Things were changing so fast—girls getting engaged, joining up, saying goodbye at train stations. Life was moving, and they were moving with it.

That evening, when Jenny got home, she said to her mother, "Oh, I'll be late home on Wednesday, Mum—we're going to the café for tea and cakes to celebrate Ruth's engagement."

"Oh, that's nice, dear. Just you and Ruth?"

"No, a couple of the girls from work too—Ruby and Sheila."

"Oh well, have a nice afternoon."

"Yes, we will. Ruby and Sheila wanted to go to the pub in the evening, but Ruth and I said no, so we're going to the café instead."

Veronica looked horrified. "Go to a pub? Four young girls on your own—in the evening? Certainly not, Jenny. That would be indecent. And you're too young to drink. So is Ruth."

"I know, Mum, that's what we told them."

"Anyway," Veronica continued, warming to her lecture, "decent young girls do not go into pubs alone. And if you came home smelling of drink, your father would be furious."

Jenny gave a patient smile. She knew where this was heading. "Yes, I know. That's why we said no. We're just going for tea and cakes—don't worry. I'll be home in time for tea."

"How old are these girls?"

"Twenty. But they'll be gone soon—they've both joined the WAAF."

"Good heavens! But surely they'd be getting their call-up papers soon anyway?"

Jenny nodded. "Yes, but they couldn't wait. They've already signed up."

"And what did their parents say about that?"

"They haven't told them. They said they'll just let their parents think it's the call-up when the papers come."

Veronica was shocked. "Lying to their parents! Good Lord. That's terrible. And wanting to go into a pub on top of it. And who would go to the bar to get the drinks, may I ask? A decent woman doesn't go to the bar, Jenny. When I go with your father, he finds me a seat and *he* goes to the bar. That's how it should be.

These girls don't sound very savoury to me—you stay away from them. Have nothing to do with them."

"But Mum, I *work* with them. I can't just avoid them. Anyway, they're in different departments—I only see them at break time."

"Well, even so. It's not decent."

"What's not decent?" Ron asked, stepping into the kitchen as he came in from the shop.

Veronica launched into a summary of the conversation. Ron looked at Jenny with a frown. "Don't you ever go into a pub alone with just a group of girls. Decent girls don't do that, Jenny."

"That's what I've just told her," Veronica added, crossing her arms.

"And lying to their parents?" Ron muttered. "Not right. You stay away from them, love. They don't sound like decent girls at all."

Jenny looked down, crestfallen. Veronica noticed, softened, and reached out to gently brush a strand of hair behind her daughter's ear. She cupped Jenny's cheek, her voice gentler now.

"It's only because we love you, dear. We don't want you getting into any trouble. If your father and I take you and buy you a pop, that's one thing. But not just with a few girls, no matter how well you think you know them. Once a girl's lost her good name, she's finished."

She sighed, her expression wistful. "You'll be eighteen in a few weeks… I suppose you'll be getting your call-up papers before long. I heard today they're thinking of lowering the age to eighteen for girls as well as boys."

Tears welled up in her eyes.

Ron looked at his daughter and felt a lump rise in his throat. His little Jenny—nearly eighteen. It felt like just yesterday he'd been bouncing her on his knee, playing peek-a-boo while she squealed with laughter. He remembered how she used to think that if *she* couldn't see *them*, then *they* couldn't see her. Time had gone too fast.

Bloody Hitler, he thought bitterly.

Jenny, too, was upset. Not so long ago, she'd have welcomed her call-up papers, seen it as a chance for adventure. But now? Now, since meeting Marcus, she didn't want to go away. She wanted to stay here, close to home—close to *him*.

Maybe I could join the Land Army, she thought. *There are farms nearby. If there's work on one of them, I could stay at home.* Or perhaps she could apply for one of the local factories. She didn't fancy factory work, but if it kept her near Marcus and her family, she'd do it.

Her father broke the silence. "Who told you they were lowering the age?"

"Some woman in the butcher's," Veronica replied. "Said her sister told her."

"Well, that's nonsense," he said quickly, trying to reassure her. "They've only just lowered it to twenty for girls. Can't see them dropping it again so soon."

But even as he said it, he wasn't sure. And he prayed the woman in the butcher's had got it wrong.

Danny saw the auburn-haired girl enter the dance hall. She was a beauty, no mistake about that—and she was attracting plenty of attention. She looked shy and unsure of herself, almost out of place. Then, just as suddenly, she turned and walked out again.

Danny followed her.

By the light of the moon, he could see her heading back

toward the village. He quickened his pace and caught up with her.

"Hi," he said casually.

She turned to look at him. Up close, she was even more beautiful than he'd first thought. Her grey-green eyes flicked up to meet his, wary, uncertain.

"Hey, it's okay. I won't hurt you," he said gently.

She looked like a frightened rabbit, and he felt a pang of sympathy. She seemed so young. So vulnerable.

"Where you headed?" he asked.

"Home, I guess," she said softly.

"Home? But it's still early. Didn't you come for the dance?"

She nodded.

"Then why leave so soon at least stay and have a dance and a drink." "Oh no I don't drink; my dad would kill me if I drank." Danny grinned, "Well, a pop then, he won't mind you having a pop, will he?" she shook her head, "No." "Okay then, I'll escort you back to the dance hall, and we'll have a pop and a dance, how about that?"

She looked at the handsome young American; he had jet black curly hair and brown eyes, taller than she was but not by much, and a lovely smile, he was holding his arm out to her, waiting for her to make up her mind, she smiled at him and put her arm through his, he patted her hand, "Right mam a pop and a dance it is." Heads turned when they entered, several of the other men groaned, trust Butchers to grab the best-looking free girl in the place the other great looker they all agreed was Lieutenant Potter's girl, but that was clearly a long-standing relationship. They had seen her come in alone and leave again but had not noticed Danny go after her.

As they danced, Danny held her close. She smelled sweet,

like lavender soap and something softer underneath—warm, comforting. She clung to him as if he were her lifeline, and in that moment, he felt something stir deep in his chest. This—*this*—was what he wanted. A soft-hearted woman, a home, children one day. A life like the one he'd once known, back when his mother was alive and everything had still felt safe.

He looked down at her, gently brushing a loose strand of hair away from her face.

"I don't know your name," he said softly.

She looked up at him with those beautiful grey-green eyes, shy but steady.

"Maureen. Maureen Blackford. What's yours?"

"Danny Butchers. Nice to meet you, Maureen Blackford"

She smiled, a light blooming on her face.

"Hello, Danny Butchers."

They danced the night away, turning slowly beneath the dim lights, as if the world outside no longer existed. Danny didn't want to let her go, and Maureen—for the first time in her life—didn't want to be let go.

She'd never felt so safe. So serene. So at peace.

This was what she longed for: affection, tenderness… not the brutality she'd lived with all her life. Her father's anger had filled every corner of their home. The shouting, the threats, the cold disapproval. He hadn't hit her in years, but as a child, she'd endured more than her share of beatings. Her poor mother still suffered them—less often these days, but still enough to make Maureen flinch at every raised voice.

And it wasn't even drink that caused it. He wasn't a drunk—far from it. He went to the pub every Friday night, had exactly two pints, and came home. No, his cruelty wasn't fuelled by alcohol. It came from something colder, darker. He was just a brute—a vicious, bullying brute.

She used to wish she had brothers—someone to stand up to him, someone to protect her and her mother. But she didn't. She was an only child. And the burden of silence had always been hers alone.

At the end of the night, Danny turned to her as they stepped out into the crisp night air.

"I'll walk you home," he said.

The sheer look of panic that swept across her face melted his heart.

He took her hand gently, speaking in a low, calming voice.

"Hey, I'm not gonna hurt you, sweetheart. Not in the blackout, not ever. You'll be perfectly safe with me—I promise."

"No—it's not you," she whispered. "It's my father. You… you can't come to the house."

Danny frowned. "Why not? Surely he'd be glad someone saw you home safe?"

She shook her head. "No. He doesn't even know I went to the dance. And if he saw me come home with a… a soldier, he'd be furious."

Danny chuckled, trying to lighten the mood.

"Well, that's alright then—because I'm not a soldier. I'm an airman."

But she didn't laugh. Tears welled up in her eyes.

"You know what I mean… a Yank, as he calls you. He just wouldn't like it."

Danny's grin faded. He didn't like the sound of her father one bit.

"Has he ever done anything to you?" he asked carefully.

"What do you mean… 'done anything'?"

"Well… anything you didn't like."

"Oh. Yes. He used to beat me when I was younger."

Danny's jaw clenched.

"Is that all? Anything… since you got older?"

She frowned in confusion. "I don't know what you mean."

Danny realised then that he was treading into dangerous territory—too deep, too soon.

"It's okay. I was just wondering, that's all."

She paused. Looked at him. Something clicked behind her eyes—some dawning realisation of what he *was* trying to ask. Her eyes widened and she shook her head quickly.

"Oh, no—nothing like that. Just beatings."

"Right," Danny said quietly. "Well, that's bad enough. But if he ever *did* try anything like that—*anything*—you let me know. Me and a couple of the boys, we'd teach him a lesson in how to treat a lady. Especially his own daughter."

He tried to keep his tone light, but inside he was boiling. He might have been a lot of things in his life, but one thing Danny Butchers never tolerated was men who hurt women or kids. A slap on the leg for a naughty child was one thing—but beatings? And hitting your *wife*?

He wanted to throttle the man.

Back home, the boys he ran with had a way of handling that kind of coward. Even they—tough, street-hardened men—knew you never laid hands on a woman.

"Well," he said more gently, trying to soothe her nerves, "how about I walk you *almost* home? Just to the bus stop, maybe? That close enough?"

Maureen nodded. "That would be great. The stop's just

across the road from our house."

Danny offered his arm again, and she slipped hers through his.

As they walked slowly through the darkened village, a dusting of snow beginning to fall around them, neither of them spoke much—but both knew something had shifted. When they reached the bus stop, Danny leaned in and gently kissed Maureen on the forehead.

"Goodnight," he murmured.

She smiled up at him. "Goodnight, Danny. And thank you… for a lovely evening."

As she turned to walk away, he called softly, "Hey—do you want to catch a movie this week?"

She paused, her face lighting up. "Oh, I'd like that. Yes, thank you."

"Right then—how about Tuesday? I'll meet you here at six-thirty."

"Okay," she said, her voice light with excitement. "See you Tuesday."

Danny stood watching her as she walked the short distance to her house. Just before stepping inside, she turned and gave a little wave. He waved back, a smile tugging at his lips.

On the quiet walk back to base, Danny's thoughts spun. He'd never felt this way about a girl before. Normally, all he wanted was a bit of fun—some quick company, nothing complicated. If a girl was willing, that was fine; if she wasn't, he found one who was. He never forced himself, never needed to.

But Maureen… Maureen was different.

There was a softness about her, a vulnerability that stirred something protective deep inside him. He didn't want to touch her—he wanted to shield her. He could picture her in a warm kitchen, sunlight streaming in, laughter, a gentle touch. His mother would've liked her, he thought. No question.

No—he wouldn't so much as try anything with her. Not Maureen.

Still, he wanted to keep seeing her. And if he could, he'd get her away from that cold, brutal man she called her father. She deserved better. She was the kind of girl he could build a future with—the kind of girl who could give him the home he missed so much since his mother died.

Later that night, Danny lay in his bunk, staring up at the ceiling, unable to sleep. His mind drifted—backward through the years—until it settled in the hazy warmth of his earliest memories.

Back when life still made sense.

His father had disappeared not long after he was born, vanished like smoke in the wind. But his mother… she had been everything. A small woman with strong hands and tired eyes, she worked herself to the bone to provide for him. Cleaning houses, scrubbing floors, doing laundry—three different jobs at one point. They never had much, but their little apartment was always spotless. She made sure Danny went to school every single day. She believed in education like other women believed in prayer.

Sometimes, when the people she cleaned for had a party, they'd let her bring home leftovers—things Danny had never even seen before, delicate pastries and fancy cheeses. He'd eat them wide-eyed, as if they were treasures.

He worked hard at school, determined to grow up and earn good money—enough to give her a better life. He promised himself that one day, he'd take care of *her* the way she'd always taken care of *him*.

But fate had other plans.

When she fell ill, it seemed like just a cold at first. She kept going, kept cleaning, wouldn't hear of stopping. But the cough got worse. The colour drained from her cheeks. She lost weight. Finally, she couldn't work anymore. The money stopped. And there was no money for doctors. No medicine. No help.

That's when Danny met Sister Angelica.

He'd been trying to steal an orange from a fruit stand—something he'd heard was good for colds. Vitamin C. The man at the stall had looked away for a moment, and Danny reached for it—just one orange. That was all.

But someone grabbed his arm.

"What do you think you're doing?" a stern voice demanded.

He twisted in panic. "I need it!" he cried.

"You don't steal, boy. If you need something, you pay for it."

"I can't," he wailed. "I ain't got no dough!"

She folded her arms, her expression exasperated.

"I don't have any money," she said flatly.

His eyes widened, unsure if she was mocking him.

"You ain't got no money neither, Sister?"

She sighed. "Yes. I do. That's not the point."

He frowned, not understanding.

"Why do you need the orange so badly?" That's when he told her about his mother and that he'd heard oranges were good for colds because they had vitamin C.

Finally, she relented.

“Alright. I’ll buy you the orange. But in return, you’ll take me to see your mother. And we’ll see what can be done for her.”

He hesitated—but nodded.

She was the first person in his life who saw past the scruffy clothes and defiant face. And from that moment on, Sister Angelica became a kind of anchor in the chaos. A voice of reason. A hand reaching out when everyone else looked away.

As they stepped into the apartment, a harsh, rasping cough echoed from the bedroom. Sister Angelica’s brow furrowed—the sound of it unsettled her immediately. It was the kind of cough that lingered too long, the kind that meant trouble.

Danny led her quietly through to the bedroom. When she stepped inside, she was shocked by what she saw. The room was stifling, the air thick and heavy, with no hint of freshness. She crossed to the window and pulled it open, letting in a cool breeze. It stirred the curtains and carried the faint scent of the city streets, but anything was better than the stale air trapped inside.

Then she turned to the frail figure in the bed. The woman’s skin was ashen, her cheeks sunken, her eyes dull with fever. Sister Angelica stepped closer and gently laid a hand on her brow—it was burning. The woman’s lips parted in a weak smile, her eyes grateful. She was relieved, Sister Angelica realised. At last, someone had come.

“I’m Sister Angelica,” she said softly, offering a kind smile.

The woman gave the faintest nod. Her eyes closed briefly, as if the simple act of acknowledging her visitor had exhausted her.

Turning to Danny, Sister Angelica asked gently, “What food do you have in the apartment?”

He shook his head, eyes wide. "None, Sister."

"Show me the kitchen."

She followed him through to a cramped, bare space. One by one, she opened each cupboard and the icebox, finding only a few crumbs, a jar of something cloudy, and a box of crackers that had long since gone stale. Her heart ached.

"Right," she said firmly. "Try to get your mother to eat a little of the orange—not too much, just small bites. Give her sips of water in between. I'll be back in a few hours."

While she was gone, Danny did as he was told. He peeled the orange carefully, segment by segment, feeding his mother slivers of fruit and coaxing her to swallow. He offered water in between and dabbed her forehead with a damp cloth.

True to her word, Sister Angelica returned later with Sister Bridget and the orphanage's doctor—a kindly old man with a gentle manner—and a small bag of groceries. While Sister Angelica busied herself in the kitchen making something warm for Danny to eat, the doctor and Sister Bridget went into the bedroom to examine his mother.

When they came out, their faces were sombre.

The doctor sat down beside Danny and placed a comforting hand on the boy's thin shoulder. "Danny," he said softly, "your mother is very ill."

"I know," Danny whispered. "But you're going to make her better... aren't you?"

The child's blind faith tugged at every heartstring. The doctor's voice was quiet, pained. "I'm sorry, son. There's nothing I can do now—only make her comfortable."

Danny shook his head, his voice rising in desperation. "No—you're a doctor. You're supposed to make people better!"

"Sometimes we can," the doctor replied, "but not always. I'm not God, Danny. I can't work miracles."

Danny's gaze shifted to the two nuns. Surely they could help. They were holy. They knew God.

"But you can... can't you, Sister? You're a nun—you can make a miracle happen?"

His voice was so full of hope, so innocent, it nearly undid them all. Sister Angelica swallowed hard, searching for the right words.

"No, Danny. We can't perform miracles. Only God can do that. But we will pray for one. We'll ask Him to help your mother."

"And He'll do it?" Danny asked, eyes brimming with tears. "He'll make her better?"

"I don't know," she whispered, "but I hope so."

The doctor cleared his throat gently. "Danny, do you have any other family we should contact? Perhaps your father?"

"I ain't got no father," Danny muttered. "He ran off when I was born."

"What about grandparents? Aunts or uncles?"

"Just me granny and me aunty. But they don't come round no more. All they ever did was tell mum she shouldn't've married my dad. Said he was no good, that she'd regret it. They were his family, but they never liked him. They don't care about us."

The three adults exchanged glances, the gravity of the situation sinking in. This boy had no one.

The doctor gently opened his bag. "Alright, Danny. I'm going to leave some medicine for your mother. I need you to listen carefully while I explain how to give it to her. Can you do that?"

Danny's face tightened with worry. "But we ain't got no money. I can't pay you, and the Sister, she ain't got none either... so who's gonna pay you?"

Sister Bridget turned to Sister Angelica, confused. "I don't understand—what does he mean?"

Sister Angelica smiled faintly and waved her concern away. "I'll explain later, Sister."

But in her heart, she was already committed. This boy had touched something deep inside her. He was rough around the edges, a little wild, but he was brave, loyal, and kind. And right now, he needed someone to fight for him. She would be that person.

Whatever it took.

For two weeks, the sisters came regularly to the apartment, helping care for Danny's mother and supporting him as best they could. But no amount of comfort or medicine could stop what was coming.

When she died, Danny was inconsolable.

Grief twisted into rage, and he turned on the very people who had tried to help him.

"Your God is no good!" he shouted at them, tears streaming down his face. "He let my mum die! Why? She was a good person—she worked hard! I hate Him!"

The sisters crossed themselves and bowed their heads, silently praying for forgiveness—not for Danny, but for a world where such pain was possible. They knew his fury came from heartbreak, not blasphemy. It was easier to rage at God than to face the crushing finality of loss. Still, their hearts broke for him.

The funeral was a quiet, sparse affair. A few neighbours came, and so did Danny's grandmother and aunt—but their presence was cold, perfunctory. After the service, Sister Angelica approached them gently.

"Will you take Danny?" she asked softly, hopeful that perhaps blood would mean something—mean enough.

But their faces told her all she needed to know. They looked at the boy as though he were a burden, an inconvenience, something discarded.

"We don't have room for a growing boy," the aunt said flatly. "You can take him to the orphanage, Sister."

And with that, they turned and walked away without a backward glance.

So the sisters took him in.

At the orphanage, they tried their best with him. They gave him a warm bed, clean clothes, and regular meals. They enrolled him in school and prayed over him daily. But the grief and anger inside Danny ran deep—too deep.

He would disappear for days at a time, running away to wander the city streets like a stray. When he came back, he looked like a street urchin—dirty, hungry, and worn—but they always welcomed him. Sister Angelica would wash his face, fix his clothes, and make him something warm to eat. For a little while, he would settle. He'd focus on his lessons, sit quietly in chapel, even smile now and then.

But it never lasted.

The pain in his heart would rise again, and he'd be gone—another vanishing act. Still, the sisters never gave up on him. They clung to hope, fervently praying they could reach him, turn him around, help him find peace.

Then, one day, he didn't come back.

Sister Angelica scoured the city for him, walking block after block, asking after him in alleyways and on corners, checking with shopkeepers and shelters. But no one had seen him. It was as if he had vanished into the very air.

Finally, with a heavy heart, she had to admit the truth to herself:

She had failed him.

But in her heart, she still whispered prayers for him—wherever he was.

Because love like that doesn't vanish, even when a child does.

Chapter 7

The four friends sat together, sipping their tea and nibbling at the small slices of cake before them. The "celebratory" spread was a far cry from the delights they remembered from before the war—no light, airy sponge, no generous swirls of fresh cream. The meagre cream that now adorned cakes was an unconvincing imitation, and the sponge was dry and flavourless. Still, they made the best of it, pretending not to notice the disappointment on one another's faces.

"Actually," Ruby said with a small, knowing smile, "this is a double celebration."

Jenny raised her brows in surprise. "Oh, you haven't got engaged as well, have you?"

Ruby shook her head. "No. My call-up papers arrived yesterday. I handed in my notice this morning."

The other three girls stared at her, wide-eyed.

"Did they really?" Ruth asked. "Or is that just what you told your parents?"

"No, they really did arrive," Ruby assured her. "If I'd known they were on the way, I wouldn't have bothered joining up."

"Oh, I wish mine would come," Sheila sighed. "It won't be the same without you."

"I thought you were going to join up?" Jenny asked her.

"I was," Sheila admitted, "but I'd have to do it in my lunch break, and there's never enough time. Have you seen the queues?"

"Well, you could go on a Wednesday afternoon," Jenny suggested. "You'd have plenty of time to wait in line then."

Sheila shrugged, but her attention was already turning back to Ruby. "So, where are you going for training?"

"West Drayton," Ruby replied. "It's in London."

Sheila's eyes lit up with envy. "London! Ooh, I've always wanted to go—bright lights, excitement. You're lucky."

Ruby gave a half-hearted shrug. "Yes, I suppose I am."

Jenny caught the note in her voice. Ruby didn't look particularly lucky. "Are you having second thoughts?" she asked gently.

"No, of course not. Why?"

"You just don't look too happy about it. Now it's real—not just talk—you'll be a long way from home. You'll miss your family… and us."

Ruby gave a wry smile. "Yes, I suppose it did come as a bit of a shock. Suddenly it's not an idea—it's happening. But I'll be fine once I'm there and settled in."

"When do you go?" Ruth asked.

"I report for duty next Thursday."

"Crikey, that's quick! You haven't even been able to give a week's notice?"

Ruby shook her head. "No, just a couple of days. They had to accept it—nothing they could do about it. Old Mother Smithers wasn't happy, but she didn't have much choice."

Miss Smithers, the fearsome supervisor in the perfume department, was infamous for her sharp tongue and icy glare. All the girls detested her. Jenny and Ruth counted themselves lucky to be working in dresses under Miss Penheart, who, though strict, was fair and easy to get along with.

"One thing's for certain," Ruby said with a laugh, "I won't miss Old Smithers."

Jenny smiled but hoped, for Ruby's sake, that there wouldn't be a Miss Smithers waiting for her in the WAAF—or worse, someone even stricter.

When Jenny arrived home, she went straight into the kitchen where her mother was shelling peas.

"Ruby's call-up papers came this morning," Jenny announced.

Her mother tilted her head, studying her daughter. "Really, Jenny? Did they actually come, or is that just what she's told her parents?"

Jenny laughed. "Oh, Mum, that's exactly what I said to her! But apparently, they really did arrive yesterday. She has to report for duty next Thursday—in West Drayton."

"Where's that?" her mother asked.

"London, apparently."

"London?" Veronica's eyebrows rose. "Gracious. I wouldn't be happy for you to be going all that way on your own."

"No, I expect her parents aren't either, but there's not much they can do about it. Sheila's green with envy—she hasn't had her papers yet, but I think she just wants to get away from here and see the 'bright lights,' as she called them."

"Mmm." Her mother's mouth tightened. "That girl sounds like trouble to me. A bit too fast and loose. Once she's away from her parents' supervision, I shouldn't wonder if she goes wild."

"No, surely not. The people in charge won't allow that—

they'll keep a strict eye on her, I'm sure."

Meanwhile, in another part of the village, Maureen sat on the edge of her bed, hands clamped over her ears. *Oh dear God—would the shouting never stop?*

Her father's voice thundered through the thin walls, relentless, like a drumbeat, while her mother's muffled sobs tried to break through. Then, at last, the sound of the front door slamming shut made her jump.

Maureen hurried to the window and peered out. She caught sight of her father striding down the path, his shoulders hunched, his cap pulled low. Off to work. That meant her mother would have a few blessed hours of peace.

She darted down the stairs. In the kitchen, her mother sat hunched at the table, her face buried in a tea towel, shoulders shaking.

Maureen crossed the room in two quick steps and wrapped her arms around her. Her mother clung to her like a drowning woman to driftwood.

Maureen kissed the crown of her mother's head. "I'll put the kettle on," she murmured.

By the time the tea was poured and steam curled in the air, her mother had regained her composure, though her eyes were still red. They sat together at the small kitchen table; hands wrapped around their mugs as if the warmth might seep into their bones.

"If I had the money, Mum," Maureen said quietly, "I'd take us away from here. Leave him to rot on his own."

Her mother sighed, staring into her tea. "I want you to go anyway, love. It's not right for you to have to put up with this. You've had his bullying all your life, and it's not fair."

Maureen shook her head firmly. "No. I'll never leave you alone with him. I promise you—if I go, you go. We'll go together."

Her mother patted her hand with a sad little smile. "Oh, love, if only we could. But it takes money to leave, and we haven't got any."

Maureen nodded. "I know. I've a little put away in the Post Office, but nowhere near enough to start again."

They sat in silence for a while, the ticking of the kitchen clock the only sound between them. Then Maureen spoke quietly.

"Was he always like that—bullying, I mean, and shouting?"

Her mother shook her head slowly. "No, not really. He was never popular when we were young—kept to himself, didn't have many friends—but he never raised his voice to me, never hit me or tried to control me. Not until after we were married. It started about six months in."

Maureen frowned. "But why didn't you leave then? Why stay all these years and put up with it?"

Her mother gave a small, tired smile. "Because I was pregnant with you. I couldn't leave. Where would I have gone? How could I have supported us?"

Maureen's eyes widened. "He hit you while you were pregnant?"

"Yes," her mother said simply. "He has a cruel streak in him; one he kept hidden until we married."

Maureen's stomach turned. "Oh, Mum, that's awful. I wish he were dead."

Her mother's hand stilled on her teacup. "Don't, love. You shouldn't wish people dead—not even him."

"Why? Nobody would miss him. We certainly wouldn't."

Three thousand miles away, in New York, Sister Angelica sat at her desk, her mind drifting to thoughts of Danny Butchers. She had been genuinely pleased to hear from him— even if his call had come in the middle of the night. It comforted her to know he was doing well. The Air Force was a respectable career, and if he had any sense, he might even stay on after the war.

But then her thoughts darkened. She remembered the two men who had come looking for him—rough, dangerous men whose very presence had unsettled the orphanage. She had no doubt what they were: mafia. She wasn't so naive as to believe otherwise. Men like that had long arms, their reach stretching across the country. If Danny returned to America, even to another city, they would find him sooner or later. She prayed he would stay safely in England for as long as possible.

Sister Angelica had liked Danny from the very beginning—even when she caught him stealing an orange. At least, she thought, he had done it for the right reasons. She remembered his mother too, a gentle woman worn down by life. And she remembered the small package the woman had entrusted to her for safekeeping. She had stored it in the cellar years ago, intending to give it to Danny when he was grown, but the opportunity had never come.

Now, feeling a sudden pull, she went down to the cool, dim basement. The faint smell of polish and damp stone greeted her as she searched the shelves until her hand closed around a small box marked *Danny Butchers.*

It wasn't large; there had never been much to put in it. Carrying it back upstairs, she sat at her desk and carefully lifted the lid. Inside were fragments of a life cut short too soon: a few family photographs of Danny as a baby in his mother's arms, and later at various ages up to ten years old—before his secure little world had collapsed. His christening certificate. His birth certificate and his mother's. Her marriage certificate, folded and yellowed with age.

At the very bottom, tucked away like a hidden treasure, lay the most exquisite little silver-enamelled box she had ever seen. The lid was an azure blue, inlaid with mother-of-pearl, and bore the delicate image of a ballerina mid-dance. Turning it over, she examined the hallmark—this was no trinket; it must be worth something.

She opened it, and inside was a tiny silver case lined with red velvet. Resting within was a beautiful crucifix, its fine details depicting the Holy Mother cradling the infant Jesus. Sister Angelica held it reverently before placing it gently back in its casing.

Beneath it lay a wedding ring and an engagement ring. She lifted them into her palm, the metal warm from her touch, and wondered if Danny even knew they existed.

The years seemed to melt away, and Sister Angelica was once more in the stifling little bedroom of Muriel Butchers, Danny's mother. She remembered the scene as clearly as if it had been yesterday. It was a lovely summer's afternoon—too warm, even with the window thrown wide to coax in the slightest breeze.

Muriel lay propped up in bed, her breathing shallow and laboured. Suddenly, her dull eyes fluttered open, fixing on the nun seated beside her.

"Danny," she whispered, her voice no more than a thread of sound.

Sister Angelica rose and leaned over her. "He's at the market, Muriel. He'll be back soon."

"The box… for Danny."

The sister frowned slightly. "Box? What box, dear?"

With great effort, Muriel lifted one frail, bird-like hand and pointed towards the bureau. "In the drawer."

Sister Angelica crossed the room and opened the top drawer, but Muriel gave a faint shake of her head. The second drawer yielded a small treasure—the exquisite, enamelled box. Sister Angelica lifted it carefully and held it up so Muriel could see. The woman nodded faintly.

Bringing it to the bedside, the nun watched as Muriel, with trembling fingers, opened the lid. One by one, she laid the contents on the thin, worn sheet covering her.

"The box was my grandmother's," she said, her voice catching, "but the jewellery was my mother's. Will you see Danny gets them when he is older, Sister?"

Sister Angelica was momentarily taken aback. These were not trinkets. The craftsmanship spoke of quality; the stones glittered even in the dim afternoon light. There must have been money in this family once.

"Yes," she said at last. "I will keep them safe until he is grown, and I promise I will make sure he gets them."

"The photos, too?" Muriel asked.

"Yes. I'll go through the apartment and take whatever I think Danny should have."

Muriel gave a soft sigh. "Thank you, Sister. That's all I ask."

"Was she your mother's mother?"

"No—my father's. I was very close to him, and he to his mother. They were gentle people."

Her voice faltered as a coughing fit took hold. Sister

Angelica quickly helped her to a sip of water, then eased her back against the pillows. She slipped the box into her bag just as the front door banged open and Danny burst in.

"I got the groceries, Sister!"

She smiled at him and patted his head. "Good boy, Danny. But keep your voice down—your mother's sleeping."

Now, all these years later, she sat at her desk and stared at the rings. Somewhere, at some time, there had been money in Danny's family. Even the engagement ring alone was worth a small fortune—a large, clear diamond encircled by six tiny rubies. The wedding band was solid and thick, made to last.

If only she could find some family for him. She picked up the marriage certificate, tracing Muriel's maiden name with her fingertip. *Potter.* It meant nothing to her.

Gently, she placed each item back in the enamelled box and closed the lid. Folding her hands, she bowed her head in prayer.

"Dear Lord, please watch over Danny, and all the young men and women fighting this war. And please, Lord... bring them all home safely. Amen."

Making the sign of the cross, she rose and crossed to the window. Below, the children were playing in the orphanage yard, their laughter rising in the summer air. Sister Angelica prayed silently that they would never know the horrors and heartache of a world at war.

The object of Sister Angelica's prayers was, at that very moment, sitting on a grassy riverbank, watching a family of ducks teach their downy young how to dive for food. The scene was peaceful, but Danny's thoughts were anything but.

They kept drifting back to Maureen. She had slipped under his skin in a way no girl ever had before. For a moment, his mind flicked to Sister Angelica, and he wondered what she would make of the *new* Danny Butchers—not the angry, uncontrollable boy who had caused her so many sleepless nights, but the man he was trying to become.

Once, he had meant to stay on the straight and narrow, just as he had when his mother was alive. But the speed and shock of her death had knocked the legs out from under him. He'd been so certain that the sisters' prayers would work—that God would grant them a miracle and his mother would recover. After all, if God listened to anyone, surely He listened to nuns and priests.

Only... He hadn't.

The bitterness from that disappointment had festered. Danny remembered the long spells when he would run away from the orphanage, vanishing for days, sometimes weeks, until hunger drove him back. The sisters never turned him away. They would clean him up, fill his belly, give him a warm bed—and for a while, he'd settle into the routine. But it never lasted.

It was during one of those absences that he met Jake Costello. Or rather, Jake's right-hand man.

Danny had picked the wrong pocket.

A meaty hand had shot out, gripping him by the throat and shaken him until his teeth rattled. "What the hell do you think you're doing, kid?"

When the man finally let go, Danny crumpled to the pavement, gasping for breath. The man hauled him upright by the arm and bent to meet his eyes.

"Well? You gonna tell me what you think you're doing?"

"I need money," Danny croaked.

The man snorted. "Yeah, we all need money, kid. So why do you need it bad enough to steal?"

"I ain't got none… and I'm hungry."

The man—Jimmy the Bulldog, though Danny didn't know it yet—gave him a long look. The kid was thin as a rail, all elbows and knees. *Could be useful,* Jimmy thought.

"Alright, here's the deal. I'll buy you some food, then we'll talk about your future."

"My… future?"

"Yeah. I think you and me are gonna make a great team. I can find you work, which means money. But first, let's get you fed."

He marched Danny through the back door of a restaurant. "Hey, Luca, give this kid some food, will ya? He's half-starved."

The chef eyed him with disgust. "Jimmy, get that ragamuffin out of my kitchen—he'll pollute the place."

"Yeah, yeah… come on, kid. We'll be in the office. Luca, send in some food, yeah?"

Jimmy led him to the back office where a man sat behind a desk. The man raised an eyebrow.

"Who's this?"

"Some kid who tried to pickpocket me," Jimmy replied.

The man laughed. "Oh, kid, *that* was a big mistake. So what's he doing here?"

"Luca's sending in some food—he's half-starved. Then we're gonna talk about his future. Ain't that right, kid?" Jimmy said, glancing at Danny.

"So, does this kid have a name? Or should we just keep calling him 'the kid'? Maybe 'Charlie,' like *Charlie Chaplin.*

Remember that film *The Kid*? Great film."

Jimmy rolled his eyes. "What's your name, kid?"

Danny wiped his sleeve across his nose. "Danny."

Jimmy slapped his arm away. "Don't do that—it's filthy. Use your handkerchief."

"Ain't got no handkerchief."

Both men exchanged a look.

"When's the last time you had a bath?" the man behind the desk asked.

Danny shrugged. "Dunno. Last time I was at the orphanage, Sister Angelica made me have one."

"The orphanage, huh? So why are you running around filthy and picking pockets?"

"I run away. But I go back now and then."

"Why? Don't they feed you?"

"Yeah, but they make me go to school and church. And the other kids get on my nerves."

A waiter arrived with a tray, and Danny fell on the food like he hadn't eaten in weeks. When he was finished, Jimmy stood.

"Alright, kid—come with me."

He led Danny upstairs to a small bedroom. "Through that door is a bathroom with soap and fresh towels. Get yourself cleaned up—properly—or you'll be back in there until you do, got it?"

"Yeah, I hear you."

"Leave your clothes here—I'll get rid of them."

"What'll I wear if you get rid of these?"

"Don't worry, you'll have clothes. Oh, and there's a spare toothbrush and toothpaste in the cabinet. Use them."

The bath was hot, the soap rich with lather, and the dirt of weeks slid away. Danny had to admit—it felt good to be clean again. He glanced at the bed. It looked impossibly soft, like the beds back at the orphanage on a cold night. Surely five minutes wouldn't hurt.

He pulled back the covers, slid beneath them, and was asleep within minutes.

Jimmy returned later with clean clothes, only to find the boy curled on his side, breathing deeply. For a moment, Jimmy just stood there, noting how young he looked—too young, too fragile for the life ahead of him.

Still... the kid had potential. And in the morning, they'd discuss his future.

Chapter 8

When Jenny opened the door to Marcus that Sunday lunchtime, he stood there smiling, holding out a small posy of wildflowers.

She took them and lifted them to her face, breathing in their delicate scent.

"Oh, Marcus, they're lovely—thank you."

"Well, they looked so pretty growing by the roadside, I thought, why leave them there for cars and lorries to plough into? I figured you might like them more."

"I do. I love them—thank you."

He grinned and reached into his pockets. "I also managed to get hold of these. I'm sure your mother can use them." He placed a tin of Spam and a tin of peaches into her hands.

Jenny's eyes widened. "Good lord—where did you get these?"

"The government sends us crates of the stuff—Spam and canned fruit. I just... diverted a couple in your direction."

They stepped into the dining room, where Betty was sitting at the table. She looked up and beamed at Marcus.

"I drawed you a pictured of your airplane."

"Drew, dear," her mother corrected gently.

"Yes, but I *drawed* it, Mummy," Betty insisted.

Veronica raised her eyebrows at Marcus. He chuckled, leaning down to pat the little girl's head.

"Well, that's lovely, Betty—oh yes, that looks *just* like my plane."

The picture, scrawled in every colour of the rainbow, bore little resemblance to any aircraft in existence, but Marcus accepted it with solemn courtesy. Betty held it out to him.

"It's for you."

"I'll treasure it—and put it on my wall," he said warmly. Betty's smile grew even wider.

"Mrs Jackson, thank you so much for inviting me to lunch," he said. "But are you sure you've enough to go round? I'd hate to think one of you would go without to feed me."

"Oh, don't give it a second thought. You're welcome to share whatever we have."

Jenny held up the tins he'd brought. "Well, these might help, Mum—Marcus brought them."

Veronica's brows lifted in surprise. "Good lord. Oh, Marcus—thank you. That's very kind, and they're most welcome."

"Think nothing of it," he said with a shrug. "We get plenty."

During lunch, Jenny asked, "When are you going on leave?"

"Not yet. Leave's been cancelled for a while."

"Oh—why?" Veronica asked, but Ron looked up sharply from his plate.

"We shouldn't be asking that, love. Careless talk, remember? The less you know, the better."

Marcus nodded. "He's right. And even if I did know—which I honestly don't—I couldn't say."

"Of course. I shouldn't have asked."

"No harm done," Marcus replied easily. "All I can tell you

is, it's all been cancelled."

Jenny was secretly thrilled—but then felt a pang of guilt. His cancelled leave meant he wouldn't see his own family.

After lunch, Jenny began clearing the table, but her mother waved her away.

"No, Jenny love—it's a lovely afternoon. Why don't you two go for a walk? I can do the washing up, and if your father's feeling generous, he can help with the drying." She winked at them.

Ron gave a mock groan. "It's not enough that I work all week to provide—now I have to dry dishes as well?" He grinned. "Go on, you two. Too nice a day to be stuck indoors."

They didn't need telling twice. Jenny fetched her coat, and soon they were strolling down the road, hand in hand.

As they walked, they spotted Danny and Maureen on the other side of the road, also walking hand in hand. Jenny glanced up at Marcus.

"Goodness—I didn't know they were going out together. Did you?"

Marcus shook his head. "No, I didn't. But I don't think he's a suitable companion for her—whoever she is. Do you know her?"

"Yes—that's Maureen Blackford. And if her father sees them..." Jenny grimaced. "He'll go mad."

"Is he strict?"

"Strict isn't the word. He's a real bully—always shouting at her and her mother. When we were younger, Maureen often came to school with bruises. She'd claim she'd fallen, but there were too many—too often—for that to be true. And her mother... she often had a black eye, bruising on her face."

Marcus stopped dead in the middle of the pavement, staring

at her.

"He beats them?"

"I don't think he beats Maureen anymore—but I'm sure he still beats her mother. And she's a lovely woman. It's such a shame."

"Good lord." Marcus's voice hardened. "Well, I'll be having words with Butchers. If he hurts that girl, he'll answer to me. Sounds like she's been through enough."

Jenny nodded. She hated passing Maureen's house—it was almost certain she'd hear her father's angry voice bellowing inside. Jenny's own parents were strict, but they never shouted like that, and certainly never raised a hand. The worst she'd ever had was a quick slap on the leg, bottom, or hand if she'd been truly naughty—and it had never left a bruise.

Maureen suddenly stiffened mid-step and came to a halt. Danny, still holding her hand, glanced down at her.

"What's wrong, honey?"

She nodded to the other side of the street. "That's Jenny Jackson with her beau—and I think they've seen us."

Danny followed her gaze and spotted the "skip" with his girl. He gave a casual shrug.

"So what of it? They're just taking a walk like us."

"Yes, but if she talks, my dad will get to hear—and he'll go mad."

Danny let out a slow sigh. That bloody father of hers again. Sliding his arm around her shoulders, he said firmly,

"Maureen, we're not doing anything wrong—we're just taking a walk. How can he object to that?"

"Because he objects to everything I do," she said, her voice tight. "You don't know him, Danny. He likes to control everyone and everything. He's awful. The other day, before he went to work, he was shouting at Mum—she was in a terrible state when he left."

Danny's jaw set. "Well, he'll have to lump it, because I will *not* stop seeing you. And anyway, you'll soon be old enough to leave and get married. What's he going to do then? He can't stop you."

She sighed. "I know. And if this war's still on when I turn twenty, I'll get my call-up papers—he won't be able to stop that. Then I'll leave and take Mum with me. I'll never leave her alone with him."

The next morning, during break, Maureen spotted Jenny sitting alone in the staffroom. She crossed the room quickly, tea mug in hand.

"Mind if I sit?"

Jenny looked up, smiling. "Of course not."

Maureen sat, but didn't touch her tea. "Actually, Jenny—I wanted a word."

Jenny tilted her head. "Oh? About what?"

"Yesterday afternoon."

Jenny's eyes flickered, but her face stayed neutral. "What about it?"

"I know you saw us—me and Danny."

Jenny leaned in slightly. "Yes, I did. And who you see is your business. But… be careful. Danny's got a reputation on the base. I'd hate to see you hurt."

Maureen shook her head. "He's not like that. Not when you really know him. He's kind, gentle… nothing like what people say. What I'm worried about is you telling anyone—especially my dad."

Jenny's voice lowered. "Walking down the high street on a sunny Sunday? Half the village saw you. Your dad's bound to hear."

"I know," Maureen admitted, her voice catching. "But there's nowhere else to go."

Jenny's gaze softened, but her tone stayed steady. "Just be careful. I remember school, Maureen—I remember the bruises. Your dad's a bully. A nasty one."

Tears pricked Maureen's eyes. "Yes, I know. But I can't leave until I'm twenty-one—and when I do, I'm taking Mum with me. I'll never leave her alone with him."

Jenny reached across the table and squeezed her hand. "I hope Danny's all you say he is. Just… don't let your guard down."

"I won't. And thanks, Jenny."

Jenny managed a small smile. "Anytime. But I'd better get back before Miss Penheart has me for breakfast."

While Jenny and Maureen were having their quiet heart-to-heart, Marcus was having a far less gentle one with Danny.

"Butchers, I want a word with you."

Danny looked up from what he was doing. "Oh—hi, Skip. What's up?"

"I'll tell you what's up. What are your intentions towards that young girl we saw you with yesterday?"

Danny blinked in surprise. "Blimey, Skip—what are you, her father now?"

Marcus's eyes hardened. "Don't get smart with me, Butchers. I want a straight answer."

Danny exhaled. "I like her. We get on well."

"And that's all there is to it?"

Danny gave a small shrug, wondering why the skip was taking such an interest—then the penny dropped.

"Wait—are *you* interested in her?"

Marcus felt an instant urge to flatten him. "No, I am not. I've got Jenny. But I *do* know something about this girl's background—and she's been through enough. I won't stand by and watch you take advantage of her and leave her in the lurch. Do you understand me?"

Danny sat down heavily, rubbing the back of his neck. "I guess Jenny told you?"

Marcus nodded. "She did. And it wasn't pretty."

"I know. Maureen's told me about her father. Look, Skip—believe it or not, I love her. I've every intention of marrying her and taking her far away from here. But until she turns twenty-one, my hands are tied. As long as I live, I'll take care of her. And if that father of hers lays another hand on her, I'll make him sorry he was ever born."

Marcus was taken aback. This was a side of Danny he'd never seen before—and in his eyes, he saw the truth of it.

"Well," he said slowly, "I actually believe you. But if you let her down, *I'll* make you sorry you were ever born."

"Believe me, Skip, I won't let her down. From the minute I saw her, I just felt like we belonged together. When I held her and danced with her—it felt right, you know?"

Marcus gave a small nod. "Yes. I know."

As Marcus turned to leave, Danny called after him.

"Oh—just one more thing, Skip. Don't tell the others about this. I wouldn't want them thinking Danny Butchers was going soft." He winked.

Marcus laughed. "You're one crazy guy, Butchers—you really are."

When Jenny got home, she told her parents and Marcus about her conversation with Maureen.

"Well, I hope she's right, love," her mother said softly. "As you said, she's been through so much—I'd hate to see her hurt anymore."

"I had a talk with Danny today," Marcus added, leaning back in his chair, "and I must say, I was pleasantly surprised."

"Oh? Why?" Veronica asked.

"Well, he seemed genuinely fond of her. Told me he wanted to marry her, but that he had to wait until she turns twenty-one."

Jenny raised her eyebrows. "And you believe him?"

"Yes," Marcus said with quiet certainty. "There was something in the way he spoke about her... and in his eyes. I think he really does care."

Veronica gave a slow nod. "Let's hope you're right. I'd hate to see her hurt again."

That evening, Maureen told Danny about her talk with Jenny. He grinned.

"Oh, she's just looking out for you, sweetheart."

"Yes, I know. She's actually quite nice."

"Well," Danny said, "I had a chat with the Skip today—or rather, he had a chat with me. Wanted to know if my intentions towards you were honourable."

Maureen laughed. "And are they?"

"Hell no," he teased, grabbing her and nuzzling her neck.

She giggled, but he quickly grew serious. “But honestly, I promise I’ll never hurt you, Maureen. You do believe that, don’t you?”

“Yes, I do. That’s what I told Jenny—that you’re nothing like your reputation. Anyway, why do you have such a bad reputation on the base?”

He shrugged. “Dunno. Probably because it keeps people at arm’s length. I don’t like getting too close.”

“Why? You’re close to me.”

“You’re different. But I don’t want them knowing too much about me. I like to keep my life private—especially the years before I joined up.”

“Why? Was it so terribly bad?”

Danny studied her face, wondering what she’d say if he told her the truth. “Yeah… it wasn’t good. Best left in the past.”

She hesitated. “Danny… you weren’t in prison, were you?”

He could see the concern in her eyes. Leaning forward, he kissed the tip of her nose. “No, honey, I wasn’t.” *But I came pretty damn close,* he thought.

Sensing she needed more, he offered, “My mother died when I was young, and I ended up in an orphanage.”

Maureen’s eyes softened. “Oh, Danny… I’m so sorry. But what about your dad? Didn’t he take care of you?”

“He was long gone—walked out just after I was born. Mum worked three jobs to make ends meet, and when I was ten, she got sick and died.”

Tears welled in Maureen’s eyes. Her life had been hard, but at least she still had her mother. “Was the orphanage bad? Were they cruel?”

“Oh no—nothing like that. The sisters were kind and caring.

But it wasn't the same as having a home. I went off the rails a bit—nothing too bad," he lied. "They just had to set me straight again."

"I suppose that's understandable—you were angry and grieving."

"Yeah… I was. But now I have you. Something to hold onto. That's why I keep my distance from the others on base—if I got close and they were killed; I couldn't take it. But you… you'll always be here."

She smiled faintly. "Yes. I'll always be here, waiting for you. And when all this is over and I can marry without my father's permission, we will. And we'll go far away from here—take Mum with us if she wants to come."

Danny already had it planned. He had enough put aside to start fresh somewhere else. Ireland, maybe—he'd always fancied it.

Maureen noticed his faraway look and nudged him in the ribs. "Hey—what are you thinking so deeply about?"

He squeezed her hand. "Nothing much. Just our future when this bloody war is over."

She tutted. "Language, Danny."

He grinned. "You sounded just like my mum—and Sister Angelica—then."

"Well, don't swear, love."

"Yeah, sorry. But we will make a fresh start, far from here. Your mum too, if she wants."

"In America? New York?"

He shook his head. "No, not New York. I thought… Ireland."

"Ireland? Why?"

"No reason. I've just always wanted to go."

"Well, I don't mind where we go, so long as we're together. Yes… Ireland. Why not?"

"Then Ireland it is. They say there are more than fifty shades of green there, you know."

She laughed. "I don't believe that—how can there be more than fifty shades?"

"Don't know. That's just what they say."

"Hmm… I think Ireland will suit you. You're full of the blarney."

He pulled her close and kissed her before stepping back with a sigh. "I'd better get you home before I lose control of myself. Anyway, it's nearly ten—we don't want your dad getting hot under the collar because you're late."

He stopped, his hands resting firmly on her shoulders. "Maureen—you *would* tell me if he ever hit you, wouldn't you?"

She nodded. "Yes, I promise. I'll never let him hit me again."

"That's alright, then. Because if he ever does, he'll regret it."

He walked her to the bus stop and kissed her goodnight, watching until she was safely inside. Only then did he turn back toward the base, his jaw set. One day, he would make that man regret every cruel thing he'd done to Maureen and her mother.

Chapter 9

"Why does Butchers look so familiar?" Marcus asked suddenly.

Alvin glanced at him over his coffee. They were sitting outside the hangar, soaking up the early spring sunshine, watching Danny polish his boots a short distance away. Alvin frowned.

"He's our tail gunner, Skip. That's why."

The answer was simple enough—but Alvin's stomach tightened. Why was Marcus asking that now? Butchers had been part of the crew for months. Was the Skip losing his memory? Because if he was, that meant he wasn't safe in the air. Alvin's mind was already running through whether he ought to speak to the station commander.

"You okay, Skip?" he asked carefully.

Marcus caught the concerned look on Alvin's face and realised exactly what he was thinking. He gave a small, reassuring grin.

"Yeah, sure. I don't mean I don't know who he is—I mean I can't shake the feeling I've seen him somewhere before. Not here. Before he joined us. I just can't put my finger on it."

Alvin let out a slow breath of relief. "Oh, right. Well, maybe you bumped into him on the subway. You ever go to New York?"

Marcus nodded. "Yes, many times. But no—it doesn't feel like that. I get the sense it's... closer to home." He sighed, shaking his head. "Oh well, I'm sure it'll come to me eventually. Anyway—how's your family doing?"

Alvin's expression brightened. "Great. Martha sent pictures last week—little Davy's growing fast. He's started to talk, and he's walking round the furniture now. Won't be long before he's off on his own."

"That's great. You must miss them—and I'm sure they miss you."

"Yeah, I do. But he won't even know me when I get home. I'm missing all his formative years." Alvin's mouth tightened. "Bloody Hitler. I wish he'd drop dead."

Marcus gave a dry chuckle. "We'd all like that—but would it end the war? I'm not sure. Someone else would just take his place, and we'd go right on killing each other."

Alvin shrugged. "Yeah... I guess so."

Jenny glanced around the staff break room. It was practically deserted. The store was running on a skeleton crew now—so many of the girls had gone, and the boys too. Even the lift boy had gone; she hadn't realised he was eighteen. He'd looked so young.

Ruby was gone now, and Sheila wouldn't be far behind—her call-up papers had finally arrived a few days ago. Jenny had expected her to be excited, but Sheila was mostly furious.

"Can you believe it?" Sheila had complained, her voice full of outrage. "I get out of one dump only to end up in another! Innsworth—a little village outside Tewkesbury, in Gloucester.

Why couldn't I go to London like Ruby? It's so bloody unfair."

Jenny and Ruth had tried to console her.

"Well, maybe it won't be so bad once you get there," Ruth suggested. "If there's a training camp, it'll be busy enough. There'll still be dances, and there must be a town nearby—you can go to the pictures."

But Sheila wouldn't be placated. Every break was the same—complaints, moaning, muttered insults about "backwater postings." The other girls were starting to avoid her. Jenny sighed inwardly. Oh well—she'd be gone in a few days.

"I must admit, it's Murphy's Law," Ruth had said with a little shrug.

Jenny frowned. "Murphy's Law? I don't know what you mean."

"Well, Ruby would have preferred Innsworth and Sheila London—but they got it the other way round."

Jenny smiled faintly. "Yes... that sounds about right."

"Oh, I see—yes, as you say, Murphy's Law. Maybe the powers that be know more about us than we think, and know exactly who would be best suited to which area."

"Yes, that's true. At least Ruby will behave. But Sheila—if she ever got sent to London—I think she'd go wild."

Jenny smiled faintly. "My mum said pretty much the same thing, and she's never even met her."

"Well, let's hope she doesn't get herself into trouble and end up back here," Ruth said.

Jenny gave a little shudder. "Oh Lord, let's hope not."

Just then, the subject of their discussion swept into the room. Spotting them, Sheila strolled over with an air of smug anticipation.

"Well—only a couple more days and I'm out of this dump," she announced, dropping into a chair with a dramatic sigh. "I've resigned myself to going to that backwater. It's only for a few weeks anyway, then I'll get posted—and I've heard you can even get a posting abroad."

She bit into her sandwich, eyeing the other two. "Still—never mind. Your turn will come soon enough."

"No, thank you," Ruth replied firmly. "I'm quite happy where I am."

Jenny nodded in agreement. "Me too."

Sheila looked scandalised. "You can't be serious! Do you really want to spend the rest of your lives in this dump?"

"There are worse places to be. And anyway, my family and friends are all here," Ruth told her.

Sheila shrugged dismissively. "Oh well—there's no accounting for taste, is there?"

Jenny lay in bed, luxuriating in the rare pleasure of a full day off. With so many of the girls gone, whole days off were scarce, replaced by a series of half days. But today was different—today was her eighteenth birthday.

She knew it wasn't as significant as turning twenty-one, but it was still special. She'd asked Miss Penheart if she might swap shifts to have the whole day free, half expecting a sharp refusal. Instead, Miss Penheart had looked at her over the rim of her glasses and said:

"I was young once myself, Miss Jackson, and I'm not so old that I don't remember what that feels like. I remember my eighteenth birthday well—and I would have loved the day off, but couldn't. That's no reason to stop you. If you can get one of the girls to change with you, then yes—you may have the day."

Jenny had been so touched she'd almost hugged her. She'd rushed to tell Ruth, who agreed at once to swap.

"I'll do the same for you on your birthday," Jenny promised.

"Alright," Ruth grinned. "I'll look forward to it."

This evening Marcus would be coming for tea to help her celebrate. Jenny could hardly believe her luck. Her mother had even said she could have a proper bath—not the long, steaming soak she'd enjoyed before the war, but more than the usual wash in the sink.

She slid out of bed, slipped into her dressing gown and slippers, and padded downstairs.

"Oh, Jenny, sweetheart, I was going to bring you breakfast in bed—a special treat for a special day," her mother said warmly.

"That's lovely, Mum, but I'm up now."

Her mother hugged her and kissed her cheek. "Happy birthday, dear."

Jenny smiled. "Thanks, Mum."

"There are cards and presents on the table. I hope you like them."

Jenny found several cards—from her grandparents, aunts, uncles, and parents. Her grandparents had sent a silver charm bracelet with two tiny charms already on it. One aunt and uncle had given her a pair of delicate earrings; another, a pretty little onyx trinket box.

Her parents' gift made her gasp. Nestled in a small box was a beautiful signet ring with a tiny ruby in the centre. She slipped it on—it fitted perfectly.

"Oh, Mum—it's beautiful."

Her mother's eyes shone. "I'm glad you like it. Everything's so scarce now, we didn't know what to get. But when we saw that, it just felt right."

Betty came toddling in, clutching a sheet of paper. "I drawed us," she announced proudly.

Jenny bent to hug her. "Oh, Betty—it's beautiful."

The child pointed to the matchstick figures. "That's Mummy, that's Daddy, that's you, that's me—and that's Marcus."

Each figure was a different colour, the whole picture bright and cheerful.

"I'm going to frame it and keep it always," Jenny told her.

Later, Jenny revelled in her bath—even if it was only four inches deep—sprinkling in the last of her Christmas bath salts so the water was soft and delicately scented.

By the afternoon, the family had gathered. Each person brought something—bread, buns, a trifle—and soon the table held a birthday tea that could almost have belonged to pre-war days. Her mother had even managed a cake.

Ruth arrived with a neatly wrapped gift. Inside was a small porcelain elephant.

"For luck," Ruth said with a smile. "But you must keep his trunk facing the door or window—so the luck comes in."

Jenny laughed. "Then I'll make sure he's always facing the right way."

When Marcus arrived, he stepped into the hallway with his familiar, easy smile and handed Jenny a small red velvet box.

Her breath caught. She took it carefully, the velvet soft under her fingers, and eased it open.

Nestled in a bed of white satin was the most exquisite string of pearls she had ever seen. The glow of them seemed to catch the light and hold it, each bead smooth and perfect.

"Oh, Marcus… it's beautiful." Her voice trembled slightly. "But it must have been so expensive."

He smiled, leaning close to kiss her cheek. "Price doesn't matter. I wanted you to have it."

"But where did you get it?"

"It was my grandmother's," he said softly. "I know she would want you to have it."

Jenny's brow furrowed. "I can't take it—if it was hers, surely one of your sisters—"

He shook his head before she could finish. "No. She left it to me, and I'm giving it to you."

He lifted the necklace from the box, the pearls cool against his skin, and gently fastened it around her neck. Stepping back, he studied her for a moment with quiet satisfaction.

"It suits you perfectly. My grandmother would approve."

Her family gathered to admire the gift, their exclamations of surprise and praise warming the moment. Jenny's cheeks glowed, though a part of her felt the weight of the gesture. Pearls were not just a gift; they were a statement.

Later that evening, after the cake crumbs had been swept away and the last of the guests had gone, Marcus found himself alone with Ronald in the sitting room. The blackout had deepened the quiet outside, and the faint hum of the wireless carried from the kitchen where Jenny and Veronica were washing up.

They sat in the fire's soft glow, each with a beer in hand.

"That was a fine necklace you gave her," Ronald said after a moment. "Are you sure you want her to have it? It's a family heirloom—from your grandmother, no less."

"Yes, sir, I'm sure. I want Jenny to have it."

Marcus paused, feeling his heartbeat quicken. "There's something else... something I'd like to ask you. I'd like your permission to ask Jenny to marry me."

Ronald's eyes didn't leave his. "I see. You realise she's only just turned eighteen—still young. And with this war..." His gaze dropped briefly to the fire. "I'd hate to think of her as a young widow. We all hope you'll come through unscathed, but you fly a bomber, Marcus. Anything could happen."

Marcus held his gaze. "I know. But I wasn't thinking of marriage straight away. We could get engaged, and then marry in a couple of years. That way there's no rush, and she can stay here with her family until the war's over."

"I see." Ronald leaned back, the firelight sharpening the lines on his face. "In that case, I've no objection. But remember—an engagement doesn't give you the rights of a husband. You'll be engaged, not married. I trust you understand that."

"Absolutely, sir. I'd never take advantage of Jenny—I have far too much respect for her." Marcus hesitated, lowering his voice slightly. "I wasn't planning to ask her just yet. I'm due furlough soon, and I'd like to tell my family about her before I propose. It may be a couple of months yet... but I thought I should ask for your blessing while we have the chance to talk alone."

For a long moment, Ronald was silent, studying him. Then his mouth curved into a dry smile. "So—you believe in striking while the iron's hot. Seizing the moment, eh?"

Marcus grinned faintly. "I don't often get the chance to

speak to you alone. It seemed like a golden opportunity."

Ronald chuckled, the tension between them easing. "Quite right. Well then—in that case, welcome to the family."

They shook hands, a firm, measured clasp that carried more than words.

Just then, Veronica and Jenny came in from the kitchen, the scent of soap still clinging to them. Veronica glanced between the two men. "And what are you two plotting?"

"Nothing," Ronald said, the corner of his mouth twitching. "Just man's talk."

Danny couldn't stop turning it over in his mind — how the hell was he supposed to marry Maureen without her father's permission? She was only eighteen, and the law was on the old man's side until she turned twenty-one. But he wanted that ring on her finger now.

It wasn't just for love, though that was a big part of it. If something happened to him, being his wife would give her protection: a widow's pension, whatever money and property he left behind — more than enough to keep her for life. And if they were lucky enough to have a child, well... that would be something worth leaving behind. A son to carry on his name. Or a daughter, even. But a son would be better.

He thought of her father — and felt the same dark heat in his gut that used to rise when someone tried to push him around back home. If they were in New York, Jimmy would have sorted him out in an afternoon. Jimmy...

That thought pulled him backward in time, all the way to that first meeting.

Back then, he hadn't known who Jimmy really was — or the kind of men he worked with. He only knew they'd fed him, cleaned him up, given him a soft bed to sleep in and clothes that weren't falling apart. For a kid used to damp blankets and meals that didn't always come, it felt like striking gold.

He remembered waking after one of the best sleeps of his life, finding a pile of clothes — even socks and underwear — waiting on a chair. The old rags he'd come in wearing were gone. The shoes, too. These were real clothes, well-made and warm.

Following the smell of frying bacon, he'd found his way to the kitchen, where Luca, the chef, had looked him over.

"Well, you've cleaned up, and no mistake. Didn't recognise you. Guess you want feeding again, eh, kid?"

Danny nodded, and soon he was faced with the biggest breakfast he'd ever seen. He'd just mopped up the last of it when Jimmy walked in with another man, Vito. The two of them bickered like old dogs until Danny cut across them. "You shouldn't take the Lord's name in vain. Sister Angelica says it's wrong."

That got their attention. Vito eyed him as though noticing him for the first time. "So this is the kid you told me about?"

"Yeah," Jimmy said.

"And if I want to swear, kid, I will," Vito told him. "No nun's gonna tell me different. Anyway, who's Sister Angelica?"

"She runs the orphanage. Gets mad if we swear."

"Yeah, well, she ain't here, is she? And if she was, it wouldn't make no difference." Vito turned back to Jimmy. "So what are we gonna do with him?"

Jimmy's mouth twisted into a grin. "He's gonna help us get into the warehouse on Pier Forty-Four."

Vito frowned. "Why?"

"Because, genius, the boss wants back what the Feds took last week."

"What'd they take?"

Jimmy sighed. "The liquor. The boss wants it back."

"So why not send the boys down there to get it?"

Jimmy cuffed him across the head. "Because, idiot, if we try breaking in, we get pinched. But the kid —" he nodded toward Danny — "can get through the side window and open the door. Then all we gotta do is load the truck and drive."

Danny had been listening, weighing things up. "What do I get out of it?" he asked.

Both men stared at him. Kids didn't usually bargain.

Jimmy's grin widened. "What do you want?"

Danny thought for a moment. "That bedroom. Mine. No one else uses it."

Vito burst out laughing.

Jimmy tilted his head. "That's it? Just the room?"

Danny frowned. "For starters. And food. And maybe some money… so I can buy stuff when I need it."

"What kind of stuff?" Jimmy asked.

Danny shrugged. "Dunno. But I'll think of something."

Jimmy started laughing. "You're one hell of a weird kid, you know that?" Then he nodded slowly. "Alright. The bedroom, food, and some money. How much?"

Danny hesitated — then took a gamble. "Five dollars a week."

Jimmy raised his brows. Five dollars was a fortune to a street kid. For a moment Danny thought he'd pushed too far. Then Jimmy nodded. "Five a week it is. Plus the room and your meals. You in?"

Danny couldn't believe it. He'd landed on his feet — and if he played it right, he'd be set for good.

That night, they'd driven to the wharf, and Danny had done exactly what was asked — slipping through the window, picking his way through the dark until he found the bolts, then stepping back while the men rushed in.

And that was when he'd asked for his first payment. Not for himself — but for flowers. Gardenias, his mum's favourite. He wanted to lay them on her grave, which they'd passed on the way. Jimmy had bought every last bloom in the shop, paying with a fifty and telling the woman to keep the change.

At the cemetery, under the narrow beam of Jimmy's flashlight, Danny had knelt by the grave. "It's me, Mum. Danny. I brought you your favourite." He'd introduced Jimmy like he was a proper friend, and promised to come back.

Jimmy had stood there, silent, watching a boy try not to cry. And Danny had ridden home with his face to the window, tears tracking down but making no sound.

Now, years later, the memory burned in him — not just the ache of losing his mum, but the sharp awareness that protection was rare. Real protection. Someone willing to put themselves between you and the worst of the world. Jimmy had done it, in his own rough way.

And that was exactly what Danny was going to do for Maureen. One way or another, he was going to put himself between her and the man who'd made her life hell. And if he had to find a way around the law to make her his wife before twenty-one, he'd damn well do it.

Chapter 10

The war news was a mixed bag; some were good, and others were not. The raid on Nagoya Tokyo, which became known as the Doolittle Raid because it had been masterminded by Lieutenant Colonel James Doolittle, brought a great boost to troops and was in retaliation for Pearl Harbour. Towards the end of April, the German Luftwaffe conducted raids on various towns such as Bath, Exeter, Norwich, and York. These sporadic attacks would last until June the sixth. The Air Force retaliated with heavy bombing of Rostock in Germany.

People were tired and weary, but they continued to boost their morale by listening to the wireless, programs such as It's That Man Again, commonly known as ITMA, and Workers Playtime, which housewives and factory girls would sing along with so long as they could hear it over the noise of the machinery. The Cinema too helped; people could lose themselves in the films and forget the war for a couple of hours. They laughed at films such as My Favourite Blonde with Bob Hope and Madeleine Carroll.

Jenny and Marcus spilled out of the cinema into the cool evening air, still laughing so hard they were clutching their sides. Tears of mirth streaked down their cheeks.

"Oh, lord," Jenny gasped, dabbing at her eyes with a handkerchief, "I can't remember the last time I laughed so much."

Marcus grinned, still catching his breath. "Me neither — but it felt good to just let go."

"It really did," she agreed. "At least the film stars keep us sane."

"That's true," he said, slipping his hand into hers. "Come on, let's head to our favourite café."

They strolled along the lamplit street, their fingers intertwined, until the warm glow of the café windows beckoned them inside. Once seated in their usual corner with steaming cups of coffee before them, Jenny asked, "Have you heard anything more about your leave?"

Marcus shook his head. "No, not yet — but hopefully soon."

She didn't answer straight away, but the faint shadow that crossed her face didn't escape him. Reaching across the table, he took her hand and said softly, "Honey, it's not that I want to get away from you. Quite the opposite — I'd take you with me if I could. But I do want to see my family… and there's something important I need to do while I'm there. So I need to go — and soon."

Jenny sighed. "I know. I'm sorry. Of course you should see them. They must miss you terribly."

"They do. I ring when I can, but it's not easy — they're five hours behind us, so I have to catch them at the right time. Still, I suppose it could be worse — they could be seven or eight hours away."

She thought of his family, picturing them waiting for his letters and brief calls, their son and brother fighting a war an ocean away. "I wonder what the world will be like in a hundred years," she mused.

Marcus raised an eyebrow, a slow smile tugging at his lips. "Whoa — a hundred years? I can't even imagine what it'll be like in fifty."

"I know. It's hard to picture. But I was thinking… our great-grandchildren will be alive then. Imagine — the year 2043. What will their lives be like?"

"I've never thought about it," he admitted. "We won't be here."

"But don't you ever think about the future?" she asked.

"Sure," he said with a small shrug. "But our future. During our lifetime — not the next century."

He studied her, curiosity in his eyes. "So… what brought that on?"

She shook her head lightly. "Oh, I don't know. I was just wondering what kind of world future generations will inherit."

Marcus squeezed her hand. "Well, whatever it's like, let's hope there's no war — that they never have to fight."

Jenny gave him a wry smile. "There's always been war, Marcus. Look back over history — I can't think of a time when there wasn't some sort of conflict."

"Maybe this will be the last one," he said.

"I doubt it. They said that about the last war — the 'war to end all wars' — and twenty-five years later, here we are again. And with the same country starting it, too."

He leaned back in his chair. "Well, it won't be our problem. That'll be for someone else to deal with."

There was a short pause before he added, "I never realised you thought about things like this. There's more to you than meets the eye, Jenny Jackson — you're quite the philosopher when you want to be. But come on — if we dawdle much longer, you'll be late home, and your dad will roast us both."

As Jenny and Marcus stepped off the bus, the glow from the streetlamp lit up the small shelter ahead. The bus wheezed away into the night, leaving behind a faint tang of petrol in the cool air. The blackout curtains in the shop windows along the high street turned the row of buildings into a dark, silent wall. Under the lone streetlamp by the bus shelter, Danny and Maureen sat close together, their fingers laced. The lamp's light caught in her hair, turning it to a dull bronze against the shadows.

"Hello, you two," Marcus called, his voice breaking the muffled quiet. He and Jenny walked over, the soles of their shoes clicking softly on the damp pavement. "What are you doing here?"

Danny gave a short shrug. "Maureen's old man won't let me in. Doesn't even know I exist."

Jenny's eyes moved to Maureen. The pale glow showed her drawn face, her mouth tight, as if she was holding something in.

"You're so lucky, Jenny," Maureen said quietly. "Your parents are happy for you to see Marcus — and bring him home."

Jenny's chest tightened. "Well don't stay out too late or your dad will go mad."

Maureen nodded. "I know. I was just going in."

They wished them both goodnight, but as Jenny and Marcus walked away, they noticed Danny stayed in the shelter, watching Maureen's back until she disappeared inside.

Danny's jaw was tight as he turned towards the base. He hated this — the secrecy, the stolen moments, the feeling of being kept in the shadows. He longed to walk her home openly, to sit with her parents over tea, to be seen as a man who cared for her.

He quickened his pace and caught up with Marcus.

"You okay?" Marcus asked.

Danny gave a humourless laugh. "Maureen's old man — boy, I'd like to throttle him."

Marcus's voice was steady. "Look, I get it. But you'll only make things worse if you confront him. Best to leave it alone."

"That's easy for you to say. Jenny's dad's fine with you. I can't even walk Maureen to her door. I've got to watch her from the bloody bus stop."

Marcus laid a hand on his shoulder. "I know it's rough. But you challenge him, and he'll take it out on her. I think she's had enough to deal with, don't you?"

Danny's eyes narrowed, but he gave a short nod. "Yeah... you're right, skip. But I swear, if he ever lays a hand on her again, I'll kill the bastard."

Inside the house, Maureen found her mother in the sitting room, knitting needles clicking softly. She looked up and smiled.

"Hello, love. Have a nice evening?"

"Yes, thanks," Maureen said, slipping off her coat. "It's getting warmer — spring's on its way at last."

"Well, there's tea in the pot if you want one."

From behind his newspaper, her father's voice cut in, flat and cold. "Where have you been?"

"Out with a friend."

"What friend?"

"One of the girls from work. You don't know her."

His tone sharpened. "And where did you go with this friend?"

"Just walked around a bit, then went for a coffee."

At last, he lowered the paper and looked at her. For a long moment, their eyes locked — and he was startled by what he saw. Naked hatred. Loathing. It hit him like a physical blow. My God, he thought. Does she hate me that much? And in his gut, he knew the answer. Yes. And he had put it there.

His voice grew harder. "Well, keep away from that Jackson girl. I saw her with a bloody Yank tonight. She'll bring trouble to their door; you mark my words. Going with Yanks... I don't know what her father's thinking. Must be soft in the head. Always was — too soft on her."

"Jenny would never get into trouble," Maureen said sharply. "She's not like that. And her boyfriend is a good man."

"You just stay away from her, you hear?" he snapped. "I don't want trouble at my door. You bring it here; I'll beat the brat out of you. There'll be no bastards born in this house — and certainly not a bloody Yank's."

Maureen and her mother exchanged a brief glance, a silent understanding passing between them. One day, she vowed, she would get herself — and her mother — away from him. She prayed that day would come soon.

Back at the base, Danny thought about Maureen's father, Danny often thought that if his father were still alive—and Jake and Jimmy too—they would have known exactly how to deal with Maureen's brute of a father. He could still recall, with chilling clarity, how those men "dealt" with people—sometimes those who had crossed them, sometimes those they simply didn't like.

They had known his father. Worked with him. That revelation had been a shock. And it hadn't come from a confession or a story—it had been something he overheard entirely by accident.

It was only a few days after they had taken the flowers to his mother's grave. Danny had been lingering outside the office when Jimmy, in the middle of some idle chatter with Jake, suddenly asked, "So, what's your surname, kid? I assume you *do* have one?"

Danny frowned. "Yeah, of course. It's Butchers—Danny Butchers."

Both men stared at him. "Butchers?" Jimmy repeated slowly. "Your surname is Butchers?"

"Yeah… why?" Danny asked, suspicious now.

"How old did you say you were?" Jimmy pressed.

"I didn't. Why, is it important?"

"Just answer the question," Jimmy said.

"Ten. I'm ten years old, okay?"

Jimmy and Jake exchanged a glance—silent, but heavy.

Then Jimmy reached into his pocket, pulled out some coins, and handed them over. "Go to the kiosk down the road and get me a pack of cigarettes, will you?"

Danny took the money and left, but he didn't wander far. As he reached the corridor, he noticed the door hadn't quite closed behind him. Voices drifted out.

Jake's low growl came first. "Butchers… why is that name familiar to me?"

Jimmy's reply was quieter, but the words landed like a hammer blow. "Because that's the guy we sent to the bottom of the Hudson ten years ago—Rocco Butchers."

"I remember now," Jake said slowly. "He stole from me. Come to think of it, he was always stealing."

"Yeah, that's the guy," Jimmy said. "And I'm telling you—he's the kid's old man. I remember Rocco begging me for his life. Said his wife had just had a baby boy. Said he wanted the money for them and wanted to see the kid grow up. I didn't believe him. Thought he was just whining to save his miserable skin."

Jake's voice was dismissive. "Well, nothing we can do about it now. You'll see the kid's okay." Papers rustled as he turned back to his ledger.

Danny stood frozen outside the door, his heart hammering in his ears. So his father hadn't "left" them at all. He'd been murdered. Sent to the bottom of the Hudson by the very men who had taken Danny in. They were the reason his mother had been forced to work herself to exhaustion at three jobs. They were the reason she had died. He didn't yet know *how*, but one day—*one day*—he would make them pay.

For now, he forced himself to keep his head down, to obey every order, to give them no reason to suspect what he knew.

When he returned with the cigarettes, his mind was still reeling. Only then did he notice he'd bought the wrong brand. He feigned ignorance, handing the packet over.

"They didn't have your usual ones, Jimmy," he said lightly. "I got these instead—but I can go back and change them if you want."

Normally, Jimmy would have torn strips off him for that. But today, he simply shrugged. “That’s okay. These’ll do. Here—want to try one?”

Danny shook his head. “No, thanks.”

“Go on,” Jimmy insisted, lighting one and handing it over.

Danny took a cautious drag—and nearly choked himself into oblivion. Coughs wracked his chest until his eyes streamed. Jimmy chuckled, patting his back, while Jake scowled.

“What the hell are you trying to do—kill the kid?”

But in truth, Jimmy had done him a favour. That first cigarette was also his last. He never touched another one in his life.

Jenny and Ruth sat in the staff room, their tea steaming gently in the cool air, half-eaten sandwiches resting on paper napkins. The conversation, as it often did these days, had drifted to Maureen and Danny.

“I think it’s sad,” Jenny said quietly. “Danny seems like such a nice person. Even Marcus has changed his opinion of him.”

Ruth nodded. “I know. I saw them together the other day. You could tell—just by the way he looked at her—that he genuinely cares.”

For a while they ate in silence, the soft rustle of sandwich paper the only sound between them. Then Jenny spoke again.

“I wonder why he’s got such a bad reputation on the base. He must have done something—but Marcus swears he hasn’t. Not really. Just… rubs people the wrong way.”

Ruth shrugged. “Maybe it’s deliberate. Some people like to keep everyone at arm’s length—especially now. If you don’t let people get close, it’s easier when they don’t come back from a mission."

"Mmm. Could be," Jenny murmured. She tapped her fingers on the table, thinking. "But coming back to her father—I can't see any future for them. She's only nineteen. She's still got two years before she turns twenty-one, and by then the war could be over... Danny might be back in America."

"Or," Ruth said, lowering her voice, "she could run away with him. Go to America. I wonder what the age of consent is over there. Do you think it's still twenty-one?"

Jenny shrugged. "No idea. I'll ask Marcus. But even if it's lower, she can't leave without her father's permission."

"She could lie," Ruth suggested. "Pretend she's lost her birth certificate... find a way."

Jenny gave a small, hopeful smile. "Maybe. I just hope it works out for them. It's such a shame, having your life ruined by someone else's selfishness."

Maureen, meanwhile, had Danny on her mind—almost constantly these days. She had decided it was time to tell her mother about him. She was sure her mother would understand.

On Wednesday afternoon, her half-day from work, she knew she would have the perfect opportunity. Her father would still be at work, and they could talk without fear of interruption.

When she got home, the smell of freshly cut bread and butter greeted her. Her mother was in the kitchen, slicing bread and layering sandwiches.

Once they were seated with their lunch and mugs of hot tea, Maureen took a breath.

"Mum... if I tell you something, will you promise not to tell *him?*"

Her mother's knife paused mid-air. She knew exactly who "him" meant. Maureen hadn't called her father "dad" in years—only "him." The knowledge stung, though she couldn't blame her daughter. He had earned her hatred.

"That depends on what it is, love," she replied carefully. "Are you in trouble?"

Maureen shook her head. "No, Mum. I'm not. But... I've met someone. And yes—before you ask—he's an American airman. But he's so nice, Mum. Gentle. Caring. He really cares about me. We've been seeing each other for a couple of months now."

Cynthia stared at her daughter. "Oh, Maureen... if your dad finds out, he'll go mad."

"Yes, I know. But he *won't* find out."

"So when you go out and tell me you've been with a friend—it's him, isn't it?"

Maureen nodded.

Cynthia studied her daughter's face. The light in her eyes, the warmth in her voice—it told her everything. Her heart softened.

"Maureen, love, no good can come of this. You know your father will never allow it."

Tears sprang to Maureen's eyes. "Oh, I wish he was dead," she burst out.

"Don't, love," Cynthia said sharply, shocked. "Don't wish people dead—not even him. Curses come home to roost."

She watched her daughter's head bow, tears dripping silently into her tea. Then she spoke again, more gently.

"I'll tell you what—we've got a couple of hours on Friday

nights when he's at the pub. Why don't you invite this young man round for a cup of tea then? I'd like to meet the boy who's put such a sparkle in my daughter's eyes."

Maureen looked up, astonished. "You really mean it? He can come here?"

"Yes, love—but one condition. He'll have to come through the back gate and leave the same way. If anyone sees him coming in the front door, they'll tell your dad, and we'll both be for the high jump."

Maureen jumped up and hugged her. "Oh, Mum—thank you!"

"Well, he can't come until after your dad goes out at seven, and he has to be gone sharp by ten, understand?"

Maureen nodded, joy bubbling inside her. She couldn't wait to see Danny and tell him the news.

That night, when Maureen told Danny the news, he could hardly believe it.

"Really? She actually said I could come round while your dad's out?"

Maureen nodded, smiling. "Yes. She wants to meet you—but you can't come until after seven, and you have to be gone sharp by ten."

He brushed his fingers gently along her cheek. "That's fine by me. As long as we get time together, I don't care how short it is. I'll wait at the bus stop and watch him leave."

Friday night came, and Danny sat hunched in the bus shelter, the damp chill creeping in under his collar. He kept glancing toward the house.

"Jeez," he muttered under his breath, "will the guy never

leave?"

It was already past seven before the front door finally opened. Maureen's father stepped out, walking down the road toward the pub.

Danny slipped quietly from the shelter, keeping to the shadows as he made his way down the back alley. He wasn't sure which house it was—until he saw Maureen's figure in the gloom, her pale face just visible in the dim light. She beckoned him urgently, and he followed her through the back gate.

"I thought he'd never leave," Danny said in a low voice.

"Neither did we," Maureen replied with a quick smile.

Inside, she introduced him to her mother. The sight of Cynthia Blackford made him stop for a moment. She had the same delicate features and grey-green eyes as her daughter, but her beauty had been worn thin by years of hardship. Her once-auburn hair was streaked with grey, her skin pale, her figure slight—almost birdlike. There was a faded grace about her that spoke of better days long gone.

Danny took her hand gently. "It's nice to meet you, ma'am. I'm Danny—Danny Butchers."

He smiled warmly, and Cynthia instantly understood why her daughter had fallen for him. "Well, it's nice to meet you too, Danny."

Reaching into his pocket, he pulled out two bars of chocolate and handed one to each of them. Their eyes widened in astonishment.

"Oh, Danny—where did you get these?" Maureen gasped.

"We get plenty of stuff like that," he said with a shrug. "I should've given you some sooner, but I will from now on."

Cynthia clasped hers like treasure. “Thank you, Danny. I haven’t had chocolate since before the war. I don’t even know where I could keep it so he doesn’t find it.”

“In my bedside cabinet, Mum,” Maureen said quickly. “He never goes in my room, and you can eat it while he’s at work.”

“Oh, I will, love—but best put it away now before we forget.”

Maureen darted upstairs and tucked the precious chocolate away.

“Sit yourself down, lad, while I put the kettle on,” Cynthia said.

Danny sat, glancing around the little kitchen. The place was spotless, but everything was worn thin—table legs scuffed from years of use, curtains faded by sun and smoke. He vowed, then and there, that one day Maureen and her mother would have a better home than this.

The evening passed far too quickly. They chatted over tea, and Cynthia couldn’t remember the last time she’d enjoyed herself so much. Danny spoke about his life in New York—at least, the parts he wanted to share. She was saddened to hear how young he’d lost his mother, but comforted that the nuns had been kind to him. He kept the darker details—Jake, Jimmy, and the rest—safely to himself, focusing instead on Sister Angelica, Sister Bridget, and the others who’d looked out for him.

Before they knew it, the clock struck ten. Danny rose reluctantly, taking Cynthia’s small, bony hand in his.

“Thank you, ma’am, for a lovely evening.”

“And thank you, Danny. I’ve loved every minute—and for the chocolate, too. You *will* come again, won’t you?”

He smiled. “I’d like that very much.”

Maureen walked him to the back door, and they stepped into the cool night air.

"I'll see you tomorrow, sweetheart," he murmured—and for the first time, he kissed her on the lips.

Just then, the faint creak of the front door reached them.

"Danny—you have to go!" Maureen whispered urgently.

He slipped quickly through the gate, and she closed it behind him, heart pounding. She dashed into the kitchen, snatched up the tea towel and hand towel from the line, and stepped back outside just as her father came in.

"What the hell are you doing out there, girl?"

"Oh—Mum just remembered the tea towel and towel she put out to dry, so I'm bringing them in for her."

"Well, shut the door and throw the bolt. I don't want to be burgled."

Danny walked back toward the base under the cold stars, his jaw set. He was more determined than ever to get Maureen and her mother out of that house. He didn't yet know how—but he would find a way.

Chapter 11

The following morning, after her father had left for work, Maureen turned to her mother.

"What did you think of him, Mum?"

Cynthia smiled faintly. "I think he's a lovely, handsome young man."

"I know," Maureen said, her cheeks warming, "but above all, he's kind to me. He treats me properly—with respect—and I love him, Mum. And I know he loves me."

"Yes, I can see that," Cynthia replied softly. "Just the way he looks at you—it's obvious."

But inside, her heart ached. Would her daughter ever be allowed the chance to be happy? In that moment, she wanted her husband gone from their lives. She didn't care how—just gone.

Jenny and Ruth were delighted for Maureen when she told them that Danny had met her mother.

"And your mum liked him?" Ruth asked eagerly.

"Yes, she did—and he brought us chocolate. A whole bar each! We haven't had that since before the war."

"Well, no wonder she liked him," Ruth laughed. "So would I, if he brought me chocolate." Then she glanced at Jenny with a teasing look. "Does Marcus ever bring you chocolate?"

"Sometimes," Jenny said, smiling. "But I share it with Mum, Dad, and Betty." She paused, a pang of guilt flickering in her chest. "I'll tell you what—next time I'll let you have it, and you can share it with your mum and dad."

"No, don't be silly. That's not fair—after all, he brings it for you."

"We don't do so badly," Jenny said. "But you can have the next one, I promise."

Sister Angelica couldn't sleep. She lay in the darkness, her mind restless, something niggling at her that she couldn't quite shake. It had to do with Danny Butchers.

That boy will be the death of me, she thought with a weary sigh. He had been a handful from the very start, and now—ten years later—he was still capable of keeping her awake at night.

Sister Angelica loved all her charges, but now and then one would creep deeper into her heart, making themselves at home there permanently. Danny was one of those children.

Her unease had started weeks ago, after a telephone call from him. He had sounded... troubled. She couldn't put her finger on it, but the worry had stuck with her. Was he in trouble again? Had he fallen in with the wrong people? And if so—how could she possibly help him from three thousand miles away in England?

She thought back to the last time he had vanished.

He had been gone for months, and when he finally appeared again, she had barely recognised him.

He had swaggered into her office like a boy playing at being a prosperous businessman—neatly cut hair, an expensive suit that fitted him like it was tailored, polished shoes gleaming under the light.

"Good heavens, Danny," she had said, staring at him. "Where on earth have you been? And where did you get those clothes?"

He had grinned and held his jacket wide, giving her a slow turn on his heel. "Waddaya think, Sister? Great threads, ain't they?"

She gave him a hard look. "Where did you get them, Danny?"

That grin—charming enough to melt the iciest heart—flashed again.

"Sit down, Danny."

When he made no move, she repeated, more firmly, "Sit down. Now."

At last, he dropped into the chair.

"I didn't steal them, if that's what you're thinking, Sister. I paid for them—shoes too."

"Paid for them? How? Where did the money come from?"

"I've got a job."

Her heart sank. "A job? You're supposed to be in school, not working. And what kind of job pays a boy your age enough to buy such things?"

"I'm working for someone. He pays well—so I buy nice things."

Her unease deepened. "Who is this man? What kind of business is he running?"

"All sorts. He does a lot of different things."

"I want to meet him," she said firmly. "He needs to know you're underage and should be in school."

"No, Sister. I don't want to be in school. I like what I'm doing, and I'm going to keep working for him."

The words hit her like a slap. He had never spoken to her with such defiance before.

"Danny," she said, softening her tone, "I'm worried about you. What exactly do you do for him? What kind of work is it?"

"Like I said—lots of things. I run errands, pick up stuff, deliver stuff."

She sighed. There was no reaching him. "At least tell me his name—or the name of his business."

He knew she was fishing for something to take to the police. He shook his head, stood up. "No, Sister. I'm sorry—but I can't."

Then he reached into his pocket, pulled out a twenty-dollar bill, and tossed it onto her desk.

"That's to help you get whatever you need right now."

She picked up the note and held it out to him. "No, Danny. I don't want this—not if it came from illegal practices."

"You need it, Sister. I know you do."

And with that, he turned and walked out.

That had been the last time she saw him for years—until a few months ago, when he'd appeared again with five hundred dollars in cash, telling her he was going away and not to tell anyone she had seen him.

Over the intervening years, money had arrived in the post from time to time—always with no note, no return address. But she always knew who it was from.

"Bombs away, Skip," Marcus' bombardier called over the

intercom.

"Right—let's head home, then," Marcus replied. "Great work, everyone. Well done."

"Yeah," Patterson said, his voice crackling in Marcus' headset. "We hit our target. There'll be a lot of unhappy people down there right now."

Marcus's tone cooled. "Let's not gloat. There'll be a lot of innocent civilians suffering too."

"Well, they started it, Skip—what did they expect?" Patterson muttered.

"No," Marcus said firmly, "one maniac started it, Patterson. That's the difference."

"Yeah, I guess you're right," Patterson conceded, "but all the same, I could be back at home with my girl if it wasn't for this lot."

"Yeah—milking cows," Danny chipped in over the radio.

"Nothing wrong with working on a farm," Patterson said. "Good healthy life, outdoors, fresh air."

"I get plenty of fresh air," Danny shot back. "But what about the smells? Don't they turn your stomach?"

"What smells?" Patterson asked.

"Well—farmyard smells. Cows, and… things."

Patterson chuckled. "You ever been on a farm, Butchers?"

"No—and I don't intend to."

"You don't know what you're missing," Patterson said. "It's a great life, and I only hope I live to get back there."

The next moment, the plane lurched violently to the left, and all hell broke loose. The engines roared under strain as tracer fire sliced through the air.

"Bandits—two of 'em!" someone shouted.

A Messerschmitt 210 and a Heinkel HE 219 had appeared

out of the grey sky, one on each side. Both opened fire, the deafening hammer of their cannons reverberating through the fuselage.

Danny swung his turret, the twin Browning chattering as he locked onto the Heinkel. Bullets tore into its fuselage, and the German fighter sheared away—only to bank hard and return with a vicious parting volley. Glass shattered around him. Danny kept firing until the enemy peeled away for good.

The B-17 was still taking heavy fire. Danny scanned frantically—then caught sight of the Messerschmitt appearing out of nowhere on his flank. He squeezed the trigger, and a burst of fire stitched across the fighter's nose. It veered sharply and was gone.

"Everyone okay back there?" Marcus called.

"Yeah—all okay, Skip," came the reply.

Danny was about to answer when he noticed a dark red drip on his flight suit. He glanced down. Blood. Then he saw the neat bullet hole in the glass of his turret—and the matching groove in his right arm.

"Jeez," he muttered. "The bastard got me."

Chuck, stationed nearest to him, scrambled over as best he could. "Where are you hit?"

"In my right arm," Danny said, almost casually.

Chuck exhaled sharply in relief. At least it wasn't life-threatening. Butchers might be a pain in the backside, but Chuck didn't want to see him dead.

Back on the ground, they hustled Danny straight to Sick Bay. The medic peeled back the torn sleeve and inspected the wound.

"Well, you'll be pleased to hear you'll live to fight another day, Butchers," the doctor said. "Just a scratch—your flying jacket took most of it."

Danny grinned. "Yeah, I'm like a cat, Doc—I've got nine lives. I'll see this war out and die an old man in my bed."

The doctor smiled faintly at the bravado, though he doubted the truth of it. Tail gunners had the shortest life expectancy of all—six to eight weeks, on average. Butchers had already beaten the odds by months. In the doctor's mind, the man was living on borrowed time.

Maureen's eyes filled with worry the first time she saw Danny after the mission.

"Oh, Danny—you could have been killed. Can't you ask to do something else, something not so dangerous?"

Her voice trembled, and tears welled in her eyes. Danny reached up, brushed them away with the back of his hand, and kissed her cheek.

"It doesn't work like that, honey," he said gently. "It's my job—and that's that."

"But you won't fly again until it's healed, surely?"

"No. I'll be grounded until the doc gives me the all-clear. But it's only a surface wound—it won't take long."

Jenny, too, was unsettled when Marcus told her what had happened.

"Oh, Marcus, he could have been killed. You all could have been killed."

He caught the tear that slipped down her cheek and wiped it away with his thumb.

"I know," he said softly. "But it's our job. It's what we do—to keep you safe."

"Oh, I hate this war," she whispered. "I wish it was over."

Marcus pulled her close. "So does the rest of the world," he murmured.

For Danny, those Friday nights at Maureen's—if there wasn't a dance on the base—were the brightest part of the week. He relished the hours in that small, threadbare kitchen, talking with Maureen and her mother. Over time, he and Cynthia built a quiet, mutual respect.

He admired how she never complained about her lot, never whined or sought pity. She bore life with a quiet stoicism, always cheerful, always grateful for the little things he brought—candy, chocolate, nylons for both her and Maureen.

She never wore the nylons herself. There was nowhere to go where she could dress up, and Albert would have demanded to know where she got them. Instead, she slipped them to Maureen after Danny left.

The more he visited, the more determined he became to get them away from Albert Jackson.

Sometimes, sitting in that kitchen, Danny would think back to his own childhood—back when his mother was alive and healthy—and anger would rise hot in his chest. If it hadn't been for Jake and Jimmy, maybe she'd still be alive.

If not for them, his education wouldn't have been cut short. He might have gone to college—become a doctor or a lawyer. He could have taken care of her, got her out of the cramped, dirty apartment they called home.

At least, he thought with grim relief, she had never known that his father was tangled up with the Mafia. That knowledge alone would have broken her.

Even after learning the truth, Danny kept working for Jake and Jimmy, never letting on that he knew they'd killed his father. He always sensed that Jimmy carried a heavy weight of guilt about it.

Jimmy had a way of looking out for him—almost like a father would. At Christmas and on birthdays, Danny would find expensive gifts waiting for him.

Some of the others didn't see it that way. They whispered about Jimmy's motives—dark, ugly insinuations.

One man, Nico Costa, had the gall to say it aloud, thinking Jimmy was out of earshot.

He wasn't.

Jimmy had come into the room like a storm, eyes blazing. In two strides he had Nico by the throat, one big hand clamped tight.

"You disgust me, you little creep," Jimmy snarled. "There's nothing wrong with being fatherly to the kid. He's got no father. And if you ever—ever—say what you just said again, neither will your kid."

Nico's face went purple. His legs kicked weakly as Jimmy shook him like a rag doll, then hurled him to the floor. Danny thought for a moment he'd actually killed him.

"Jeez, Jimmy—you've killed him," Danny blurted.

Jimmy looked down at the gasping, writhing heap. Then he kicked him—hard enough to make Nico cry out.

"He's not dead," Jimmy growled, "but he will be if he ever repeats it."

The message stuck. No one ever dared voice such accusations again.

On Danny's sixteenth birthday, Jimmy had decided it was

time to "make a man" of him.

He took him to the brothel they ran and handed him over to Lola. Danny never knew her real name—she was just "Lola" to everyone.

"Here you are, kid," Jimmy said, clapping him on the shoulder. "Your birthday present. Lola, I give you this kid—you give me back a man."

Danny stared at her. She was only a few years older than him, with a practiced smile that didn't quite hide the weariness in her eyes.

"This your first time, kid?" she asked, cocking her head.

Danny nodded.

She rolled her eyes. "Come on, Jimmy—an innocent kid? Why can't you give him to one of the others?"

"Because I want you to teach him," Jimmy replied. "I'll make it worth your while."

She sighed, resigned. "Okay, come on, kid. Let's get this over with."

"I'll be back in two hours," Jimmy told her.

"Two hours? That's a hell of a long time. Make it half an hour."

"Two hours," he repeated firmly. "He's got a lot to learn."

After that first time, Danny visited Lola regularly—not always for sex. Sometimes they just sat and talked. In those moments, he learned they had more in common than he'd expected.

"Why 'Lola'?" Danny asked one afternoon.

She shrugged. "It's as good a name as any."

"So... what's your real name?"

Her expression changed instantly—eyes hard, voice sharp.

"Don't ever ask me that again. I don't use any other name but Lola. Got it?"

"Yeah," Danny said quietly. "I got it."

"Good. Then we understand each other."

"Okay, no real names," he said after a pause. "But judging by your accent, I'd say you're from Wisconsin."

Her face darkened. "Get out. Just get the hell out."

Danny blinked. "Hey, take it easy—I'm just making conversation. I thought we were getting to know each other."

"You ask too many bloody questions I don't like. Just get out, Danny."

Shaken by her sudden anger, he'd picked up his jacket and left. He stayed away for a couple of weeks, figuring she needed time to cool off.

When he finally returned, she was back to her old self—smiling, teasing, acting as if nothing had happened.

"I didn't mean anything by it," he told her. "I was just making conversation."

"Yeah, I know. I'm sorry," she said, her tone softening. "I just don't like to talk about my life before I came here."

"Okay, I get it," Danny said. "So… is it okay to ask how you ended up here?"

She hesitated, then shrugged. "I came to New York looking for work. It didn't work out. I was desperate—starving. Then I met Jimmy, and he said he could help me."

She stopped, clearly uncomfortable.

"So, he brought you here," Danny guessed. "How long have you been here?"

"Too bloody long. Four years."

"How old were you when you came?"

"Eighteen."

In that moment, Danny's stomach turned. He hated Jimmy for it. It seemed the man had a talent for taking advantage of every vulnerable soul he crossed paths with.

"I'll get you out of here," Danny said quietly. "I promise. We'll both get out one day."

She grinned, but there was no real hope in it. "Yeah? And how are you gonna do that?"

He shrugged. "I don't know. But I will."

A thought struck him. "Do you have any money? Or do they take it all?"

"I've got some. They let me keep a bit, and I've got a few private clients."

"So... do you spend your life in here, or do you ever get out?"

She laughed. "I'm not a prisoner, Danny. I can come and go as I please—so long as I'm here when I'm supposed to be."

"They know you go out?" Danny asked, still unsure how it worked.

"Sure, they know. They're not all bad."

"Then why don't you just leave? Get on a train. Go."

"Because I don't have enough money yet. But when I do..." She gave him a small, fierce smile. "I'll leave."

Danny nodded, relieved she had a plan. Still, the thought of her spending the rest of her life here—until she was too old to draw in clients, only to be tossed onto the street—made his chest tighten.

Chapter 12

Jenny and Ruth sat in the staff room, half-listening to the hum of conversation around them. At the next table, a cluster of girls were huddled together, giggling over something. One of them finally spoke up, her voice loud enough to carry.

"It's great, but it does go on a bit," she said, waving a bundle of typed sheets. Then, turning to Jenny with a sly smile, she added, "Hey, Jenny—you're dating a Yank, aren't you?"

Jenny and Ruth exchanged a glance. "Yes," Jenny replied evenly. "What of it?"

"Well… have you heard this?" the girl asked.

"Heard what?" Jenny said, her tone cautious.

The girl straightened the papers and began to recite in a singsong voice, as though performing for an audience:

We dreaded invasion, well it came,
But it wasn't the beastly Hun—
The god-damned Yankee army's come.
In admiration, we would stare
At all the ribbons that they wear
And wonder at all their deeds so bold and daring,
Won the medals that they're wearing.
But that pretty ribbon just denotes
They crossed the sea, brave men in boats.

We see them on the tram or bus,
There isn't any room for us.
We walk to let them have our seats,
Then get run over by their jeeps.
They love your hair, your eyes, your curls—
Your teeth are like the brightest pearls.
"I love you, darling, please be mine..."
It's the same old Yank with the same old line.
You are their life, their love, their all,
But for your mother they would fall—
In a different town, in a different place,
To a different girl with a different face.
It's the same old Yank with the same old line.

By the end of the recitation, Jenny's cheeks were burning—not with shame, but with anger.

Ruth shot to her feet, her voice cutting through the room like a whip. "That's enough! You're disgusting. Not all of them are like that—there are some decent ones. Anyway, how do you know our lads aren't carrying on exactly the same way wherever they're stationed?"

The girls shifted uneasily, their amusement fading. One of them muttered, "Sorry, Jenny. I didn't mean any harm."

Jenny didn't respond. Yes, she knew plenty of people thought that way, but as Ruth had said, they weren't *all* the same. And she knew Marcus wasn't.

That evening, Ruth told her mother what had happened.

"That's awful," her mother said, looking genuinely horrified. "And so cruel. Poor Jenny. But I think her young man's different. I know there are some terrible ones, but he's not like that."

Ruth nodded. "I know—that's exactly what I told them. At least they had the grace to look ashamed."

"Well, you're a good friend," her mother said warmly. "It's good you stood up for her."

"She would have done the same for me."

"Yes," her mother agreed, smiling. "She would."

A few doors down, Jenny was also telling her mother about the incident.

Veronica reached over and patted her daughter's hand. "Don't take any notice, love. They're probably just jealous. Marcus is a very attractive young man, and didn't you say all the girls liked him?"

Jenny nodded reluctantly.

"Well, there you are then. And it was nice of young Ruth to stand up for you. She's a good friend."

"Yes, she is. But she knows I'd have done the same for her."

"I know you would, dear," Veronica said firmly. "Now sit down and eat your tea while it's hot. Forget all about them."

Maureen, too, had heard the poem, and the hurt it carried lingered in her mind.

"Danny isn't like that, love," her mother reassured her. "What chance does he even have to cheat on you? If he's not with you, he's at work. And I've seen the way he looks at you—he's bowled over. Believe me, you've nothing to worry about."

Just then, the front door opened, and her father stepped in from work. He stopped and eyed them both suspiciously.

"What doesn't she have to worry about?"

They both jumped; neither had heard him come in.

"They're thinking of closing some of the departments at the shop," her mother said smoothly, "because they can't get enough staff now the girls are being called up. Maureen was worried she might lose her job, but I told her she's very good at what she does, so she's got nothing to worry about."

He studied them for a moment, as if weighing the truth of it, then moved into the other room without another word.

Once he was gone, Maureen gave her mother a grateful smile. "Thanks, Mum."

"No need to thank me, love," her mother replied quietly. "The less he knows, the better."

Danny lay on his bunk, hands folded behind his head, staring up at the ceiling. His mind was far from the barracks. He was turning over the same thought he'd been wrestling with for days—how to get Maureen and her mother away from her father. They were too good, too kind, for the miserable life they endured with him.

The simplest answer—wait for the man one night and kill him—came easily enough. But Danny dismissed it almost immediately. They hung murderers here in England, and if they didn't, the Americans would haul him back home and strap him into the electric chair. Either way, Maureen and her mother would be left worse off than before. No, he had to find another way—something clever, something that would work without leaving a trail.

"Hey, Butchers—what are you doing?"

The voice yanked him out of his thoughts. Jerry Patterson

stood in the doorway with his inseparable shadow, Stu Parnell, both wearing the same lopsided grins.

"I was trying to think something through," Danny said, "until you interrupted me."

Jerry laughed and glanced at Stu. "You hear that? He *thinks*. Who'd have thought it—Butchers can think."

They both erupted into laughter.

"Yeah," Stu said, "does it give you a headache when you do that?"

Danny swung his legs over the side of the bunk and gave them a flat look. "Boy, you two crack me up. Who do you think you are—Laurel and Hardy?"

Jerry grinned, instantly picking up the cue. Running a hand through his hair, he said in his best Oliver Hardy impression, "That's another fine mess you got me into, Stanley."

They roared again, clearly enjoying themselves at his expense.

Danny's patience was running thin. "Why don't you two go and be infantile somewhere else?"

"Infantile—hear that, Stu? He thinks we're infantile."

"Does he even know what it means?" Stu asked with mock seriousness. "I didn't think he knew any words of more than one syllable."

The laughter rolled on, but Danny wasn't smiling. He got to his feet, and his expression made both men take notice.

Stu began backing away. "Hey, look, Danny—we're just having a bit of fun, that's all. Jerry doesn't mean anything by it, do you, Jerry?"

Jerry glanced at him and realised they'd pushed too far. "Nah, just letting off steam."

"Well, bugger off and let off steam someplace else before I

get *really* mad," Danny said evenly.

They didn't need telling twice. Butchers was unpredictable, and they weren't about to test his limits. They left quicker than they'd come in.

After they'd gone, Danny lay back on his bunk with a sigh. Guilt pricked at him. He knew they meant no real harm—they were good guys, both of them—and after all, they faced death every day. Letting off steam was part of how they kept their sanity. He'd buy them a beer in the mess later to make it right. They'd think he'd gone soft, but what the hell.

Still, his mind wandered back to the world he'd left behind. He thought about how Jimmy would have handled the situation. Jerry and Stu wouldn't have been laughing—hell, they might not even have been breathing. Jimmy never took prisoners. His motto was simple: kill first, ask questions later.

Then there was Jake. Odd thing, that—Jake was the boss, but it always seemed Jimmy ran the show. The boys paid their respects to Jake, treated him with the proper deference, but when it came to taking orders or solving problems, they looked to Jimmy.

Danny had once asked him about it. "Hey, Jimmy—how come Jake's the boss, but you're the one running everything?"

Jimmy had narrowed his eyes. "So what's it to you, kid?"

Danny shrugged. "Nothin'. Just wondered, that's all."

That had been the first time anyone had questioned Jimmy's growing grip on the organisation, and he hadn't liked it. Danny was smart—too smart for his own good, in Jimmy's opinion. The kid noticed things the others didn't. Where the rest of the crew just took orders without question, Danny always wanted to know the whys and wherefores.

And men like Jimmy didn't much care for curious kids.

Jimmy weighed his words carefully. The kid wasn't the type to swallow half-truths, and if he didn't hear it now, he'd figure it out sooner or later. Better to come clean on Jimmy's terms than risk Danny piecing it together on his own.

"Okay, kid—come with me."

Danny followed him out to the car without a word. Jimmy pulled the Packard out of the garage, tyres crunching over the gravel, and steered them through the gates.

"Where we going?" Danny asked.

"You'll see."

They drove down to the wharf, the fog rolling in off the river, wrapping the old warehouses in a damp, ghostly haze. Jimmy parked outside one of them and unlocked a heavy steel door. Inside, the air smelled of dust, wood, and something faintly metallic.

Rows of racks stretched into the gloom—men's suits, women's dresses, furs. Stacks of boxes. Crates of jewellery glinting under the single bare bulb. In one corner, rows of bootleg liquor bottles stood like soldiers at attention. Danny stared. "What is all this?"

Jimmy's mouth twitched into a small, tight smile. "My future. My insurance."

"And Jake doesn't know about this?"

Jimmy shook his head slowly. "Nobody knows—except you and me. So if he *does* find out, I'll know exactly who opened their mouth."

Something in his tone made Danny's blood run cold.

Whatever loyalty Jimmy felt toward him, it wouldn't stop him pulling the trigger if he thought he'd been betrayed.

"He won't hear it from me," Danny said quickly. "No one will hear it from me."

"That's good, kid." Jimmy's eyes stayed on him a beat longer before he added, "You want to know why?"

Danny nodded.

"I thought you two were like brothers," he said, sweeping an arm toward the piled riches.

"We were," Jimmy said flatly. "But Jake's going soft—acting strange, losing his grip. There's a family in Chicago sniffing around, looking to take over. Sooner or later, they will. And when it happens, it'll be either a takeover or a war. Jake hasn't got the stomach for a war. When it comes, I'm cutting and running."

"You don't want to work for the Chicago outfit?"

Jimmy snorted. "No. Don't like 'em. Don't trust 'em. They'd slit their own grandmother's throat for a few bucks. Ruthless. If I were you, Danny, I'd get out too. I'll keep you posted so you've got time to vanish."

Danny nodded but kept scanning the warehouse. He'd never seen so much loot in one place. "You got an inventory for all this?"

Jimmy shrugged. "No need. You and me are the only ones who know it's here. No one's taking it."

Danny's mind was already turning over possibilities. He noticed a small window high on the side wall—big enough for him to squeeze through. Easy to open. Easy to close again without anyone noticing. Yeah, this could be useful. He thought of Lola—she could turn some of this into good money.

A week later, the opportunity came. Jimmy was out of town for a few days.

Danny waited until nightfall, then drove down to the wharf. The small window yielded to a careful twist of his screwdriver. Inside, the warehouse was silent except for the echo of his own footsteps. His flashlight's beam skated over racks of clothing, stacks of crates.

The jewellery caught his eye—glints of gold and silver, stones flashing under the light. There had to be thousands of dollars' worth here. He opened the bag he'd brought and slipped in a handful of pieces—didn't even check what they were. The less time he spent in here, the better.

He slid back out the way he came, eased the window shut, and drove away.

Back in his room, he shoved the bag into his closet and threw a blanket over it. Out of sight, for now.

Three days later, he went to see Lola. Her room was locked.

"Where's Lola?" he asked one of the other girls.

She smiled slyly, running a painted fingernail down his cheek. "Why d'you want Lola when you can have me?"

He brushed her hand away. "Where is she, Sadie? Just tell me—I need to see her."

"Well, if you're *that* desperate, honey, I'm available—"

He caught her wrist, maybe a little too hard. "Just tell me. I need to speak to her, okay?" He let go, and she rubbed her arm, glaring.

"No need to be like that. What's got into you?"

"Nothing. Just give Lola my message. I'll be back later."

When Lola finally called him, her tone was wary.

"Hi, Lola. Fancy a coffee? Luigi's, half an hour."

"Danny, have you lost your mind? Coffee? Sadie said it was important—you damn near broke her arm."

"Yeah, she got on my nerves. Sorry about that."

"You alright, Danny?"

"Yeah. Just feeling fed up. Thought we could talk over a cup of coffee."

There was a pause. "Okay. Half an hour. Luigi's."

When Danny slid into the booth beside Lola, he placed a small canvas bag on the seat between them.

She raised an eyebrow. "And what's this?"

"Have a look," he said quietly. "But don't take anything out. Not here."

Lola glanced around the café before unfastening the zipper. She peeked inside —and drew in a sharp breath. Her head snapped up.

"Danny… where the hell did you get these?"

"Never mind that," he said, his tone clipped. "I just need you to keep them safe until I find a buyer. Then we split the proceeds."

Her eyes narrowed. "Why, Danny?"

"Because you'll be able to get out of here a whole lot sooner than if you keep saving nickels. And changes are coming, Lola—changes you won't like."

She leaned closer. "What sort of changes?"

"A Chicago family's moving in. Jake will roll over and let them. Believe me, you don't want to work for those people. Before I go, I want to make sure you're gone too."

"What about the other girls?"

Danny's expression hardened. "Too bad. They'll have to take

their chances. You can't tell them. If Jake or Jimmy find out I told you anything… I'm dead. Understand? You keep this to yourself."

Lola studied him for a moment, then nodded. "Sure, Danny. I understand."

"You got somewhere safe to keep it?"

"Yeah. I've got a locker at the bus station—keep my money there for a quick getaway."

"Good. Come on. We'll stash it now."

Fifteen minutes later, the bag was locked away, hidden behind a battered metal door at the station. As they walked back, Danny said, "We need a code—something to let you know when I need to see you."

Lola gave a small laugh. "This is all very cloak-and-dagger—like a spy picture."

"It's not a game, Lola. If Jimmy finds out we've got that jewellery, he'll kill us both."

She stopped in her tracks. "You stole it from Jimmy?"

"Don't worry. By the time he notices, we'll be long gone."

Her voice dropped to a whisper. "I hope to God you're right. I don't want to end up at the bottom of the Hudson."

That evening, Danny pushed open the bar door and spotted Stu and Jerry leaning on the counter. He strolled over.

"You two want a beer?"

They both eyed him suspiciously. "Why?" Stu asked.

Danny grinned. "You don't want one?"

"Yeah, sure—but why you asking?"

"Look, I was out of line earlier. Thought I'd buy you a drink to make it up."

They exchanged a look. "Alright—thanks."

As the bartender pulled the pints, Jerry said, "You still seeing that pretty little redhead?"

"Yeah," Danny said.

"So what's the score there?"

"What do you mean, 'the score'?"

"How serious are you?"

Danny didn't hesitate. "Let's put it this way—I intend to marry her when this lot's over."

Both men looked surprised.

"Danny Butchers, settling down," Jerry said with a low whistle. "She must be something special."

"She is."

"Well, I hope you'll be happy."

"Thanks. I know we will."

"I wouldn't have taken you for the family-man type," Stu said. "Settling down, kids... So, you taking her back to New York to meet your folks?"

Danny's face shadowed. "No. We won't be going back there. And I don't have any folks."

Stu frowned. "Jeez—that's rough. Nobody at all?"

"My old man was killed just after I was born. My mother died when I was ten—working three jobs wore her out."

The two men exchanged a glance that said they understood more about Danny now.

"So who raised you?"

"The Sisters of Mercy orphanage."

Jerry let out a low whistle. "I knew a kid raised by nuns—said they were brutal."

"Not Sister Angelica," Danny said. "She was kind. Compassionate."

Jerry nodded slowly. "That's good. Bad enough losing your parents without the people looking after you making it worse."

"So will you stay here after the war?" Stu asked.

"No," Danny said firmly. "I'll get Maureen as far away from her old man as possible—and take her mother too. He's a real brutal bastard."

Stu's face darkened. "Yeah... hard to say which is worse—being hurt by strangers or by your own family."

Chapter 13

Ruth's emotions were a knot of excitement and dread.

Raymond was coming home—badly injured, but alive. The army was sending him to Berrington Hospital in Shropshire for treatment. She longed to see him, yet a constant worry gnawed at her: how badly hurt was he?

Getting to Shropshire would be difficult, but she was already turning over in her mind the ways she might manage it.

When she told Jenny, her friend's face softened with sympathy.

"But when he's discharged," Jenny asked, "will he come home for good… or go straight back to fight?"

Ruth hesitated. "I… I assumed he'd stay. You think they might send him back?"

"Well," Jenny said carefully, "I suppose it depends on how bad his injuries are. If he can still fight, they might."

Ruth felt her chest tighten. "But that's awful. If he's injured, surely he's done his bit?"

Jenny reached for her hand. "Oh, Ruth… I don't think it works like that. They need every man they can get. If a soldier can still fight, they send him back."

That evening, Ruth turned to her father. "Dad… do you think they'll make Raymond fight again once he's discharged? Jenny said if they can still fight, they have to go back."

Stephen Mitchell studied her face—the hope in her eyes made him ache. He wanted to reassure her, but lies would be crueller in the long run.

"I don't know, love," he said at last, "but I do know in the last war, if a man was able, he was sent back. Some poor blokes went back more than once."

"What do you mean, more than once?"

"Some got wounded, sent home to recover… then sent straight back to the trenches."

Ruth stared at him, horrified. "That's awful. Cruel."

"That's war, love. Awful and cruel."

Her mother, Gillian, reached across the table. She knew exactly what her daughter was feeling—she had lived through the same fear twenty-five years earlier. "Oh, love… I know. But you have to hold onto hope that he'll come back to you safe. That's all any of us can do—for him, and for all the boys."

Ruth nodded, but the dread in her stomach only deepened.

When she and Victoria finally stepped onto the hospital ward, the sight that met them stopped Ruth in her tracks.

Rows of beds stretched out before them, filled with young men broken by war. Some were swathed head to toe in bandages, others hobbled on crutches, their sleeves or trouser legs pinned where limbs had once been. One man stared sightlessly at the ceiling, his face pale and drawn. The air smelled faintly of antiseptic, starch, and pain.

Ruth's stomach turned. She wanted to run—escape the sight of so much suffering—but she forced herself to cling to

Victoria's arm.

Victoria gave her hand a firm, reassuring squeeze. "It's alright, love. I'm here."

A nurse led them to a bed near the far wall.

Raymond lay still against the pillows, his skin as pale as the sheets. For a moment, Ruth could only stand and stare. This quiet, fragile figure bore little resemblance to the laughing boy she'd known from schooldays. Tears stung her eyes. She hated Hitler, hated the Germans, hated everything that had put him here—and she wanted them to suffer as he had suffered.

Raymond's eyes opened slowly, and when he saw them, he smiled faintly.

Ruth and his mother both bent to kiss him.

"Well, you've got yourself into a pickle and no mistake," Victoria said gently.

Ruth clasped his hand. Her throat felt too tight for words.

"Hello, Ruth," he whispered.

She smiled through her tears. "Hello, Raymond."

They simply looked at each other, their silence saying more than any words could.

Victoria's own heart ached. Seeing her only son like this broke something deep inside her, and she silently wished every possible evil upon Hitler himself.

All too soon, a nurse appeared. "I'm sorry, but visiting time is over."

Victoria bent to kiss Raymond's forehead. "I'll try to come again soon, son, but I'll need to get time off work. It's a long way… but I'll be here as soon as I can. I love you."

"I love you, Mum."

Ruth leaned down and kissed his lips. "I'll come again soon

too. I love you, Raymond."

"I love you too," he whispered.

Victoria was silent on the train home, her gloved hands resting in her lap. The rhythmic rattle of the carriage wheels only seemed to echo the pounding in her head. She couldn't lose Raymond—not after losing his father in the last war. Surely life wouldn't be that cruel, not twice. Then she gripped Ruth's hand and held it the whole way, drawing comfort from the girl's presence. Whatever happened, she would always treasure Ruth—not just for the steadfast love she gave her son, but for the hope she had planted in his heart.

When Ruth reached home, the walls of her own house felt too close, too heavy. She went straight to Jenny's.

Veronica opened the door and took one look at her pale, tear-streaked face.

"Oh, sweetheart… come in."

She called for Jenny, and between them they eased Ruth into the sitting room.

"I'll put the kettle on," Veronica said gently, and headed for the kitchen.

As she filled the kettle, her own eyes brimmed with tears. *Dear God… must we really go through all this again, and so soon after the last war?*

In the sitting room, Jenny wrapped her arms around her friend. Ruth broke down, sobbing until her shoulders shook and her body felt limp. By the time Veronica came back in with the tea, her voice was thick with emotion.

"Here, love—drink this. It'll help, just a little."

Ruth took the cup in both hands. "Oh, Mrs Jackson, I'm

so sorry. I just couldn't let go in front of Mrs Merrett… and Mum and Dad are out. I didn't know where else to go."

"You did right, love," Veronica assured her, patting her hand. "Where else *would* you go? You're among friends here."

Jenny's voice was tentative. "Is he… in a very bad way?"

Ruth swallowed hard. "Yes. He looked so frail, lying there under all those bandages. And Jenny—you should have seen some of the other men. Some with no legs, some with no arms. Others… just lying there, wrapped up like mummies. It's awful."

Jenny squeezed her hand. "And Mrs Merrett?"

"She's putting on a brave face, but I can tell she's struggling."

Veronica straightened suddenly. "I'm going round there. This is no time for her to be alone. Jenny, when your dad comes in, tell him where I am. Tea will be a bit late tonight."

"That's fine, Mum. I'll see to it—and I'll feed Betty and get her ready for bed."

After Veronica had gone, Jenny turned back to Ruth. "When will your parents be home?"

"I don't know. They didn't expect me back so soon. We thought we'd have more time with Raymond, but the nurses said visiting hours were over and that was that."

"Then you're having your tea with us," Jenny said firmly.

"Oh no, Jenny, I can't impose—"

"Nonsense. You'd do it for me. And you *need* to eat. I'll make us some spam sandwiches—Marcus gave us a couple of tins—and we've still got some butter."

When Mr Jackson came in from the shop, Jenny told him where his wife had gone. He sighed, his face heavy with sympathy.

"Oh, the poor woman. She must be beside herself. And that poor lad—what he's been through."

He rested a warm, fatherly hand on Ruth's shoulder and gave it a gentle squeeze. "I'm sorry you had to see him in that state, lass."

She managed a watery smile. "Oh, Mr Jackson... you should have seen him. And the other men. I was just telling Jenny—it's dreadful."

"I know, lass. I saw it in the last lot. Some men came home barely recognisable."

Jenny frowned. "But why didn't you get more time with him? You left in good time."

"It's much further than I thought. And the train just crawled. I had no idea how far it was—it took ages."

That evening, when Jenny told Marcus, his expression hardened with determination.

"I'll see if I can get a car on Sunday," he said. "We'll drive Ruth and Mrs Merrett up there—it'll be quicker, and if we leave early enough they can have a proper visit. We'll make a day of it."

Jenny's eyes lit up. "Oh, Marcus, really? You think you can get one?"

"I'll try. But don't say anything to Ruth until I'm sure. I wouldn't want to disappoint her.

Ruth wrote to Raymond every single day. She wanted him to know that, even though she couldn't visit often, he was in her thoughts constantly. At first, she didn't expect a reply—he was so ill, and writing might be impossible—but when the first letter came, her heart leapt.

"One of the nurses writes them for him," she told Jenny, eyes shining. "They do it for all the men who can't write for themselves because of their wounds."

Jenny smiled warmly. "Oh, Ruth, that's lovely. And so kind. They must be rushed off their feet, yet they still find the time to do that."

"Mrs Merrett's had a couple too," Ruth added. "She's over the moon."

On Friday night, Marcus told Jenny that he'd managed to get a car for Sunday's visit. The next morning, on the way to work, Jenny broke the news to Ruth.

Ruth stopped in her tracks, beaming. "Oh, Jenny—that's so good of him!"

The moment she reached the store, she hurried to the haberdashery to tell Victoria.

"Oh, Ruth, that's wonderful," Victoria said, her face softening with relief. "It means we can see him for longer—that's cheered me right up. I'll pop out in my lunch break and get him something nice."

"Well," Ruth said, "it'll be quite an early start. Jenny said we'll leave just after half eight. The drive's about three hours."

Victoria laughed lightly. "Sweetheart, that's more than fine. No Sunday lie-in for me, but I'd trade it for an extra minute with my boy."

Marcus was waiting for them on Sunday morning, leaning casually against the car, a grin on his face. As they approached, he handed each of them a bar of chocolate.

"Goodness, Marcus!" Victoria exclaimed. "Are you sure? This must be your whole ration."

He shook his head. "Only one's mine. I had a word with

some of the lads—they gave me theirs for you. I've got a couple more for the chaps in the hospital."

"That's so kind," Ruth said. Then, without hesitation, she held hers out to Victoria. "Here—give mine to the lads. They deserve it more than I do."

Jenny followed suit. "Mine too. Marcus brings me chocolate often enough. Let the men have it."

Victoria looked from one to the other, touched. "You girls… You haven't had a taste of this in ages, yet you're giving it away."

Marcus didn't say anything, but in that moment his respect for them deepened.

They arrived in the town too early for visiting hours, so they strolled through the quiet Sunday streets, peering into shop windows. Everything was closed, but the morning air was fresh, and the walk was pleasant. They found a small café and had a light lunch before Ruth and Victoria made their way to the hospital.

When they stepped into the ward and saw Raymond propped up in bed, Ruth's heart lifted. He was still pale and clearly unwell, but he looked stronger than before.

"I've brought you a few things," Victoria said gently, setting a small paper bag on his lap. "Some nice apples from the grocer—and this."

Raymond's eyes widened. "Chocolate? Where did you get that?"

"Jenny's young man," Victoria explained. "The men at his base donated their rations for you lads."

"You should keep some for yourself, you haven't seen chocolate since before the war." Raymond told them. Both women shook their heads. "No, love," Victoria said firmly. "You all deserve it far more than we do. You've been through too much already."

Ruth took one of the bars and crossed the room holding the chocolate out to the one-armed man.

"For me?" he asked, blinking at her.

"Yes," Ruth said simply.

"Why?"

"Because you deserve it."

He eyed her for a long moment. "It's only the Yanks who can get chocolate. You been with a Yank?"

Ruth's cheeks coloured, but her voice was steady. "No. I'm engaged to Raymond—that's his mother over there. My friend's courting an American, and the lads at his base sent these for you."

The man's face softened. "I thought you were Raymond's sister. Well… in that case, I'll take it—thank you, lass. But could you do me a favour?"

"Of course."

"See that chap in the wheelchair? Break it in half and give him the other piece. We were in the same lot—got hit the same day."

Ruth's throat tightened. "That's so sad."

"That's war, pet."

She took the half bar to the man in the wheelchair, who looked at it warily until his friend called over, "It's alright, Charlie—it's from an American Air Force base."

Charlie took it then, smiling faintly. "Thanks, lass."

"You're welcome," Ruth said softly.

Back at Raymond's bedside, she said, "I've one more. Jenny gave me hers—who should have it?"

"Any one of the lads would be glad of it. Tell you what—give it to the nurse. She'll know who needs it most."

Ruth carried the last bar to the nurse's station. "Could you see one of the men gets this? Or split it between two?"

The nurse smiled as she took it. "Haven't seen one of these in a while."

"Then share it with a colleague—you deserve a treat too, for what you do."

The nurse shook her head. "No, they need it more. But thank you."

Back at the bed, Victoria said quietly, "Raymond reckons they might let him come home once his stitches are out."

Ruth's eyes lit up. "Oh, that would be wonderful! I could see you every evening after work."

"That's what I told him," Victoria said. "And I'll take some time off to look after him."

When they left the hospital, the air seemed warmer, the sky a little brighter. They walked back to the car with lighter hearts than when they had arrived.

The war machine rumbled on; on the third of May, the Japanese had landed unopposed in Tulagi, opening the battle of the coral sea. General Joseph Stilwell evacuates Burma, deciding there is nothing more they can do. On the fifth, Exeter is bombed by the Germans, another Baedeker raid. So-called because the name came from a series of German guidebooks for tourists, showing detailed maps used to select targets. General Stilwell's party arrives in Indaw after abandoning their trucks as they keep getting stuck in the mud; they go by jeep, which does much better. And so on it goes. On the ninth of May, three soldiers are executed for mutiny on Horsburgh Island in the Cocos Islands, the only British Commonwealth soldiers to be executed for mutiny in the Second World War.

Chapter 14

Danny turned the ring over slowly in his fingers, watching the way the light caught on its facets. It was, without question, the most beautiful thing he had ever held. The ruby—pear-shaped and sliced clean down the middle—glowed a deep, blood-red in the dim light, its heart crossed by a neat row of four tiny, sparkling diamonds. On either side, a flawless pearl nestled in its yellow-gold setting, soft and luminous like drops of moonlight.

He wondered idly what it might be worth. Several hundred, at least—more than he'd ever had in his pocket at one time. But the value didn't matter, not in the way it once might have. This ring wasn't for selling. It was for Maureen.

He knew she couldn't marry him yet—she was still shy of twenty-one—but he didn't care. He would ask her anyway, slip this ring onto her finger and let it speak for him. It wasn't about the timing; it was about the promise.

He remembered the moment he'd first seen it, glinting among the other treasures in Jimmy's warehouse haul. At first, his instinct had been purely practical—find a buyer, turn it into cash. But something had made him pause, made him pocket it with a different kind of care. He couldn't have said why at the time, but now he understood. He'd been saving it—waiting for the girl who would make him want to give it away.

He'd kept his promise to Lola too. From that first night they'd plotted in Luigi's, they'd shared the spoils. Most of the jewellery he'd ferried quietly over the border into Canada, where buyers didn't ask awkward questions. The money was split evenly, just as he'd said it would be.

Sometimes, though, he kept a piece back. Something too pretty to let go, too perfectly suited for Lola—a silk dress in midnight blue, a pair of Italian shoes with heels like sculpture. He never said where they'd come from, and she never asked.

Whenever he had something for her, he'd call with their signal: "Luigi's—half an hour." Then they'd meet, and after a quick coffee and a few quiet words, they'd walk together to the bus station. The locker swallowed whatever prize he'd brought, and Lola would turn the key with a little smile, the kind that said she was one step closer to the day she'd walk out of New York for good.

The next time Danny called, Lola was gone.

He'd been with her just the night before, slipping her a few more pieces from Jimmy's stash, and now he was on the phone asking for her.

"She's not here," the girl at the brothel said.

"Well, when she gets back, tell her Danny called—tell her I'll be in Luigi's tomorrow at three o'clock."

"No, you don't understand," the girl replied, with a note of amusement in her voice. "She ain't here no more."

Danny's grip on the receiver tightened. *Not here anymore?*

"What do you mean, not here anymore? Where is she?"

A shrug he couldn't see came down the line. "Dunno. She left with a bag one day and never came back."

Danny's chest tightened. *The bitch has run out on me—with my stash.* "When was this?"

"About three weeks ago. Took all her stuff, cleaned her room out. Oh—yeah—almost forgot. She left a note for you. It's on her dressing table. I saw it when we went in to see why she wasn't answering her door."

He didn't wait for more. Slamming the receiver down, Danny was out the door and into the car in seconds. The drive was a blur—his pulse hammering, mind racing through every way this could play out.

By the time he reached the brothel, he knew he had to slow down. If he looked too eager, too desperate, they'd start asking questions he couldn't answer. He walked in as casually as he could manage, but once inside, he took the stairs two at a time.

Lola's room felt strangely empty, it was also a mess, the faint trace of her perfume lingering like an echo. On the dressing table sat the envelope. He tore it open.

As he read, the tightness in his chest eased.

Dear Danny,

When you hear I've gone, I know what you'll think. But I haven't taken your stuff—only mine, and what we agreed. Yours is still in the locker. I've paid two months' rent on it, so hopefully you'll get it before it expires. I've left the key with reception, in an envelope with your name on it. Just go and ask for it.

I'm sorry I didn't tell you in person, or say goodbye, but I just couldn't take it anymore. I have enough now to start over somewhere else. I might go to Canada. I've thought about going back to college to finish my education... or maybe I'll enlist. I don't know yet. But I'm done with this life.

I took a beating—from a client. First time it's ever happened to me, but I've seen it happen to others. I'm not waiting around for a second time. The next day, I packed and left.

I wish you well, Danny. You're one of the good ones. Don't stick around too long—get out before it's too late. Who knows, maybe we'll meet again. I'd like that. I'll miss you. You've always been good to me, and I'll always be grateful for that.

Take care, Danny.

All my love,

Lola xxxx

By the time he finished, Danny was smiling faintly. She hadn't crossed him. She'd just… escaped. And good for her. Still, he'd like to meet the bastard who'd laid a hand on her. That was something he couldn't forgive.

He drove to the bus station, and collected the envelope from the receptionist. "Danny Butchers?" she said, handing it over without a glance. Inside was the locker key.

The metal door swung open, revealing exactly what Lola had promised—his stash, untouched. He stood looking at it for a moment, the thought whispering that he could take it all right now and disappear. But there was still one thing he needed to do before leaving.

Snapping the locker shut again, he returned to the desk. "How long have I got on this?"

"Just over a month," the woman said. "The young lady paid

for two months in advance—runs out end of next month."

"Right. I'll keep the key."

She gave a little shrug. "Okay, honey."

He drove straight back to the house, heading for his room without a word. He needed to think—really think. One wrong move and he could tip his hand, and if Jimmy even suspected, it would be over.

That night at dinner, Jimmy broke the silence.

"Seen Lola lately?"

Danny looked up, casual as he could manage. "No. Why?"

"She's disappeared. No one knows where she's gone. You've been pretty cosy with her—I figured you might know."

Danny shook his head. "No idea. We used to grab coffee sometimes at Luigi's. I rang today—they said she'd left."

"I hear she left you a note." Jimmy's gaze locked on him, hard and searching.

Danny kept his voice light. "Yeah, she did."

Jimmy didn't blink. "So, what did it say?"

Danny feigned a frown, as if trying to remember. "What did what say?"

Jimmy's jaw tightened. "The note, Danny. What did the note say?"

"Oh—*that*. Nothing much. Just said she was going. Didn't say where or how. Can't have gone far though—how much money could she have?"

Jimmy leaned back, still studying him. "I don't know. Maybe she's been holding out on me about what the guys have been paying her."

Danny shrugged. "Maybe. But that'd only be a few dollars—you can't get far on that."

Jimmy's shoulders eased slightly. Maybe his suspicions about Danny had been wrong after all.

"Well," he said coldly, "if I find her—she's dead."

Danny forced himself to chew, to nod, to look unconcerned. Inside, he prayed she was already across the border, far beyond Jimmy's reach.

Two days later, his chance came. Jimmy and Jake were both out of town for several days. Apart from Luca rattling pans in the kitchen, the house was his.

Danny moved quickly. He packed his bags, carried them to the car, then slipped into the office. He knew exactly where Jake kept the spare safe key.

The lock clicked open, and his eyes widened. Stacks of bills filled the shelves. He counted quickly, whistling under his breath. *Three thousand dollars.*

Grabbing a scrap of paper, he scrawled a note in quick, hard strokes:

I know what you did to my old man, which means you're responsible for my mother's death. Nothing I can do about that now—but the contents of this safe will go a long way to compensate.

Danny.

He stuffed the money into his bag, shut the safe, and left without looking back.

At the bus station, he cleared out the locker. Then he drove to the orphanage, pressing five hundred dollars into Sister Angelica's hands. She protested, of course—he'd expected that—so he lied about how he'd come by it, knowing she'd never take more.

From there, he stopped at the cemetery, buying flowers on the way. He laid them gently on his mother's grave, brushing his fingers over the stone.

"I have to go away for a bit, Mum," he murmured. "But I promise I'll be back one day. I'll come and see you. I love you."

He drove all day, pushing the car hard until nightfall. In Indiana, he ditched it—no point keeping something that would have every roadblock looking for him. The rest of the journey would be by train.

As the train pulled out, Danny allowed himself a low, humourless laugh. He could almost see Jake and Jimmy's faces when they came home to find the safe cleaned out and the locker empty.

No—Danny Butchers wouldn't want to be in that house when they got back. The boys left behind were in for hell.

Danny Butchers was only eighteen, yet he held more money than most men twice his age would see in a lifetime. The jewellery he'd lifted from Jimmy's hidden stash was still being sold off, piece by piece. The cash was too much to keep stuffed in his closet, so he began slipping it into a bank account—slowly, carefully, never too much at once. Big deposits made people curious, and curiosity could be deadly. Over weeks, the money sat there quietly, earning interest, as safe as it could be.

Then, the world exploded.

One cold December morning, as Danny sat enjoying the pace of the cafe, the door to the café banged open and a man burst in waving a newspaper, shouting so wildly that no one could make sense of him. It took several minutes before the story spilled out—Pearl Harbor had been bombed. President Roosevelt had declared war.

Danny snatched the paper from the man's hand, scanning the headline. In that instant, he knew exactly what he was going to do. It was his patriotic duty—and his ticket out of Canada. Because no matter how far he'd run, Jake and Jimmy's reach was long, and he'd always known it was only a matter of time before they caught up to him.

By the next morning, he was across the border, back on American soil, walking into the first recruitment office he saw. He signed up without hesitation.

Now, almost a year later, he was in the UK—alive, in love, and wanting to marry Maureen. He glanced at the pale scar on his arm where a bullet had grazed him. Two inches to the left and it would have been over. As a tail gunner, he knew the odds—weeks, maybe months at most—and he had already outlasted many.

A grim thought struck him: what would happen to his money if he didn't come back? He wanted Maureen to have it, but without marriage, the law wouldn't recognise her. He slipped the ring back into its box, hiding it in the bottom of his locker. The station commander would know what to do.

The clerk at HQ looked him over like something scraped off his boot.

"What do you want, Butchers?"

"To pummel your head," Danny thought. Out loud, he said, "I need to speak to the commander."

"What about?"

"It's personal."

"He's busy."

"Then I'll wait."

Danny dropped into a chair, settling in for a long sit. But luck was on his side—the commander stepped out of his office a moment later.

"Oh—waiting to see me, son?"

"Yes, sir, if you've got a minute."

"Of course. Come in."

Danny shot the clerk a wink as he passed; the man glared after him.

Inside, the commander gestured to a chair. "Well, sit down. What can I do for you?"

"I was wondering, sir… who would get my belongings if I died?"

The commander studied him. "I see. Well, what family do you have?"

"None, sir. My parents are both gone."

"That makes it awkward. I suppose the courts would decide."

Danny leaned forward. "And if I wanted someone in particular to have it all?"

"Then you'd need to make a will."

"How do I do that, sir?"

"I can have one drawn up. We'll get it signed and I'll hold it for you."

"Could we do it quickly? Before we go out again?"

"I don't see why not."

The clerk was called in, the will typed, read, and approved. Danny signed, the witnesses signed, and he left with a sense of calm he hadn't felt in weeks. Whatever happened to him,

Maureen would be taken care of.

That evening, he met her by the river. The early summer air was warm, the water calm, the long grass swaying gently in the breeze.

They sat on the bank, and Danny reached into his pocket. "Maureen… will you marry me?"

Her eyes softened with sadness. "Oh, Danny, if only I could. But you know my father—he'd never give us his blessing."

"I know. But if we got engaged now, then when you're twenty-one, we could just go away and get married."

She thought for a moment, then nodded. "Yes. But I can't tell anyone or wear a ring. If he saw it, he'd go mad."

"Then don't wear it Just keep it. I want you to have this."

He opened the box. The ruby caught the light, flaring deep red, the diamonds winking, the pearls glowing softly.

Her breath caught. "Danny… it's beautiful. It must have cost a fortune. Where did you get it?"

He didn't blink. "It was my grandmother's. Passed to my mother when she died. And now—to you."

He slipped it onto her finger. Tears shimmered in her eyes as she threw her arms around him. One kiss turned into another, and before either of them thought to stop, they were making love in the grass, the river whispering beside them.

Afterwards, she lay curled against him, his arms wrapped around her.

"Oh, Danny… I love you so much."

"And I love you, sweetheart. Always remember that."

That night, as he said goodbye, he held her tightly before watching her walk to her door. She turned and waved, smiling at him in the moonlight. But in her chest was a terrible, unshakable feeling—that she would never see him again.

Three days later, in a raid over Germany, Danny Butchers was shot and killed.

Chapter 15

What began as a routine bombing mission turned into disaster.

Danny had been in high spirits that morning, whistling as he checked his gear, trading jokes with the crew.

"What's got into you, Butchers? Been drinking?" Chuck asked, grinning.

Danny's smile stretched from ear to ear. "No—much better than that. I'm engaged."

The men stared at him.

"You mean that pretty redhead actually agreed to marry you?"

"Okay—how much did you have to pay her?" someone snorted.

Danny rolled his eyes. "Ha, bloody ha. She loves me."

Alvin clapped him on the shoulder. "Well, I'm glad for you, kid. Just treat her right. I think she'll be good for you—keep you on the straight and narrow. Just what you need."

The raid itself went smoothly. Targets hit, no serious damage to their own ship, and spirits were high. If they kept their pace, they'd be back on base before the bar closed.

Then, without warning, two Dornier Do 17s dropped out of the clouds like vultures. Marcus threw the bomber into evasive manoeuvres, but the German pilots were relentless, darting in and out of sight.

Danny swung the tail guns, tracking one, then the other, but they were playing a deadly game of cat and mouse—first appearing on the port side, then vanishing and reappearing to starboard with no warning. Sweat poured down his back as he tried to keep up.

Bloody hell, at this rate they'd never shake them.

Glass shattered. A burning sting tore through him. For a heartbeat, he didn't register it—then the warmth spreading down his side told him. He was hit. Bad. The copper taste of blood filled his mouth.

His vision blurred.

From somewhere far away, he heard Jerry's voice. "Jesus—Danny!"

To Marcus: "He's hit, Skip!"

"How bad?"

"I don't think he'll make it—he's bleeding out fast."

"Hold on, Danny—we're nearly home. Just hold on."

Danny forced his eyes open one last time. His voice was faint; a whisper carried on his last breath.

"Maureen… tell her I love her. And Sister Angelica… thanks… for everything."

Then his eyes closed, his body going limp in Jerry's arms.

Two B-17s roared into view, guns blazing. The Dorniers peeled away and vanished into the clouds. But the fight was already over for Danny.

When they touched down, the medics rushed to meet them,

but there was nothing to be done. Danny Butchers had died before they ever left the sky.

They never made it back before last orders. Instead, the crew went to Marcus' room, opened his whiskey, and raised their glasses to Danny. He could be a pain in the neck at times, but he was one of their own—and every man there was thinking the same thing: he had died just when he had everything to live for.

At one o'clock in the morning, Maureen was dreaming of him. She could see Danny's face, his crooked grin, the warmth in his eyes—then, suddenly, the vision shifted. His face dissolved, replaced by rivers of blood.

She heard his voice.

"I love you, honey."

She woke with a gasp, her nightdress damp with sweat, her heart hammering in her chest.

"Danny!" she cried into the darkness.

Then she turned her face into the pillow, clutching it to her as if it could hold her together. Silent sobs shook her body. She knew. She didn't know how, but she knew. He was gone. The certainty cut through her like a blade.

Three thousand miles away, in an orphanage in the Bronx, Sister Angelica had only just gone to bed, nursing a migraine. She had barely drifted into sleep when she saw Danny's face in her mind's eye.

He was smiling, just for her.

"Thanks," he said softly.

Then—blackness.

She woke with a start, her heart heavy, her eyes wet.

No. She mustn't cry. She must pray.

Slipping from her bed, she knelt on the cold floorboards and clasped her hands. She prayed for the soul of Danny Butchers—the boy she had loved like a son, the boy she had fought to keep on the straight and narrow.

And the boy she feared she had failed.

When Jenny heard, the news hit her like a blow.

"Oh, Mum—poor Maureen. She'll be devastated. They'd just got engaged. He gave her such a beautiful ring—his grandmother's."

"Good Lord," Veronica said. "Her father gave permission?"

Jenny shook her head. "No. He doesn't know. She never wears the ring. But she brought it to work once and showed us."

"Oh, love… that poor girl."

"I know. I ought to go and see her, but her father doesn't know anything about Danny. I don't know what to do."

"I know, love. It's hard. That man… I could kick him."

Ruth was just as shocked when she heard.

"Oh, Jenny—it could have been any one of them. Oh, how I hate Hitler. We ought to go and see her."

"I know. That's what I said to Mum. But we can't."

"I wondered why she hadn't been at work the last couple of days."

"Yes. Her mother rang and said she had a bug. But it's not illness—it's grief."

Danny's belongings were gathered up and taken to the station commander so a letter could be sent to his family along with his effects. But there was no family—only one name and address in his records: Maureen Blackford. Among the items was a sealed envelope containing his will.

When the letter arrived, telling her of Danny's death and asking her to contact the station commander, Maureen knew she couldn't let him come to her house. Even with Danny gone, her father would make her life a misery if he found out.

She was thankful she'd been at home when the postman came and could intercept the letter before her father saw it.

She walked to the base and asked to see Colonel Withers.

When she was shown into his office, Roy Withers was struck by how pale and fragile she looked. He gestured to a chair and sat opposite her.

"Miss Blackford... I can't tell you how very sorry I am about Gunner Butchers' death."

"Thank you," she murmured.

"There's something else. He left everything he owned to you. Did you know that?"

She shook her head. "No... he never said."

"I've looked into his finances. He's left a considerable amount of money. I assume it must have been an inheritance. Did he ever mention one?"

Again she shook her head. "No... but he gave me this ring when we got engaged. He said it was his grandmother's. It's clearly worth a great deal—so perhaps his family was wealthy."

The colonel glanced at the ring. It was, indeed, valuable.

"Would you like me to help you access this inheritance, Miss Blackford, or will your father handle it?"

Her voice was quiet but firm. "No—he won't. I'd be grateful if you would help me."

"Very well. I'll set the wheels in motion. You should hear from the solicitor in a day or so."

"One more thing, Colonel… I don't want any letters sent to my house. Could they go to my friend's address instead?"

"Yes, of course."

She gave him Jenny's details, thanked him, and left.

On her way home, Maureen stopped at the shop. Veronica came out from behind the counter as soon as she saw her.

"Maureen—oh, my dear, I'm so sorry. How are you?"

Maureen managed a watery smile. "I'm not sure… I still feel numb. But I wanted to ask if it would be alright to have some letters sent here. Danny's left me everything—apparently quite a considerable amount—and the colonel's arranging it. But I can't have the solicitors writing to me at home. If Dad saw, there'd be trouble."

"Of course, dear. That's no problem. And if you need anything—anything at all—we'll help."

"Thank you."

Veronica watched her go, her heart aching. Poor girl—she couldn't even grieve openly. Her mother might comfort her as best she could, but everything would have to be kept hidden, locked behind closed doors.

Cynthia sat in the kitchen and froze as she listened to her daughter retching in the bathroom. This was the third morning in a row. A cold wave of dread swept over her.

When Maureen came downstairs, she looked pale as paper.

"Are you alright, love?" her mother asked gently.

"I think I've caught a bug. I feel awful."

"Maureen… I need to ask you something. And I don't want you getting upset—but I need to know."

Maureen looked at her warily. "What?"

"Did you and Danny ever… make love?"

Maureen's cheeks flamed, and tears filled her eyes. She gave a tiny nod.

"Often?"

She shook her head quickly. "No. Just once—the last time I saw him. The night we got engaged. Why?"

Cynthia exhaled slowly. "Because… I think you're pregnant."

If it was possible, Maureen went even whiter. "No—that's not possible. It was just the once, I told you."

Her mother took her hand. "Oh, love… once is all it takes. For some people it can take months—others, just once."

Maureen's tears spilled over. "Oh, Mum—what am I going to do? He'll kill me."

"No—we'll think of something."

Maureen's head came up sharply. "I'm not getting rid of it. It's Danny's baby—and I won't kill it. I won't."

She broke down, sobbing uncontrollably in her mother's arms.

Later that day, in the staff room, Jenny spotted Maureen sitting alone. She was deathly pale, her eyes red and swollen. Jenny walked over, sat beside her, and took her hand.

"Oh, Maureen… you can't go on like this. They won't let you keep working here if you're in this state. Customers can't see you like this."

Maureen's gaze lifted to hers. Her voice was so soft Jenny almost thought she'd imagined the words.

"I'm pregnant, Jenny."

Jenny froze. When she finally found her voice, it was barely above a whisper.

"Oh, Maureen... what are you going to do? Your dad will go mad."

"I know. But it was just the once... the last night I saw him. He proposed, and we... we just got carried away. Then he was killed. He never knew about his baby."

Tears spilled down her cheeks. Jenny glanced around the empty room, making sure no one could overhear. Just then, the door opened and Miss Penheart came in.

She took one look at the girls and crossed to them, sitting down beside Maureen and gently taking her hand.

"Oh, my dear," she said softly. "I know exactly what you're going through."

The two girls stared. How could she possibly know? She was old—surely she'd never been in love like this, never lost someone.

Amelia saw the doubt in their faces and smiled faintly, though her eyes were sad.

"I was young once," she said. "And I had a young man in the last war. We were engaged. He was killed in 1916. I never had another beau after that—I couldn't replace Thomas. So you see... I do understand, my dear."

Jenny and Maureen were stunned. They had never heard a word of this before.

"I'm so sorry, Miss Penheart," Jenny said gently.

"Thank you, dear. But it was a long time ago. Time heals, a little. Still... I never thought your generation would have to face the same fate. For that, I am truly sorry."

Maureen squeezed her hand. "Thank you for telling us. And I'm so very sorry you lost your young man."

"Well, life goes on," Amelia said quietly. "The pain will fade in time, but the memories will stay. Hold on to those, dear."

That evening, Jenny told her parents what Miss Penheart had told them.

"Oh, Jenny love, that's so sad," Veronica said, her voice thick with sympathy. "The poor woman."

"Yes… but I think it helped Maureen to hear it. She realised she isn't alone in her grief." Jenny hesitated. "Actually… Maureen told me something else."

Her parents looked at her expectantly.

"She's going to have a baby."

Veronica's fork clattered onto her plate. Ronald looked up sharply.

"Good Lord," he said at last. "And what does Albert Blackford have to say about that?"

Jenny shook her head. "He doesn't know. And he can't know—Dad, he'll kill her. Her mother knows, but Maureen is determined she won't get rid of it. It's Danny's baby. She said they only made love once—the last night she saw him, when he proposed. But her mother says sometimes once is all it takes."

"That's right," Veronica murmured. "Sometimes just once." She sighed. "Oh, Jenny… what will she do? The poor lass."

Jenny shook her head. "I don't know. I'll speak to Marcus. Now she has this money, maybe she can get away."

"But she's only nineteen," Veronica said. "She's not of age yet."

Ronald cleared his throat. "Well… for what it's worth, I have to say—though it goes against the grain—I agree with Jenny. The girl has to get away from that brute of a father of hers."

Both Veronica and Jenny stared at him in shock. They'd never thought they'd see the day when Ronald Jackson would back an unmarried, pregnant young woman defying her father.

Veronica reached across the table and took her husband's hand.

"Oh, Ron… I thought you'd be against her for what she's done."

"Normally I would, love—if she were the type to sleep around. But like Jenny said, it was just the once. They got carried away in the moment. I'm not saying it was right, but even I can understand it. After all… Danny was the only person who ever showed her any love or affection. People need that."

When Jenny told Marcus, he was visibly shaken.

"Dear Lord… what will she do?"

"She has to get away, Marcus. Her father will kill her—literally. He's vicious, and he hates Americans with a passion. He's even told her that if she ever got pregnant, he'd beat the baby out of her."

Marcus rubbed a hand over his eyes. Something had to be done—and quickly—before she began to show.

"Is there any way you could get her some of the money Danny left her, so she can leave?" Jenny asked.

He shook his head. "How?"

"I don't know…" Jenny began, but then Marcus's expression changed.

"I know who can help—my father. He's in banking. I'm sure he can do something."

"Oh, Marcus—do you really think so?"

"I don't know... but it's worth a try." He glanced at his watch. His father never left the office before seven in the evening, and it was just after nine now—which meant it was only five o'clock in Vermont.

"Jenny, love, I have to leave you now. I want to catch my father before he leaves the office."

She nodded. "I understand. Do you think he can help?"

"I'm sure he can. I'll see you tomorrow and let you know. I love you, Jenny. Sweet dreams, sweetheart."

He kissed her gently and left, his mind already racing ahead to the phone call that might decide Maureen's future.

Back at the base, Marcus wasted no time. He put a call through to his father's office.

Celia, his father's long-time secretary, answered.

"Good afternoon, Mr. Potter's office."

"It's Marcus. I need to speak to my father urgently."

Within moments, his father's voice came on the line, tinged with concern.

"Marcus—what's wrong, son? Do you need help?"

"No, Dad, but I know someone who does. And they need your help."

"Alright," his father said, "I'm listening."

Marcus told him the whole story—about Danny, his death, and about Maureen's situation. When he finished, there was a low whistle on the other end.

"That's quite a story, son. The poor girl."

"But can you help, Dad?"

"Yes, I can. Here's what I'll do: I'll have the paperwork

drawn up immediately and send it to you. You get this girl to sign it and send it back to me, and I'll take care of the rest. She should be able to access her money in a week or two."

"She's only nineteen, Dad. Will she need her father's signature? She does here."

"Don't worry about that, Marcus—I own this bank. I can do what I want. And if I'm willing to take the risk of opening an account for an underage girl, that's my business. From what you've told me, there's plenty of money, and I'm sure she'll be sensible with it—especially with a baby to take care of."

Marcus gave him Maureen's full name, then added, "There's one thing, Dad—you can't send it to her home address because of her father. Could you send it to Jenny's address instead?" He read it out.

"Of course. Jenny's your young lady, isn't she?"

"Yes, she is. You and Mum are going to love her. I'll be home on furlough soon—it should come through any day now. Love to Mum and everyone. I have to go."

"Alright, son. Take care, and we'll look forward to seeing you. Keep safe, Marcus."

When the call ended, Mr. Potter rang his secretary.

"Celia, could you do a little overtime for me this evening? I'll make it worth your while."

She smiled—he was a good boss, generous and fair. "Of course I can, Mr. Potter. What do you need?"

"I need some papers drawn up urgently, and they must go in the post as soon as they're ready." He outlined the situation briefly, gave her the names and addresses, and waited while she worked.

When she brought the completed documents in for his approval, he nodded.

"Yes, that's perfect. Thank you, Celia—I appreciate it. Send them to my son. I think they'll get there quicker if the address is on a base rather than a civilian one; their post seems a bit more reliable. You can go now—oh, and would you mail them on your way home, please?"

"Certainly, Mr. Potter. See you in the morning."

Chapter 16

As Danny had no surviving relatives in the United States, the decision was made to bury him in the American War Cemetery in Cambridge. Jenny, Ruth, and Maureen were given time off to attend the funeral, and even Miss Penheart had joined them. After the service, she returned to work with Jenny and Ruth, but Maureen was in no state to face the day. Veronica quietly took her and Cynthia back to her own home.

"You shouldn't be alone at a time like this," she said gently.

Betty, noticing Maureen's tear-stained face, tilted her head in curiosity.

"Why is that lady crying?" she asked.

"Because she's feeling very sad," came the reply. "It's like when you cry because you're not feeling well. Why don't you take your dolly in her pram for a walk around the garden? It's such a lovely day, and dolly could use the fresh air."

Betty looked back at Maureen. "Do you want to come? It might make you feel better."

Through her tears, Maureen gave the child a faint smile.

"No, she doesn't, love," her mother said kindly. "Now off you go, young lady."

Betty pouted in protest until Veronica stepped in with a bright suggestion.

"I'll tell you what—why don't we go and see if Daddy has a nice shiny apple you can take with you? Then you can sit under the tree and eat it. How does that sound?"

Betty's face lit up. She slipped her hand into her mother's and followed her into the shop.

"Mummy said you have a bright shiny apple for me, Daddy," she announced, looking up at her father with her big brown eyes.

Ronald glanced down at the tiny figure before him and felt his heart melt.

"Oh, did she indeed? Well, we'll just have to see what we can do, won't we?"

Taking her small hand, he led her over to the neatly arranged boxes of fruit. Selecting a deep red apple, polished to a glossy sheen, he held it out to her.

"Here's one I think will be just right. Look—this one has your name on it."

Betty turned the apple over in her hands, studying it carefully.

"Where's my name, Daddy?"

He chuckled and scooped her up into his arms, hugging her close. This tiny child brought him so much joy. Both his daughters did—but Betty was different. She was their miracle.

After Jenny's birth, they had never thought they would be blessed with another child. And then, suddenly, this little bundle of mischief arrived, filling their lives with laughter after so many years of hoping.

"Thank you, Daddy," Betty said. "I'm going to the garden to take Lucy for a walk."

"Lucy? Who's Lucy?" he asked with a puzzled frown.

Betty gave a theatrical sigh, surprisingly comical coming from such a small person, and rolled her eyes.

"My dolly, Daddy. Her name's Lucy."

"Oh, right—of course. I'll remember," he promised, patting her head.

"You've got to member her name, Daddy," she insisted.

"I will, love. I promise."

And with that, she was off, running back into the house.

"Look, Mummy, I got one!" she called, proudly holding up the apple.

"Oh yes, dear—it's lovely," her mother said warmly. "Now off you go with dolly; she's waiting for you."

Once Betty had disappeared into the garden, Veronica straightened up.

"Right, I'll put the kettle on," she said briskly, heading for the kitchen.

The familiar rattle of crockery and the hiss of boiling water soon filled the air. She returned a few minutes later, balancing a tray of tea. As she set it down, her eyes fell on Maureen.

The girl sat motionless, her face pale as porcelain, still clutching the folded American flag she had been given from Danny's coffin.

"What will you do with the flag, dear?" Veronica asked gently.

Maureen's gaze lifted slowly. "I'll keep it… and give it to the baby when it's older—so I can tell them about their father."

"That's a lovely thought," Veronica said, hesitating. "But… should you take it home? What if your father sees it?"

The idea seemed to strike Maureen for the first time. She

faltered.

"She's right, love," Cynthia said quietly. "You can't take it home."

"But what will I do with it?" Maureen's voice trembled. "I don't want to get rid of it."

"You don't have to," Veronica reassured her. "You can leave it here. It will be perfectly safe until you want it."

"Can I? You wouldn't mind?"

"Of course not. You can leave it in Jenny's room—she won't mind at all."

"Thank you," Maureen whispered. Tears spilled down her cheeks.

Veronica's heart ached for her. Maureen had truly loved Danny, and it was a cruel twist of fate that they would never have the long, happy life they had imagined. He hadn't even known he was to be a father.

"Maureen, love, why don't you go and lie down in Jenny's room? You'll feel better after a little rest. Come along—I'll take you and settle you."

Veronica led her upstairs. In Jenny's room, she said softly, "Take off your frock and shoes, love—you'll be more comfortable."

Maureen obeyed, moving as if in a daze, and lay down on the bed. Veronica drew a blanket over her, pulling the curtains so the light fell dim.

"You get some sleep, love. It will do you good," she murmured before slipping quietly from the room.

Downstairs, Cynthia gave her a grateful look. "This is very good of you, Veronica."

"Not at all. The girl is grieving. I'd like to think that if it were Jenny, you'd do the same for her."

"Of course I would." Cynthia sighed, her brow creasing. "I'm worried. I really don't know what she's going to do. I just wish she could get away."

"Well, Jenny said Marcus had an idea and was going to help," Veronica replied. "Let's hope he can come up with a solution. Now—how about a fresh pot of tea?"

When Jenny came home, Veronica told her about the flag now resting safely in her room, and how Maureen had fallen asleep on her bed.

"Oh, Mum, I felt so sorry for her this morning," Jenny said softly. "I've never seen anyone in such a state. I do hope Marcus can help her."

A few days later, Marcus received the documents his father had sent.

"Jenny, we need to get Maureen here so she can sign these," he said, tapping the papers.

"Alright, I'll pop along and see if she can come now—the sooner, the better."

When Jenny knocked at the Blackford house, it was Albert Blackford himself who opened the door. His face hardened immediately; he had long disapproved of her relationship with an American, and his dislike coloured every glance.

"Well, what do you want?" he snapped.

"I'd like a word with Maureen, please, Mr. Blackford."

"She's busy," he said curtly, beginning to close the door.

But Maureen, having heard Jenny's voice, appeared in the hallway.

"Don't be so rude," she said sharply, her eyes full of loathing as she looked at her father. The look seemed to make him recoil, and without another word he withdrew.

"I'm sorry, Jenny," Maureen murmured once he was gone

"It's not your fault," Jenny replied. Then, in a quieter voice, she added, "Can you come to my place now? Marcus has some papers for you to sign."

Maureen's face lit with sudden hope. "Already? That's wonderful, Jenny. Yes, I'll come now."

She took her coat from the peg, and together they walked quickly back to Jenny's.

Marcus greeted them and spread the papers out on the table.

"The sooner these are signed and returned to my father, the sooner we can start the process of getting you out of here," he explained.

He pointed out where Maureen needed to sign, then he and Ronald added their names as witnesses. Sliding the papers into the return envelope, Marcus said, "I'll send these back through our postal system—it'll be quicker that way. Once my father receives them, he can contact the bank in Canada and arrange for the transfer of all the money. Then you're home and dry. A couple more weeks, Maureen, and it will all be over."

Maureen exhaled a long, shaky breath. "Thank you, Marcus. I can't begin to tell you what a relief this is."

"Well, Danny was one of my crew," Marcus replied quietly. "It's the least I can do for you—and for his child."

That night, Maureen slept more soundly than she had in weeks. In her dreams, Danny came to her—smiling, his voice warm and familiar.

"Not long now, honey, and you'll be free," he said. He blew her a kiss, and then he was gone.

When she awoke the next morning, the heaviness in her chest had lifted. For the first time in days, she felt calm.

Meanwhile, when Marcus's father received the signed papers, he made a decision of his own: he would go to Vancouver personally to speak with the bank about Danny's account.

As Jeanette Brownlow stood in the queue, waiting to cash her check, her attention was caught by the man ahead of her. He had just spoken to the teller—and she was almost certain she had heard him mention the name *Danny Butcher*.

Her pulse quickened. Could it be? Had someone finally caught up with him?

She studied the man more closely. No—this wasn't the type she had feared. He was well dressed, with the polished air of a businessman. The girl behind the counter pressed a small buzzer, and almost instantly the bank manager appeared, shaking the man's hand warmly before ushering him into his office.

Jeanette cashed her check and stepped outside, but she didn't go far. Sliding into a seat at a café next door, she ordered coffee and kept watch. Two cups later, the man emerged from the bank.

She quickly paid her bill, stepped into the street, and caught up with him.

"Excuse me," she said.

The man turned, smiling politely as he lifted his hat. "Can

I help you?"

She returned his smile. "I know this is a little presumptuous of me—and I don't usually accost strangers in the street—but I was in the bank just now, and I thought I heard you mention a friend of mine. I was curious."

"I see. And who is your friend?" He raised his eyebrows slightly.

"Danny Butcher."

The man regarded her with new interest. "I see. Perhaps we could find somewhere quieter to have a coffee, and you can tell me about your friend."

They chose a small corner table in another café. Once their coffees were served, he leaned forward.

"So—how do you know Danny?"

"We worked for the same company in New York several years ago," Jeanette replied. "I haven't seen him in some time—or even heard anyone mention his name—so I was surprised when I overheard you asking about him in the bank."

"I see. And what kind of relationship did you have? Just colleagues—or something closer?"

If only you knew, she thought with a flicker of amusement. Out loud, she said smoothly, "Just work colleagues. And how do you know him?"

"I'm helping his girlfriend gain access to her inheritance."

For a moment Jeanette could only stare. "I'm sorry—I don't understand. Girlfriend? Inheritance?"

"Oh… my dear, you don't know?"

"Know what?"

"Danny was killed in a bombing raid over Germany several

weeks ago."

She swallowed hard, forcing back the scream that rose in her throat. Her face drained of colour, and Marcus thought she might faint.

"Are you alright?"

She nodded faintly, her voice barely above a whisper. "Danny's… dead?"

"Yes, I'm afraid so."

Her hand went to her throat as tears welled in her eyes. "Oh no… poor Danny. You said a bombing raid over Germany? Are you telling me he was in the Air Force?"

"Yes. He was my son's tail gunner. He was badly wounded in a dogfight and died from his injuries."

"Oh, dear Lord… that's awful. He was so vibrant, so alive. I can't believe he's gone."

"My son said much the same—he was a very vibrant character."

Jeanette frowned slightly. "But you said you were helping his girlfriend claim her inheritance?"

"Yes. Apparently, he left a not inconsiderable amount to his fiancée in England. She's expecting a baby, so she needs it. My son has asked me to do what I can for her."

"Danny was going to be a father? Oh—he would have been thrilled by that."

"Unfortunately, he died before he knew. He never had the chance to find out."

"That's… that's so sad. He would have loved that."

"Then why can't this girl just claim her inheritance?"

Marcus hesitated, then decided there was little harm in telling her—after all, she didn't know Maureen.

Jeanette listened in silence, shocked by the revelations

about Maureen's father. *The bastard,* she thought grimly.

"Is there anything I can do to help her?" she asked at last. "Danny once helped me—in fact, I wouldn't be where I am today without him. The least I can do is help his fiancée and child."

She thought of her thriving hairdressing business, now boasting several salons across Canada with more in the works. All of it had begun with the money Danny had given her—and the jewellery. She knew he would be pleased for her success, but she had never forgotten that without him she might still be stuck in the Bronx, working for Jimmy and Jake, edging closer to the end of her usefulness. At twenty-five, she had already been nearing the point where the punters would want younger girls.

"Well, I can give you an address where you can contact her," Marcus said. "It's not her home, of course—it's the address of a friend."

"I see. Well, thank you. And thank you for telling me about Danny. He died a hero, really. I'm proud to have known him—and to call him my friend."

"Yes, I'm sure."

"So… he left quite an inheritance?"

Marcus nodded. "Yes. We believe he must have inherited it himself. There are also some unique pieces of jewellery. According to my son, the engagement ring he gave Maureen belonged to his grandmother—it's very unusual."

"Oh? What's so unusual about it?"

Marcus described the ring in detail, repeating what his son

had told him. Jeanette listened intently. She knew the ring he was describing—the last time she had seen it, it was in her locker, waiting for Danny to collect along with several other pieces. So, he had made it to the locker in time. She was glad; she hated the thought of the bus station staff finding it and Danny losing it after the risks he'd taken to get it.

"Well, I must be going," he said at last. "It was pleasant to speak with you—and I'm truly sorry I couldn't have given you better news." Then he smiled faintly, "I don't believe I caught your name?"

"It's Jeanette. Jeanette Brownlow."

He offered his hand. "A pleasure to meet you, Jeanette. I'm Marcus Potter."

They parted, and Jeanette made her way back to her apartment, her thoughts heavy with memories.

Sitting in her penthouse suite, the harbour lights shimmering beneath her window, Jeanette cradled a glass of whiskey and stared out at the dark water. The amber liquid caught the glow of the city beyond.

It seemed a lifetime ago now—yet it had been only a year.

She thought back to that morning. After the beating, she had decided she'd had enough. Enough of the bruises. Enough of the fear. Enough of *him*. She knew she had enough money to run, and enough jewellery to sell if she needed more.

She had showered to wash away the stench of his touch, then dressed quickly. Before leaving, she scribbled a note to Danny—she didn't want him thinking she had simply run out on him. She packed the few belongings she kept there and slipped out.

Some of the other girls saw her in the corridor.

"Where are you going at this time of the morning? It's only six o'clock," one asked.

"Yes, I want to get to the cleaners early. Got a lot on today—see you later," Jeanette lied, forcing a casual tone.

Sophie eyed her more closely. Jeanette had tried to hide the bruises beneath makeup, but the shadows on her skin still showed.

"Bloody hell—did he do that?"

"Yeah."

"I thought I heard you yell… I figured maybe it was just excitement. I had no idea he was beating you." Sophie gestured to the other girls nearby. "We'd have come to your rescue if we'd known. I'm sorry, Lola."

Jeanette shrugged as though it were nothing. "Not the first time, and I guess it won't be the last."

"Well, just because we do what we do doesn't mean they have the right to use us as a punch bag."

"I guess not. Anyway, that's why I need to get these cleaned—get the blood off."

She wanted them to believe the bag she carried held dirty laundry. In truth, everything she owned was still upstairs—this was only her personal belongings.

At the bus station, she unlocked the storage locker she shared with Danny and emptied its contents into the bag. Handing the key to the woman at the reception desk, she said, "I'd like to pay for two months up front and leave this for my friend. His name's Danny Butcher—he'll be collecting it soon."

"Alright," the woman said, tucking the key away. "But if he doesn't come before the two months are up, we'll have to clear it out and toss the lot."

Jeanette prayed Danny would make it before then—but she knew his routine. He would.

She boarded the first bus leaving the city. She didn't care where it went—so long as it wasn't New York. It was heading for Nebraska. That was far enough. From there, she could change for Canada, or take the train. It didn't matter, so long as she was free.

In Nebraska, she stayed just long enough for her face to heal. Then she took a train to Canada, drifting west until she reached Vancouver.

For several weeks she kept to herself, selling a few pieces of jewellery to boost her funds—not that she needed to. She had more than enough to last almost a lifetime. But she wanted her next move to be deliberate.

She decided to cut her hair short and dye it back to its original colour. She'd been blonde in New York, but her true shade was a deep, almost-black brunette. The transformation was striking. She doubted even those who came looking would recognise her now.

It was in that hair salon, sitting under the bright lights, that she realised what she wanted to do.

The stylist made conversation as she worked. "So, what do you do?"

"Well… I was training to be a hairdresser, actually. But my training got cut short because of family problems."

"Ever thought of finishing it?"

Jeanette shrugged. "I've thought about it. I only had eighteen months left before I qualified."

"Well, why don't you finish? Once you're qualified, the world opens up to you."

"I'd need a placement in a salon, though."

"That's where I can help. I've got an opening at the moment. I was going to advertise, but since you've already got experience, you'd be better than starting with a complete novice. I pay reasonably, and the tips are good."

Jeanette mulled this over as the scissors snipped. Finally, she smiled. "You know what—I'll take you up on that offer. When can I start?"

"That's great! How about Monday?"

"I look forward to it. My name's Jeanette, by the way—Jeanette Brownlow."

"I'm Margaret Hoffman. Well—welcome aboard."

Jeanette had thrived at the salon. Over the months, she and Margaret became firm friends. When Margaret retired a few months later, Jeanette bought her out, keeping the salon's reputation intact and building on its success.

Through long hours, determination, and a keen business sense, she expanded, opening more salons across the country. Within a year, she had built a small empire, and her wealth and standing in the community soared.

She often thought about how the money and jewellery Danny had given her had been the foundation of it all. Without that start, she wasn't sure how far she might have got.

Margaret still visited regularly to have her hair done, and over time she became the only person Jeanette trusted with the truth about her past.

One evening, as they sat over dinner at Margaret's home, Margaret leaned back in her chair and asked, "So—what happened to make you abandon your training?"

Jeanette hesitated. "It's not pretty. You'll be shocked."

Margaret gave a dry little smile. "I don't shock easily. I've heard some tales in my time, believe me. But if you don't want to talk about it, I understand."

Jeanette stared at her wine glass for a moment, then nodded. "Alright. I never knew my father, he isn't even named on my birth certificate. My mother had a succession of men, then through my training, she took up with a real nasty piece of work. He was brutal. Never laid a hand on me—he knew better. I think he could see I'd kill him if he tried.

"Then one day, they had one of their usual fights. He hit her. She went down hard, smacked her head. And then… he just left.

"There was something about the way she was lying. I knew. I checked for a pulse—nothing. She was gone. I knew he'd go to the bar, get drunk, and come back for another round. So I packed up, took whatever money I could find, and got on the first bus out of town. It took me to New York."

Margaret's expression was grave. "So why didn't you finish your training in New York?"

Jeanette let out a small laugh—without humour. "Because I had no place to stay and no money. Then I met a man who said he could help me. And he did—by help I mean dumping me in a brothel. Called it a 'place to stay.'"

For once, Margaret looked genuinely shaken. She poured more wine, took a deep swallow before speaking. "Bloody hell. The bastard."

"Yeah. Anyway, I was there four years. Then I met a man who helped me get out. But not before I took a beating from some client. That's when I knew I had to leave. I wasn't going to be a punch bag like my mother. And here I am."

"So where's the man who helped you now?"

Jeanette shrugged. "No idea. But I hope wherever he is, he's doing as well as I am."

"Did he work for this man too?"

"Yeah. But he was a good one. We got close—good friends."

Margaret raised an eyebrow. "Just friends? Nothing more?"

Jeanette shook her head. "No. There was nothing like that between me and Danny."

Margaret smiled faintly. "Well, I take my hat off to you. A lot of girls wouldn't have survived what you've been through." She raised her glass. "Here's to you—and a great future."

Jeanette clinked her glass against hers. "I'll drink to that."

Chapter 17

Raymond returned home two weeks after Ruth and Victoria's last visit. He was still fragile—his skin pale and his movements slow—but at least he was home, safe in their care, and on the mend.

"They'll kill the poor lad with kindness, the way they're going on," remarked Gillian, Ruth's mother, watching the girls fuss over him.

"Well, it's understandable, love, after what he's been through," Stephen replied. "They were so worried they might lose him. And after young Danny going like he did—well—who knows how long Raymond's got once he's sent back?"

"Yes, I suppose you're right. But let's hope this war ends before that happens."

"Oh, not much chance of that, love," Stephen said grimly. "Not with the battle for Stalingrad in full swing, the *Laconia* torpedoed, and fighting breaking out everywhere. I reckon we've got another year of this at least—unless someone shoots Hitler."

"I'd readily volunteer for that job, believe me," Gillian replied, her voice sharp.

Ruth and Victoria were over the moon to have Raymond home, but in the quiet moments they both wondered how long they would have him before the military called him back. They desperately wanted him restored to his old self—but secretly, they hoped his recovery would take time. Perhaps enough time for the war to be over.

That evening, Ruth sat close to him on the couch, her hand wrapped gently around his. His pallor was still alarming, and every now and then a flicker of pain crossed his face. She longed to throw her arms around him, but fear of hurting him held her back.

Oh, how she hated Hitler. The vicar always preached that they should love their enemies, but how could anyone love a man capable of such evil? Surely no one did. Her mother called him the devil incarnate—and Ruth believed her.

But it wasn't just Raymond's physical injuries that troubled them—something deeper had changed. The bright-eyed, laughing boy they had known at school was gone. In his place was a quiet, withdrawn young man who spoke only when spoken to and refused to talk about where he had been or what had happened to him.

Ruth and Victoria worried constantly. Would they ever see the old Raymond again? Would he return to them when this terrible war finally ended, or was he destined to remain locked inside himself forever? They prayed, with all the hope they had left, that the Raymond they loved would come back to them.

One evening, Ruth broke the silence.

"Would you like to go to the pictures one evening this week?"

Raymond looked at her and managed a faint, almost apologetic smile.

"If you like, love."

"Alright—I'll see what's on."

He nodded, then sighed. He knew he was different; he could feel it in every part of himself. But how could anyone return from what he had endured unchanged? He had fought in the battle for El Alamein—where over thirteen thousand men had died, and a hundred and fifty thousand more were wounded. He was one of the latter.

He had watched his best mate torn apart by an explosion, and the image would never leave him. They had struggled to gather enough of him for burial. Even now, the memory made his stomach turn. When he closed his eyes, he saw it all again—the noise, the heat, the smell of cordite, and the terrible silence that followed.

How could he tell his mother—or this beautiful girl sitting beside him—about those horrors? How could they ever understand? This was his burden, his alone, and there was no escape from it. Once, he had shared everything with his mother. Lately, he had shared with Ruth too. But this… this he would carry in silence.

And so he prayed, with all his heart, that the next generation would never know what he had seen.

Ruth watched the changes flit across his face—the tightening of his jaw, the flicker of pain in his eyes. She squeezed his hand.

"Raymond, are you alright? Are you in pain?"

He blinked, dragged from his thoughts, and looked at her. The despair in his gaze made her throat tighten, but she forced herself to stay composed. He needed her to be strong enough for both of them.

She gave him a small, watery smile. "I'll get the local paper and see what's on at the pictures."

He nodded, grateful for a few minutes to compose himself.

When she returned, she scanned the listings. "What we need is a comedy—something to take us out of ourselves. There's a Gert and Daisy picture; they're always good for a laugh. Or there's Will Hay. What do you think—Gert and Daisy versus Will Hay?"

"I don't mind, love—you choose."

She studied him for a moment, then said as brightly as she could, "Alright—Will Hay it is. We'll go tomorrow night, if you're up to it."

"Yes," he said quietly. "I'd like that."

The next morning at work, Ruth confided in Jenny.

"Oh, Jenny, I just don't know what to do—and his mum is just as worried."

Jenny reached across the table and took her friend's hand.

"He's been through so much, Ruth. He just needs time."

Ruth nodded, though tears shimmered in her eyes. Jenny's heart went out to her.

"Look, I tell you what—why don't Marcus and I come with you? It might help having someone else there. Unless, of course, you'd rather be alone with him?"

"No… I think that would be a good idea."

When Jenny told Marcus, he readily agreed.

"Yes, that would be fine. As you say, it might help him. Sounds like he's in a pretty bad way."

"He is. Ruth and Mrs. Merrett are so worried. He was the life and soul at school, but now Ruth says he just sits there, hardly speaking. They can't seem to get through to him. Oh, Marcus, it's so sad—all these men's lives being blighted by one man. How can one person cause so much distress and unhappiness?"

Marcus pulled her into his arms and held her close.

"I know, honey. But it's not really just one man—it's all the people who follow him and carry out his bidding. And don't forget Mussolini—he's just as bad."

"I know... Oh, Marcus, will this war ever end?"

He kissed the tip of her nose. "I sure hope so, honey."

That evening turned out to be the best they'd had since Raymond came home. He had actually laughed—first at the antics of Will Hay and Thora Hird, then with real gusto through the second feature. For a short while, he had been able to forget the nightmares. He and Marcus got along well, and his mother was visibly pleased.

"Oh, Ruth, thank you for taking him," Mrs. Merrett said warmly. "I think it's done him the power of good. Bless you, dear." She kissed Ruth's cheek.

"I enjoyed it," Ruth replied, smiling. "It was good to see him relax and laugh again."

When the letter arrived, Maureen stared at it in disbelief.

"It's from Canada," she said to Jenny at work. "But I don't know anyone in Canada."

"Well," Jenny replied, handing it over, "unless you open it, you never will. No good just sitting there looking at it—go on, open it."

Maureen broke the seal and began to read. As her eyes moved down the page, they misted over.

"What is it?" Jenny asked, her tone full of concern.

"It's from a friend of Danny's," Maureen said softly. "She heard about his death and wanted to tell me how sorry she is. It's… it's a lovely letter, Jenny. Here—you read it."

"Only if you're sure. It's not too private?"

"No, honestly—go ahead."

Jenny took the letter and read aloud:

Dear Maureen,

I hope you don't mind me being so informal. I heard about Danny, and I'm so sorry. He was my friend—oh, don't worry, there was never anything between us except friendship.

I also heard that you are having his baby. That's wonderful. He would have been so happy. But I heard he died without ever knowing, and that is so very sad. All he ever wanted was a family.

I guess he never mentioned me, but he was very good to me at a time when I needed a friend. He had a good heart and would have made a wonderful husband and father.

I know how desperately you must miss him. I hope you don't mind me saying this, but I heard about your father and know you need to get away. If there is anything I can do to help you, please let me know. I owe it to Danny to help the girl he fell in love with.

I will send this to the address I've been given—I know it's your friend's address, since you can't have mail coming to your own. I'd like to keep in touch and be friends. It would be nice to watch Danny's child grow. I hope all goes well for you. Keep safe and well.

Warmest regards,
Jeanette Brownlow

When Jenny finished, she looked up. "Oh, Maureen—that's lovely. Will you write back to her?"

Maureen nodded. "Yes. I'd like to hear more about Danny—he clearly meant a lot to her."

"Yes. She says he was there for her when she needed a friend. That means a lot. You know what they say—'A friend in need is a friend indeed.' That's what Danny was to her, obviously."

Maureen's eyes filled again. "Yes—and like she said, he had a good heart." She swallowed hard. "I miss him so much, Jenny. Sometimes the pain is so bad I can't bear it."

Jenny hugged her gently. "I know. I don't know what I'd do if anything happened to Marcus. But we mustn't get maudlin—they wouldn't want that."

Maureen hesitated, then asked, "I wonder how she knew... Who told her?"

Jenny frowned. "I don't know. I hadn't thought about that. But yes—it's odd. How would she know about you and your father, and to send the letter to me? Yes... curious."

That evening, when she told Marcus about the letter, he was just as puzzled about how Jeanette had come by such personal details.

A few days later, Marcus received word that he'd been granted furlough—two whole weeks at home.

"Oh, Marcus, I'll miss you so much," Jenny said, trying to smile for him. "But you should go and see your family—you haven't seen them in so long."

He stroked her hair, his voice low and warm. "I wish I could take you with me. But two weeks will fly by—you'll see."

There was more to his trip than a family visit. He intended to travel to New York while he was Stateside, to see if he could trace any of Danny's relatives. If there was family to be found, they deserved to know what had happened to him—and about Maureen and the baby.

Two days later, Marcus was back in Vermont. His family greeted him with open arms, overjoyed to have him home. His brother came down from college for a few days to join the reunion, and everyone noticed how tired Marcus looked. His mother clucked over him like a mother hen, making sure he ate well and rested.

His sisters were full of questions.

"What's England like?" Susan asked eagerly.

"Well, apart from the small village and town where I'm based, I haven't seen much of it," Marcus replied. "But I did discover that there's a Norwich in England—which they pronounce 'Norritch.'"

"Really? What's it like? Is it anything like here?" Susan pressed.

"I don't know—I haven't been yet. But one day, when I get some time off, I'll go. Jenny said she'd show me."

"Jenny?" Susan tilted her head. "Who's Jenny?"

Marcus grinned. "My girl back in the UK."

"You have a girl over there? What's she like? Is she pretty? Do you take her to the dances?" Susan's questions tumbled out in a rush.

"Hey, slow down!" Marcus laughed. "Well… she's very pretty. And yes, I take her to the dances. You'd like her—I know you would."

His mother spoke up then. "She is very pretty—and she looks nice, too."

Susan turned to her in surprise. "You know about her?"

Her mother nodded. "Yes. Marcus told me—and he sent a picture."

Susan's eyebrows rose. "And you didn't tell us? Or show us her picture? Why not?"

"I don't know… time just slipped by. You were at school, and I've been so busy, I just put it away and never thought to show you."

Susan turned back to Marcus. "Do you have a picture?"

"I sure do." He took his wallet from his pocket and pulled out the photograph of himself and Jenny, handing it to her.

Just then Sally came in and peered over Susan's shoulder. "Who's that?"

"Marcus's girlfriend," Susan said.

Sally's eyes widened. "Girlfriend? You kept that quiet! How long have you known her?"

Marcus shrugged. "A few months. Mum and Dad knew about her—I thought they would have told you."

"No, they didn't," Sally replied. "But you know Mum and Dad—always on the go. They probably just never thought about it."

When Richard first heard about Jenny, his brow furrowed.

"What does she do?"

Marcus raised his eyebrows. "Do? What do you mean, what does she *do*?"

"Well, for a career. Or doesn't she work?"

"Of course she works. She's in the dress department at a department store."

Richard stared at his brother as if he'd suddenly grown a second head.

"She's a shop girl?"

Marcus felt the hackles rise on the back of his neck. "As I said—she works in a department store." His eyes locked on Richard's, daring him to push the matter.

Richard gave a dismissive shrug. "Well, I suppose it's fine to amuse yourself with the local girls. If I were in your place, I'd do the same—a distraction, and who knows how long you've got."

He patted Marcus on the shoulder and turned to walk away, but Marcus caught his arm and swung him back around.

"I am not amusing myself with her I intend to marry her and bring her back here. And if you ever speak about her like that again, I'll make you sorry."

Richard was too stunned to reply—so much fuss over a shop girl.

Susan, sensing trouble brewing, stepped in. "Well, I think she looks lovely, and I'm very happy for you, big brother."

Sally agreed. "So do I—and I'm looking forward to meeting her."

"What does her father do?" Richard asked now, his tone deliberately casual.

Marcus's gaze never wavered. "He owns a grocery store in the village."

Richard almost choked. "A grocery store? You mean like Johnson's on Lexington?"

"Yes—like Johnson's on Lexington. Is that a problem?"

Richard raised his eyebrows and gave a nonchalant shrug. "Not for me. But then, I'm not the one planning to marry her."

Before Marcus could reply, he was gone. Marcus loved his brother—but there were times he didn't much *like* him.

Susan followed Richard, catching his arm as he started up the stairs.

"What the hell is wrong with you?"

Richard tried to pull free. "What do you mean, what's wrong with me?"

"Marcus hasn't been home five minutes, and you're already being your usual obnoxious self. After everything he's been through—fighting this war for you—this is how you repay him? By insulting his girlfriend?"

"I didn't ask him to fight," Richard shot back. "He joined up."

Susan's eyes hardened. "You know, Richard—sometimes I dislike you intensely. Maybe one day you'll grow up and stop being so damned high and mighty. Not everyone is born into wealth. Some people have to work for a living—but that doesn't make them less important. You might try it sometime—it could do you good."

She turned and walked away. Richard shrugged and continued up the stairs. He honestly couldn't see what all the fuss was about—a shop girl and her grocer father? Was Marcus seriously planning to marry into trade?

The thought nagged at him. He wondered if their father knew—and what he thought about it.

He turned and went back down the stairs, heading straight for his father's study. Knocking once, he entered.

Marcus Sr. looked up from his desk. He had heard the raised voices earlier and had a fair idea what this was about.

"Yes, Richard—what can I do for you?"

"Did you know about this girl Marcus is planning to marry?"

"Yes, I knew. What about it?"

"Well… how do you feel about it? I mean, he'll take over from you one day. Do you really think she's suitable to be the wife of the head of the company?"

His father studied him for a long moment. Richard was the image of his grandfather—and had inherited far too much of the old man's attitude.

"Yes, actually, I do. She's down to earth and grounded—that's what's needed in a wife in my position. That's what your mother is. And she'll teach Jenny, train her. I foresee no problem."

"Really, Father? We'll be a laughing stock—a common shop girl whose father is a grocer. *Trade*, Father—that's what they are. Trade! Will she even know which knife and fork to use at dinner? I doubt it."

Marcus Sr. stood abruptly, planting his fists on the desk and leaning forward. His voice was low and dangerous.

"Richard—you are my son, and I love you. But if I ever hear you speak like that again, I will make you sorry. You need a hard lesson to knock some of that arrogance out of you. Now get out of my office and let me get back to work."

Chapter 18

The next morning, as Marcus came down the stairs, the warm aroma of freshly ground coffee and pancakes drifted up to meet him. Oh, how he had missed that smell.

He stepped into the breakfast room to find his mother sitting alone at the table, the morning light spilling across the white tablecloth. Leaning down, he kissed her cheek.

"Good morning, Mother."

"Good morning, my dear," she said, patting his hand. "Did you sleep well?"

"The best night's sleep I've had in a long while—no sirens or raids to keep me awake."

Her eyes darkened with concern. "Oh, Marcus… is it very bad over there?"

He didn't want to frighten her. Smiling, he said lightly, "No, not really. Just noisy—it keeps us up sometimes."

She sipped her coffee. "So, what are you planning to do today?"

"Actually, I think I'll go to New York. I need to see if I can find any family for Danny—they have a right to know what happened to him, and about Maureen and the baby."

She frowned, puzzled. "Danny? Maureen? Baby? Marcus,

dear, you're not making any sense."

He looked up sharply. "Dad didn't tell you?"

She shook her head. "Tell me what?"

"About my tail gunner, Danny Butchers."

"No—I've never heard of him."

So, over coffee and cooling pancakes, Marcus told her. He spoke of Danny's service, his death, and of Maureen—her impossible situation with her father, and the baby she was carrying.

"Oh, that poor girl," his mother murmured. "Marcus, is there nothing you can do for her?"

"Dad's already working on it. We'll help her—don't worry."

"Is there anything *I* can do for her?"

"Not from here. If you were in England, yes—but she'll be alright. Danny left a will, and she's inherited a considerable sum. The challenge is getting it to her. Under British law, she needs her father's consent to open a bank account, and that's... not going to happen. But Dad's finding a way around it."

She nodded slowly. "So why do you need to go to New York?"

"Well, as I said, I want to see if Danny has any family. Maybe they can help her. But they also deserve to know about him."

"How long will you be gone?"

"Just a couple of days. I'll be back as soon as I can—I promise. Is my car still in the garage?"

"Yes—Burton's been keeping it serviced and ready for you."

"That's good. I'll need it to get to the airport."

"Burton can drive you."

"No, that's alright. I don't know exactly how long I'll be

away, and if I finish my business quickly, I'll head straight back—it might be late. Easier if I have the car."

"Well, as you wish, dear."

When Marcus arrived in New York, he had no clear plan—no idea where to start. He decided to begin simply: find a bar, buy a beer, and talk to the barman. If Danny had been known in the city, someone behind a bar would have heard of him.

He had no idea how many places he might have to try before he struck gold.

The bar he stepped into was dim and almost empty. A few solitary drinkers hunched over their glasses, and in the far corner two men sat talking quietly. Marcus didn't like the look of either of them. He doubted even Danny would have frequented a place like this. Still, he had to start somewhere. Sometimes, you had to turn over a rock to see what might crawl out.

He ordered a beer and leaned casually against the counter. The barman gave him a measuring look—not the usual type of customer, clearly—but smiled.

"You're not local," the man said. "I haven't seen you in here before."

Marcus took a sip of his beer. "Have you worked here long?"

"Yeah. I own the place. Been here twenty years."

That was promising. If Danny had ever been here, this man would know. "Then maybe you can help me. I'm looking for someone."

"Maybe. Who you looking for?"

"Anyone who knew a man named Danny Butchers."

The barman's expression shifted—his face paled slightly, his shoulders stiffened. Out of the corner of his eye, Marcus saw the two men in the corner sit up, listening.

The barman studied him more closely. "You don't look like the sort who'd be mixed up with Danny Butchers. What's your interest in him?"

Marcus ignored the question and asked his own. "So you *did* know him?"

"Sure. I knew him."

One of the men from the corner rose and came over. Marcus didn't like the look of him—hard eyes, the kind of man who'd do violence without thinking twice.

"So," the man said, "what's your interest in Butchers?"

"I'm trying to find his family."

"He ain't got no family. Anyway, what's it to you?"

"He was my tail gunner."

The man stared at him. "Tail gunner? Wait—you telling me Butchers is in the Air Force?"

"He *was*," Marcus said quietly.

"Was? Where is he now?"

"Lying in a cemetery in a small Suffolk village in England."

They both looked as if they'd been slapped. "Dead? Danny's dead?"

Marcus nodded. "Yes. He was killed on a raid over Germany."

"That's too bad... but maybe just as well. Anyway, like I said—he never had any family. His parents died when he was a kid."

That explained, Marcus thought, why Danny had left everything to Maureen.

The man lost interest and returned to his table. Not long after, both men left. The barman leaned in slightly.

"Lieutenant, it's not a good idea to ask too many questions about Danny around here. But if you really want to know more, go to the Sisters of Mercy Orphanage and speak to Sister Angelica. She can tell you about him."

"Sisters of Mercy Orphanage—where's that?"

"Left out of here, two blocks. Then turn left again for another couple. You can't miss it."

Marcus thanked him, left money on the counter, and walked out into the cold city air.

Sister Angelica studied the young lieutenant before her. He seemed far too young to be flying a warplane, let alone dropping bombs. She didn't believe in war. To her mind, there was no problem that couldn't be solved by sitting down, talking, and finding a compromise. Naïve, perhaps—but it was a conviction she held to firmly.

Marcus, for his part, saw a woman of perhaps sixty or seventy—it was hard to tell. Her face was lined, but softly, as if the years had been kind. She had the gentlest eyes and the sweetest smile, and now that smile was directed at him.

"What can I do for you, Lieutenant?" she asked.

"I understand you knew Danny Butchers, ma'am."

Sadness clouded her eyes. She nodded. "Yes, I knew him. So… he is dead, isn't he?"

"Yes, ma'am. I'm afraid he is."

"How did he die?"

"In a raid over Germany. He was my tail gunner. He was shot during a dogfight."

She made the sign of the cross, bowing her head in silent prayer. Marcus waited patiently until she looked up again.

"I believe you knew him well, ma'am. I wondered if you could tell me about him—about his family. I'd like to let them know."

"I'm afraid he had no family," she said. "We were his family—on and off."

"On and off?" Marcus frowned. "I thought he was raised here."

"In a manner of speaking, yes. But he kept running away. He'd be gone for weeks, sometimes months. Then he'd come back... until one day, he didn't. That last time, he'd fallen in with the local mafia. After that, I never saw him again—until he came here one day to say he was leaving New York. He gave us five hundred dollars. I never saw him again, except for a phone call a few months ago. That's when he told me he was in the Air Force, in England. And now you tell me he's gone."

"I'm sorry," Marcus said quietly. "He left a fiancée—a young woman expecting his child. I thought if I could find some family, she might have somewhere to go after the war."

Her brows rose. "Good heavens—an illegitimate child? How old is she?"

"Oh... so young. Will her family help her?"

"No. Her father's a brute—he'd make her get rid of the baby. Her mother's kind, but too frightened of him. He never even knew she was seeing Danny, and certainly doesn't know about the child."

"Oh, dear Lord... is there anything I can do?"

"Not from here, ma'am. But Danny left her a considerable inheritance—he'd made a will. I assumed it meant he came from a wealthy family."

She shook her head. "No, Lieutenant. It would have been from the proceeds of crime. I know he stole a great deal from his mafia boss when he left. They came looking for him—but I didn't know where he was. And even if I had, I wouldn't have told them."

Marcus rose to leave. "Thank you, ma'am. I appreciate your time."

"Wait—there is one more thing." She went to a cabinet, unlocked it, and took down a small box. "Before his mother died, she entrusted this to me. She said the contents belonged to her grandmother. Now they belong to Danny's unborn child. I'd like you to take it to the young woman."

Marcus accepted the box. "Of course, ma'am."

"There are photographs inside, and a trinket box—it's quite exquisite. It suggests there was money in the family at one time."

He nodded. "Thank you."

"I shall pray for you, Lieutenant," she said softly. "And for the young woman and her child."

"Her name's Maureen," Marcus told her.

"Maureen…" She smiled faintly. "I shall remember her in my prayers."

As she watched him walk away, she wondered if he would live to see home again when all this madness ended. She hoped so—sincerely.

Marcus decided it was time to head home—there was nothing

more he could do in New York.

When he stepped through the front door that evening, his mother beamed.

"Oh, Marcus, you made it back in time for dinner!"

"Yes—it didn't take as long as I thought, so I came straight back."

He was unusually quiet through the meal, his thoughts clearly elsewhere. When dinner was over, he excused himself and went up to his room, setting the small box Sister Angelica had given him on the bed.

Inside were pieces of jewellery—clearly valuable—and beneath them, a marriage certificate and a birth certificate for Muriel Butcher. His eyes lingered on her maiden name: Potter. Not unusual, perhaps, but strange all the same. Danny had never mentioned it—not that Danny had ever struck Marcus as someone interested in family history.

He examined each piece in turn. The silver trinket box was finely made, and among the contents lay a faded photograph of a small group of people. A young man in the picture bore an uncanny resemblance to Danny, and in his arms was a baby girl—judging by the clothing—though the image had clearly been taken decades before Danny was born. Could it be Danny's mother as an infant, held by her father? That would explain the likeness if the man was Danny's grandfather.

A knock at the door interrupted his thoughts. His father appeared in the doorway.

"Can I come in, son?"

"Of course—come in, Dad."

Marcus Senior stepped inside, his gaze falling on the array of jewellery spread across the bed. He picked up the engagement ring, turning it in his fingers.

"This is a fine piece. Where did it come from?"

"Danny Butcher's mother," Marcus replied, and then told him about his visit to Sister Angelica. Finally, he handed over the photograph.

His father studied it, frowning. "Good heavens—I know this photo. Where have I seen it before?" After a moment he straightened. "Wait here. I'll get the old album—it could be in there."

He returned with a large, red leather-bound album Marcus remembered from childhood, a fixture at family gatherings. Leafing through the stiff pages, he stopped suddenly. "Yes—here it is. That's the same photograph."

The two men compared the images. They were identical.

"But why would we have a photograph of Danny's family—or why would he have one of ours?" Marcus asked.

"It doesn't make any sense," his father agreed. "But I know who might be able to help—your great-aunt Clementine. She'll know who these people are. And with any luck, she'll know why Danny had this."

The next morning, Marcus and his father drove to Clementine's house. She was breakfasting on the patio, the summer sun casting a warm glow across a riot of colourful blooms. Marcus realised, with a pang, how much he'd missed such simple beauty while overseas.

Clementine sat beneath a striped awning, looking fresh as a

daisy. In her early sixties, her skin was remarkably smooth, her eyes bright with intelligence. Her once-glorious auburn hair was now elegantly streaked with grey. She wore a flowing silk kaftan patterned with large mauve and peach flowers.

The butler announced them with ceremonious formality: "Mr. Potter Senior and Young Mr. Potter, madam."

"Ah, Henry," Clementine smiled, "please send out fresh coffee and two more cups."

"Certainly, madam."

"Well, this is a pleasant surprise," she said, holding out her arms. "Come here and give your old aunt a kiss."

They obliged, and once the maid had set the coffee tray down and left, she leaned back.

"So—what brings you here so early in the morning?"

"We have a bit of a dilemma," Marcus Senior said. "We were hoping you might shed some light on it."

"Oh good—I do love a puzzle. So, what is it?"

"I think Marcus should tell you," his father said. "It's really his story."

"It's a long one," Marcus warned, "but you'll need the whole picture."

"Of course—no good going off half-cocked," she replied. "Go on, then."

Marcus began. "My tail gunner was a young man named Danny Butchers. He was killed in a raid over Germany a couple of months ago."

"Oh, Marcus dear—I'm so sorry. How old was he?"

"Nineteen."

"Good heavens. So young. This terrible war is taking far too many. But please—go on."

"Yesterday I went to New York to see if I could find his

family. There wasn't any—both parents dead—but I met a nun at the orphanage where he was raised. She gave me a box his mother had left for him, to be given when he was older. He was only ten when she died."

"Oh, the poor boy," Clementine murmured. "How very sad. Forgive me for interrupting."

"In the box was a silver trinket box, some jewellery, and an old photograph. When I showed it to Dad, he recognised it. He fetched the family album—and there it was. The exact same photograph. We were hoping you could tell us why Danny had a picture from our family, or why we would have his. Also—his mother's birth and marriage certificates both show her maiden name as Potter."

Clementine's brows rose. "Well... that *is* a puzzle. And you've brought the photograph?"

"Yes—and the trinket box."

Marcus's father took them from his briefcase and set them on the table.

Clementine drew in a sharp breath. Her hand hovered over the box before she touched it gently, her eyes misting.

"Oh... I never thought I'd see this again. It's been so many years."

Marcus and his father exchanged a glance.

"You recognise it?" Marcus Senior asked.

"Oh yes," she said softly. "It was my mother's."

The two men glanced at each other, then at Clementine, then back again. For several moments, no one spoke.

Finally, they both began at once.

Marcus Senior said, "Your mother's—you mean this belonged to Grandmother?"

Marcus Junior spoke over him. "Great-grandmother's? This was hers?"

"Yes," Clementine replied softly. "And it had been *her* mother's before that. It's a family heirloom, passed down through the generations."

Marcus Junior frowned. "But how did Danny's mother have it? She told the nun it was *her* grandmother's."

"I don't know..." Clementine's voice trailed off as her gaze shifted to the photograph. She reached for it, but as she picked it up, her hand began to tremble.

The two men exchanged a worried glance. For a moment, Marcus Junior thought she might faint.

"Here, Aunt," Marcus Senior said gently, pouring a glass of water and guiding it into her hands. She took a few slow sips, her colour gradually returning.

When she set the glass down, Marcus Senior asked quietly, "You know who they are... don't you?"

She nodded. "Oh yes. I know exactly who they are. The man holding the baby is my older brother—Clarence. The young woman beside him is his wife, Charlotte Benson, as she was then. And the baby in his arms..."

She paused, her voice tightening. "...is their daughter."

The shock that passed through the two men was palpable.

Chapter 19

For a long moment, no one spoke. The revelation hung in the air, heavy and astonishing.

Marcus sat back, his mind reeling. *So that's why he sometimes seemed familiar...* Somewhere deep in his subconscious, he must have remembered the photograph from the old family album—the same one now lying on the table between them.

He found his voice before his father did. "So… what you're saying is that the man in this picture is my great-uncle?"

Clementine nodded. "Yes, he is."

"But why would Danny have it? His mother told the nun it belonged to *her* grandmother. And why," Marcus frowned, "have I never even heard of Great-Uncle Clarence?"

Her gaze softened. "Because his name was never mentioned after we lost touch. I think it was too painful for Mother to talk about him, and Father…" She hesitated. "…Father would not allow his name to be spoken in the house."

Then she asked, "What was Danny's mother called?"

Marcus shook his head. "I can't remember. It was on her birth certificate—and her marriage certificate—but I didn't think to bring them. I could call Sister Angelica. She might remember."

“I suggest you do, dear.”

Marcus went inside. Lifting the receiver, he dialled the number for the orphanage. Sister Angelica answered on the third ring.

“Oh, Sister—it’s Marcus Potter. I visited yesterday about Danny Butchers.”

“Yes, Lieutenant Potter, of course. How are you?”

“I’m fine, thank you. And you?”

“Busy as usual. How can I help you?”

“I was wondering… do you recall Danny’s mother’s first name?”

“Oh my… it’s been so long. Let me think. Miriam… Margaret… no, it began with an M…” She fell silent for a moment, then said suddenly, “I have it! Muriel. Yes—that was it. Muriel.”

“Thank you, Sister. I appreciate it. And my father will be making a donation to the orphanage soon.”

“Oh, Lieutenant, that would be so kind. Thank you.”

Marcus returned to the garden and told his aunt.

Clementine’s eyes widened. “Good heavens—yes, that was it. Muriel. Then that young man who died in your plane… he was Clarence’s grandson. My great-nephew.”

They sat in silence for a while, each absorbed in private thoughts. Finally, Marcus Senior broke it. “So that makes him my cousin.”

“Yes,” Clementine replied, “and young Marcus’s first cousin once removed.”

Marcus Junior’s mind leapt to Maureen. “I wonder what the baby will be…”

Clementine's head tilted. "Baby? What baby?"

"Oh—I didn't tell you. Danny's girlfriend is pregnant."

Clementine blinked in surprise. "Good heavens." Then, with a sigh: "How very sad. Did he know?"

"No. That's the worst part."

"Well," she said, folding her hands in her lap, "I can't say I approve of babies outside marriage—but during wartime... I suppose I can understand it. It happened often enough in the last war."

She paused, calculating aloud. "That child would be your first cousin once removed, Marcus. And young Marcus's second cousin."

They both stared at her.

"Heavens, that does sound complicated," she admitted with a faint smile. "But the point is—you served with your own blood. Removed, second cousin—it doesn't matter. You shared the same family line."

Marcus felt a hollow ache in his chest. He wished with all his heart he had known that while Danny was still alive. He should have been more than a comrade—he should have been a brother to him.

They sipped their coffee in thoughtful silence, each lost in their own reflections, until Clementine set down her cup and said quietly,

"Well—you'd better speak to Edward Lavender about his inheritance."

Both men stared at her.

"Inheritance?" Marcus Senior's brows drew together. "What inheritance?"

Clementine gave a faint, knowing smile. "Goodness, Marcus, I really do need to have a long discussion with you one day. There's so much you don't know. But fortunately, Edward does."

"Yes," Marcus Senior replied dryly. "So it would seem."

She continued, "When Mother died five years ago—she was ninety-three, you know, quite incredible—she left her money equally among all her children. That included Clarence. James, of course, had been killed in the Great War, and he had no children, so his share reverted to the rest of us. Your father, Clarence, and I each took a third. Charles tried to have the will overturned so Clarence would not inherit, but it was watertight.

"Anyway, Charles, your father, and I received our shares, but nobody knew where Clarence was. We knew he had gone to New York, but not where exactly. And if someone truly doesn't wish to be found, they can vanish quite effectively."

"So what happened to his share?" Marcus Senior asked.

"Edward placed it in trust, as Mother had instructed. She was determined Clarence and his descendants would receive their portion. It was spelled out very clearly in her will."

Marcus Junior frowned. "But what I still don't understand is why they were cast out of the family. What actually happened?"

Clementine's expression softened with sadness. "Oh, it was all so foolish and unnecessary. Clarence and Charlotte had been walking out for several months. Our families were very close—we'd grown up together. Then Father and Mr Benson decided to go into business. They each had their own ventures, but this was to be a joint enterprise. I was still quite young, so I don't know all the details, but Father accused Mr Benson of cheating him.

"It even went to court. There was a terrible to-do; I remember Mother crying a great deal. But Father could be very austere—and bull-headed. Charles is much like him in that regard. Father forbade Clarence ever to see Charlotte again. Mother disagreed; she said it wasn't the girl's fault, which of course it wasn't, and that they were in love and should be allowed to marry.

"Mr Benson, for his part, forbade Charlotte to see Clarence and refused them permission to wed. So when Charlotte turned twenty-one, they eloped. We kept in touch for a while, but then… I don't know what happened. The letters stopped. We lost contact.

"Mother never forgave Father, and in her will she divided her estate equally between her surviving children and their descendants. Charles sided with Father, but there was nothing they could do about it. And as Father died first, Mother inherited his share of the estate. She had also inherited a great deal from her own father, who never liked Father and had structured his will so Father could never touch her money."

Clementine reached out and ran her fingers gently over the trinket box. "Mother gave this to Charlotte as a wedding present. The rings inside were Charlotte's wedding and engagement rings."

For several minutes, no one spoke. Then Clementine broke the silence. "So—tell me about England. Is it truly as bad as they say?"

"Yes, Aunt, it is," Marcus replied. "Rationing is severe, and the air raids... but somehow they keep going. They're stoical, with grit and determination. I admire them immensely."

"Yes, I'm sure. I feel so sorry for them. I don't know how I would cope with being bombed every night and never getting any sleep. But tell me about *you*. Are you still courting that blonde girl—oh, what was her name?"

"Millicent. No, Aunt—we parted ways before I enlisted."

"Well, I can't say I'm sorry. She wasn't right for you. So... do you have a young lady now?"

Marcus grinned. "Oh yes. And when I get back, I intend to ask her to marry me. I've already spoken to her father—he's given his permission."

Clementine's eyebrows arched. "An English girl?"

Marcus took Jenny's photograph from his wallet and handed it to her. "That's Jenny. And I intend to marry her."

Clementine studied the smiling young woman in the picture. "She's very pretty, Marcus—and she has a pleasant face. What does her father do?"

"Her parents own a grocery store in the village. Jenny works in the dress department of a department store in town."

Clementine chuckled. "Oh dear—Charles and Richard won't approve. But I think it's wonderful. Bring her here as soon as you can. I want to meet her."

"Well, I don't know about Grandfather—I haven't spoken to him yet. But Richard's already in a rage. Like I said, it's none of his business who I marry."

"Well," Clementine said with finality, "I think it's wonderful. And as long as you're happy, Marcus, that's all that matters."

Meanwhile the war was raging on; operation Jubilee had ended in disaster for British and Canadian forces, most of the men are either killed or captured by the Germans. Brazil declared war on the Axis countries in response to riots in their streets over the sinking of Brazilian ships. One thousand Jews are massacred at Stanislau in Poland in a reprisal action. The Germans launched a massive air raid on Stalingrad.

Raymond stood at his bedroom window, staring out over the garden without really seeing it. His thoughts were miles away.

It had been six weeks since he'd come home, and he knew—deep down—that when he saw the doctor, the verdict would be inevitable. They would send him back.

He didn't want to go back. He wanted to stay here, safe with his family. He wanted to marry Ruth and settle down—not be sent back as cannon fodder. But he also knew there was no avoiding it.

A thought had crossed his mind more than once: if he swallowed some silver paper, it would show up on an X-ray, make it look as though he had lung trouble, and they might discharge him. But no—he couldn't do that. Not to his mates. It wouldn't be right or fair. It would be cowardly, and he would have to live with that shame for the rest of his life.

No, he would go back. He would fight alongside his friends—for King, for country, and for freedom from tyranny.

There was a knock at the door. His mother's head appeared around it.

"You alright, son?"

He nodded. "Yes, Mum, I'm fine."

They held each other's gaze. Two breaking hearts, both

wearing brave faces.

"Well," she said quietly, "I think it's time we went. You don't want to be late."

On the bus, neither spoke. Both prayed silently that the doctor would say Raymond wasn't fit to return—but neither truly believed that would happen.

At the army hospital, Victoria sat on the hard, unforgiving chair in the waiting room, praying harder than she had ever prayed in her life.

The doctor's examination was done in silence.

"You can get dressed now, Private," he said at last. When Raymond sat back down, the doctor looked him over.

"Well, I think you can rejoin your regiment. You've healed well."

"Yes, sir."

The doctor was an elderly man with kind eyes. He studied Raymond for a moment.

"I know it's hard, son. I fought in the last one myself, and I know how you feel. But I have no choice but to register you fit for active duty." He placed a hand on Raymond's shoulder. "I wish I didn't have to send you back—but then, who would defeat Hitler? I'm sorry, son."

"I know, sir. I understand. And… thank you."

When Raymond had gone, the doctor slumped back in his chair. This was the part of the job he hated most—sending young men back to be killed or maimed. He prayed they would all return unscathed, though he knew it was impossible. Those who came back whole in body would still carry the scars in their minds.

When Raymond stepped back into the waiting room, Victoria didn't need to ask—she could see it in his face. Still, she smiled and asked softly,

"How did it go, son?"

"I have to go back, Mum. I'll get my orders in a day or so."

Her heart sank. Every instinct screamed to burst into the doctor's room and tell him he couldn't send her boy back—but wasn't that what every mother, wife, and sweetheart felt? She would have to accept it… and pray.

When Ruth heard, she felt exactly as Victoria did.

"But you're still not right—you still get pain. Did you tell him that?"

Raymond took her hand so tightly she thought he'd stop the blood from flowing.

"Yes, but it's only twinges. They'll subside in time."

Tears filled her eyes. She didn't want him to see her cry, but she couldn't help it. What if he didn't come back? What if he was killed—or came home like those poor men in the hospital, missing limbs?

Jenny was gentle when she heard the news.

"Oh, Ruth… I'm so sorry. Poor Raymond. When does he go?"

"In a few days. His travel papers will come through, along with orders telling him where he has to go."

When those papers finally arrived, Victoria and Ruth took the day off to see him off. At the station they clung to each other, unwilling to let go, until at last Raymond boarded the train. And then—he was gone.

The two women walked home together, sobbing. The house felt unbearably empty. Would he come home safe—or had they just seen him for the last time?

Veronica came over to comfort them, but there was little comfort to be had.

Would this bloody war never end? The evil they wished upon Hitler knew no bounds.

Marcus was still reeling from the revelations his aunt had shared. He could hardly take it all in, but he was grateful she had told him. She had also advised him to speak with the family solicitor—something he had already intended to do. He wanted to ensure Jenny would be provided for, should anything happen to him

But before that, there was something else—something far more personal—that he wanted his mother's help with.

He knocked on the door to her sitting room and stepped inside. She looked up from the guest list she was working on for his father's upcoming business dinner, and smiled warmly.

"Oh, Marcus, come in, dear."

"Sorry—am I disturbing you?"

"Of course not. Do you want some tea?"

"No, thank you. Are you busy tomorrow morning?"

"I'm always busy, but for you, I'll make time. What do you need?"

"I was hoping you might come and help me choose an engagement ring for Jenny."

Her eyes lit with pleasure. "I can do better than that. I can give you one of your grandmother's rings—unless you really want to buy a new one. It's up to you."

"One of Gran's would be wonderful. Jenny would love that."

"Very well—come with me."

She led him upstairs into her bedroom and opened the closet, taking several small jewel boxes from the shelves. Setting them on the bed, she said,

"There you are. Help yourself. They're not engagement rings as such, but still very pretty—and any one of them would make an excellent engagement ring."

Marcus studied the small collection. There were four rings in total, but one immediately caught his eye: a heart-shaped sapphire set in yellow gold. It was simple—no diamonds—but he knew Jenny would adore it.

He picked it up, turning it gently between his fingers. His mother watched him closely.

"This is it," he said at last. "She'll love it."

"Yes, I thought you'd like that one. It's one of my favourites, too."

"Then you should keep it, Mum. It's not right to take it from you—it belonged to your mother, and it's only right that you keep what you want. I can choose another."

She closed his hand around the ring. "No, Marcus. If this is the one you think she'll like, then this is the one she shall have. Please—take it. I have plenty of rings, and I never wear this one."

"Only if you're sure."

"I'm sure. Now—there's a ring box in here somewhere."

She rummaged through the drawers and produced a red velvet box. "Here—perfect."

Marcus placed the ring inside and closed the lid. He could

hardly wait to see Jenny's face when he gave it to her.

The object of his thoughts, at that very moment, was having her afternoon tea break in the staff room at Findley's Department Store. Ruth was clearly bursting to share some news and had been since returning from her lunchtime shopping trip.

As soon as they were seated with their tea, Ruth leaned forward eagerly.

"You'll never guess who I ran into in town at lunchtime."

Jenny eyed her friend's excited expression. "Ronald Colman," she said with a teasing smile.

"Oh, Jenny, be serious."

"Well, go on, then—if I have to guess, we could be here all day."

"Sheila—from Shoes."

"Oh—is she home on leave?"

Ruth shook her head. "No. She's been thrown out of the WAAF."

Jenny's eyes widened. "Thrown out? What for?"

"You'll never believe it—she's expecting a baby."

If it were possible, Jenny's eyes grew even wider. "A baby? So—she's married? That was quick work."

"No—she isn't married. She's just expecting."

Jenny stared. "But... she's going to get married, isn't she?"

"No. Apparently, the father wants to marry her, but she said no. She says she'll have the baby adopted so she can 'live her life.'"

Jenny was speechless. "That's terrible. What do her parents

think?"

"They want to take the baby and raise it themselves—but she's not sure. She thinks they'd use it to keep her here."

"But it would be better off with its grandparents than in an orphanage! What if no one adopts it? I think that's awful."

"I know—so do I. Maybe once it's born, she'll change her mind."

"Not Sheila. She was always selfish."

Ruth sighed. "Anyway—let's change the subject. When's Marcus due back?"

"In a couple of days. I can't wait to see him—I've missed him so much."

Then she caught the shadow that crossed Ruth's face and felt a pang of guilt for speaking so thoughtlessly.

"Oh, Ruth—I'm sorry. That was unkind."

"It's all right—I know you didn't mean anything by it."

"Have you heard from Raymond lately?"

"Yes. Mrs Merrett and I both had a letter the other day. He can't say where he is, but he sounds all right—says he's back to his old self. The wounds have healed, and he's feeling fine."

"Well, that's good. When you write to him, give him my love—and tell him to take care of himself."

Chapter 20

After dinner that night, Marcus knocked on his father's office door and leaned in.

"Do you have a minute, Dad?"

"Of course—come in. I've been hoping to get a moment alone with you; I need to talk to you."

"Yes, I want to talk to you too—but you go first."

His father sat back in his chair. "Well, I want to speak about this young woman of Danny's—Maureen. I've been to Canada and arranged for all the money to be transferred into the account here, so she can access it."

"Ah—yes, that's exactly what I wanted to ask you about. Thanks, Dad. But how will she access it? She can hardly run around England with an American chequebook."

"No, I've thought of that," his father said, reaching for a document. "I've written this letter of introduction and authorisation for her to take to a bank in England so she can open her own account. Once that's done, we can transfer money to her as and when she needs it."

He handed Marcus a sealed envelope.

"Oh, that will make her life much easier. I think she's been wondering how she was going to get hold of it."

"Will she know how to open an account?"

"No—but I can help her. This letter will certainly smooth the way."

"Well, I sincerely hope so. From what you've told me; it sounds as if she needs all the help she can get."

"Yes. Now, all I have to do is speak to Mr Lavender and find out about Great Grandmother's will."

Marcus sat before the imposing desk, facing the kindly solicitor he had known all his life—a man who was not only the family's legal adviser, but also a trusted friend.

Edward Lavender smiled warmly. "Well, young man, how are things in the Air Force?"

"Good, sir. A bit hair-raising at times—but good."

"I'm pleased to hear it. So, what brings you to me?"

"Two things, really. First, I want to make a will."

Edward raised his eyebrows. "I see. A sensible decision, given your profession and the times we live in. And the second?"

"I need some advice about my great-grandmother's will."

Edward's gaze sharpened. "Your great-grandmother's will? You weren't in it—you weren't even born when it was written."

"No, sir, I know. But my great-aunt Clementine told me to speak to you about it. It's for a friend of mine—well, more for his child. I think they may have been included, indirectly."

"I see. If Clementine sent you to me, she must have had a good reason. Start from the beginning and tell me about your friend."

Marcus recounted Danny Butchers' story, much as he had told Aunt Clementine, and explained about Danny's unborn child.

"Ah," Edward said at length. "En ventre sa mère."

Marcus frowned. "I'm sorry, sir?"

"It's a legal term—French. It means 'in the mother's womb.' An unborn child can inherit under that rule, provided the will is correctly worded."

"I see. Do you think this child could inherit?"

"I'll have to review your great-grandmother's will, but as I recall, it's possible."

He pressed a buzzer, and when his secretary appeared, he asked her to bring Henrietta Potter's will from the archives. Once it was placed before him, Edward read it in silence while Marcus waited.

At last, Edward looked up. "Did you say Danny Butchers made a will before he was killed?"

"Yes, sir—he left everything to his girlfriend, Maureen."

"Then she inherits, not the child."

Marcus stared. "Maureen inherits? I don't understand."

"Under the will, Danny's grandfather—Clarence Potter—inherited upon Henrietta's death. But Clarence had already died, so his daughter, Danny's mother, inherited. When she passed away, everything she owned went to Danny. His own will leaves it all to this young woman—so she now inherits."

Marcus sat back, stunned. Maureen was a wealthy woman. "I see. But is it too late to claim? My great-grandmother died five years ago."

"No. She planned for such delays. She was a determined woman—adamant that your grandfather should never get this money—so we placed it in trust with a long lifespan. She left it nominally to Clementine, with instructions to hold it in trust for Clarence and his descendants. And that's precisely what we did."

"Can the money be paid into Maureen's bank account?"

Edward tilted his head. "Bank account? She has one here in the States?"

"Yes. Danny's money was in a bank in Canada, but my father arranged for it to be transferred to his own bank. He sent the papers to England, and Maureen signed them so he could open an account for her."

"I see. Well, yes—I can make payments if your father sends me the account details. There's been considerable interest accrued. I'll speak with him about it. Now—about your will."

Marcus nodded. "It's quite simple, sir. I want to leave everything to Jenny—my fiancée."

Edward studied him closely. "Marcus, I would be failing in my duty to you and your family if I didn't strongly advise you to reconsider."

"I understand, sir. But that's what I want. If anything happens to me, I want Jenny to benefit. If I come home safe, I'll marry her and provide for her then. But if I don't, I want to know she'll have a secure future."

"Your trust fund is substantial," Edward said gravely. "Whilst I appreciate your feelings, you've only known her a few months. Given the circumstances of your meeting—and your current life—are you quite certain this isn't just the infatuation of a young man far from home?"

Marcus shook his head. "No, sir. Being home hasn't changed how I feel about her."

Edward sighed. "Very well. What are your instructions?"

"In the event of my death, she inherits everything. If I'm posted missing, I want her to receive something immediately—the rest once I'm declared dead."

"I see you've thought this through."

"Yes, sir. And time is of the essence—I return to England in a few days, so I'd appreciate having it ready by then."

"Have you spoken to your father about this?"

"Not yet. I'll tell him and Mother at dinner tonight. I wanted to consult you first."

"In that case, I will draw it up as you've requested—but I strongly advise discussing it with them before signing. And how much would you want her to receive if you are merely posted missing?"

"Fifty thousand."

Edward's eyebrows lifted slightly. "Marcus—that's a great deal of money. Are you certain?"

"Yes, sir. That's what I want her to have."

"Very well. I'll have my secretary prepare the draft and let you know when it's ready. In the meantime, have your father contact me regarding the other matter so we can finalise it."

They shook hands, and Marcus left. Edward sat back in his chair, troubled. The young man was of age, and the decision was his—but the solicitor could only hope his parents might persuade him to reconsider.

Over dinner that evening, Marcus told his parents about his plans for his will. Before either could reply, Richard burst out angrily,

"Have you gone mad? You hardly know this girl, and you intend to give her everything? Does Grandfather know?"

"No—and he's not going to know. I'm old enough to make my own decisions, and I've made this one. I don't need yours—

or Grandfather's—approval."

Richard turned to their parents. "Surely you're not going to allow this? Letting the money go out of the family to a perfect stranger—who's probably only with him for his money anyway! And given his job, his life expectancy isn't exactly good, is it?"

The table froze. Richard had always been a hothead, but this time he had gone far beyond acceptable.

Marcus's cutlery clattered to his plate. He pushed back his chair with such force it toppled over, and in two strides he was across the table, seizing Richard by the lapels. Before he could strike him, his father stepped in and prised Marcus's hands free.

"That's enough!" he barked through clenched teeth.

Marcus's eyes blazed. "If you ever speak about Jenny like that again, I'll hit you so hard your teeth will rattle. And for your information—she knows nothing about my wealth."

Their mother's face was pale with shock. To speak so bluntly of her son's possible death at the dinner table—she knew it was true, but hearing it said aloud was unbearable.

"I think you'd better go to your room, Richard," she said coldly.

"I'm not a child to be sent to my room," he snapped.

"Do as your mother says—and don't you ever talk back to her again, do you hear me?" their father roared.

Richard stalked from the room.

Marcus righted his chair, sat down, and took a long swallow of wine. "Do you think I'm doing the wrong thing?" he asked quietly.

His father hesitated. “For what it’s worth, I’m not exactly thrilled—but if you’ve thought it through, and this is truly what you want, then I have no objections.”

His mother studied him. “You must love her very much.”

“I do.”

“What did Edward advise?”

“He tried to talk me out of it. But I’d like you to meet her—whether I’m with you or not. Once you know her, you’ll understand why I’m doing this.”

“Very well,” she said at last. “I promise that whatever happens, we’ll go and see her. I’d like to meet the girl who’s captured my son’s heart.”

When Charles Potter heard what his grandson was planning, he was incensed.

“Davies!” he bellowed.

The butler appeared in the doorway. “Yes, sir?”

“Tell Pinkerton to bring the car round immediately.”

“Certainly, sir.”

Marcus’s butler, Harold, was wondering who was ringing the bell so violently when the door flew open and Charles Potter stormed inside, nearly knocking him over.

“Where’s my son?” he barked.

“I believe Mr Potter senior is in his office, sir. Shall I announce you?”

“Certainly not—I’ll announce myself. Now get out of my way.”

He strode down the hall.

Sally and Susan appeared, drawn by the shouting.

“Oh, Grandfather—whatever’s the matter?” Susan asked.

"Matter? The matter, young lady, is none of your business. You'd best go to your room—this isn't going to be pleasant."

"But what happened?" Sally pressed.

"You too—go to your room, both of you."

Just then Richard came down the stairs.

"Ah—Richard. You're here. Come with me," his grandfather ordered.

As the two disappeared down the hall, Sally seized Richard's arm.

"You told him, didn't you? How could you? In a few days Marcus will be going back to fight—he could be killed—and you've burdened him with all this unpleasantness. If anything happens to him, I will never forgive you. Never."

"Neither will I," Susan added fiercely. "Sometimes I hate you, Richard—I really hate you."

Sally spun on her heel, stormed out the front door, and jumped into her car. She roared down the drive and out through the gates.

At Clementine's house, Henry barely had time to open the door before Sally swept past him.

"Oh, Henry, where's my aunt?"

"In her sitting room, miss. Is something wrong?"

"Oh, yes—everything is wrong."

She hurried on without waiting for an answer.

Clementine looked up from her book as the door burst open. "Good heavens, Sally—whatever is the matter?"

"Aunt Clementine, you have to come—quickly, please, now." She grasped her aunt's arm, trying to pull her up from the chair.

Henry, who had followed, was aghast.

Clementine gently removed her niece's hand and held it. "Henry, could you bring another cup, please?"

"Certainly, madam." He glanced at Sally. "Will you be all right, madam?"

"Yes, I'll be fine."

Turning back to Sally, Clementine said, "Now, dear—sit down and take a deep breath, and tell me what's going on."

"Oh, Aunt, we don't have time—I'll tell you on the way—"

Clementine's voice, calm but commanding, cut across her. "Sit down, Sally. Now."

Henry returned with a tray, placing the cup and saucer before the girl.

"Oh, Aunt, we don't have time for tea—please—" Sally's voice trembled on the edge of tears.

Once Henry had left, Clementine said quietly, "Take a deep breath and compose yourself."

When Sally had mastered herself, Clementine added, "Now, start at the beginning and tell me everything. And drink that tea—it's camomile, very soothing. It will do you good."

Sally forced herself to speak calmly as she told her aunt about Marcus's will, the row at dinner, and her grandfather's furious arrival.

Clementine listened, sighed, and shook her head.

"Oh, really—this is just too much. Sometimes I could wring your grandfather's neck."

"I'm sorry, but you're the only one he listens to—the only one who can make him see sense. He's so angry, and he's shouting—"

"That won't do his blood pressure any good at all," Clementine said crisply. "Very well, I'll come and see what I can do. Now—you stay here and finish your tea. I want you completely calm before you drive me back. I've no wish to end up in hospital—or worse. And we will *not* be driving fast, young lady. Do you hear me?"

"Yes, Aunt Clementine, I hear you."

When Charles and Richard burst into Marcus senior's office without so much as a knock, he leapt from his chair.

"What's the meaning of this? How dare you burst in here unannounced!"

Richard at least had the grace to look down at the carpet, unable to meet his father's eyes. Charles, on the other hand, met his son's gaze without flinching.

"Where's Marcus?" he demanded.

"I believe he's taking tea with his mother in her sitting room. Why?"

Without answering, Charles strode from the office, Richard at his heels.

In Gloria's sitting room, she and Marcus junior looked up sharply as the door burst open.

"What's the meaning of this?" she said coldly. "How dare you come barging into my sitting room like this? Marcus, what's going on?" she asked her husband.

Marcus junior could only stare, stunned into silence. Charles turned on him.

"Have you lost the use of your legs, boy? Don't you stand when your elders and betters enter a room?"

Marcus rose. "Yes, sir—of course. I was just surprised, that's all."

"Well, you might be," Charles snapped. "What's this nonsense I've been hearing about you leaving your estate to some gold-digging little piece in England?"

Marcus's temper flared. "She is *not* a gold-digger. She doesn't know I'm wealthy, and if she did, she wouldn't care. She's not that sort of girl. And with respect, Grandfather, I resent the way you've just spoken about her. I will not tolerate it."

"You arrogant young pup—I'll thrash your hide for that—"

"Oh, don't be ridiculous, Charles," a firm voice cut in. "You'll give yourself a coronary at this rate."

All eyes turned to the doorway. None of them had heard Clementine and Sally arrive, drawn by the shouting.

"Clementine is quite right," Gloria said sharply. "And I'll thank you not to behave in this disgraceful way. This is my sitting room, and I won't have it defiled like this."

"Quite right, too," Clementine added, seating herself in the nearest chair and fixing her brother with a cool gaze. "Oh, Charles, you are so like Father—he had no soul either. These two young people are in love, and with luck they'll marry. This young girl may be the mother of your great-grandchildren, and there's nothing you can do about it. So stop ranting before you burst a blood vessel. Think of your blood pressure."

"To blazes with my blood pressure! I'll put a stop to this. I'll go and see that fool Lavender—I don't know what in blazes he's thinking, allowing this idiot to sign away his fortune from the family."

"That's enough!"

The voice, sharp and commanding, stopped him cold. It was Gloria—and none of them had ever heard her raise her voice in anger before.

"I shall ask you to leave now Charles."

He stared at her, taken aback, but she went on, her tone quieter and icier.

"And the only fool in this room is not my son—but you. Now go."

Chapter 21

When Charles had gone—followed closely by his son and grandson—Gloria let out a long sigh.

"Oh, Newman, could we have some fresh tea, please?"

"Certainly, madam."

As he passed Clementine, she gave him a quick wink. He grinned in return. When she and Sally had arrived earlier, Sally had dashed through the door without waiting for Harold to open it, while Clementine had followed at her usual unhurried pace.

"Good afternoon, Newman."

"Good afternoon, madam."

There was a mutual respect between the two. Harold admired Clementine's spirit—she never let her brother browbeat her, and Harold privately suspected Charles Potter might even be a little afraid of her. She never raised her voice, but she always knew exactly how to handle him.

For her part, Clementine valued Newman's discretion and his unfailing sense of the household's undercurrents. He always seemed to know precisely what was happening, and with whom.

"I believe my brother is here," she said now.

"Yes, madam, though I'm afraid Mr. Potter is… a little agitated."

Clementine smiled faintly. "Yes, I can hear that. And where exactly is he being agitated?"

Even at this distance, Charles's voice was a steady rumble of outrage.

"In Mrs. Potter's sitting room, madam."

Clementine's brows lifted. "Oh dear. Gloria won't like that. A lady's sitting room, Newman, is sacrosanct—one does *not* raise one's voice in it."

"No, madam."

"Well," Clementine said, "I suppose I had better go and calm him down before he has an apoplexy."

Now, with the storm over and the tranquillity of Gloria's sitting room restored, the two women overlooked the rose garden and drank soothing camomile tea. Clementine gave a contented sigh.

"I'm so sorry, Gloria dear, about Charles. I don't know what gets into him. Father was the same—he could work himself into a rage over the most trivial things."

"Is it trivial?" Gloria asked quietly. "What if he's right, and this girl is only after Marcus's money?"

Clementine's gaze sharpened. "Surely you don't believe that? Marcus is a good judge of character, and he's known this girl for months. If she were that sort, she'd have found another prospect long ago. And didn't he say she knows nothing of his wealth?"

Gloria sighed and nodded. "Yes, you're right. It's just that Marcus is so in love with her—I don't want him to be hurt."

"I'm sure he won't be," Clementine said. "He's a sensible

boy. It will work out for the best. Don't let Charles plant ideas in your head."

Charles was very fond of his daughter-in-law. She was, in his eyes, the perfect wife for his son—born to the right background, from a family with both wealth and standing in the community. He regretted their quarrel, but in his mind he *had* to prove to her that young Marcus was wrong about this girl. After all, it wouldn't be the first time a gold-digger had wormed her way into a Potter heart. And Charles knew all too well what that could mean—his own heart had once been smashed to smithereens by one.

Determined, he stormed into Edward Lavender's office, striding past the reception desk without so much as a glance at the secretary. Without knocking, he went straight into the inner office.

Edward's secretary, Lavinia Wentworth, hurried after him. "I'm sorry, Mr. Lavender—he just walked in."

"It's all right, Lavinia. That's fine." Edward leaned back in his chair, eyeing Charles with mild exasperation. "Well, Charles, I don't need to ask why you're here. This is about young Marcus's will."

"Of course it is. You didn't think I'd ignore it, did you?"

"Not for a moment," Edward replied evenly, "but there's nothing you can do. He's of legal age, and it's all perfectly above board."

"I'll go to court and have it overturned."

Edward sighed. "You know that's nonsense. No judge in his right mind would overturn it—there's no reason."

"I'll *find* a reason. Say he's not in his right mind after all he's been through in England."

"And you think his commanding officer and fellow airmen would attest to that? Don't talk rubbish, Charles."

Charles glared at him. "Why didn't you talk him out of it?"

"I *tried*. The boy was adamant. If I hadn't drawn up his will, he'd simply have gone somewhere else to do it."

Charles's shoulders slumped; at last, he admitted defeat. Dropping heavily into the chair opposite, he sighed. "Yes… I suppose so. So what do we actually know about this girl?"

Edward shrugged. "Nothing—except that Marcus is smitten with her."

Charles rose to his feet. "Well, I just hope this isn't history repeating itself." Without another word, he walked out of the office looking like a broken man.

"Amen to that," Edward murmured quietly to himself.

Not long after his grandfather had gone, Marcus Junior arrived to review his will and sign it.

Before the pen touched paper, Edward made one last attempt. "Are you *quite* sure, Marcus, that this is what you want?"

"I've never been more certain of anything in my life, sir. Yes—this is what I want."

"Very well."

Edward pressed the buzzer on his desk. Lavinia appeared.

"Oh, Lavinia, I need you to witness Mr. Potter's signature."

"Yes, sir."

Marcus signed the document in a firm hand. Edward and Lavinia added their own signatures, and with that, the matter was settled. Lavinia slipped quietly back to her desk.

"I spoke to your father about that other matter," Edward

said, "and I'll arrange the transfer in a day or so."

"Thank you, sir. Father's given me a letter of recommendation for Maureen so she can open an account in England. Then he'll start sending money over."

"That's good. I understand she needs to get away from her father."

"Yes—he's quite brutal. She wants to take her mother with her, get her away too. And now she'll have the money to do it."

Edward gave him a thoughtful look. "I'm sure you'll help her."

"Yes. I owe it to Danny to make sure she's safe."

Edward extended his hand. Marcus took it, and they shook firmly.

"It was good to see you again, sir, and thank you for everything."

"Yes—it was good to see you too, Marcus. Take care, and come back to us safely."

"I will, sir. God willing."

Edward stood at the window and watched the young man walk down the street. He prayed silently—not only for Marcus, but for all the young men—to come home safe.

Jenny was as jumpy as a kitten. She had asked for the afternoon off so she'd have plenty of time to get ready for Marcus's return. She knew he would be back at the base by three o'clock and would come straight to her, so she wanted everything perfect.

Her mother had let her indulge in the luxury of a proper bath—no hurried wash at the sink today. She'd washed her hair until it shone, slipped into her newest dress, and carefully pulled on a pair of real nylons Marcus had given her—not just the usual black pencil line drawn up the back of her leg.

Every time a sound came from outside, Jenny jumped.

"Was that the door?" she asked for the twelfth time.

Veronica, amused and sympathetic, shook her head. "I'll make you a cup of tea. You need to relax—you'll be worn out before he even gets here."

Finally, a knock came at the door. Jenny was across the sitting room and in the hallway in a heartbeat—Veronica had never seen anyone move so fast. And then she was in his arms, being hugged and kissed until she could hardly breathe, tears of pure joy spilling down her cheeks.

"Oh, Marcus—I've missed you so much."

"I've missed you too."

Marcus felt a small tug at his trouser leg and looked down to see a tiny child clutching at him. Smiling, he bent to lift her into his arms.

"And I've missed you too, Betty."

"Where did you go?" she asked solemnly.

"I went home to see my family."

"Is it a long way away?"

He laughed. "Yes—a very long way away."

Veronica greeted him warmly. "Welcome back, Marcus. How was your leave?"

"It was very good, thank you."

"Your family must have been pleased to see you."

"Yes, they were. It was good to catch up with everyone—I even visited my great aunt, who I hadn't seen in a while."

"Oh, that's wonderful. I bet she was pleased."

"She sure was. Still sprightly—slower than she used to be,

but still very much on the ball."

Ronald welcomed him back as though he were his own son, shaking his hand and clapping him so heartily on the back that Marcus half-suspected he'd been bruised in the process.

Once the greetings were over, Marcus turned to Jenny. "I have a letter from my father and a cheque for Maureen so she can open an account. Will you give it to her?"

"Of course I will. Oh, Marcus, that's wonderful—that means she and her mother can finally get away."

"Yes. The letter is a recommendation, so she won't need her father's permission to open the account."

"Well, that's just as well. He would never give it—and he can't know about Danny and the baby."

"Exactly. Also… I'd like to speak to her. There's something I think she should hear from me."

"Oh? What?"

"I'd rather wait until I've spoken to Maureen."

"All right. I'll ask her to come round tomorrow evening."

After tea, they strolled through the park. The evening was one of those fine September nights when summer still lingered, but the first hints of autumn glimmered in the golds and browns of the turning leaves. The season was poised between warmth and chill, and the soft breeze still carried a trace of late-summer gentleness.

The park was quiet—just a few couples taking advantage of the weather before winter closed in. Birds called softly in the trees. Jenny, who had always loved autumn, breathed it all in, thinking how perfect the evening felt.

As they approached a bench, Marcus nodded toward it. "Shall we sit for a while?"

They sat, watching squirrels chase each other up tree trunks and dart across the grass. Then, without warning, Marcus stood, pulled a small box from his pocket, and opened it. Dropping to one knee, he looked up at her.

"Jenny," he said, "will you do me the honour of becoming my wife?"

Tears of pure joy welled in her eyes. She nodded, her voice trembling. "Yes—I will marry you."

He slipped the ring onto her finger, then pulled her into his arms for a tender kiss.

"But my father—you'll have to ask my father," she said when they parted.

Marcus smiled. "I already did, before I went on furlough. He gave us his blessing."

"He never said a word."

"I suppose he didn't want to spoil the surprise."

She looked down at the ring, turning it so it caught the light.

"You do like it, don't you?" Marcus asked. "It was my grandmother's."

"Oh, Marcus, I love it. But shouldn't it go to one of your sisters?"

"No. Mother said she wanted you to have it—it was her mother's."

"Then I should write and thank her. Your parents know you were planning to ask me? They have no objection?"

"None whatsoever."

When Marcus and Jenny returned home, she showed her parents the ring. Veronica hugged and kissed them both, tears bright in her eyes—she had suspected Marcus's intentions, and her happiness for them was genuine. Her father embraced Jenny and shook Marcus's hand warmly.

"I think we still have some sherry left from Christmas," Veronica said. "This deserves a toast." She disappeared into the pantry and came back with a half bottle. Glasses were filled, and the young couple were toasted.

The next morning, Ruth and Maureen were delighted for her.

"Oh, Jenny, it's beautiful," Ruth said, admiring the ring.

Maureen echoed her, and both women hugged her, wishing her every happiness.

Jenny pulled an envelope from her handbag. "Marcus wanted me to give you this, Maureen—it's a letter of recommendation from his father for you to open a bank account, and a cheque. Now you can finally be free."

Maureen's eyes widened as she read. "Oh, Jenny—this is wonderful news, thank you."

But as she continued reading, her expression changed to shock.

"Is everything all right?" Ruth asked.

"I... I can't believe it. Here—read it."

Ruth and Jenny leaned over the letter. When they finished, they looked at each other, then back at Maureen.

"Did you know he had all this money?" Jenny asked.

Maureen shook her head. "No, he never said. Mr Potter says it's an inheritance. I knew Danny must have had something when he died, but I never realised how much."

"Yes—but how odd he never mentioned it. Oh—and Marcus wants to talk to you. I don't know what about, but can you come round this evening?"

"Yes, of course. I wonder what he wants."

Then her eyes shone, and her voice trembled. "Oh, heavens—you realise what this means, don't you? We can finally get away from him. Finally be free."

She didn't know whether to laugh or cry. Tears spilled down her cheeks as her friends hugged her.

"Oh, Maureen—we're so happy for you," they said.

That evening, when Maureen arrived, Marcus told her gently what he had discovered during his trip home.

"So you and Danny were related—and you never knew?"

Marcus shook his head. "No, we never knew. I wish I had. But it means I'll be related to the baby."

Her face softened. "Oh, that's wonderful. I'll keep in touch with Jenny, and hopefully we can meet occasionally."

"Where will you go? Do you have any idea?"

"I thought of Ireland—Danny talked about going there—but until the war ends, I don't think that's an option. It's too dangerous; they're sinking ships."

"Yes, I know. I wouldn't recommend it."

"So I think we'll go to Scotland. It's far enough away for him not to find us."

Marcus nodded, then reached into his pocket. "There's one more thing. This was given to me by Sister Angelica, one of the nuns at the Sisters of Mercy orphanage where Danny was raised after his mother died."

He handed her a small trinket box and an envelope containing certificates and photographs.

Maureen traced her fingers over the box. "It's beautiful. Was it Danny's mother's?"

"Well, it originally came from his grandmother, then down to his mother."

Her eyes shone with unshed tears. "I'll treasure it always. And when the baby grows up, I'll give it to him—or her—and tell them about their father. Thank you, Marcus, for everything you've done for me."

"I'm glad I could help. It's what Danny would have wanted me to do."

When Maureen got home, she told her mother. Cynthia's face lit up with joy.

"So you mean—we can really go?" she asked, almost breathless.

"Yes, Mum, we can really go. How much money do you have?"

"Not much, love, but I know where he keeps some, and we can get it. Why—if you have the cheque, surely you can just cash it?"

"I can't open an account until we reach Scotland. I can't risk him finding out. I have a little saved, but we just need enough for the train and a couple of nights in a hotel until I can open the account and cash the cheque. Once we get to Scotland, it'll be fine."

Her mother patted her hand. "Leave it to me, love. I know he's got plenty stashed—he thinks I don't know, but I'm not as stupid as he likes to think."

"Right—tomorrow, after he's gone to work, we'll get packed up and go. Is that all right with you, Mum?"

"All right? It's more than all right! Oh, I won't be able to sleep tonight knowing this will be the last night I have to put up with him."

Maureen looked at her mother, a knot of worry forming. She couldn't risk her father guessing what they planned.

"Mum, you must act normally. He can't know. If he finds out—you know what will happen to both of us. Can you do that?"

Her mother's face grew serious. She knew better than anyone what he was capable of. "Yes, love, don't worry. I'm sorry—I just got carried away."

"I know, Mum. I did too—for a while."

The following morning, as soon as her father had left, Maureen said, "Right, Mum—where's this money?"

Cynthia went to his bureau, opened the top drawer, and lifted out a small cash box.

"Do you have the key?" Maureen asked.

"No—but we'll break it open. Fetch the carving knife—that should do it."

After some effort, the lock gave way. When they lifted the lid, both women were shocked by the contents. They counted the notes and coins—twenty-five pounds, seven shillings, and sixpence.

"Good heavens," Cynthia said. "I hadn't realised just how much he was keeping back. He's always kept me short of money—but this? Well, he'll have a shock when he gets home tonight."

"Have you got the ration books?"

"Yes, don't worry—they're in my bag. Right—let's get packed. Leave the breakfast dishes—he can do them when he gets home. One more thing for him to moan about."

In less than an hour, they were making their way toward the train station. Their cases were light—just the essentials they could carry—but their steps were quick and determined.

On the way, they stopped at the shop to say farewell to Jenny and her family, who wished them luck and embraced them warmly.

"Jenny, I'm sorry to ask you to do this," Maureen said, "but could you let them know at work? Just say it was last minute."

"Of course," Jenny replied without hesitation.

They stood together on the platform, exchanging quick hugs, the whistle already calling passengers to board. Maureen climbed into the carriage and found a seat beside her mother. As the guard's flag waved, she turned to look back through the open window. Jenny stood there, waving, her smile holding back the worry in her eyes.

Maureen lifted her hand in return, wondering—would she ever see her friend again? She hoped so, with all her heart.

The train jolted forward, gathering speed, the station slowly slipping away. Only when the last rooftops of the town vanished from view did Maureen and Cynthia finally let out long, shuddering sighs of relief.

Somewhere, she thought, Danny would know—and perhaps be glad—that they were free at last.

Chapter 22

When Albert Blackford arrived home that evening, the first thing he noticed was the darkness. Not a single lamp was lit. A prickling sense of unease crawled over him as he stepped inside. The air felt oddly still, empty.

He walked through to the kitchen, his boots heavy on the linoleum, and stopped dead. The breakfast dishes were still scattered across the table, the crusts of bread and cold tea just as they'd been left that morning. No smell of supper hung in the air—no stew bubbling, no bread warming.

Then his gaze fell on the bureau. The top drawer gaped open, and on the table beside it sat the cash box—smashed open, its jagged edges bent and twisted.

Rage surged through him. He stormed upstairs two steps at a time. In the bedroom, the wardrobe door swung ajar, empty hangers clinking faintly against one another. Drawers had been yanked out and rifled through; everyone was empty. His wife's clothes were gone.

He barged into his daughter's room. The sight was the same—wardrobe bare, drawers pulled out, suitcases missing. The beds looked oddly neat, stripped of anything personal.

Albert roared in fury, the sound bouncing off the walls.

Where the bloody hell had they gone? Wherever it was, he'd make them sorry. He'd drag them back—kicking and screaming if he had to.

Someone must know. His mind ticked over quickly. Yes—the Jacksons, down at the greengrocer's. Maureen was friendly with that little madam of theirs. She'd know.

He snatched his coat and marched down the street, rage in every step.

When Albert burst into the shop, Ronald was serving the last customer of the day—Mrs. Frances Davies—before closing up. Both looked up in surprise at the sudden crash of the door.

"Where are they?" Albert bellowed.

They stared at him.

"Well? Where are they? That slut of a girl of yours must know!"

"There's no call for that kind of language," Mrs. Davies said sharply.

Albert turned on her, eyes blazing. "Oh, shut up, you stupid woman!" he roared.

Her mouth fell open. "How dare you speak to me like that—"

Ronald came out from behind the counter, his voice low and dangerous. "Right—that's enough. Out, before I call Constable Peters."

"Call him if you want," Albert snarled, "but I still want to speak to that slut of a daughter of yours—"

Before he could finish, Ronald seized him by the lapels, dragging him forward.

And then another voice cut through the tension—an American voice, cool and deadly calm.

"I'd advise you to watch your language. You're talking about my fiancée. And if Mr. Jackson doesn't hit you, I will."

Albert swung round, finding himself face-to-chest with a man a head and shoulders taller than he was.

Mrs. Davies, standing stiff-backed, said coldly, "He's a foul-mouthed bully, that's what he is. And I'll be reporting you to Constable Peters for the way you spoke to me. I'll have you locked up."

With that, she swept from the shop, the bell over the door jangling sharply in her wake.

After Mrs. Davies had swept out, the fight seemed to drain from Albert. His shoulders sagged, and he slumped heavily into the chair by the counter, glaring at the worn floorboards.

Ronald crossed his arms. "Right… maybe you'd like to tell me what this is all about, Albert."

"They've gone," Albert muttered, his voice tight with a mix of disbelief and fury. "Taken everything and gone. No tea for me—didn't even clear the breakfast table. Dishes still sitting there, cold as ice. And they've taken all my money from my cash box."

Marcus and Ronald exchanged a glance—one of those silent looks that carried a whole conversation.

"Well," Ronald said at last, "what did you expect? It was only a matter of time before they'd had enough. After all these years of being downtrodden… you've only yourself to blame."

Albert looked up at them, and for the briefest moment there was something almost pitiful in his expression—confusion, perhaps even hurt. For a split second, they almost felt sorry for him.

Almost.

Then they remembered why Maureen and her mother had gone, and any trace of sympathy evaporated.

"Do you know where they've gone?" Albert asked, his voice rising again, edged with desperation.

Ronald shook his head. "No, I don't. And before you ask—neither does Jenny. Now, I'm trying to close up. It's well past closing time, and I need to get the blackout up before the ARP comes round. So, I'll ask you to leave."

Albert stared at him for a moment, jaw tight, but said nothing more. He rose slowly and walked out, the bell above the door giving one last sharp jangle as it shut behind him.

While Albert Blackford was raging in the greengrocer's, his wife and daughter were seated side by side in a softly lit dining carriage, enjoying the best meal they'd had in years aboard the night train to Scotland. The rattle and sway of the train was almost soothing, the scent of roast beef and warm bread filling the air.

"I'd love to have been a fly on the wall when he got home," Maureen said with a wicked grin, buttering a roll.

Her mother chuckled. "Me too. I know he'd have gone mad—especially over the money. And no tea ready, breakfast dishes still on the table..." She shook her head with a satisfied sigh. "Well, he's had it coming for years. Serves him right."

"The sad thing is," Maureen said, her voice softening a little, "if he'd been different, he could have had contact with his grandchild. Now... he'll never even know he has one."

Her mother reached over and squeezed her hand. "That's

his loss, love. Not ours. We're going to have a good life—you, me, and this baby."

Maureen smiled faintly, feeling the train carry them farther and farther from the life they had left behind—and toward the one they were finally free to build.

In September, the battle of Stalingrad began in earnest, and there was an Irish Republic Army riot in Belfast. Australian and US forces defeated the Japanese forces at Milne Bay, Papua. The Black Sea port of Novorossiysk is taken by the Germans. A Japanese plane drops more incendiaries on Oregon but with little effect. Hitler spoke to his people and boasted that Stalingrad would be taken. October saw a minor victory when British Commandos raided Sark, one of the Channel Islands, capturing one German soldier. By mutual arrangement, the Allies agree on a strategy whereby Americans will bomb in the daytime and the RAF at night. Second Battle of El Alamein begins with massive Allied bombardment of German positions. By November the second Battle of El Alamein ended when German forces under Erwin Rommel were forced to retreat at night. The United States Combat Command "B" of the 1st Armoured Division lands east and west of Oran as part of Operation Torch. And Churchill makes a speech telling the people, "This is not the end. It is not even the beginning of the end. But it is, perhaps, the end of the beginning."

In December, gasoline rationing was introduced in the US, and President Roosevelt received a coded message telling him "The Italian navigator has landed in the new world." This message told him that Enrico Fermi and his team, at the

University of Chicago, had initiated the first nuclear chain reaction, which could turn the tide of the war.

"Do you think the war is nearly over?" Jenny asked, her eyes bright with cautious excitement.

Marcus gave a small shrug, his arm tightening around her shoulders. "I don't know, honey," he said quietly, "but I sure hope so."

That Christmas carried a different feeling from the ones before. Rationing still kept tables sparse—tiny portions of meat, carefully saved sugar, and eked-out butter—but there was something new in the air. People smiled a little more readily in the streets, sang carols with more warmth in their voices, and lingered over cups of tea as though the world might just be softening again.

Hope had crept in, tentative yet stubborn.

Maybe by next Christmas, it would all be over.

It was a thought everyone clung to—like a candle burning in a long, dark winter, flickering but refusing to go out.

January forty-three saw the tide turning, with many small gains for the allies and Russia, even the Jews in the Warsaw ghetto rose up for the first time. Suddenly Hitler was not getting it all his own way.

Winter softened into spring, bringing with it the familiar optimism of longer days and gentler skies. For Maureen and Cynthia, life had finally settled into a quiet, steady rhythm. They rented a small but cosy house in a sleepy rural community where everyone seemed to know everyone else.

Maureen had opened her bank account without difficulty, and the funds from America now arrived in regular intervals.

For the first time in their lives, money was no object. They could afford good food, warm clothes, and little luxuries that once would have been out of reach. Slowly, they began to make friends and were, in time, welcomed into the life of the village.

Maureen told their new neighbours she was a widow; her husband having served in the Air Force and been killed in action. The story—part truth, part necessity—earned her much sympathy, particularly as she was expecting a child. Officially, she kept her own surname, but unofficially she introduced herself as *Mrs Butchers*. Even the postman never questioned the occasional letter addressed to "Mrs Blackford."

In early May, Maureen gave birth to a healthy, bouncing baby boy. She named him Danny Marcus Butchers. He was the very image of his father—soft black curls framing his tiny face, eyes the warm brown of polished chestnut.

As she cradled him in her arms, she smiled through her tears.

"Hello, little Danny. How your daddy would love you."

She tilted her head back, whispering silently into the quiet room.

Well, Danny, here he is—your son. Thank you for him. At least I still have a piece of you. I will always love you, and I'll tell him all about you. He'll know your face, your smile. We will never forget you.

When Jenny received Maureen's letter announcing the birth,

she was delighted.

"Oh, Marcus—she's named him after you as well as Danny. Isn't that lovely?"

Marcus blinked in surprise. "After me? Why on earth?"

"Because she wanted to thank you—for everything you've done for her," Jenny replied warmly.

Jenny wrote back at once, sending Maureen their heartfelt congratulations, along with those of her parents and Ruth. In her letter, she also shared news of Maureen's father—how, since their departure, his life had unravelled. He spent every evening in the pub, drinking heavily, and had eventually lost his job. Not long after, he was forced out of his house. One day he simply left the village, and nobody had seen him since.

In early June, devastating news reached the base—and, soon after, the village. Marcus's plane had been shot down over Apeldoorn in Holland during the return leg of a bombing mission on Düsseldorf.

The raid itself had gone well. The target was hit, and the crew were heading home, their spirits high, when, without warning, two Messerschmitts swooped in from the cloud cover.

"We've got company, Skip," Chuck called over the intercom.

Kevin, the new tail gunner who had replaced Danny, opened fire, trying to drive them off. But the enemy pilots were toying with them, darting in and out of range in a cruel game of cat and mouse. Marcus banked hard, weaving and diving to spoil their aim, but the constant manoeuvres made it harder for Kevin to get a clean shot.

Then—disaster. One engine coughed, sputtered, and died. The bomber lurched, nose dipping toward the ground. Marcus fought the controls, wrestling the great machine back into line, but he knew the truth—she wasn't going to make it home. A fresh burst of cannon fire tore through the fuselage, and that was the end.

"Bail out!" Marcus ordered, his voice firm despite the chaos.

One by one, the crew jumped. Only Alvin remained with him.

"Come on, Skip—you too. Just leave it!"

Reluctantly, Marcus grabbed his chute and leapt. Alvin followed moments later, and as he drifted down, he spotted Marcus tangled in the branches of a tall tree just to his right. Alvin hit the ground running, shedding his parachute and heading toward him. He had no idea where the others had landed, but Marcus was closest, and he had to get him down before the enemy arrived.

Then he heard it—shouting. Figures were racing through the trees toward Marcus. Alvin froze, straining to make out the language. It wasn't English. It sounded like German… but maybe, just maybe, it was Dutch. He dared not go closer. Moments later, they had cut Marcus free and carried him off into the woods. Alvin's only hope was that they were Dutch Resistance and not German soldiers.

Back in the village, Jenny started at every sound.

"Was that the door?" she asked her mother for what felt like the hundredth time.

"No, dear, I don't think so. Settle down, love. He's probably just held up—he'll be here as soon as he can."

By ten o'clock, she knew he wasn't coming. Her parents

exchanged a troubled glance. Her father put a reassuring arm around her shoulders.

"It'll be work, love, I promise you. Like your mum said—he'll be here when he can."

"But it's been two days, and no word," she whispered.

"I know, love. But it was the same in the last war—sometimes we went days without knowing anything, and then suddenly your dad would appear as if nothing had happened. And remember—careless talk costs lives. They can't just tell you where they are."

That night, Jenny slept fitfully, tossing and turning, waking with a pounding headache. She dragged herself out of bed and dressed for work, hoping the routine would steady her nerves.

When Ruth saw her, she frowned. "Jenny, you look awful. Are you sure you're up to working?"

"Yes. I can't sit around the house all day waiting—it'll drive me mad. I'll be better at work."

Miss Penheart took one look at her and shook her head.

"Jenny, go home. You can't be here looking like that—and frankly, you're no good to us in this state."

Tears filled Jenny's eyes. Miss Penheart's voice softened. She led her to the staff room and pressed a cup of tea into her hands.

"My dear, I know exactly how you feel—but you must have hope. I'm sure there will be a perfectly logical explanation. Now finish your tea and go home."

When Jenny stepped through her front door, her mother looked up in surprise.

"Jenny—what are you doing home in the middle of the

morning?"

Jenny sank into the nearest chair and broke down. Her mother gathered her into her arms, holding her until the sobs subsided. Then she fetched her an aspirin, a fresh cup of tea, and tucked her into bed.

When Ruth came home from work, she stopped by the Jacksons' to check in.

"Still no news, I'm afraid," Veronica said quietly. "Jenny's still in bed—but I have to say, Ruth, I fear the worst."

"I know, Mrs. Jackson." Ruth's voice was heavy with worry. "I don't know what else we can do except be here for her."

By the next day, whispers were moving through the village—word that a plane had been shot down. For those who knew, it was enough to confirm their worst fears. It had to be Marcus's crew. Marjory was distraught; her budding romance with Chuck had been one of the bright spots in recent months. They had been spending more and more time together, and she had begun to imagine a future with him. Now she was terrified she would never see him again.

Meanwhile, in occupied Holland, Alvin remained hidden among the undergrowth, watching helplessly as Marcus was cut free from the tree and carried away. The men weren't in uniform, but that meant nothing—they could still be German collaborators. The language they spoke sounded like German to his untrained ear, and he dared not risk approaching. For now, his only certainty was that he needed to find a way back to England and report what had happened. Where the rest of the crew had landed—or whether they were even alive—he could only guess.

As dawn's pale light began to spread through the trees, Alvin knew he couldn't linger. The Germans would have seen the plane come down and would be combing the area. He crept out of his hiding place, moving slowly, pausing often to listen. At the sound of a rustle nearby, he dropped flat to the ground, willing himself invisible.

Then—voices. One in particular caught his attention.

"Shit—these bloody brambles."

Alvin's head shot up. "Chuck? That you?"

Chuck froze, scanning the bushes until he spotted him. "Alvin!" he whispered back, relief washing over his face. "Boy, am I glad to see you. Have you seen any of the others?"

"No—just the Skip. He got tangled up in a tree and was cut down by some locals. I don't know if they were Germans or not."

Chuck let out a low whistle. "Bloody hell. Well, let's hope the bastards stick to the Geneva Convention and treat him properly."

"I wouldn't bet on it," Alvin muttered

"Either way, we can't stay here. Let's move."

They crawled out from the undergrowth and began walking, keeping low where they could. By midday, they had covered several miles.

"Don't know about you," Alvin said, "but I'm starving—and parched."

"Yeah, me too." Chuck pointed ahead. "Look—farmhouse. Smoke from the chimney. Might mean a hot meal."

"You reckon they're friendly?" Alvin asked.

Chuck shrugged. "Only one way to find out. We need food, water, and maybe help. If they call in Jerry, well… at least we'll end up in a POW camp instead of shot in the woods."

Alvin didn't like the odds, but Chuck was right—there weren't many choices.

As they approached the farmhouse, a young boy burst out the front door. He stopped short when he saw them, staring for a moment before bolting back inside. Moments later, he reappeared with a man in tow. The boy spoke quickly in a language neither airman understood, pointing toward them.

The man looked them over, then beckoned. *"Kom snel, kom binnen."* He gestured toward the open door.

Inside, a woman stood at a table, her hands dusted with flour. She glanced from her husband to the strangers.

"Wie zijn deze mannen? Engels?"

"Volgens mij, ja," her husband replied.

"English?" Alvin asked cautiously. "Do you speak English?"

Both shook their heads. *"Nee, geen Engels."*

"I don't think they do," Chuck muttered.

Alvin tapped his lips and mimed lifting a spoon to his mouth. "Food?" he said, pointing toward the pot on the stove.

The woman nodded. *"Ja, zit."* She motioned for them to sit, then turned to her husband.

"Jan, ga Anton halen, breng hem hier."

Jan wiped his hands on his trousers, grabbed his coat, and left.

While they waited, the woman ladled stew into bowls and poured strong, dark coffee. The two airmen ate hungrily, the warmth of the food seeping into their chilled bones, wondering who "Anton" was—and whether he would be friend or foe.

Chapter 23

When Jan returned, he brought with him a wiry, sharp-eyed man who stepped forward and introduced himself.

"I am Anton. So—you are not English, but Americans? Jan say you English."

"No, we're Americans, but stationed in England," Chuck explained. "Why has he brought you? Can you help us?"

Anton gave a short nod. "*Ja,* but first—you must change clothes. You cannot walk around in uniform." He turned to Jan. *"Kleding. Zij hebben kleding nodig. Hebben wij wat?"*

"Ja, kom."

Anton gestured toward the back room. "Go—Jan will find clothes."

The two airmen followed him and returned a short while later in worn but serviceable civilian clothing. Anton gave an approving glance. "*Nu* we wait for dark—then we go."

"Where are we going?" Alvin asked.

"Katwijk. I have a friend—he take you to England in his boat."

"Is it far?"

"One hundred kilometres."

"That's a long way. Do you have transport?"

"I have truck, but we can take only short way. Then—we walk."

While waiting for nightfall, Alvin and Chuck stretched out on benches near the stove. They hadn't slept in more than twenty-four hours and were utterly spent. The quiet murmur of voices and the gentle crackle of the fire lulled them into a deep, dreamless sleep.

When they woke, the room was dim, the windows already covered. A tall, gangly youth—no more than eighteen—stood near the door, shifting his weight nervously.

"Mijn zoon, Willem," Anton said by way of introduction.

Alvin and Chuck shook his hand, then climbed into the back of the truck alongside Anton and Willem. They thanked the farmer and his wife warmly before leaving.

"What about our uniforms?" Alvin asked. "If the Germans find them, they'll know you helped us. You could be in trouble."

"They are already burned," Anton said simply.

Chuck gave a wry laugh. "Uncle Sam's not gonna like that—burning military uniforms."

"Where are we, anyway? What's this place called?" Alvin asked.

"Apeldoorn," Anton replied. "We are in Apeldoorn. No more talk. Quiet now."

By morning, the truck rattled to a stop on the outskirts of Gouda. Anton climbed out and motioned for them to stay put.

"You wait."

He disappeared into a large, weathered brick building,

leaving Willem behind to keep watch. A few minutes later, Anton reappeared with a woman in her mid-twenties. Willem hopped out, grinning, and kissed her on the cheek.

"Mijn zusje," Anton told them.

"Your sister?" Alvin guessed.

"Ja, kom," Anton confirmed, beckoning them to follow.

They stepped inside the building and were instantly enveloped by a heady wave of fragrance—rows upon rows of flowers in every hue stretched out before them. The air was thick with the scent of fresh blooms, sweet and almost dizzying. Men and women worked quickly at long tables, sorting blossoms into bundles and packing them carefully into boxes bound for the German markets.

The woman led them quietly through the bustle, up a narrow staircase worn smooth by countless feet. They emerged into a series of plain rooms above the flower hall. Anton and the woman exchanged a few hushed words in Dutch, then she slipped away.

"What happens now?" Chuck asked.

"Now we wait until dark," Willem replied. *"Mijn tante*—my aunt—she will bring food."

The room was sparsely furnished: a plain table, three chairs, and a pile of burlap sacks in the corner. True to Willem's word, the woman soon returned, carrying a basket of bread, cheese, and smoked fish. They ate in silence, hunger overtaking any need for conversation.

When the meal was over, Anton stood. "We sleep," he said simply. They stretched out on the sacks, letting the warmth and the food lull them into uneasy rest.

Night fell, and with it came movement. Anton roused them quietly. "We go now—on bikes. No more truck. We leave truck here."

Four bicycles appeared from the shadows, and within minutes they were riding along narrow country lanes under a star-pricked sky. The air was cold and smelled faintly of damp earth and salt from the distant coast.

Within a couple of hours they were approaching their destination. "We go round Leiden," Anton warned. "Not safe to go in."

"Are there many Germans here?" Alvin asked.

"Yes. And NSB also."

Chuck frowned. "NSB? What's that?"

"Nazi collaborators," Anton said grimly. He spat on the ground. "When war over, they pay."

At last, they rolled into the quiet fishing village of Katwijk. Anton led them to a weathered house by the harbour and knocked—three times, then twice, then three times again. The door swung open to reveal a large, broad-shouldered man with a thick beard. Without a word, he ushered them inside.

The interior was dark; only when the door was bolted did the man light a small oil lamp. He studied the two airmen. *"Engels soldaten?"*

"Nee, Amerikaanse vliegers. Zij komt uit Engeland. Misschien mogelijk jij deze mensen meenemen?" Anton asked him.

"Natuurlijk," the bearded man replied.

Anton turned to Alvin and Chuck. "This is Kees. He will take you to England. He has a boat. *Nu wij gaan—success.*"

Alvin extended his hand. "Thank you for everything. We

owe you a lot."

"You are not the first," Anton said, "and there will be more."

With that, Anton and Willem were gone.

Kees gestured. *"Kom."* He led them through narrow, twisting alleys down to the darkened harbour, where a small fishing boat bobbed gently in the water. He motioned for them to climb aboard, then untied the mooring rope and jumped in after them.

The engine coughed to life, and the boat eased forward into the open water. Kees pointed to the narrow stairs leading below deck. "You go—Duitse Lichten."

They hesitated, but his expression sharpened. *"Snel, nu."*

A bright beam slashed across the dark water, fixing on the boat. The two men ducked below as Kees waved lazily to the German patrol. *"Vis!"* he called, holding up a bucket. Laughter echoed back across the water, and the light blinked off.

By mid-morning, the chill of the North Sea gave way to the pale outline of the English coast. Great Yarmouth lay ahead, grey and familiar. Kees nosed the boat as close to shore as he dared.

"We here," he said.

The two airmen grinned their thanks, then leapt overboard into the frigid water. The shock of it stole their breath, but they pushed through, wading ashore with soaked trousers and boots squelching.

They were back in England. Now all they had to do was find their way to base.

They agreed their best option was to head straight for the nearest police station. The moment they stepped inside, the constable on duty looked up from his desk and frowned. The sight before him was curious—two tall men, clearly not English by the look of them, dressed in odd, ill-fitting civilian clothes that looked like they belonged on the Continent.

"Hi," Chuck said casually.

The constable's eyes narrowed. "Are you… American?" he asked, his voice tinged with puzzlement.

"Sure am," Chuck replied. "So's my buddy here."

The constable's gaze travelled up and down their mismatched outfits. "And why, might I ask, are you dressed like that?"

"It's a long story," Chuck said, "but right now, we need you to contact our base and get us transport back."

"Oh aye? And where's this 'base' of yours, then?" the constable asked, clearly sceptical.

Chuck gave him the details crisply. "You need to speak to the base commander, Colonel Roy Withers. Tell him Sergeant Chuck Brierly, radio operator, and Second Lieutenant Alvin Peterson, co-pilot, need a ride back to base. We're Lieutenant Potter's crew."

The constable's eyes narrowed further. "So… if you're American airmen, why are you dressed like that? Been to a fancy-dress party, have you?"

"No," Chuck said flatly. "We got shot down over Holland. A farmer lent us these. Then we were brought back in a fishing boat."

"A fishing boat, you came back from Holland on a fishing boat?" The scepticism in his voice was almost a challenge.

"Well, I'll believe you—thousands wouldn't. Who am I calling again?"

Chuck went through the details again. The constable muttered something under his breath and disappeared through a side door. A few minutes later, he returned with a stocky sergeant in tow.

"Right, gentlemen," the sergeant said, folding his arms, "what's all this my constable's been telling me?"

Alvin and Chuck exchanged a weary look. Alvin asked bluntly, "Would you believe us if you were in our place?"

Chuck shook his head. "No. Probably not."

They went through the story yet again—shot down over Holland, rescued by a farmer, smuggled across to England by fishing boat. By the end of it, Alvin added, "Just make the call. We're tired, hungry, and soaked through. We just want to get back to base."

The sergeant didn't believe a word of it—but he picked up the phone anyway. When he returned from making the call, his whole manner had changed.

"Constable," he said briskly, "make these gentlemen a cup of tea and see if you can find some biscuits. Then get them some dry clothes."

"Really, Sarge?" Pollock asked, incredulous.

"Yes, really, Pollock. Now move it."

Back at the base, Colonel Roy Withers was still processing the message he'd just received. "Let me get this straight, Sergeant," he said slowly into the phone. "You're telling me that two of my airmen, reported shot down over Holland two nights ago, are sitting in your police station in Great Yarmouth?"

"Yes, sir," the sergeant replied. "That's about the size of it—at least, that's who they say they are."

"What do you mean, 'that's who they say they are'? They have identification, don't they?"

"No, sir. I'm afraid not."

"But their uniforms—surely they're wearing American Air Force uniforms?"

"Well… that's the thing, sir. They aren't wearing uniforms."

Withers frowned. "Then what in blazes are they wearing?"

The sergeant hesitated, as if embarrassed to say it. "Hard to describe, sir. Some sort of foreign clothing—clogs, baggy trousers, knitted pullovers…"

"I see," Withers said slowly. "But they are American? I mean, they sound American?"

"Oh yes, sir. Definitely American accents."

"Describe them."

The sergeant reeled off the description, and Withers' frown softened. "Yes… that sounds like them all right. I suppose they swapped clothes in case they ran into the Germans. Right—I'll send a jeep, but it'll take a while. Great Yarmouth's quite a trek. In the meantime, Sergeant, make them as comfortable as you can. They've been through a lot in the last forty-eight hours."

After hanging up the phone, Colonel Withers barked, "Corporal! Get me Sergeant White—on the double!"

Chalky White, as he was known across the base, was halfway through his coffee when a scrawny young corporal appeared in the doorway.

"What do you want?" Chalky grumbled. "You're disturbing

my break."

"The Colonel wants you—on the double, Sarge."

"What for?"

"Dunno, Sarge. He just said to get you."

Chalky sighed, muttering something about "no peace for the wicked," and stomped off toward the Colonel's office.

When he arrived, Colonel Withers looked up from his desk. "Ah, Sergeant. I need you to dispatch a jeep to Great Yarmouth and collect Second Lieutenant Peterson and Sergeant Brierly. They're at the police station."

Chalky blinked. "At the police station… in Great Yarmouth, sir? But I thought they were shot down in Holland a couple of nights ago."

"They were," Withers said dryly, "but somehow they've made it back to England and ended up in Great Yarmouth. I want them fetched—now."

Chalky's brow furrowed as he tried to process it.

"Yes, I'm as surprised as you are, Sergeant," Withers added. "The sooner they're back here, the sooner I can find out what happened."

Back at the motor pool, Chalky bellowed, "Dobson! Get your sorry hide in here!"

"Yes, Sarge?"

"Get a jeep with a full gas tank and head to the police station in Great Yarmouth."

"The police station in Great Yarmouth, Sarge? What for?"

"You're collecting Second Lieutenant Peterson and Sergeant Brierly."

"Right, Sarge." Dobson turned to leave, then stopped and frowned. "But weren't they shot down on a mission, Sarge?"

"Yes, Dobson, they were. Now they're back. And you get the pleasure of making sure they get home in one piece. So go."

Dobson took two more steps, then turned again. "Er... where is Great Yarmouth, Sarge?"

Chalky pinched the bridge of his nose. "I don't know, Dobson. Look it up on a bloody map. You *can* read a map, can't you?"

"Yes, Sarge."

"Then bloody well do it. On second thought, take Wilson with you—he can read a map, and you'll probably get lost."

Some hours later, Dobson and Wilson rolled up outside the Great Yarmouth police station. Inside, the desk sergeant greeted them with a nod.

"Brierly and Peterson?" Dobson asked.

The sergeant jerked a thumb toward the back. "Asleep in the cells."

Dobson's eyes widened. "You locked them up? Why?"

The sergeant rolled his eyes. "No, son, I didn't lock them up. They were tired. I *let* them sleep in there."

He sent a constable to rouse them. Alvin and Chuck emerged looking much more rested, thanked the police officers, and climbed into the waiting jeep. The engine growled to life.

Finally—they were headed back to familiar territory.

It was late when the jeep finally rolled back into the base, but Colonel Withers had left strict instructions—he was to be told the moment they returned.

Within minutes, Alvin and Chuck were seated in his office,

their uniforms replaced by ill-fitting Dutch civilian clothes, mud still crusted on their boots. The Colonel leaned forward, hands clasped on the desk.

"Right," he said briskly. "What happened—and how in God's name did you two manage to get back?"

Alvin recounted the story: the attack, the bailout, and how he'd seen Marcus get tangled in a tree.

"And the people who cut him down," Withers pressed, "you don't know if they were German or Dutch?"

"No, sir," Alvin admitted. "They weren't wearing uniforms, but... after meeting the Dutch people who helped us, I think—honestly—they were Dutch who cut the Skip down."

Withers exhaled slowly. "Let's hope to God you're right. What about the rest of the crew—did you see any of them?"

"No, sir," Alvin said. "Sergeant Brierly was the only one I met up with after we landed."

The Colonel turned to Chuck. "And you, Sergeant? Any sign of the others?"

"No, sir."

Withers' expression darkened. "Then we can only hope they've fallen into the hands of the Dutch resistance... and not the Germans. I'd better start writing to the families."

Then Alvin said, "One thing, though—Lieutenant Potter is engaged to a girl in the village. I think she ought to be told, and she should hear form someone she knows"

"Good Lord, I had no idea Potter was engaged." His eyes narrowed suddenly. "She's not pregnant, is she?"

Alvin and Chuck exchanged a glance, caught off-guard.

"No, sir," Alvin said firmly. "I'm pretty sure she isn't. Why?"

Withers leaned back. "When Butchers was killed, he left a girl pregnant. I can't have all my men running around leaving expectant mothers behind."

"No need to worry about the skip sir," Chuck put in. "That's not him."

"Well, that's a relief," Withers muttered. "Very well—who is she, and where does she live?"

"Sir... I know her quite well," Alvin said. "It might be better if I told her."

"Very well. Tomorrow then. No sense knocking on doors at this hour."

The following afternoon, Alvin knocked on the Jacksons' front door. Veronica answered.

The moment she saw him; her face drained of colour. "It's bad news, isn't it?" she asked quietly.

"I'm sorry, ma'am," Alvin said gently. "I wish I had better news. But I wanted to tell Jenny myself."

Veronica stepped aside. "She's in the kitchen. You'd better come through."

Jenny looked up as they entered—and the look on Alvin's face told her everything.

"Oh no... please, no..." she whispered, tears spilling down her cheeks.

Veronica went to her at once, wrapping her arms around her. Alvin started to speak, but Jenny's knees buckled and she fainted. He caught her just before she hit the floor.

"Where shall I put her, ma'am?"

"I'll get her to bed," Veronica said quickly.

"Would you like me to carry her for you?"

"That would be helpful, thank you."

Veronica led the way to Jenny's room, and Alvin laid her gently on the bed. As he turned to go, he felt a tug at his trouser leg. Looking down, he saw a small child peering up at him with curious eyes.

"Well, hi there," Alvin said softly. "You must be Betty."

"Why is Jenny asleep?" the little girl asked.

Veronica looked down at her youngest. "Oh, Betty—not now, love. Go and see Daddy."

Alvin glanced at her. "Would you like me to take her down to your husband?"

"Oh, would you?"

"Certainly." He scooped Betty up into his arms. "Let's go see Daddy so Jenny can sleep."

Betty tilted her head. "Can I have a shiny apple?"

Alvin smiled. "Well, I guess Daddy might just find you one if you ask nicely."

Just as Alvin stepped into the shop from the Jacksons' back door, Betty perched comfortably in his arms, Ruth came in from the street. She stopped short when she saw him.

"Goodness," she said in surprise. "I didn't know you were back. Are the others here as well?"

"No," Alvin replied quietly. "Just Chuck and me."

Her expression shifted. "Oh no… is Marcus—?" She couldn't bring herself to finish the question.

"No," Alvin said quickly. "At least… he wasn't, the last time I saw him. He was caught in a tree after bailing out. Some Dutch—possibly resistance—were bringing him down. I think he's in good hands."

Ronald, who had been serving a customer at the counter, came over, concern etched on his face.

"Good Lord. Does Jenny know?"

"Well, she knows he didn't make it back," Alvin said. "But she passed out before I could tell her what happened. She's lying on her bed now—Mrs Jackson's with her. She asked if you could look after Betty for her, sir."

"I'm busy," Ronald said, glancing around the shop. "I can't have her underfoot here."

Ruth stepped forward. "Would you like me to take her home with me, Mr Jackson? She can have her tea at my house, and even stay the night if need be."

Ronald's face softened. "Oh, Ruth—are you sure your mother won't mind?"

"Of course not," she said with a smile. "She loves little Betty."

She bent down so she was at the child's eye level. "Betty, how would you like to come home with me and have your tea at my house?"

"Ooh, can I?" Betty's eyes lit up.

"Of course. Let's go and get your colouring book and crayons, and then we'll go see my mummy."

"Thanks, Ruth. I appreciate it," Ronald said sincerely.

"It's no trouble," Ruth replied. "Tell Jenny I'll pop round later to see how she is—and if you want me to keep Betty tonight, I can pick up her night things."

When Ruth arrived home with Betty skipping along beside her, her mother looked up from the kitchen table, curiosity knitting her brow.

"Why have you brought Betty back? Is something wrong?" Gillian Mitchell asked.

Ruth set Betty's things down and explained what had happened—Marcus missing, Jenny fainting when she heard the news.

“Oh, that poor girl,” Gillian said softly. “That’s terrible. But the lad who brought the news thinks Marcus is with the Dutch resistance? Well, that’s good news, surely?”

“Yes, if they were Dutch resistance,” Ruth agreed. “But Jenny fainted before he could tell her, so she doesn’t know. I imagine her mother will tell her when she comes round. Anyway, I said we’d give Betty her tea, and later I’ll pop over to see how Jenny is. If they want us to keep Betty till morning, I’ll fetch her night things.”

“Of course,” Gillian said warmly. “That’s what friends are for—helping in times of crisis.”

Chapter 24

When Jenny came to, she found her mother sitting on the side of the bed, holding her hand.

"What happened?" she murmured.

"You passed out, dear. Feeling better?"

Jenny nodded slowly, but the fog of confusion cleared in an instant as memory came rushing back.

"Marcus... oh no, Marcus." The words emerged in a strangled whisper before the tears broke free. She began to sob—deep, racking sobs that seemed to drain the strength from her.

Her mother held her close, letting her cry until the storm began to subside. Then, when Jenny had regained a fragile hold on her emotions, Veronica gently eased her back against the pillows.

"Alvin said Marcus was taken down from the tree," she told her softly. "He thinks the people who took him were Dutch. They weren't in uniform, so he doesn't believe they were German. If he's with the Dutch, then he's in safe hands. You have to hold on to that, dear."

Jenny nodded faintly. "I know," she whispered. "But I just want him home."

"I know, dear." Her mother gave her hand a reassuring pat.

"Now, I'm going to make you a nice cup of tea. You wash your face and come down when you're ready. I'll see you in a minute."

Just as Veronica reached the bottom of the stairs, Ruth came through from the shop.

"Oh, Mrs Jackson—how's Jenny?"

"Well… as you'd expect, really, love. I'm just about to put the kettle on. Do you want one? She should be down in a minute."

"Oh yes, I'd love one, thanks." Ruth hesitated. "I wondered if you wanted us to keep Betty tonight?"

"Oh, love, I don't want to be a nuisance. Are you sure?"

"Of course. She's been no trouble at all—she's had her tea, and when I left she was sitting on Dad's lap playing clapping games. Mum and Dad are in their element having a young child in the house. They always wanted more children, but I was all they got."

"Well… it would be helpful. I don't think Jenny's up to answering the million and one questions Betty will have about why she's upset."

"If you give me her night things—and Mr Cuddles. I've had strict instructions not to forget Mr Cuddles."

Veronica smiled. "Yes, she won't sleep without him."

At that moment Jenny appeared in the doorway. Ruth stood and hugged her tightly.

"Oh, Jenny, I'm so sorry. But Alvin thinks the Dutch took him—that's hopeful."

"I know, but… if they did, why didn't they send him home with Alvin and Chuck?"

"I don't know," Ruth admitted. "But I'm sure he'll be home

soon."

Across the ocean in Vermont, Marcus's family were reeling from the news. Gloria was devastated, praying more fervently than she had in her life. *Please, God, bring my son home safely,* became her mantra day and night.

Marcus's father was equally shaken—his eldest child shot down and somewhere in Holland, fate uncertain. The fact that no one could say for sure who had taken him only deepened the torment.

In the Potter household, Clementine openly chastised her brother Charles for the way he had treated Marcus during his leave, particularly over his choice of a wife.

Sally and Susan took it even further, refusing to speak to Richard altogether, treating him as if he were invisible.

"If anything happens to him, I shall never speak to you again as long as I live," Susan declared.

Sally's words cut even deeper. "I hate you, Richard. I really hate you. You're such a snob, and because of you, he left under a cloud with Grandfather. I hate you both. Why don't you go and live with him—you deserve each other."

He returned to college and stayed away. During the holidays, he chose to stay with friends, unable to face his family's simmering wrath. Charles made attempts to reconcile with his son and daughter-in-law, but Gloria refused even to see him, and Marcus Sr. remained distant and cold. The Potter household was in turmoil—every conversation edged with tension—and no one seemed to know how to steer it back onto an even keel.

When Edward Lavender received the news about Marcus, he was equally stunned. He read and re-read Marcus's instructions concerning his will. While the provisions regarding the full inheritance would not take effect until death was officially confirmed, there was another clause—an instruction to make a payment to Jenny if Marcus was shot down but not confirmed dead.

He picked up the phone and called Marcus Sr. to explain.

"What would you like me to do, Marcus? I can wait a few more weeks, or I can pay the young woman now. It's been nearly a month since he was shot down."

Marcus sighed heavily. "No… if that's what Marcus wanted, then you should carry out his wishes. By the way, how much did he tell you to pay her?"

"Fifty thousand. The rest would be paid only if he's confirmed dead."

"Good Lord—that's a great deal of money, Edward."

"Yes, I know. I tried to persuade him to reduce it, but he was adamant. Do you want me to reduce it now?"

"No. If it's what he wanted, then we have to respect his wishes. Go ahead and pay her, Edward. I just hope his faith in her is justified."

"Amen to that," the solicitor murmured.

When the letter from America arrived, Jenny turned it over and over in her hands before daring to open it. Her parents, watching from the kitchen table, exchanged glances—wondering if she ever would.

Finally, her father said, "It won't open itself, love."

"I know… but the envelope is from a solicitor. Why would a solicitor in America be writing to me?"

"Well, like your dad said—unless you open it, you'll never know."

Jenny slit open the envelope. A folded letter slid out, and with it, a cheque. The moment her eyes landed on the amount, she gasped and dropped it as if it had burned her fingers.

Veronica and Ronald both sprang forward, half-expecting her to faint. Her mother picked up the cheque and stared at it in shock before passing it to her husband. The three of them sat frozen, staring at the slip of paper as though it might leap up and bite them.

At last, Ronald found his voice. "What does the letter say, Jenny?"

As though only just remembering she still held it, Jenny unfolded the letter and read aloud:

Dear Miss Jackson,

Firstly, allow me to introduce myself. My name is Edward Lavender, and I am the Potter family solicitor.

Whilst on leave earlier this year, Marcus came to see me in order to make his will. In the event of his death, you are the sole beneficiary. However, he also instructed me that, should he be shot down and not confirmed dead, you were to be given an amount from his trust fund. The amount stipulated was fifty thousand dollars.

As you can imagine, we are all extremely shocked to hear Marcus is missing in action. We hope and pray that he will be returned to us in good health. In the meantime, if I can be of service to you, please do not hesitate to contact me.

Assuring you of my best intentions at all times,

Yours sincerely,

Edward Lavender, Attorney-at-Law

Jenny read it twice, scarcely able to believe the words on the page. "This is unbelievable. First Danny, now Marcus… are all Americans as wealthy as this?"

She handed the letter to her parents, who read it in silence.

"I have to give it back," she blurted. "I can't keep it. I don't want it—I just want Marcus home and safe."

"Of course you do, love," Ronald said gently. "But he obviously wanted you to have this. I don't think you should do anything hasty. Besides, wouldn't giving it back be like throwing his gift in his face? First thing tomorrow, I'll take you to the bank so you can open an account and pay the cheque in. You don't have to spend a penny of it—just leave it until you decide what you're going to do. I also think you should write to this Mr. Lavender and thank him."

"I agree with your father," Veronica added. "Don't do anything rash, love. Think about what Marcus would want you to do."

Jenny sighed. "I don't know… what if his family think I only went out with him because he was rich, when I had no idea?"

"Then you should tell Mr. Lavender you had no idea," her mother said firmly. "And write to his mother as well."

That evening, when Jenny told Ruth about the cheque, her friend was just as stunned.

"Heavens, Jenny—how much is fifty thousand dollars in pounds?"

"I've no idea… but a lot," Jenny admitted, her voice low and uncertain. "What on earth am I going to do with all that money, Ruth?"

When Ruth got home and told her parents, her father chuckled. "Well, if she doesn't want it, I could put it to good use."

"Dad, that's not funny," Ruth said sharply. "Poor Jenny—she had no idea he was rich. First Danny, now Marcus... it seems they all come from wealthy families. It's incredible."

"I know, love, I was only joking. But the lad clearly wanted her to have it. Anyway, didn't you say Danny and Marcus were related?"

"Yes—so it seems."

"Well, there you are, then. That's why they both had money. Family money."

When Ronald accompanied Jenny to the bank the next morning, he asked to see the manager. The two men knew each other well, and Andrew Wolsey greeted Ronald warmly.

"Ah, I see you've brought young Jenny with you. Come to learn the finer art of banking, have you, my dear?"

"Andrew," Ronald said, "Jenny wants to open an account."

Andrew raised his eyebrows. "I see. Been saving your wages, have you? Very wise—too many young people today spend as if there will be no tomorrow. So, how much have you saved?"

He smiled at Jenny in a genial, avuncular way. Jenny simply handed him the cheque.

The smile froze. His eyebrows climbed so high they seemed to vanish into his hairline. Slowly, he removed his glasses, polished them, and set them back on his nose. For a long moment, he said nothing—then finally, in a voice that came out as a rasp, "That is..." He stopped, coughed, cleared his throat, and tried again. "That is a great deal of money. May I ask how you came by this?"

"It's from my fiancé," Jenny said quietly. "This letter came with it."

She handed him Edward Lavender's letter. Andrew read it carefully, then looked at Jenny, then at Ronald, then back again.

"I see. I'm very sorry to hear your fiancé is missing," he said at last. "I hope he returns safe and sound. In light of this letter, everything appears above board—but I had to be sure. You do understand this is an extraordinary sum of money, Jenny?"

"Yes, Mr. Wolsey, I do. In fact, I was going to send it back. I had no idea Marcus was wealthy—I just want him home." Her voice wavered, and tears welled in her eyes.

Andrew, who was already imagining how the presence of such a large deposit might look to his superiors, quickly turned to Ronald. "Is that what you think she should do, send it back?"

Ronald shook his head firmly. "No. Marcus clearly wanted her to have it, and I think she should keep it. It will secure her future—with or without him. I've persuaded her to open an account and think it over."

"Quite right," Andrew agreed. "Best not to act in haste. Now, let's get the paperwork done, shall we? I'll need your signature as well, Ronald, to authorise the account."

"Yes, I realise that—but this is Jenny's money. I won't be touching a penny of it."

"No, of course not," Andrew said smoothly. "Quite right."

Both Jenny and her father felt a measure of relief once the

money was safely deposited.

That afternoon, Jenny sat at the kitchen table and began to write to Edward Lavender.

Dear Mr. Lavender,

Thank you for your very kind letter and the cheque. I have now deposited it into an account at my father's bank for safekeeping. However, I feel I should return it, as I do not believe I am entitled to it. I had no idea Marcus was wealthy—I always thought he lived on his Air Force wages. He never mentioned his family was rich, and this, as you can imagine, has come as a great shock. All I truly want is for Marcus to come home safe and well.

Should you feel that I ought to return the money, I am more than willing to do so.

Yours respectfully,

Jenny Jackson

When Edward Lavender received Jenny's letter, he was pleasantly surprised. He read it twice, then folded it carefully and took it straight to Marcus and Gloria.

"Well," he said, handing it to them, "it seems young Marcus' trust in this young woman was entirely justified."

Marcus Sr. and Gloria read it together. Gloria's eyes softened. "Yes—and I shall make sure Richard and Father know it as well."

Edward hesitated. "Do you want me to ask her to return the cheque?"

"Certainly not," Gloria replied sharply, her voice leaving no room for debate. "This is what Marcus wanted, and I will uphold his wishes. In fact, I shall write to her myself. I always knew he wouldn't fall for a gold digger. Jenny is exactly the right girl for him."

When Clementine heard the news, she too declared she would write to Jenny, as did Susan and Sally. The Potter women, united in purpose, began planning their letters—each determined to ensure Jenny would feel a warm and unquestionable welcome into the family.

Charles and Richard, suitably chastised for their earlier distrust, kept their heads down and made themselves scarce for a while.

Chapter 25

Marcus thought his head might split in two. Never in his life had he experienced such a pounding headache. Slowly, he forced his eyes open. The room around him was unfamiliar—neither his billet at the base nor his bedroom back home.

When he shifted slightly, pain flared—not only in his head but in his leg. Glancing down, he saw it was encased in plaster. An accident? That seemed the obvious explanation—until voices reached his ears.

German.

He froze, holding his breath. The sound seemed to come closer, and then—like a blow—memory came rushing back. The mission. The Messerschmitts. The tree he had tried to avoid, but failed. The impact. Darkness.

Two figures entered—a man and a woman. They weren't wearing uniforms, and they didn't look like Germans. He quickly shut his eyes.

"Hij slaapt nog," the woman said softly.

"Moet ik de dokter brengen?" the man asked.

"Nee, geef nog een paar uren."

Marcus's mind worked furiously. They must be all right—after all, they'd had a doctor set his leg, given him a bed, and hadn't turned him over to the Germans. Hunger and thirst finally tipped the balance. He opened his eyes.

"Ah, finally you wake?" the woman said, smiling faintly.

"Yes," Marcus rasped. "Do you… have a drink of water?"

"Yes. I bring."

She returned with a glass and gently lifted his head so he could drink. When he sank back onto the pillow, pain stabbed through him and he winced.

"You have pain?" she asked.

"Yes—my head, and my leg."

"You have concussion. And leg is broken."

"Where am I?"

"Apeldoorn. In Holland."

"My crew—what happened to my crew?"

She shrugged. "I don't know. You the only one we find."

Marcus closed his eyes briefly, hoping the others had been just as lucky. "So… you're Dutch?"

"Yes. Dutch."

"Is it safe for you to have me here? What about the Germans?"

"They came. We told them you my brother. You have accident. They go."

"How long have I been here?"

"Six weeks. Maybe little longer. Time go fast."

"Six weeks?"

"Yes."

"Have I been unconscious all that time?"

"No. You sleep, then you wake for little, then you sleep some more."

"Good lord… and my leg, the doctor set it?"

"Yes, but he say you need operation. He cannot do operation here, so he do what he can. You must see doctor when you go back."

"I see… and the concussion?"

"He say time will heal. He give medicine make you sleep. He say is better to sleep."

Bits of memory returned—shadowy figures moving in and out, voices drifting around him while he lay half-aware.

"Who is Jenny?" the woman asked suddenly.

"Jenny?"

"Yes—you say 'Jenny' many times. You call me Jenny."

Marcus smiled faintly. "She's my girl. My fiancée. We're getting married."

"Ah… she is girl in wallet. Blond. Pretty."

"Yes—that's her. She must be going frantic. So… what happens now? Is there any way I can get back to England?"

"When leg heal, then we try to get you back."

"How long does the doctor think?"

"He does not know. Everybody different. Maybe week, maybe month, maybe two. Now I get you food and water. You want pain medicine? Doctor give me if you need."

"Yes, thank you—but I'll eat first."

After a simple meal, he took the tablets and, despite having slept for much of the past six weeks, felt exhaustion wash over him again. He was asleep within minutes.

The next morning, the headache had eased, but when he tried to get up, dizziness and a sharp jolt of pain in his leg drove him back to the bed. Best to stay put for now.

Time passed slowly. The doctor came often, checking his

leg and giving quiet reassurances. Even after the cast was removed, walking was difficult and painful.

One day, it struck him—he'd never even asked the couple's names.

"I don't know your name," he said apologetically to the woman. "I should have asked sooner."

She shrugged. "Is no matter. My name is Coba, and my husband—he is Hans. And you are Marcus. I see Jenny—she write to Marcus with love."

As the days slid by, Marcus regained strength. The headaches faded, and though his leg still ached at times, he could walk short distances. Then Christmas arrived—bleak, grey, and joyless. No turkey, no presents, no tree. Just the simple act of surviving felt like the only gift anyone could hope for.

While Marcus recuperated from his injuries, The war machine had been relentless, by October Neapolitans had completed their uprising and had freed Naples from German occupation. Lord Louis Mountbatten was appointed as the commander of South East Asia Command. Elsewhere the Germans conquer the island of Kos. Corsica is liberated by Free French forces, and the Allies cross Italy's Volturno Line.

The Japanese executed 98 American civilians on Wake Island, and Italy declared war on Germany. December saw one of the worst atrocities when The Germans conducted a highly successful Air Raid on Bari, Italy. A German bomb hit an Allied cargo ship carrying mustard gas, releasing the chemical, it killed 83 Allied soldiers, and over 1000 more soldiers died in the raid.

In southern Greece, German forces carried out the massacre of Kalavryta—yet another atrocity in a war already filled with them. And still, the grim news bulletins kept coming, each day bringing fresh reports of suffering from somewhere in the world.

But in towns, cities, and the smallest of villages, people refused to let the war steal Christmas entirely. For a few hours, they set aside fear and grief. Neighbours came together, communities pooled what little they had, and homes flickered with candlelight.

Jenny tried not to dwell on the previous Christmas—when Marcus had been with her. Instead, she poured her energy into making the holiday as happy as she could for her family, especially little Betty, who was still blissfully unaware of the war's cruelties. The child's eyes had widened in delight when she and her mother took her to see Father Christmas in town. At midnight mass, Jenny bowed her head and whispered a prayer: *"Please, God, wherever Marcus is, take care of him... and bring him home to me."*

Across the country, others prayed too—that by the next Christmas, the war would be over, the boys would be home, and celebrations could once again be free of fear.

When the New Year came, two letters arrived from America. One was from Marcus's mother, Gloria; the other, from his formidable great-aunt Clementine.

Gloria's letter was tender and full of feeling:

Dear Jenny,

I'm sorry I haven't written before, but the shock of hearing my darling boy had been shot down completely blindsided me. I'm sure it did you, too.

We are united in our worry and grief for him, and I believe this gives us a bond—though I wish we could meet and draw strength from one another in person. For now, letters must be the next best thing, and I hope we can write regularly.

Edward Lavender told us you wanted to return the check, and I know he has already written to say you should not. Marcus wanted you to have it, and so do we. From the way he spoke of you—and the way his eyes lit up when he mentioned you—I know he loves you deeply, and so do we.

I can't wait for this war to be over, for Marcus to bring you home as his wife, and for us to be a family again. I also look forward to meeting your family; Marcus tells me you have a little sister, just four years old. My girls will love her—they adore small children.

I hope this letter brings you some comfort. It has helped me to write it. I will write again soon.

All our love,

Gloria

xxxxx

Clementine's letter, in contrast, wasted no time on sentiment.

Dear Jenny,

I trust this letter finds you well. I know you will be concerned for Marcus—but frankly, dear, worrying is of no use. At my age, one learns to accept such trials with stoicism. I have endured many anxious times, and fretting never changes the outcome.

We are all praying for Marcus's safe return, and I feel certain he will come back to us. The question is simply when. Until that day, we must carry on in the best possible way, because that is what Marcus would want.

We look forward to his bringing you home and finally meeting you. I know you mean a great deal to him, and therefore to us. I think it only fair, however, to warn you that his younger brother Richard, and my brother Charles—Marcus's grandfather—may not be as welcoming as the rest of us. There's no sense in pretending otherwise. The women of the family, however, will rally around you, and Marcus's father will be firmly on your side.

This may sound harsh, but I believe in preparing people for reality. One person you will certainly have in your corner is this "silly old woman" whose favourite nephew you will be marrying. If he loves you, then I will love you.

Please take this letter in the spirit in which it is written. I have always believed in honesty and, at my age, I'm far too old to change now.

My warmest regards,
Clementine Potter

"Heavens… well, I'm not sure what to make of that, love," Veronica said slowly. "I mean, there's honesty… and then there's honesty. Clearly she doesn't believe in pulling her punches. But I'm sure she'll be on your side. I just wonder why they object."

Jenny shrugged. "I don't know. Maybe his grandfather had a girl picked out and Marcus refused. Or it could simply be because I'm not American. But I hope his aunt is right and the others are on my side."

"Oh, don't worry, love—I'm sure they will be. His mother certainly seems to be. You had a lovely letter from her."

"Yes, that's true."

"Will you answer them both?"

"Oh yes—it would be rude not to. But I'll have to think carefully about how to answer Clementine's letter."

Over the following weeks, Marcus steadily regained his strength. Coba and Hans had become good friends to him, and he knew he would be sorry to leave them—but getting back to England was all that mattered. He was now strong enough to help with chores around the farm, and his restlessness was growing by the day.

Finally, in early June, it was time. Marcus thanked Coba and Hans for everything they had done for him. Coba contacted her niece Marieke, who was part of the Dutch resistance, and told her about Marcus.

"Marcus is klaar voor reizen, zal jij hem naar Katwijk kunnen brengen?"

"Natuurlijk! Vanavond?"

"Ja! Goed!"

Once darkness fell, Marieke and Marcus set off, following the same route that Chuck and Alvin had taken months earlier. As before, they travelled in the farm truck until they reached the outskirts of Gouda, where the journey continued by bicycle from the flower factory. Kees was pleased to see them again. Marcus shook Marieke's hand, thanked her warmly, and wished her luck before parting ways.

Constable Pollock looked up from his paperwork when the door opened, his eyes narrowing at the sight of a limping man dripping water onto the floor.

"Hi," Marcus said, "do you think you could contact my base and ask them to send a jeep to collect me?"

Pollock eyed him suspiciously. "And what base would that be, then?"

Marcus gave the name of the base. "Ask to speak to Colonel Roy Withers—tell him First Lieutenant Potter has arrived back from Holland."

"Blimey… not another one," Pollock muttered.

Marcus frowned. "Another one? What do you mean, another one?"

"Well, a couple of months ago we had two more come in here—soaked, same as you, and dressed the same way. Said they'd been shot down over Holland and made it back."

"Two more? What were their names—do you remember?"

The constable screwed up his eyes in thought. "Well… one of 'em reminded me of that cartoon chipmunk… what was it now… oh, I've got it—Alvin. He was a lieutenant as well. And the other one was Chuck—definitely remember that, 'cause it made me think of chucking someone out of the pub."

Marcus's face broke into a relieved smile. "Alvin and Chuck made it back? That's good news. Any others?"

"No, just them two—and now you. I'll let my sergeant know."

Moments later, Sergeant Riley appeared. "Another one, Pollock?"

"Yes, sarg—just walked in."

Riley looked Marcus over and gave a low whistle. "Well, this is a turn-up for the books, and no mistake. We had a couple of your lot in here a few months ago—also dressed like Dutch peasants."

Marcus nodded. “Yes, your constable told me. Could you let my base know? They can send a jeep to collect me.”

Roy Withers could hardly believe it when the message came through that First Lieutenant Potter had just walked into a police station in Great Yarmouth.

“But he’s been missing for nearly a year,” he said, astonished. “And you’re telling me he just walked into your police station?”

“Yes, sir—he did.”

“Right, I’ll send transport. Thank you, sergeant.”

“That’s alright, sir—happy to be of help.”

Sergeant White was equally stunned when he heard. “But his plane went down months ago, sir. Where’s he been all this time?”

“I don’t know, sergeant—but I imagine he’ll tell us. Send a jeep to bring him back. The sooner he’s here, the sooner we can get to the bottom of this. And let’s hope more arrive home.”

Private Dobson stared at his superior. “Another one, sarg? But he’s been gone months—I thought he was dead.”

“Well, you’re not paid to think, Dobson. That’s way above your pay grade. Just get a jeep and go get him.”

Privately, the sergeant agreed—he’d thought Lieutenant Potter was dead too.

“Shall I take Wilson again, sarg?”

“Why—can’t you remember the way?”

“Well, it was a long time ago, sarg. And he’ll be company for the journey—give me someone to talk to.”

The sergeant rolled his eyes. Where on earth were they getting these recruits from?

"Just go, Dobson. Take him, don't take him—I don't care. Just get out of my office!"

When Marcus arrived back at the base, he was taken straight to the colonel for debriefing. The two men shook hands.

"Welcome back, Lieutenant. I must admit I was extremely surprised when I heard you'd arrived back. So… where have you been?"

Marcus explained. "I got tangled in a tree and was cut down by resistance fighters. They took me to a farmhouse where I was looked after by a kind couple. I had a concussion and a broken leg. The doctor did what he could for me, but he says I'll need an operation—hence the limp."

"Yes, I noticed. We'll have the doctor look at you once we're done here. Do you know what happened to the rest of your crew?"

"No, sir, I don't. I understand two of them made it back a couple of months ago, but I have no idea about the others. I can only hope they fared as well as I did."

When the base doctor examined him, he shook his head.

"Well, Lieutenant, you're very lucky you were found by people who had access to a decent doctor. Otherwise, you might have lost that leg. As it is, we can work with what's been done, but you'll probably have a limp for the rest of your life. There's a nasty gash down the outside of the leg—it's been patched up well enough—but as for the concussion, I don't see any lasting damage there. All in all, you've had a lucky escape. I'll get the nurse to put you to bed and we'll see what we can do."

When Chuck and Alvin heard Marcus had returned—"from the dead," as they put it—they hurried to the hospital wing. After the greetings were over, Marcus asked, "I take it Jenny was told I'd been shot down?"

"Yes—I told her," Alvin replied. "She took it pretty bad. Do you want me to go and tell her you're home?"

"If you could. She needs to know—and I can't go myself."

"No trouble, skip. I'll see she knows. In fact—" He lowered his voice and glanced around to make sure no one was listening. "I'll see if I can't smuggle her in to see you. I think she'd like that—just to see for herself that you're alive and well."

When Jenny heard the news, she could barely contain her excitement. She laughed and cried all at once.

"But why hasn't he come himself to see me?"

"Well, he has to have an operation on his leg. Apparently, he broke it in the fall, and while a doctor treated him, it still needs proper work. But I'm going to try to get you in to see him. I'll let you know when I can."

Her parents and Ruth were just as delighted.

"Oh, Jenny, that's wonderful news."

"I know—I can't believe it. After all these months of worry, and now he's home... I feel like I'm dreaming."

Two days later, Alvin returned to say he'd succeeded—he'd sweet-talked a nurse who'd agreed to help. If they got caught, she would deny all knowledge.

When Jenny stepped into the ward and saw Marcus lying in bed, she ran to him. He smiled up at her.

"Boy, aren't you a sight for sore eyes."

She kissed him and hugged him tightly. “Oh, Marcus—I thought I’d never see you again.”

“I know, honey. But I’m back now—and I’ll be here for some time before I can fly again.”

“But surely you won’t have to do any more missions?”

“Jenny, honey—it’s a war. I’m a pilot. Odds are, I will have to fly again. But that’s a long way off. For now, let’s just enjoy the time we have together.”

“I had a letter from your mother and your Aunt Clementine—now I can write and tell them how you’re doing. Oh, and I had a letter from your solicitor. Marcus, he sent me an enormous cheque. I put it in the bank and haven’t touched it. I offered to send it back, but he refused. But now I can give it back to you.”

Marcus took her hand and shook his head. “No. I want you to have it, Jenny. Use it—it’s yours.”

“But Marcus—”

“No, Jenny. I intended you to have it. I don’t want it back. Please—keep it.”

Finally, she conceded. “If you’re really sure… but it’s so much money. Why didn’t you tell me you were rich? It was such a shock.”

“Because I didn’t want to seem boastful—and here in England, where people have so little, it seemed arrogant. Am I forgiven?”

For an answer, she kissed him tenderly. “Of course—I’d forgive you anything.”

Chapter 26

There was jubilation in Vermont. The Potter family raised their glasses of champagne to toast the return of their hero.

"Oh, I wish I could go and see him," his mother said tearfully.

"Well, according to Jenny, he's doing well. The operation was a success, but he will always have a limp," Marcus Sr. replied.

Susan and Sally were partly willing to forgive Richard and their grandfather, but the rift was far from healed—their relationship would always be tinged with resentment.

January '44 brought more massacres, death, and destruction. In Italy, Count Ciano—the Italian Foreign Minister and Mussolini's son-in-law—was executed by Mussolini's revived Fascist sympathisers. The first Battle of Monte Cassino began when the British X Corps attacked along the Garigliano River, striking at the western end of the German Gustav Line. The Red Army pushed westward toward the Baltic states.

British Operation Outward accidentally claimed lives in neutral Sweden by knocking out lighting and causing a train crash. The Royal Air Force dropped 2,300 tons of bombs on Berlin.

Back in England, Marcus, Jenny, Chuck, and Marjory enjoyed evenings at the cinema, escaping into films like *The Life and Death of Colonel Blimp* and *Heaven Can Wait*—light-hearted romantic comedies that lifted their spirits. They were young, in love, and determined to snatch joy wherever they could, even under the shadow of war.

April brought tragedy for the Americans when hundreds of soldiers and sailors were killed over two days of training for the D-Day invasion.

In June, Operation Overlord—originally scheduled for the 5th—was postponed by twenty-four hours because of high seas. D-Day finally commenced on June 6th.

In July, the young Leningrad diarist Tanya Savicheva died of starvation at the age of fourteen. Her diary, recording the loss of her entire family during the siege, would later become a symbol of the war's human cost.

One evening that summer, Clementine sat across the dinner table from her brother. Dining at Charles' house was always an ordeal. In some ways, she pitied him—he had never recovered from Christine's betrayal—but that was no excuse for his attitude toward Jenny.

As was her way, she came straight to the point.

"Marcus will be home soon—with his new wife. I hope everyone will welcome her. She'll be thousands of miles from her home, her family, and friends. We need to show her good old-fashioned American hospitality at its best. Don't you agree, Charles?"

Charles speared an asparagus tip and inspected it like a

laboratory specimen.

"We'll see," was all he said.

Clementine's jaw tightened. "She's proved she's not a gold digger. She offered to return the money Marcus gave her, and I understand she hasn't spent a dime of it. She's still working in the department store, living on her wages."

"That proves nothing," Charles said flatly. "She could just be playing for time—stringing him along."

The stubborn old fool. If he carried on like this, he'd lose Marcus's trust, respect, and loyalty.

"So who would you have him marry?" Clementine asked.

"Nothing wrong with that girl he was courting before. Her parents were the right sort—money, breeding, standing in the community. That would have been a good match."

Clementine gave a sharp snort. "Millicent? By whose standards—yours? She would have bored Marcus within two weeks. He'd have had affairs before the year was out. Millicent was an empty-headed socialite shopping and parties were all she cared about. That might suit you, Charles. It might even suit Richard. But Marcus needs what he has in Jenny—a woman with substance, gumption, and above all, a brain."

She threw down her napkin and rose.

"What are you doing? We're in the middle of a meal. Father would be appalled at your behaviour."

"Oh, to hell with Father—and to hell with you, Charles. Is that really what you want for your grandchildren? To marry idiots? Don't you want them to have intelligent equals—and be happy? Just because you weren't happy in your marriage doesn't mean they can't be happy in theirs. Marcus has had a happy marriage—with a wife who is his equal in every way."

"The girl has no money or standing. She's a shop girl. Her father runs a grocery store—he's trade, for heaven's sake."

"I feel sorry for you, Charles. Truly, I do. Marcus has been through the most horrific experiences. Jenny too has faced extraordinary hardships in her country. And all you care about is standing and money. So what if her father runs a grocery store? It's honest work. You're to be pitied."

Charles shot back, "And what about you? Why did you never marry after Joe was killed? You had plenty of beaus."

Clementine took a deep breath, her voice quiet but steady. "Joe was the great love of my life. How could I ever replace him? And how dare you compare what I had with Joe to what you had with Christine?"

She straightened, turned, and walked out.

Driving home, she felt deflated and sad. The only legacy her brother seemed destined to leave was that of a bitter, vitriolic old man no one would miss. She thought of the happy, fun-loving boy he had once been—and, for the first time in years, she wept.

She wept for him.

She wept for herself.

And for the life she might have had if Joe had lived.

In July of forty-four Col. Claus von Stauffenberg attempted to assassinate Hitler, whilst Hitler was visiting headquarters at Rastenburg, East Prussia, but the plot failed. Reprisals follow against the plotters and their families, included Rommel, but the tide is turning against Hitler. In December the home guard is stood down. Bandleader and US Army Major

Glenn Miller went missing as his single-engine transport was crossing the English Channel; he was headed to Paris to work out arrangements to entertain troops in France, but neither the plane nor its occupants are found.

In January forty-five the tide was finally turning, American rangers rescued Bataan and Corregidor POWs from a Japanese prison camp. US and Philippines forces finally retook the historic Bataan peninsular. The Japanese are defeated in Burma. In April soviet forces encircled Berlin and On the 30th of April Hitler and his mistress, Ava Braun, committed suicide in his bunker in Berlin.

On May 7th, the Germans surrendered, and finally—it was over. After six long and harrowing years, the world stood at the dawn of something new.

The streets of London were packed for VE Day. Throngs of people gathered outside Buckingham Palace, cheering wildly as the royal family and Winston Churchill stepped out onto the balcony to acknowledge the jubilant crowds.

Yet the war was not fully done. It would be another four months before Japan surrendered, and then only after two horrific atom bombs were dropped on Hiroshima and Nagasaki. The devastation was unimaginable—tens of thousands killed instantly, with thousands more dying in the weeks and months that followed from burns and radiation. In Hiroshima, the estimated death toll ranged from seventy to one hundred and twenty-six thousand, including soldiers and Allied prisoners of war. Nagasaki suffered between sixty and eighty thousand deaths, with similar tragic aftereffects.

At Findley's, the staff celebrated with a party. Jenny continued working there despite the large sum in her bank account—she valued the friendships she'd formed and knew she would miss them terribly once she left for America.

Ruth, still waiting for her fiancé Raymond to return home, had agreed to travel to America with Jenny to be her chief bridesmaid. Little Betty would be a flower girl, while Susan and Sally would serve as bridesmaids.

For Veronica and Ronald, the excitement was bittersweet. They were thrilled for Jenny but dreaded the thought of her living so far away. Betty too would miss her dearly.

Marcus planned to ask Richard to be his best man, with Alvin and Chuck as groomsmen. He hoped Richard had finally accepted Jenny and would behave accordingly—but he had his doubts. Jenny and her family would follow Marcus to America in a few weeks. The sea crossing would take about a week, but Marcus had secured first-class cabins so they could travel in comfort.

At Jenny's farewell party from Findley's, Miss Penheart hugged her warmly and wished her every happiness. Even Sheila and Ruby were invited. Sheila had eventually left her child in her parents' care, but she spent most of her time flitting from place to place, dressed in increasingly expensive clothes. No one knew exactly what she did to earn her money, but it was clear she was doing well. She visited occasionally but never played a mother's role, and the little girl was being raised to believe Sheila was her sister. When the truth emerged years later, it would come as a painful shock.

The voyage to New York was smooth and uneventful. Betty could barely contain her excitement, her chatter endless.

Marcus met them at the docks and drove them to Vermont. As the car pulled up outside the sprawling mansion, Jenny and her family stared in awe. Veronica's eyes widened; Ronald instinctively moved to carry the suitcases, but uniformed staff appeared from the house and took them instead.

Gloria stepped out onto the wide front porch to greet them.

"Jenny dear, welcome." She embraced her warmly before turning to Veronica and Ronald with a gracious handshake. She then welcomed Ruth and finally bent down to smile at Betty.

"Well now, you must be Betty. I've heard so much about you, and I'm looking forward to getting to know you."

Betty, all innocence, asked, "Why have you got such a big house? Do lots of people live here?"

"Betty!" Veronica hissed, mortified.

Gloria only smiled. "Not at all," she reassured Veronica, then turned back to Betty. "Yes, dear, quite a few people do live here."

Marcus Sr. was equally warm in his greeting. Susan and Sally quickly swept Betty away with laughter and fuss.

Upstairs, Jenny and Ruth were shown to their rooms—lavish, spacious, and each with its own ensuite.

"Oh, I wish Mum could see this," Ruth breathed. "She'd never believe it. And an ensuite!"

They had just begun to unpack when a maid appeared. "Oh no, miss, I will take care of that. Please, freshen up—tea is waiting for you on the terrace."

During tea, Richard arrived. He glanced over the unfamiliar faces, his expression cool. Gloria introduced him, and he gave only a curt nod before starting to walk away.

"Richard," his father said in a tone that brooked no argument, "please sit down and be sociable. You need to get to know your future sister-in-law and her family."

Richard sat, resigned. He had to admit both Jenny and her friend were strikingly attractive. Then his eyes caught the engagement ring on Ruth's finger.

"So—are you marrying an American too?"

Ruth disliked him instantly and felt a flicker of concern for Jenny. "No," she replied evenly. "My fiancé is a British soldier. I'll be going home after the wedding, and we'll marry as soon as he's demobbed."

"I see. What did he do before the war?"

"He was a clerk in an insurance office, and that's what he'll return to. They've kept his job for him."

Richard smirked, and Ruth's dislike deepened.

"And what do you do?" she asked.

"I'm at college."

"What are you studying?"

"Business. When I finish this summer, I'll take over some of Father's business interests."

"I see. So you won't really need to work at all—you'll just inherit. You'll never have to get your hands dirty, will you?" She turned away from him deliberately and addressed Susan, who was grinning.

"Well, Ruth's got you figured out, hasn't she?" Susan said later, clearly enjoying her brother's discomfort.

Richard was furious. "How dare that common little shop

girl speak to me like that?"

"Frankly," Sally said coolly, "I think someone like Ruth is exactly what you need to keep you grounded. And she's right—you will inherit, and you'll never have to get your hands dirty."

Later that day, Betty wandered into the garden and spotted Richard lounging by the pool. She watched him for a moment, her head tilted, then strolled over with the air of someone on an important mission.

"Why are you cross?" she asked.

Richard blinked, pulled from his thoughts. He had been brooding over his disapproval of Marcus and Jenny's engagement—and still smarting from Ruth's sharp tongue.

"Who says I'm cross?" he muttered.

"No one," Betty said matter-of-factly. "But you look cross. Don't you like us?"

"Go away, kid, and leave me alone."

Betty frowned. "But why don't you like us? Don't you want Jenny and Marcus to get married?"

Richard sighed. This child was clearly not going to wander off. "No," he said bluntly.

"But why? I want them to get married. I like Marcus."

"Yes, I'm sure you do—and his money," Richard said with a sneer. "Your sister Jenny is a gold digger. That's why I don't want them to get married. Happy now?"

He pushed himself up from the sun lounger and strode away, leaving Betty standing there, puzzled.

That evening at dinner, Betty suddenly piped up, "Mummy, what's a gold digger? Richard said Jenny was a gold digger."

She turned innocently to her sister. "But you don't dig, do you, Jenny?"

The table fell silent. Every head turned toward Richard, who was trying very hard to disappear into his chair.

Chapter 27

Several things happened at once. Cutlery clattered onto plates, sharp breaths were drawn, and shock rippled around the table. Jenny's eyes filled with tears, and they began to spill silently down her cheeks.

Gloria was the first to recover. Her voice was calm, but her eyes were like steel. "Sally, dear, why don't you take Betty to the kitchen and see if Cook has any ice cream?" Then, turning to the little girl, she smiled warmly. "Betty, I think Cook might even have some strawberries to go with it. Would you like that?"

Betty nodded eagerly. As she passed Richard's chair, Sally leaned down and murmured in his ear, "Well, you've done it now. You're in so much trouble. Serves you right." Then, straightening, she said brightly, "Come on, Betty, let's go find that ice cream."

"Ooh, can I, Mummy? Please?"

Veronica managed a smile for her daughter. "Of course, dear. Off you go."

Once Betty was safely removed from the table, the full force of everyone's anger descended on Richard.

Ronald was first. His glare could have cut glass. "My

daughter," he said, his voice low and dangerous, "has never been, nor will she ever be, a gold digger. She hasn't touched a penny of the money Marcus sent when he went missing—not one penny. She even offered to return it, and offered it back to Marcus when he came home. How dare you imply she's marrying him for his money?"

Jenny sat between Marcus and Ruth, each holding one of her hands in silent support. Marcus now fixed his brother with a look of pure loathing that made Richard shrink in his chair.

"I was going to have you as my best man," Marcus said, his tone like ice. "But after that remark, you are no longer even invited to the wedding. I don't want you anywhere near it. And you will apologise to Jenny—now."

Marcus Senior's voice was even harder. "I think it best you go and stay with your grandfather. As your brother has just told you, you are no longer welcome at this wedding. I am appalled and disgusted that a son of mine could behave this way toward his brother's fiancée. Now, get out of my sight before I really lose my temper."

Richard pushed his chair back, ready to leave, when his father's voice stopped him cold.

"And another thing," Marcus Senior said. "I'm not sure leaving you at college is wise. You clearly need a hard lesson. As of next month, you will present yourself at the lumber mill and report to Mike Rathbone, the foreman. You'll work your way up from the bottom, on proper wages for the job. Your allowance ends today."

Richard gaped at him. "You can't do that! I need my allowance to run my car—and what about my studies? I'm due to graduate this summer!"

"As I said," his father replied, utterly unmoved, "you need a hard lesson. You'll be treated like any other employee. As for your car—you can trade it for a pickup. Your car stays in the garage until I say otherwise. And business studies? You won't need them. You'll learn on the job—over the years. Now, get out."

Richard left the room in shock. He couldn't believe his father meant it—surely, once he'd cooled down, he would change his mind. But when Richard came down the stairs, bag in hand, Newman was waiting at the foot.

"I'll need your car keys, Mr. Richard."

Richard stared at him. "My car keys? Why?"

"Mr. Potter instructed me to take them from you. You're not to take your car."

"This is ridiculous! How am I supposed to get to my grandfather's?"

"Roche will drive you and drop you off, sir."

Richard was speechless. Was his father really choosing *her*—that shop girl—over his own son?

When Charles Potter heard the news, he was just as outraged as his grandson. He immediately ordered the car brought round.

Meanwhile, Jenny was upstairs in her room, being comforted by Sally, Susan, and Ruth. Downstairs, her mother and Gloria sat together in Gloria's private sitting room.

"You don't believe Jenny is just after Marcus's money, do you?" Veronica asked hesitantly.

Gloria shook her head firmly. "No, my dear, I do not. I've seen them together; I know she genuinely loves him. And I understand she still hasn't spent a single dime of the money she was sent. I can't imagine what possessed Richard to say such a thing—especially to a small child. Veronica, I am so very sorry."

"But why does he feel that way about Jenny? He doesn't even know her."

Gloria sighed. "I don't know. He's so like his grandfather. And… I'm afraid we spoiled him. He was always a difficult child—tantrums if he didn't get his way. Instead of disciplining him, we gave in. 'Spare the rod and spoil the child'—it's an old saying, but a true one."

Veronica, who had never laid a hand on either of her girls, found this bluntness shocking, but she couldn't deny Jenny had never been prone to tantrums. A firm word had always been enough.

The door suddenly opened, and in swept Clementine.

"What on earth is going on, Gloria? Newman tells me there's trouble over some remark Richard made, and that he's been packed off to Charles."

Gloria rose to greet her aunt. "Oh, Aunt Clementine, you've caught us at a difficult time."

"So it would seem." Her sharp gaze moved to Veronica, and her face softened into a smile. She extended her hand. "You must be Jenny's mother. Clementine Potter—Marcus's great-aunt. How do you do?"

Veronica returned the smile and shook her hand. "It's nice to meet you at last."

Seating herself, Clementine got straight to the point. "Now, what's all this about Richard?"

Gloria explained.

"He told a seven-year-old child her sister was a gold digger?"

Clementine's eyebrows shot up. "Good heavens! What's got into that boy? I told you spoiling him would end badly. Well, his father's right—a good hard lesson is exactly what he needs, and it's about time." She clapped her hands together decisively. "Now, where is the bride-to-be?"

Veronica felt herself warming to this forthright aunt.

When Jenny was introduced to Clementine, the connection was instant.

"My, how pretty you are, my dear," Clementine said warmly. "Yes, quite lovely. Now—have you your wedding dress yet?"

"No, not yet," Jenny admitted. "We were planning to shop tomorrow. Wedding dresses in England are very hard to find, and fabric is almost impossible to come by."

"Mmm. It's not much different here, I'm afraid."

Clementine's eyes took on a distant look. "However... I may have the solution. Many years ago, I was to be married, but my fiancé was killed in the Great War." Her voice softened, and for a moment her gaze was far away. The others felt a pang of sadness for her.

But the moment passed, and her tone became brisk again. "I still have my wedding dress, carefully boxed. You are welcome to have it. Tomorrow I'll send my car to collect you, and we'll see what can be done. My dressmaker can alter it as needed. But I don't want you to feel obliged—this is your wedding, and if you'd rather buy your own gown, I'll understand completely."

"Oh, Aunt Clementine, I think that's a lovely idea. Thank you—I'd love to see your dress."

When Newman opened the door to Charles Potter, he was nearly bowled over by the older man's determined stride.

"Where's my son?" Charles barked.

"Mr. Potter is in his study, sir— with young Mr. Marcus."

"Well, that's just as well. I want a word with that young man, too."

"Shall I announce you, sir?"

"Certainly not. I'll announce myself."

Charles strode down the hall and flung open the study door without knocking. Father and son stopped mid-conversation, both startled by the sudden intrusion.

"Father—what's the meaning of this?"

"You may well ask," Charles shot back. "Why have you banished Richard from the house and the wedding? And what's this about taking his car, cutting his allowance, and dragging him out of college for some menial job? Have you taken leave of your senses?"

"No, Father," Marcus Sr. replied evenly. "If anything, I've come to them. For far too long he's been pampered and spoiled. He's grown arrogant, rude, and undisciplined. Now he needs a hard lesson—and this is the only way he'll learn."

"And you're doing all this on the word of a *child*?"

"Yes, Father—because what she said was the truth. And it hurt and upset Jenny and her family. They are guests in my house, and I will not have them treated in this way. Furthermore, Jenny is about to become a member of this family."

Charles's eyes narrowed. "All Richard said was that he hoped the girl knew what she was getting into—that life here would be very different from what she's used to. How can that possibly warrant such a punishment?"

Marcus, who had remained silent until now, turned to his

grandfather. "Is *that* what he told you? Because I can assure you, that's a lie. What he told Jenny's little sister was that Jenny is a gold digger. The child didn't even know what it meant and asked in all innocence at dinner. Grandfather, Jenny is about to become my wife, and I will not have her disrespected by anyone."

Charles's face registered surprise—clearly, Richard had not told him the full truth. Even so, he was not convinced the punishment fitted the crime, and deep down, he harboured doubts about Jenny himself. "And are you a hundred percent certain she isn't a gold digger?"

For a moment, the room was silent. Then Marcus said quietly but firmly, "Yes, I am. And if that's how you feel, Grandfather, then you are not welcome at my wedding either."

He left the study without another word, his grandfather staring after him.

In the front hallway, Marcus asked, "Is my mother in her sitting room, Newman?"

"Yes, sir, but she's entertaining."

"Entertaining? Who?"

"Your sisters, Miss Jackson and her mother, Miss Jackson's friend from England, and your great-aunt Clementine."

"Heavens. Best not disturb them, then. Thank you, Newman."

"Not at all, sir. Is there anything I can do for you?"

"Not unless you can knock some sense into my brother and grandfather's heads."

Newman only smiled and shook his head.

The next day, Jenny, Ruth, and Veronica went to Clementine's to see the dress. Clementine brought out a large box, lifted the lid, and carefully peeled back layers of tissue. From within, she drew out the most beautiful gown Jenny had ever seen—pure white organza with a high Victorian collar, fitted to the hips with tiny pearl buttons down the back. The long sleeves had matching pearl buttons from wrist to elbow, and from the hips the skirt fell straight, the fabric covered in delicate silver embroidery.

Jenny was speechless for a few moments before finally breathing, "It's divine. May I try it on?"

"Of course, my dear—that's why you're here."

It was a perfect fit, as though it had been made for her. Clementine then produced a smaller box and lifted out a veil, its fine net also embroidered with silver thread.

Veronica's eyes filled with tears—she had never seen her daughter look so beautiful. Ruth's eyes shone as well. "Oh, Jenny, you look like a fairy princess."

Clementine was pleased. The dress and veil had sat in their boxes far too long. Joe, she thought, would have approved of them being worn.

The rest of the day was spent in town, where they found bridesmaids' dresses and a charming frock for Betty. Veronica discovered the perfect outfit for herself, and shoes were bought all round. Ronald, meanwhile, had been taken to Marcus's tailor, where a morning suit was found in stock and set aside for minor alterations. Later, he joked to Veronica that he felt like a penguin.

The wedding day dawned bright and cloudless, the early sunlight turning the grand house into something out of a picture postcard. The gardens, where the ceremony would take place, were a blaze of colour—roses, lilies, and every shade of blossom swaying gently in the summer breeze. White chairs lined the immaculate lawn, and an arch woven with flowers framed the aisle.

When Jenny appeared on her father's arm, the guests rose as one. Marcus turned, and for a moment, the world seemed to stop. She was radiant—her white gown catching the light, her veil floating softly behind her, every step measured and graceful. His breath caught in his throat; words failed him.

Later, as they danced beneath strings of fairy lights to Glenn Miller's *Always in My Heart*, Marcus leaned close and whispered, "I promise I'll make you happy, Jenny. I'll spend the rest of my life making sure you never have any regrets."

She smiled up at him, her eyes bright. "I will never have any regrets marrying you, Marcus. And I'll do everything in my power to make you happy, too."

Maureen had travelled from Scotland for the wedding, bringing little Danny with her. The resemblance to his father was uncanny—it was like looking at a miniature version of the man they had lost.

Alvin stood proudly as best man, with Chuck as groomsman. Marjory had crossed the Atlantic from England to be there. She and Chuck were now planning their own wedding, and Jenny took comfort in knowing she would have a dear friend from home living nearby. It was the sort of friendship that would endure, no matter how many years passed or how far the world shifted around them.

Chapter 28

THIRTY YEARS LATER

Richard stood on the terrace, the morning sun already warming the flagstones beneath his polished shoes. Across the rolling green lawn, Jenny was walking towards him, the hem of her summer dress brushing against the grass. Her hair—still thick, still shining—caught the light, and he found himself struck by how little she seemed to have aged.

Time, it appeared, had been kind to her.

She carried herself with the same graceful confidence she had the first day he'd seen her, though back then he'd refused to acknowledge it. He had expected her to be a passing phase in Marcus's life—a mistake, a distraction. Instead, she had become the cornerstone. She had given Marcus five children, kept a warm and welcoming home, and moved with ease in both family life and his business world. She had been the steady hand that kept his brother's life anchored.

And through it all, she had remained modest. No diamonds flaunted, no extravagant displays. She'd raised her children to value hard work and to understand that money wasn't something to take for granted. She had been, he had to admit—though the words lodged like grit in his throat—

exactly the wife Marcus needed.

As she drew level with him, her eyes cool but polite, he smiled. "Good morning, Jenny."

"Good morning, Richard. What brings you here so early?"

She had never warmed to him. Oh, she got on well with Sally and Susan, her sisters-in-law—laughter came easily with them—but Richard... no, with him there had always been a careful distance.

"I was hoping to catch Marcus before he went to the office," he said.

"I'm afraid you've just missed him. He left straight after breakfast."

"Right... I'll find him there then."

But he stayed where he was. Jenny waited, patient but expectant.

"Was there something else?" she prompted.

He hesitated, looking for the right words, words he should have spoken decades ago. "Yes. Something I should have said years back but was too stubborn to admit. I want to apologise—for what I said when you first arrived. I misjudged you, Jenny. Completely. And not just me—Grandfather as well. You've proved us both wrong. I wish he'd lived to see the life you've built with Marcus, and the family you've raised. You've been... an excellent wife and mother."

For a moment she simply looked at him, her face unreadable. Then she inclined her head, her voice calm. "I see. Well... thank you. As I said, Marcus is at the office."

Her tone was polite, but she gave him nothing more—no warmth, no invitation to linger. The wound from thirty years ago had healed, but the scar was still there.

As he drove away, Richard's thoughts turned inward.

By any outside measure, his life was a success. A sprawling house run by staff, a fleet of cars, investments that kept his bank accounts comfortably full. But the truth was far less satisfying. Three failed marriages, each leaving him lighter in the pocket. Children who came around only when they wanted something. A fourth wife who, he suspected, was already looking for the exit.

He remembered the day his father had stripped away his allowance and sent him to start at the bottom in the lumber mill. At the time, it had felt like humiliation. In hindsight, it was the only thing that had taught him anything worth knowing. But the arrogance had never entirely left him, and pride still tripped him up more often than he cared to admit.

He envied Marcus—not for the wealth, but for the kind of life he had built. The laughter in his home. The way his children looked at him. The steady devotion of a woman who would walk across a lawn on a summer morning, looking exactly as she had thirty years before.

Richard tightened his grip on the steering wheel. Somewhere along the way, he'd taken the wrong turn, and now it was far too late to go back.

In England, Maureen stood on the village high street, taking in the changes. The Jacksons' grocery shop was still there, but now it was a general store selling almost anything. It had been enlarged when the neighbouring house became vacant—Jenny had paid for most of the work to help her parents expand.

Her eyes moved to her own childhood home. The sight made her shudder. A conservatory had been tacked onto the back, and the neat front garden was now a paved carport. What had once been the American base was now a drab council estate.

Turning to the young man beside her, she said, "This is where I grew up, Danny—and where I met your father."

"Yes, I know, Mother. It's… small. I knew it was a village, but I didn't realise just how small."

"Yes, it was small."

Across the street, a woman stepped out of the general store to arrange fruit on the display table. Maureen's eyes widened. "Betty…" She took her son's arm and crossed the road.

As the woman reached the doorway, Maureen called, "Betty?"

She turned, smiling. "Yes? Sorry, do I know you?"

"It's Maureen. You might not remember me—you were very young when I left—but I saw you at Jenny's wedding."

Recognition lit her face. "Of course! How are you?"

"I'm well. Oh—Betty, this is my son, Danny."

They shook hands, and Betty said, "Would you like to come in for a cup of tea? I know Mum would love to see you."

"I'd love to. How are your mum and dad?"

"Thriving, as usual. Dad still helps in the shop—he can't quite let go—and Mum keeps the house running. Jenny offered to hire a cleaner, but Mum won't hear of it."

Veronica and Ronald were delighted to see them. "My, how like your father you are," Veronica said to Danny.

"Yes, that's what everyone tells me," he replied with a smile.

Talk turned to business. "I hear your teashops are doing

well," Ronald said. "There's even one in town now."

"Yes, and that's one reason we're here," Maureen explained. "I'm thinking of opening one here in the village. We'd buy our produce from you."

"That would be marvellous," Veronica said. "The old café has closed—the building's vacant. You could buy that."

"Yes, I'll look into it. It would be nice to have a reason to come back."

After a happy hour with the Jacksons, Maureen and Danny walked down the lane to Ruth's house. Ruth was overjoyed to see them and, like everyone else, remarked on how much Danny resembled his father. Raymond was at work, but Ruth promised he would be sorry to have missed them. She knew Maureen had built her café empire from the money she inherited after Danny's father's death, and that she now owned successful shops all over the country.

They strolled on toward the old air base. Suddenly Maureen stopped. Across the road, at the bus stop, stood Danny—in uniform—looking exactly as he had the day she'd first seen him. He smiled, lifted his hand in a wave.

Maureen smiled back, her heart twisting, and waved in return.

Then he was gone.

Her eyes filled with tears. Yes… she would open a café here. This was where her Danny was, and where, in her heart, he would always remain.

Chapter 29

Printed in Dunstable, United Kingdom